The Clerk's Tale

The Clerk's Tale

MARGARET FRAZER

BERKLEY PRIME CRIME, NEW YORK

THE CLERK'S TALE

A Berkley Prime Crime Book
Published by The Berkley Publishing Group,
a division of Penguin Putnam Inc.,
375 Hudson Street, New York, New York 10014.

Visit our website at
www.penguinputnam.com

First edition: January 2002

Library of Congress Cataloging-in-Publication Data

Frazer, Margaret.
The clerk's tale / Margaret Frazer
p. cm.
ISBN 0-425-18324-6 (alk. paper)
1. Frevisse, Sister (Fictitious character)—Fiction. 2. Great Britain—History—Lancaster and York, 1399–1485—Fiction. 3. Women detectives—England—Fiction. 4. Nuns—Fiction. I. Title.
PS3556.R3586 C58 2002
813'.54—dc21

2001043124

PRINTED IN THE UNITED STATES OF AMERICA

10 9 8 7 6 5 4 3 2 1

To Leslie, who said,
"You can't die. Who else will make me laugh the way you do?"
And I didn't die, so here's another book.

[B]ut God yeve hym meschaunce,
That is so undiscreet of governaunce
That jangleth whan he shoulde holde his pees.

—G. Chaucer, *The Nun's Priest's Tale*

Chapter 1

All in all it was a warm January, as Januarys went, this year of God's grace 1446, with never a freeze nor snow after Twelfth Night, even at St. Hilary's that was supposed to be a year's coldest day and now it was coming on to St. Paul's. The nights nipped and there were ice-rims to puddles and watering troughs more dawns than not but the days were only damp and gray, the world all heavy with rain and thaw rather than stiff with cold. In some sheltered places there was even grass beginning to green, as here in St. Mary's infirmary garden where the little square of turf with the ash tree in its midst, the herb beds, and careful gravel paths were kept from the winds of the Chiltern Hills and the Berkshire Downs by nunnery buildings on three sides and on the fourth by a low turf-wall topped by a withy-woven fence.

It was a quiet place, meant not only for the growing of the infirmarian's healing herbs but for those nuns who had been ill enough they must needs stay in the infirmary but were at last able to come out to sit or walk quietly on warmer, drier days than presently there were.

That it was a place where no man should be, a place meant for the healing of bodies, not their harm, made it doubly wrong for the man to be sprawled there on the grass beneath the ash tree's bare branches.

Dead.

Master John Gruesby, on the graveled path a bare yard away, near enough that a single step forward would have let him touch him, did not make the step, but stood staring, unable to believe that it was true. The set, empty eyes. The death-grayed face. They weren't enough to make it true. Nor the bright spread of blood . . . It wasn't true.

But slowly he stepped backward from it, his gaze fixed as if somehow, even yet, there might somehow be life where there was plainly none. A single step. Then another. Beginning to believe it. Finally turning, stumbling into what he meant to be a run, unsteady shuffle though it was, his legs stiff with his unbelief, back toward the gate he had left open behind him, toward the passage away from the garden, into the stableyard where people would be. Heard himself cry out, though the voice was too shrill to be his own, "Help!" At last truly running, wanting someone else to come, to see, to make it true. "Help! Murder! Master Montfort's been murdered!"

Old wisdom held that

> *A January spring*
> *Is worth no-thing*

and over the years Dame Frevisse had found that was mostly true. A mild January too often meant a bitter February, a cruel March, a late-come spring; but just now it meant the three and more days of riding had been less of a travail than it would have been in usual January weather, at least so far as bodily comfort went. For ease of going and any haste they might have wanted to make, no, it had not been good. The roads that could have been firm with frost had been soft with mud instead, laboring the horses' going, and so it was only now at midday that their small company of riders was coming by the Thames road from Wallingford down into Goring, bound not for the Thames ferry crossing that made the town prosperous but for St. Mary's nunnery and journey's end.

Message had come two weeks ago to St. Frideswide's priory that Sister Ysobel, a nun here, was far along in the slow dying of lung sickness and had asked leave to see her cousin Domina Elisabeth, prioress of St. Frideswide's, before the end. Domina Elisabeth had immediately sent off a messenger to ask permission to go to her. If she had been an abbess, she would have needed no permission but her own, but St. Frideswide's was under the guidance, however lightly kept, of the abbot of St. Bartholomew's near Northampton, presently her own brother, who had sent back not only permission but a new gown, properly Benedictine-black but fur-lined "for warmer winter riding," he had said. But in fact, the gown was presently a closely wrapped bundle in one of the pack-hampers, safe-kept for wearing once they were at Goring, that Domina Elisabeth not compare poorly with St. Mary's prioress. For the journey both she and Frevisse had made do with heavy woolen cloaks over their usual heavy woolen gowns, with both cloaks and gowns now direly muddied around their hems despite Frevisse's efforts every morning to brush them clean after each night's drying.

Because no nun was supposed to leave her cloister unaccompanied by another nun, she was here as Domina Elisabeth's companion, her prioress's choice with no question of adding to the cost of travel by taking any woman-servant with them, so that all such duties were hers. Both for safety and dignity, however, Domina Elisabeth had been unwilling to travel with less than three men for escort despite the cost that would be to the nunnery in more than money. It would have been better to have the men at winter-work, at plowing and dunging if weather allowed and at the hedging and ditching and array of other tasks for which there was rarely time the rest of the year, so compromise had been made by way of the priory steward's son Dickon, age sixteen and near to mangrown, who would not have been at fieldwork but helping his father with priory accounts and even now after three and a half days' dull riding was still a-glow with his escape.

Rather to her regret, Frevisse had had to admit to having much the same sense of escape herself. She had not thought she would. In truth she had been displeased when Domina Elisabeth chose her for companion, both because she was content where she was and because she suspected why she had been chosen, their way south inevitably taking them close by Ewelme, where all too possibly Frevisse's near relative, Lady Alice de la Pole, would be at home to be visited. A woman of both wealth and, by marriage, high place in the world, her favor could be of use to St. Frideswide's and a visit from her cousin would serve as reminder of that. Since it was Alice's friendship, not her favor, that Frevisse valued, she had not liked the thought of being used by Domina Elisabeth. It was only when she had realized that Domina Elisabeth for now—whatever she might do later—was set on reaching her own cousin as the first business to hand, that Frevisse had been able to turn her mind fully to their journey and found herself enjoying it. She had not known how nunnery life had palled for her until, while tucking her cloak more closely around her against a chill little wind as they slogged down a muddy hill the first morning out from the nunnery, she found herself humming happily. The daily round of worship—the eight Offices of prayer and psalms through every day—were still her heart's delight and soul's joy, but the rest of it—the same duties, the same faces, the same voices, the same walls without let or change, days into weeks into months into years . . .

Without she had known it, a gray weight had settled on her mind and spirit. Only when she found herself riding a singularly graceless horse along a mud-bogged road between winter-barren hedges and raw-earthed fields under a gray sky that constantly threatened and sometimes gave rain, with the likelihood of more such days to follow, and had found she was happy, as if an unsuspected cloud was dispersing from around her, letting her mind lift into pleasure for the first time in . . . how long? . . . did she see how far she had been sunk without knowing it into accidie—into the weariness of spirit so deep it was a sin.

That was accidie's most subtle peril: it crept so slowly into mind and heart that the spirit sank down into the mire of despair without knowing it until too late to win free without terrible struggle. Frevisse had faced it before now in her life and knew she had not been far gone in it this time or she would not have slipped this easily out but that did not lessen her gratitude for her escape. Hand hidden under the enwrapping cloak, she had signed herself with the cross while making a silent prayer of thanks for mercy given.

But that she was almost the only one enjoying their journey was too plain. Domina Elisabeth was taken up with worry for her cousin and annoyance at the muddied travel. The two men, without ever saying so, made it clear they would have preferred to be at something else besides this slow going along strange roads, with strange food at meals, strange beds at night, strangers everywhere they looked, and a constant uncertainty of where they were and of how far there was to go. Only Dickon seemed to feel with Frevisse that the pleasure of constantly being somewhere else outweighed all other troubles. Even now, as they rode along Goring's High Street with its well-made timbered houses, shops, several inns, and folk busy with their day not greatly different from any number of other places through which they had ridden these past days, he was looking about with the same eagerness he had had ever since they left St. Frideswide's.

Frevisse, on the other hand, was glad to know that tomorrow she would not have to be on a horse. Pleasure or no, she was tired and ready to be done with travel for a time and was glad as they approached a cross street well into the town to see ahead of them on the right a long stretch of wall that must enclose the nunnery. At the corner, turning where the wall did to run along a wide street with narrow houses and many shops on its east side, the nunnery wall and buildings on its west, she could see at almost its far end the timber and plaster gatehouse that must lead into the nunnery yard and was tired enough she failed to be uneasy at the sight of other riders turning in through it ahead of them. Since the ferry made Goring the main crossing place of the Thames between Reading's bridge and Wallingford's, travelers must be usual here and besides the inns along the High Street, the nunnery surely had a guesthall of its own where travelers either too important or else too poor to stay elsewhere were welcome. So when Bartelme, their lead rider, said over his shoulder, worried, to Domina Elisabeth, "There's others ahead of us," she only answered, as untroubled as Frevisse, "We're expected. Place will be kept for us."

Worry came only when they reached the gateway themselves and found that the few riders they had seen were the last of maybe a dozen altogether, the yard so crowded with them that Bartelme was forced to draw rein under the gatehouse, unable to go further. Domina Elisabeth rode forward to beside him and Frevisse with her, able to see from there that the cobbled yard was narrowed by a low wall directly across from the gateway, a low-penticed gate leading through it into a grassy churchyard with the nunnery's long-roofed church and a tower along one side, a tall wall around the others. The cobbled yard itself ran to the left, between stables and what she took to be part of the nunnery's cloister and probably the guesthouse, to judge by two nuns with the look of taking charge of things just coming out the door at the head of a few steps up to the doorway there.

Eyeing the riders and horses between him and there, Bartelme said, "I'll shove through, should I, my lady? Let them know you're here?"

Domina Elisabeth shook her head. In the frame of her white wimple and black veil, her face was set with an effort not to show displeasure, Frevisse thought, though she said moderately enough, "No. These are mourners. See? Their needs should be met before ours."

She had the right of it, Frevisse agreed. Most of the riders ahead of them were darkly garbed and beside the stairs a woman in the full mourning-black gown and veils of a new widow was being lifted down from her horse by a man likewise thoroughly in black.

"But my lady—" Bartelme started unhappily.

Frevisse suspected he had come to enjoy the favors that had spilled over to him and Rob and Dickon as a prioress's servants these past few days and nights and was minded to go on enjoying them, but Domina Elisabeth said firmly, "Humility, especially in face of another's need, is a virtue to be practiced whenever the chance is given."

From the hard glint in Domina Elisabeth's voice, Frevisse suspected that humility came to her more by will than natural inclination. The question of whether a virtue was more virtuous if it was attained by effort or if it was better to be virtuous by nature, without struggle, was one that Frevisse had never been able to settle to her satisfaction and she was distracted from it here by better sight of the man who had lifted the widow from her saddle now following her up the stairs. Something about him, even from the back, was familiar but then he and the woman were both gone inside and Domina Elisabeth's fingers had begun to tap with displeasure on the broad rim of her saddle's pommel at still being ignored and from among the other riders now dismounting and the servants coming to take their horses Bartelme hailed a priory servant leading past a laden packhorse with, "Hai! What's it take to be heeded hereabouts?"

"You're not part of this lot, then?" the man asked back.

"Not nearly."

"Hoi!" the man yelled away across the yard. "Here's someone else to see to!" and with a nod at Domina Elisabeth, he tugged the horse's halter and went on his way toward the stable, leaving them to wait a little longer before a girl in a plain nun's habit and the white veil that told she had not taken the final vows of nunhood, was only a novice yet, slipped out of the crowding around the stairs and came at a hurry toward them, a maidservant following behind her.

Flushed with hurry and probably the excitement of it all, she looked quickly between Frevisse and Domina Elisabeth and rightly chose to make curtsy to Domina Elisabeth while saying breathlessly, "My lady. May we help you?"

Domina Elisabeth acknowledged the curtsy with a small bow of her head. "I'm Domina Elisabeth, prioress of St. Frideswide's. I was known to be coming, I think."

"Oh!" The girl's eyes and mouth made matching O's of dismay. "Oh dear."

"I sent word ahead," Domina Elisabeth said, a mere hint of displeasure under her courtesy.

"Oh." The girl curtsied again, more deeply this time, as if that might help. "Yes. You did." Her soft, unpretty face was flushing pink with confusion or distress or both. "Of course you're expected. We didn't know when, only that you were coming but . . ." She cast a rather desperate look around the yard. "Only, since then, there's been a man murdered, you see. These are his widow and family and all. They've come for the inquest. It's tomorrow. And now you've come, too, all at once and . . . Oh dear."

She was openly bewildered at all of it and behind her the maidservant wringing hands in apron was going to be of no help either, it seemed, but with something of the matter explained, Domina Elisabeth let go of her impatience, her skill at smoothing where there was trouble coming to the fore as she said, soothingly now, "What you mean to say is that the widow is to have the guest chamber that was to be mine. Is that it?"

The girl was grateful for the help. "Yes, please you. With her husband being dead here, that seemed the kindest thing to do. But please, I beg your pardon for it, my lady."

"No need of pardon. She should have what comfort she may at a time like this. Your hosteler"—the nun in charge of the nunnery's guests and guesthall—"surely has somewhere for Dame Frevisse and myself to be, once she has chance to see to us. In the meanwhile is there somewhere we can wait besides on horseback and here in the yard?"

"Oh!" The girl's pink flourished into embarrassed red. "I'm sorry. Of course there is." But the turning of her head from side to side betrayed she had no thought where it might be, until she abruptly brightened and offered, "Your cousin. Would you like to see your cousin? I can take you to her. She's in the infirmary. You could be at ease and in quiet and with her while everything is settled."

"That would do very well." Domina Elisabeth smiled

on the girl. "And our men and horses may go to the stable. Bartelme, see to everything here."

The yard was still a confusion of people, horses, and baggage being sorted out, no hope of easily riding through them; dismounting, leaving their men and horses to be seen to the stable by the maidservant, Domina Elisabeth and Frevisse followed the girl through the crowding and past the steps to a further door that, opened by the novice, let them into a low-ceilinged, stone-floored passageway beyond it. Frevisse paused to swing the door closed behind them, shutting out beyond the thick oak planking the fluster of noise from the yard and with a murmured prayer of thanks for the cloister-quiet, followed the other two through the passage and into the square cloister walk that, just as at St. Frideswide's, was surrounded on three sides by nunnery buildings, on the fourth by the church, and opened on its inner side over a low stone wall into a winter-barren garden that in spring, summer, and autumn would surely be bright with flowers and herbs, a haven of color and scents in the heart of the nunnery but for now merely part of the gray-brown winter-world. Two nuns hurried past with arms full of folded linens and sidelong looks to which the novice gave a nod as she led Domina Elisabeth and Frevisse the other way along the walk. The savory waft of cooking smells told the kitchen was nearby and through an open doorway Frevisse caught brief sight of long tables in a room that must be the refectory.

It was past there, at the next turning of the walk, that the novice turned aside into another low passageway and, partway along it, knocked slightly at a door and went in without waiting for an answer that would not have come because, following her in, they found no one there, only all the signs that this was the infirmarian's workroom, familiar and aromatic with hanging bundles of dried herbs and shelves of boxed and stopper-potted medicines, like

St. Frideswide's even to the battered wooden worktable in its middle where the work of making medicines for the nunnery's needs was mostly done.

"Sister Joane?" the novice asked but not as if she expected an answer, adding immediately over her shoulder, "She's probably gone to see if the widow is in need of anything." She pointed toward a shut door across the room. "Sister Ysobel is there. I'll see how she is, tell her you're here. Then you can go in. You and . . ." She looked at Frevisse, hesitating, as if uncertain what was best to do with her.

Feeling the same about herself, Frevisse offered with a nod toward a stool beside the table, "I can wait here. Or . . ." She looked toward the room's third door and the bit of sky seen through the small window set high in the wall beside it, suggesting it must lead outside, and she guessed, "Is there a garden? I could walk there, if it's allowed."

"Oh," the girl said with relief. "Yes. You could." But they both looked to Domina Elisabeth for final permission and only when she had given it with a nod did the girl add, "The key is there on that hook just by the door. Mind you leave it there, though. Sister Joane twitches otherwise."

Frevisse took the thought of an unknown but twitching Sister Joane into the garden with her, the key left carefully behind. She was careful of the door, too, closing it silently, unsure how troubled by noise the dying Sister Ysobel might be, and only when it was safely latched, turned to take a full look at where she was.

St. Frideswide's did not have the pleasure of a separate infirmary garden; this one would have delighted Dame Claire, their infirmarian. Enclosed on three sides by the nunnery buildings, the fourth side a turf bank topped by a high withy-woven fence, it was shut away from any sight of the world and the world from any sight of it, though somewhere nearby a stream was running with pleasant watery murmur. A graveled walk flanked with herb beds with the clipped skeletons of plants showing above their careful bedding-in of leaves ran around the garden's four sides, with in the middle of each side a short walk running in toward the center, joining a smaller walk around a little grassy square at the garden's very center where a young ash tree's winter-bare branches made a dark fretwork against the pale sky. The intersecting paths divided other herb beds equally closed down for the winter but in the frost-weary grass around the tree were a cheerful scattering of bold and very early snowdrops, their shining white a promise that sometime spring would happen.

Very likely these particular snowdrops would come to grief before long in a seasonable freeze, Frevisse thought, but that only meant they were to be the more enjoyed now, along with the peek of a primrose's determinedly green leaves at the edge of a bed and the dark swell of buds on the end of the ash tree's twigs. A January spring might be worth nothing but she could not help preferring it to the bitter cold there might have been and nonetheless did not choose to sit on any of the benches set along the paths but for warmth's sake and to work out the weariness of riding took her way at much the measured pace she would have used if circling St. Frideswide's cloister walk, around and through the garden, along one path and into another and back by a different way and around again, making no haste because where was there to haste to?

She was paused to watch the ash tree's highest branches moving against the sky in a wind that did not reach the garden, when from the unseen tower of the church a bell began to call bright-toned and clear, surely a summons to Nones' prayers, and she half turned in answer to it before she caught herself. If she had known her way well enough to slip into the church unnoticed, she would have gone but she wasn't even sure of how to reach the church from where she was, and with the other upsets to the nunnery's life today, the nuns did not need a strange Benedictine wandering about when their minds should be turned to prayer. When there was time for Domina Elisabeth and her to be made known properly, they would slip into life here easily enough, the differences none so great between life under St. Benedict's Rule and that of St. Augustine's that St. Mary's followed, but in the meanwhile she was better kept out of the way, and as the bell ceased its clear calling began the Office to herself, softly aloud, *"Deus in adjutorium."* God be my helper. A shortened Office was allowed when out of the nunnery and, her head bowed, she began to walk again while she said it, had finished but was still walking with her head down, still enwrapped in the soul-easing pleasure of prayer, when on the path in front of her a woman said, "There was a man murdered here lately, you know."

Chapter 2

Frevisse stopped short and raised her head but kept her surprise to herself as she answered, level-voiced, "No, I didn't know."

The woman in front of her nodded as if pleased to hear it. Elderly but standing straightly, her age-faded eyes bright amongst the deep-set wrinkles of her long-boned face, she pointed with a short, leaf-carved walking staff of polished oak toward the ash tree.

"Over there. Stabbed to the heart. Four days ago. His clerk found him."

"Indeed?" Frevisse ventured.

"Indeed. Though I doubt the clerk did it, if that's what you're thinking."

"I wasn't."

"Ah." The woman apparently found that both a surprise and a lack. Though white-wimpled and black-veiled, she was no nun; her gown of dark-dyed green wool with darker-dyed high-standing collar and wide cuffs told that, but while Frevisse had no guess who she might be—not the grieving widow, assuredly—the woman said with complete certainty, "You're Sister Ysobel's cousin. The prioress. Domina Elisabeth."

Her certainty made Frevisse pleased to answer, "No. She's with Sister Ysobel."

"Ah. Then you are . . . ?"

"Dame Frevisse. I companied her here. And you?" Since questions could go both ways.

"Lady Agnes Lengley," she answered readily enough, with a pause to see if Frevisse found that significant. Frevisse did not and Lady Agnes went on a little more briskly, "I come sometimes to sit with Sister Ysobel but she'll enjoy fresh company and I'll leave them to it for today." She jerked the tip of her walking staff toward the ash tree again. "So if you didn't know about him, you weren't praying for him just now?"

"No."

"Pity. He was an unpleasant man. He's probably in need of prayers."

She started forward, needing her walking staff a little but not much and clearly expecting Frevisse to join her.

As much for curiosity as courtesy, Frevisse did, tucking her hands up her opposite sleeves and shortening her steps to match the older woman's, saying, "His widow rode in a little while ago with a great many people."

"Ah, yes. I saw that. And probably none of them much caring he's dead but not about to miss for anything the funeral and the sport of mourning him."

Dryly Frevisse asked, "He wasn't much liked?"

"Liked? Morys Montfort? Not by anyone who knew him as far as I've ever heard."

"Montfort?" Frevisse stopped, startled and not hiding it. "The crowner Montfort? Is that who's dead?"

Lady Agnes, gone a step onward, stopped and looked back over her shoulder, surprised in her turn. "Yes. That's him. You knew him?"

"Somewhat." And had not liked him. As crowner he was a royal officer, charged with looking into any sudden deaths, to learn if they were accident or if there was blame, and if there was blame, then to call in the sheriff and collect any fines there might be due to the king. The office carried both power to do good or ill and the chance for profits both just and unjust, and the few times, too many, that Frevisse had had dealings with Master Montfort had not been pleasant. That he was violently dead was neither a surprise nor a distress but she asked, "Who's thought to have killed him?"

"There's never even a good guess, so far as I've heard. Or maybe I mean there are too many guesses." Lady Agnes walked on, prodding her walking staff into the gravel. "He made enough men angry at him over the years he was crowner. Or it was maybe something he's done since he became escheator. Much good that's done him."

"Escheator?" Frevisse was again in step at Lady Agnes's side. "When did he leave off being crowner?"

"Last Michaelmas. Well, he was serving under Walter Wythill, who's properly escheator, but Wythill has been none so well, as Montfort well knew when he agreed to serve him, and so Montfort was seeing to much of his duties these few months past. With an eye to succeeding him, I'd warrant, and hope of going on to be sheriff afterwards, surely. That's the way it goes, often enough. But that's all it got him." She pointed her staff toward the tree.

Escheator was another royal office, its main duty to determine the lawful heir or heirs of inheritances and see to them having their properties—with due fines paid to

the king. As with the crowner, there were profits to be
had from the work, but as Lady Agnes said, it was also
often a man's last step to becoming sheriff of a shire, with
such wide-reaching power that the thought that Montfort
might someday have ranged so high made Frevisse
slightly ill, and to cut off the half-made thought that it
was better he was dead, she asked, "But what was he
doing here in this garden at all?" An unlikely place for
any man to be, let alone Montfort.

"Now that's a question that's been asked," Lady Agnes
said. "No one knows. As a place to kill someone, it's
private enough, that's sure." She gave a brief look around
the garden, as Frevisse already had. To one side there was
only the blank, windowless back wall of what Frevisse
guessed was a barn or byre. To the other side a single
narrow window looked down from high in the gable-end
of some cloister building, while from the infirmary there
were only two small windows set well up under the eaves,
too high for easy looking out of. As for ways into the
garden, there was only the door from the infirmary and
another through a tall wooden wall across the gap between
the infirmary and what she supposed was barn or byre,
which raised a question . . .

"But who he met here and why he was killed . . ." Lady
Agnes sniffed disdainfully, as if being killed was an ill-
mannered thing to do. ". . . no one knows."

"He likely had enemies enough," Frevisse suggested.

"In plenty, I'd guess. Nor had he made any friends
lately around here, either."

"He was in Goring as escheator, then?"

"He was."

Lady Agnes's answer was clipped short enough that
Frevisse held back from asking more that way; asked instead, "The inquest is tomorrow, I think I heard. Has the
crowner learned anything, do you know?" Whoever was
crowner now.

"Ah." Lady Agnes brightened. "That I don't know, though word is he's been busy enough these two days past with questions and all. Having his mother here will likely slow him down a bit but that can hardly be helped."

"His mother?"

"Montfort's widow. The crowner is Montfort's son, God help him. Succeeded to the office when Montfort moved up to escheator, worse luck for him now. A grieving mother on one hand—supposing she's grieving all that much, which I wouldn't be—and a murdered father on the other. He'll be wishing himself anywhere but here before this is done, I'll warrant."

They were taking the turn of the path back toward the infirmary from one of the far corners of the garden, in time to see the infirmary door open and a nun stand aside to let Domina Elisabeth go ahead of her into the garden.

"Ah," Lady Agnes said with satisfaction. "Here comes Domina Matilda, and that's your Domina Elisabeth with her, I take it."

Frevisse murmured agreement. The afternoon was waning, with more shadows than sunlight within the garden walls now, but they joined the two prioresses on the path outside the infirmary door where the light still fell most golden and almost warm. Names were given, with much bowing of heads and a curtsy of respect from Frevisse to St. Mary's prioress, a gaunt, crisp woman in a faultless Augustinian habit and firmly starched and sharply pressed veil, whose deepened lines around eyes and mouth looked more likely to laughter than ill-temper as she said, "I've already given apologies to Domina Elisabeth for your poor welcome. Unhappily, I'm not sure I can better it, we're so suddenly crowded. More folk came with Mistress Montfort than we expected and—"

"Now there's no trouble," Lady Agnes interrupted. "The both of them are welcome to stay with me."

Domina Matilda gave her a considering look before

saying, "That's kindly offered," adding to Domina Elisabeth with a smile, "Lady Agnes's house is nearly opposite our east gate. You'd be well seen to there, I promise, as well as be able to come easily to most of the Offices if you choose." Her smile deepened. "I can also speak well of her character."

"Hah," Lady Agnes said.

"Besides," Domina Matilda went on, "she can show you the back way to and from the infirmary and let you use her key, to visit Sister Ysobel as you choose."

"Her key?" Domina Elisabeth said, too surprised to hide it. Back ways into nunneries were simply a common fact; keys to them in lay hands were not.

"That she may see Sister Ysobel as she wishes."

"It's what I came for today," Lady Agnes put in, "but you were here already and pleased Sister Ysobel surely was to see you."

"You're friend to my cousin, then?" Domina Elisabeth asked.

"For some years now. She was the infirmarian's help when I once fell ill enough"—and once had better be the only time it happened to her, her tone said—"to need all the care St. Mary's could give me."

"And gave it gladly, fair recompense for all your kindnesses to us," Domina Matilda put in.

Lady Agnes acknowledged that with a slight nod and a smile. "The care included Sister Ysobel keeping watch over me through the worst hours of my ailment and sitting with me for company through the days it took me to recover. Now, in her need, I return the favor as best I may. Though not to so good an outcome, I fear."

"I fear not," Domina Elisabeth agreed quietly, and the four women made the sign of the cross on themselves before she added, "Dame Frevisse and I would be pleased to stay with you, my lady. Thank you for the courtesy."

Domina Matilda smiled with relief—it was no little

matter to have strange nuns sleep in a nunnery's dorter, probably the only place she had left to offer, unavoidably distracting and disturbing the others from their usual ways—and Lady Agnes said briskly, "Best we be off then. You'll have to keep their men and horses," she added to Domina Matilda. "I've not the room for them, but you'll give orders to let their people know where they are and where to bring their baggage?"

"Assuredly," Domina Matilda agreed.

They made their farewells and thanks to her then and parted at the infirmary's door, Lady Agnes promptly turning away along the walk toward the garden's other door, saying to Domina Elisabeth beside her and Frevisse following after, "She's a good woman, is Domina Matilda. Keeps a firm hand on everything and takes no nonsense from anyone, including me. Here's our way."

The door in the wooden wall was narrow and latched by a short wooden bar fastened to the door and swung down into a wooden hasp on the frame. It opened into the gap between the buildings, with another wooden wall and door at its other end. "The gardener's way into the garden," Lady Agnes said, standing aside to let them go ahead of her, "for when he's needed here, and if a doctor is wanted in the infirmary, without need to bring him through the nunnery. A moment please." Having followed them into the alleyway, she paused now to almost but not quite shut the door and then fish a long, broad-teethed key from her sleeve.

"You see how it works," she said, crowding aside as best she could to let them both see as she jiggled the key into the lock on this side of the door. "The key goes in here, and when I turn it, it turns a latch on the garden side that lifts the bar out of its catch, letting me open the door. To lock it from here, I have to turn the key to lift the latch to lift the bar so I can pull the door shut and then turn the key to lower the latch, setting the bar into its catch. Done," she added, wiggling the key from the lock and tucking it back into her sleeve.

"Then from inside there's no need of a key," Frevisse said. "The bar can just be lifted by anyone on that side of the door."

"Even so."

The alleyway, closed in between walls and under the eaves of the barn—a byre would have had a smell of animals, Frevisse decided—was dark and chill but short and at its other end the other door had no lock nor was it as well made as the other, loose on its hinges as Frevisse swung it open and went through into what she guessed was the nunnery's kitchen garden, a long stretch of rough earth beds and low wicker fences overlooked by the back of nunnery buildings and separated on one side by a waist-high willow-woven fence from a large, open yard. Not the foreyard by which they had come into the nunnery but one of byres and barns, a haystack, a long woodpile, and men at work at the varied tasks that made possible the nuns' life of prayers.

The only idle man in sight was sitting on a bench, leaning against the kitchen garden's gatepost, but as Lady Agnes led them the shortest way toward him, he stood up, straightened his doublet, and bowed to Lady Agnes, who waved a hand at him and said, "I'm going home, Lucas. Move out."

He bowed again but took a good look at Domina Elisabeth and Frevisse before he set off along the yard, the women following. The well-trod mud made easy going except where a cart had lately rutted it raw and Lucas paused while they managed across it with careful feet and lifted skirts. No one paid them any particular heed that Frevisse noticed, though Lady Agnes asked pardon for bringing them such a back way with, "It's convenient to my purpose when I go to see Sister Ysobel. No getting caught up in talk in the cloister and so forth on days when I don't have time for it."

Following Lucas, they turned through a plain, double gateway, one gate set open, into the foreyard they had left to enter the cloister at the first. It was quiet now, guests and their horses and baggage all sorted out and away, only two men left, cleaning the cobbles with shovel and broom. Now Lucas fell back to a few paces behind Frevisse, still following Lady Agnes and Domina Elisabeth, along the foreyard and out the nunnery's front gateway to the street again and into the hurry of people about their end-of-day shopping or home-going. With no riders or carts coming, Lady Agnes crossed it a-slant to the right, saying to Domina Elisabeth beside her and a little over her shoulder to Frevisse, "I live just there," pointing with her staff along the street to an overhanging housefront set, unusually, longwise rather than narrow to the street.

Like most of its neighbors, it rose two tall stories and, like them, was half-timbered, the plastering between the wide timbers scored into cross-hatched and swirling patterns, while the roof's thick thatch was golden with newness. At street level, set back under the upper storey's overhang and thereby protected from weather when it came, two narrow shops fronted the street, their shutters down to make counters out into the way of passersby, the better to show their goods. One of them was selling gloves ranging from plain cloth to fine leather, the other had baskets of many-colored embroidery thread set out on display and skeins of fine-dyed wool hung on a bar above them. Their keepers were both women who gave smiling greeting to Lady Agnes, who gave it smiling back and said low-voiced to Domina Elisabeth, Frevisse barely able to catch the words, "Widows, like myself, the both of them, but not so fortunate in their husbands. They don't pay much rent to me but they make a living and that's better than having them poor and on the parish's hands. Besides, they're quiet. I'd not have men loud under my solar day in and out for anything I might be paid."

Lucas lengthened his stride to go ahead of them and open a door set in a gateway between Lady Agnes's house and the next. They passed through into a cart-wide, cobbled, clean-swept passage leading back between the houses, chill and deep-shadowed in the fading afternoon but opening into a small, cobbled yard with a blank wall of the neighboring house down one side, the rear wing of Lady Agnes's house down the other, the yard cut off at its far side by a head-high wattle-and-daub wall, neatly capped by thatching, and a closed gate, while the main part of the house rose between them and the street now.

That much Frevisse took in before a kerchiefed, aproned bundle of a woman flurried out of a doorway from that main part of the house and came clucking like a flustered hen toward Lady Agnes, thrusting a cloak at her while Lady Agnes fended it off, saying, "Letice, there's no need. I'm about to be indoors, aren't I?"

"You shouldn't have been out this long without it and the day's turning colder by the minute. If you've taken cold, it's no fault of mine. I saw you coming and have Emme building up the fire this very minute but this will see you warm until then."

Still fending off the cloak and moving toward the door, Lady Agnes said, "Letice, this is Domina Elisabeth of St. Frideswide's near Banbury, Sister Ysobel's cousin. Remember I said she was coming? And Dame Frevisse. They're my guests for this while. St. Mary's is overcrowded."

Letice made a quick, respectful curtsy their way without slacking her heed of Lady Agnes but leaving off with the cloak to go ahead of her up the stone step and open the door, saying, "I saw them crossing the street with you, my lady, and thought that might be the way of it and I've sent Cook word. I'll tell Emme to see to airing Master

Stephen's room when she's done with the fire, shall I?"

"Yes," Lady Agnes agreed, adding to Domina Elisabeth, "Stephen is my grandson. We keep his room ready even though he mostly stays with his wife's family since he married. And here we are."

With Letice standing aside to let them pass, she led them through the carved wooden arch of the doorway into the darkness of a wooden-walled booth that served to hold off the worst draughts from the rest of the house and through its smaller inner doorway into the house's hall, a high-raftered room running the house's full length, stone-floored and well-lighted by a pair of tall windows looking out into yard they had just left, with a fireplace in the wall between them and beyond them another doorway that led away into the wing along the yard. At the far end a narrow stairway made of thick oaken slabs went steeply up to an open gallery above, with shut doors at either end to private parts of the house, Frevisse supposed, the one on the left probably into the solar Lady Agnes had said was above the street-facing shops, and it was indeed to the stairs that Lady Agnes went, saying to Domina Elisabeth, "Now for it. Pray, pardon me my slowness." For the first time the need for her staff was plain as she leaned to it heavily while gripping the stairs' rope railing with one hand and pulling herself upward. Letice had hurried to catch up to her but the stairway was too narrow; she could not help her lady from beside her, only climbed close behind, ready to be needed, and at the top give her a push up the last step that Lady Agnes seemed not to mind, only turned, flushed with effort and a little short of breath, to say down to Domina Elisabeth, "There. I only hope your knees are better than my poor old ones."

"You could save your knees," Letice muttered, laboring up the last step herself, "if you'd have your room below instead of up here."

"There's nothing to see from any room down there ex-

cept the yard and there's nothing goes on there," Lady
Agnes answered as if this were something said between
them more often than once. "Come," she added to Domina
Elisabeth now climbing after her. "I'll show you my
chamber. You'll see for yourself why I mean to keep it."
    "They might better like to see their own," Letice said.
    "Before Emme has seen to it? Nonsense." Thudding her
short staff solidly on the gallery's wooden floor with
every step, Lady Agnes headed for the nearer door, and
with a well-heaved sigh Letice hustled ahead of her to
open it.
    Frevisse, following Domina Elisabeth up the stairs and
then along the gallery, knew as soon as she entered the
solar why Lady Agnes favored it. Besides being of goodly
size, it had a long window set under the front eave, thrust
out over the shopfronts and the street, with glass in the
middle two lights so that even on days too cold to have
the wooden shutters open on the unglassed ends, Lady
Agnes could still look out at whatever might be passing
in the street, if not over the nunnery wall. More than that,
the chamber was amply furnished toward comfort, not
only with Lady Agnes's tall bed hung with cream-colored
curtains embroidered in twining green vines and crimson
flowers but thick rush matting underfoot to warm the
floor, a wide-topped table with a bench along one side,
two backed chairs, a pair of heavy chests along one wall,
and painted wall-hangings of ships with wind-bellied sails
and strange cities perched on rocky coasts. There were the
usual joint stools, too, and the clutter of everyday living—
an embroidery frame with some three-quarters finished
piece of tapestry work in bold colors beside one of the
chairs; three books in a pile on one end of the table; folded
linen in a basket beside one of the chests, waiting to be
put away—but best of all just now was the deep-hearthed
fireplace where a woman in servant's gown and apron,
gray hair wisping out from under the back of the neatly

wrapped linen kerchief covering her head, was presently laying kindling carefully onto an old fire's coals, with three logs ready to join them when there was fire enough.

That was where Frevisse would have gone, for choice, but Lady Agnes was beckoning both her and Domina Elisabeth to come with her to the window where the shutters stood wide to the afternoon's thinning light, saying as they joined her, "You see? I should sit downstairs with four walls and nothing but servants to watch when there's this?"

She had the right of it, Frevisse silently agreed. The nunnery wall was indeed too high for her to see anything except nunnery rooftops and the church tower, but the street was all hers to watch and the nunnery's main gate and whoever came and went through it.

But Lady Agnes was drawing the shutter closed at one end of the window with a nod for Frevisse to do the same at the other, turning when she had finished to say, "Emme, haven't you that fire going yet?"

"Takes time, my lady," Emme said as if she had said it uncounted times before now and was resigned to saying it patiently many times more. But Frevisse was coming to suspect that Lady Agnes's servants were probably good at patience or they'd not be her servants for long. Certainly Letice took patiently Lady Agnes's flurry of orders to set the two chairs and a joint stool nearer the fire and that she must tell Lucas the tables needn't be set up in the hall tonight because she and the nuns would dine here and bring some hot spiced cider as soon as might be because, "It's perishing cold in here. Emme!"

"Done, my lady," Emme declared, standing up and back from the fire now licking up cheerily around the logs laid on the kindling she had been tending.

"Off with you, then, and see to airing my ladies' bed. A pan of hot coals now and another at bedtime, I'd say, to be sure of it. Go on."

Letice and Emme both went, and Lady Agnes, settling herself into one of the chairs, gestured Domina Elisabeth to the other and Frevisse to the joint stool which, being nearest to the warmth spreading out from the fire, suited her very well. Left to herself, she would have been content simply to sit and be warm, but Lady Agnes, hands folded on the rounded top of her staff, leaned forward in her chair and said to Domina Elisabeth, "So. You've heard how this widow comes to be in your way. You've heard about our murder?"

"Only that there had been one."

"Ah. Well, then." With no doubt that Domina Elisabeth would be as eager to hear as she was to tell, Lady Agnes started in again on all that Frevisse had already heard of Montfort's death. Not interested in hearing it again, Frevisse turned her gaze and mind to the fire, watching the flames at their dance and play and the slow settling of the logs into a bed of coals that had been kindling and in a while would be only ashes, just as the logs would be before the evening was done, with new logs brought to take their place, to burn to ashes in their turn. Like human lives. A brief, bright flourishing and then an end.

She ought to feel more for Montfort's death than she did.

She prodded at her feelings but nothing stirred. There was no regret in her that he was dead, only that he had died so badly, a mean-minded man come to a mean end. She would pray for his damned soul but that was the most she could do and even then with no eagerness, only duty. If anything, she would pray more readily for his murderer. Whatever reason he had had for killing Montfort—and knowing Montfort, he could well have had a great one— murder was among the worst sins and the murderer as much in need of prayer as Montfort was.

The bell from St. Mary's church tower began to sound its clear calling to Vespers. Lady Agnes broke off her telling of the clerk raising an outcry at finding the body and Domina Elisabeth paused her dismay to cross themselves, but to Frevisse starting to rise to her feet in answer to the bell's summons, Domina Elisabeth raised a hand and said, "We needn't go tonight. We've had a long day," and turned back to Lady Agnes, leaving Frevisse caught all unexpectedly into anger that Domina Elisabeth so lightly dismissed the Office as if it were something to be bothered over or not, as one chose.

But anger was a sin, too, and Frevisse quenched it, instead slid around on the joint stool to face the fire and put her back as much as possible to the other women, leaving Lady Agnes to go on, "Still, the inquest is to be here in my hall tomorrow, did I tell you? When that's done, we'll know as much as almost anyone about it all, but in the meanwhile people are saying . . ." while she silently began Vespers for herself.

Chapter 3

he morning was wearing on at too fast a pace for all that must needs be done, and Master Gruesby with an untidy bundle of papers clasped to his chest with one arm, a cushion tucked under the other, and quills and ink bottle in his hands shuffled more quickly than was his wont up the hall toward the table at its head, slowed by his left shoe having come undone while he crossed the street and no way to refasten it until he could set everything down and that he could not do until he reached the table. He had been here earlier, to be sure the table would be where it was needed and to learn how many benches there would be. Most of those who would crowd in to the inquest would be there just to gawk. They could stand and be welcome to it but for the

jury and the witnesses there must be places to sit. And
for Mistress Montfort, too. Master Christopher had urged
against her being there but she had insisted, in her quiet
way. That she would be.

She was always quiet, was Mistress Montfort. That was
something Master Gruesby had always liked about her
because a quiet woman was a seemly woman. Or so it
was said. On his own account, he rather thought it was
not the seemliness of it he liked so much as the relief it
had always been from Master Montfort's ceaseless *un*-
quiet. He wondered, as he had before, if she had made
any unquiet grieving over Master Montfort's death but
could not imagine that she had. No one seemed much
grieved over it really. Even this morning, all she had been
was quietly firm when telling Master Christopher she
would come to the inquest and Master Christopher had
given way and so Master Gruesby had this cushion from
the nunnery, both to save a place for her on one of the
benches and to make that place more comfortable.

"Somewhere near the front, that people can't turn
around to stare at her," Master Christopher had said. "But
not at the very front. Nor directly in front of me. Well to
the side and a little back would be best."

But first there were the papers and quills and ink with
which to deal and there was no one to ask for help because
just for the moment Lady Agnes Lengley's hall was
empty, even of her servants. But they had set up the six
benches just as he'd told them, facing up the hall toward
the table, three and three, and Master Gruesby supposed
it did not matter that none of them was there because
Master Christopher already had one of his own men
guarding the door, to keep out anyone who shouldn't
come in yet. Still, there was no one to help . . . With a
sidewise lean and twist, Master Gruesby laid the quills
down without damage to their neatly trimmed points; was
able then to set down the ink bottle; laid the cushion to

one side on the table; stacked the papers at Master Christopher's place; took up the cushion again; and after a careful moment to choose, went to the far end of the second right-hand bench and laid it there for Mistress Montfort.

Only then, after a long look around to be sure everything was to satisfaction for now, did he sit down himself to see to tying his shoelace, first pulling up his shoe's soft leather top to around his ankle, then wrapping the leather lace around it twice before neatly tying a bow. A double knot would be more sure, he knew, but he was never able to bring himself to it, because what if the lace should become wet and swell? He'd not be able to undo it easily, might even have to cut it and what a waste that would be. No. Better to make a simple knot and hope for the best.

Pleased, as usual, with his decision, he wiggled his foot, to be sure the knot was tight enough but not too tight, and stood up. One of his own little jests—kept to himself because he never presumed to be so bold as to make them aloud—was that he had given up any thought of becoming a monk or friar because his feet chilled too easily and so he could not have endured wearing sandals.

Of course it was only a jest because no monk or friar was expected to go only sandaled in England's bitter weather. Nor had he ever thought at all of becoming a monk or friar. But then, he'd never really thought much about becoming anything, really. He'd come to be a clerk because he was good with ink and paper and writing down words and liked doing it. If that wasn't what God had wanted of him, well, God had not yet seen fit to tell him otherwise. Clerking agreed with him and that was the sum of it. Or he agreed with clerking. But it came to the same, he supposed. Or did it? He wasn't certain. But then he was certain of so few things. Or at least not deeply certain. He managed to be reasonably certain about a great many things, yes, but not deeply certain because there were so many questions in life and so few reasonable answers.

Answers, yes. Somebody was always ready with answers. It was reasonable answers that seemed in short supply. Such as . . . such as why did the sky change color at sunrise and sunset? Nobody seemed even to wonder about that but there had to be a reason. God's will, of course, was supposed to be answer enough, but it wasn't, was it? Or maybe it was. When Roger Bacon had sought answers beyond that, he'd put himself into all manner of trouble, hadn't he? So maybe, Master Gruesby thought, now that he thought about it, he was fortunate that he seemed only good at questions, not at answers. And fortunate in that he liked clerking, liked keeping order where otherwise there would be disorder, liked taking care of small matters that otherwise would have no care taken of them.

He looked to the table again and realized he'd done it wrong. The pens and ink, those were right, they belonged there, but the papers . . . Those were his and should not be there and he hurried back and gathered them together quickly, before anyone could come in and see what he'd done. Trying to make them somewhat more orderly, he tapped them edge-on to the table, but the pieces were too many sizes and rough-torn shapes ever to be tidy and having done what he could, he looked around for somewhere to put them and found himself at a loss. For too many years his place at a crowner's inquest had been here, at a table's end or somewhere equally aside but close to the main way of things, taking notes and reading out things when they were demanded of him. He was used to being a part of everything, though not a part that anyone noticed, and that had changed not at all when Master Montfort became escheator. It was unsettling that today would be different. Today he wasn't anyone's clerk but had merely offered to help Master Christopher's young Denys, had brought things here and set them up for him while he and Master Christopher went over today's regrettable business. His own place wouldn't be here at the table but there—he looked sideways at the left-hand benches where the jury would sit—because this time he was a witness, of all things, because he had found Master Montfort's body and would therefore have to give evidence and answer questions. Instead of being out of the way, he was going to be noticed and he didn't know . . . he really didn't know . . . how he was going to bear that.

And what did he do with his notes between now and then if he couldn't have them on the table? He had made them as soon as might be after Master Montfort's death. It was important to do that; to set things down before the mind began to change things. He knew how that happened from the years he'd spent making record of everything people said when questioned by Master Montfort as crowner and lately as escheator. Most people's minds and memories were very unsteady, so at the very first chance he'd had, he'd written down everything. Not that there was much. He'd added some other papers to his few to give him more to hold. If he couldn't be writing, he liked having papers to hold. It gave his hands something to do.

Now, as if some of his papers might have lost themselves in the little while they'd been lying on the table, he ruffled through them. Then, for lack of anywhere else to put them, he rolled them tightly together and tucked them into his close-cinched belt with unsteady fingers. It always made him uneasy when things weren't as they'd always been. He liked things to be as they'd always been. He wanted—he admitted it to himself—he wanted to be safely behind a pen at the end of the table or off in a corner, unnoticed, hardly looked at. Today people were going to be looking at him. Not only looking at him but *seeing* him. He wasn't used to being seen. He was used to not being seen. He liked not being seen. It was safer.

But like and unlike had nothing to do with duty. He knew that as well as he knew anything, and with a bracing little sigh he gave a last look around to be certain yet again that everything was as it should be for now, then made to leave the hall, quickly before any servants should come back and maybe want to talk to him, only to be brought up short at the doorway by the need to step aside from a woman coming in. With his eyes down, as usual, he saw only the hem of her black gown—of good-quality wool, he noted; a lady, not a servant, surely—and murmured, eyes still down, "Pardon, my lady."

She should have simply gone past him. Instead she hesitated and Master Gruesby looked up, supposing she might have some order to give him, whoever she was, and was surprised to find she was a nun. Not that nuns were uncommon, certainly, but—in his unease at being noticed he looked her in the face, and gasped before he could stop himself, "Dame Frevisse!" Then dropped his eyes and slid past her and out the door and away, all haste and no courtesy at all.

Frevisse turned to stare after him as he scuttled out the outer door, startled both to know him and to realize that she had no thought at all of what his name might be. She had seen him often enough in Montfort's company but that he had a name he might be called by had never crossed her mind; he was simply the grubby-dressed clerk with ink-stained fingers who sat off to one side with ink-pot and pen, scratching away at bits of paper and parchment. She had probably seen more of his stooped shoulders and the top of his balding head than she had ever seen of his face and didn't remember that she had ever heard him even speak until now. She had not even thought of him when Lady Agnes said Montfort's clerk had found his body. But then, Montfort had likely had other clerks; why should it be this one who found him? And it hardly mattered anyway, and if it did she'd know soon enough, once the inquest began.

Meanwhile, her hope was for a little time alone in the chamber she and Domina Elisabeth had shared last night. Though she had awakened in the night at the hour for the Offices of Matins and Lauds, there had been no hope of going to them, of course, but she had said their prayers and psalms silently to herself, despite Domina Elisabeth's even breathing across the wide bed that told she slept on, unnoticing the hour. They had both risen in time to go to Prime, though, slipping into the church's nave with a few devout townswomen, rather than trying to join the nuns in the choir. They had been noticed nonetheless and afterward Domina Matilda had sent a servant to invite them to dine with her nuns in the refectory. Brief explanation of them had been made then and they had returned to the church with the nuns for Mass, Frevisse pleased for the day to have some familiar shape.

As in St. Frideswide's, the nuns' chapter meeting had come then, where the nuns dealt with nunnery matters, no place for outsiders, and Domina Elisabeth had gone to spend the time with her cousin. Frevisse, not minded to return to Lady Agnes's, had refuged in the church, trying for prayer but never managing to lose herself in it among the too much coming and going by others, most distractingly Montfort's widow who, draped in trailing black and accompanied by a maidservant, came to kneel below the altar with bowed head and clasped hands, staying until the bell began to call the nuns to Tierce. Without ever raising her head enough to give Frevisse clear sight of her face, she had left then and Frevisse had gone into the choir, to wait until she and Domina Elisabeth were shown where they might sit since there were more choir places than nuns in St. Mary's to fill them, just as at St. Frideswide's.

Frevisse had been deeply grateful to be able to join in the Office and to know she could again whenever else she so chose the while they were in Goring, but what she was hoping for now was a chance to sit quietly alone for a time before the inquest and she was not pleased as she reached the top of the steep steps from the hall, intent on the intricate effort of holding to the rope railing and managing her skirts, that Lady Agnes came at that moment out of her solar, saw her, and exclaimed gladly, "Ah! Dame Frevisse. You're here. Domina Elisabeth isn't with you?"

Tucking her feelings away, Frevisse answered evenly, "She stayed to talk with Domina Matilda."

"Who's already sent word she won't be here, but Domina Elisabeth won't miss the inquest, surely?"

"She means to be here, yes," Frevisse agreed.

"She'd best not linger or she'll have to push her way through the crowd to come in. They're starting to gather, aren't they?"

Having noticed clusters of people in the street outside the house and others coming as she came from the nunnery, Frevisse agreed they were.

"More than there'll be room for, likely," Lady Agnes said. She gestured behind her to two men and a young woman come out of the solar behind her. "We saw them from the window. But we'll see all from up here in the gallery and no trouble. I've sent word to Mistress Montfort that she's welcome to join us, rather than be crowded around by folk down there. Better for her son, too, if she's not there, weeping in front of him while he's trying to be crowner."

"There's no 'try' about him being crowner," protested the younger of the men, joining her. "He *is* crowner, and he'll know she's here whether he's looking at her or not."

"If she's not in plain sight in front of him," Lady Agnes said tartly, "he won't think about her at all. That's how it is with you men and don't tell me it isn't, Stephen my boy, because I've lived long enough to know better." She turned to waggle a finger at the young woman. "You take heed, Nichola. Out of sight is out of mind with men."

Nichola came forward, laughing, to take hold of Stephen's hand. "That's why I take care not to be out of sight."

Despite she was wimpled and veiled like a married woman, Frevisse saw with surprise that she was, like her laughter, very young, a girl hardly old enough to have come to her womanhood yet.

"And how can you think you're ever out of my mind and heart, Grandmother?" Stephen asked, keeping hold of Nichola but taking Lady Agnes's hand to raise and kiss. He looked to be as much as ten years older than the girl, a well-grown man in his early twenties.

"I only believe it because I want to, not because it's true," Lady Agnes returned, still tart but smiling on him before she turned to the older man on her other side, gesturing him forward as she said, "Dame Frevisse, before you meet my graceless grandson, I pray you let me introduce Master Philip Haselden to you."

Because Lady Agnes gave him no particular title but his dark red houppelande, short-hemmed and slit for riding, was amply cut, deep-pleated, and trimmed in black fur at wrists and hem, Frevisse guessed him to be an well-landed esquire, plainly somewhere in hale middle-age, with the high coloring and firm bearing of someone who ate well and spent much time out of doors, probably in the saddle.

As he bowed with a smile, Lady Agnes went on, "With my husband's death, Master Haselden became first man of our corner of the shire."

"But alas, ever second in your heart, my lady," he said.

Lady Agnes rapped him lightly on a booted ankle with her staff. "Flatterer. This, on the other hand, is my grandson and heir, Stephen Lengley."

The younger man let go of Nichola's hand to give Frevisse a bow that showed off his legs in their dark hosen below his short-cut, cream-colored houppelande trimmed in thick brown fur. His grandmother took advantage of his bow to tap him lightly behind with her staff and warn, "Don't show off," before adding, "And this is his wife, Nichola. Master Haselden's daughter."

Frevisse bent her head in answer to the girl's low curtsy, understanding now how the girl had become so young a wife. The wedding of the heir of an obviously wealthy widow to a daughter of a well-landed, possibly equally wealthy squire was likely to be of profit all the way around. And though it had possibly not been a consideration when the match was made, Stephen and Nichola seemed to agree well together because, her courtesy to Frevisse done, Nichola smiled warmly up at Stephen who smiled warmly down at her, and it crossed Frevisse's mind that although Nichola's pretty little face was still more child's than woman, her softly rounded body under her pale blue gown with its many-pleated bodice and spreading skirts, was probably not.

"Ah! Here's Letice come back from Mistress Montfort," Lady Agnes said and moved to the gallery's waist-high railing to call down into the hall, "Letice, is she coming?"

Letice, dressed for going out with a short veil over her kerchief and a fresh-pressed apron over her gray gown, called back, "She begs your pardon and sends her thanks but she's not ready to keep company yet and will sit below."

Lady Agnes slapped an impatient hand on the railing. "Fie! I was hoping for the chance to meet her. I'd like to see what sort of woman could be married to Morys Montfort and not kill him herself long before this."

Nichola giggled and Lady Agnes turned to point a finger in mock warning at her. "You just wait. You'll know what I mean. There's not a wife who hasn't thought sometime of being rid of her husband."

"You never thought of being rid of Grandfather, did you?" Stephen asked with unlikely innocence.

"Not often. But mind you, if he'd been anything like Montfort, I might have done more than think about it."

Letting her curiosity have its way, Frevisse asked, "How well was Master Montfort known around here?"

"Too well," Lady Agnes said. "A few years back he bought a manor north from here, toward Wallingford, and began trying to make himself felt among the gentry."

"He was crowner in northern Oxfordshire all the time I knew of him," Frevisse said. "I supposed that was where his interests lay." But in truth, when she came to think about it, she had known very little about him at all.

"His interests lay in his purse," said Master Haselden with open bitterness. "He began to take interest hereabout because he was hoping to win in with Suffolk."

He meant the marquis of Suffolk, who had been earl of Suffolk until somewhat over a year ago and was rumored to be aiming for a dukedom and was likely to get it, with all the influence he had come to have with King Henry these past few years. The rumors also ran, but more quietly and no one wanting their name attached to them, that influencing King Henry was not all that difficult; all you needed was to be in talking distance of him. Even in St. Frideswide's, out of the way though it was, they had heard the talk: that his father King Henry V had won the French crown and a French bride by strength of arms and victory in battle but this King Henry looked likely to give it all back for the sake of making his own French wife happy. A French wife whom Suffolk had urged on him. A French wife who after over a year of marriage had yet to birth an heir to the throne.

Frevisse, who for various reasons knew more than she wished she did about Suffolk, be he earl or marquis, held quiet but Lady Agnes took up what Master Haselden had said with, "I thought Montfort was aligned more with Lord Lovell."

"So did Lord Lovell," Master Haselden answered. "But power looks to lie with Suffolk right now and Montfort liked power more than he liked good sense, that's sure."

"Following power isn't good sense?" Stephen asked.

"Good sense is to follow someone steadier than whoever is the chance-chosen man of the moment," Master Haselden said. "There's no steadiness in Suffolk. He doesn't understand government, doesn't understand the war, doesn't . . ."

"But didn't he fight in France?" Stephen asked, sharing a glance and glimmer of a smile with Nichola.

Master Haselden rose to the bait, fuming, "What Suffolk did in France was *lose*. Give him troops and no challenge and he was fine. Let there be trouble of any kind and he didn't know which way was up. Thank all the saints the Council had sense enough to make York lord lieutenant there . . ."

"Philip, hush," Lady Agnes said, laughing with Stephen and Nicola now. "You've let Stephen rustle you again."

Master Haselden reached out to punch his son-in-law lightly in the upper arm, admitting good-humoredly, "I know. But that doesn't mean you shouldn't heed what I say. Suffolk in power is going to be trouble and . . ."

A thickening of sound from the hall's outer door made him break off and turned them all toward it, Frevisse as readily as the rest, to see two men step in and aside, flanking the doorway with halberds in hand, clearly gurards against who might and might not come in but immediately bowing their heads to the man who followed after them.

Chapter 4

Even from the steep angle of the gallery, Frevisse knew him. Master Christopher, Montfort's eldest son. When she had first met and last seen him, over five years ago, he had been a very young man in his father's service but capable even then of standing out against his father's authority if he saw the need, something no one else around Montfort dared to do so far as Frevisse had ever seen. Now he was crowner himself, come to the authority somewhat young perhaps but he strode up the hall through the bands of thin winter sunlight through the hall's windows with all the certainty of someone ready to face and deal with whatever came. He was suitably gowned in black, his houppelande three-quarters long and severely plain over black hosen and plain, low-cut black leather shoes, his hat equally black and plain, without padded roll or liripipe, only a dark blue, silver-set jewel pinned to its left side.

Frevisse had no clear view of his face before he reached the table at the head of the hall and turned his back to the gallery, laying down a leather case that he then opened and stood looking at while others took their places around and in front of him, beginning with another young man far more simply dressed, carrying papers and obviously his clerk, who went to a place made ready for him with pens and ink at one end of the table. While he was sorting things there to his satisfaction, another man in Montfort livery was seeing eight men into places on two benches, one behind the other, in front of the table. They were the jurors, Frevisse guessed, brought together to rule on Master Montfort's death—its cause and his murderer, if so much was known. It was the jurors' task to have learned as much as might be about the crime before the trial, that they might more sensibly judge the evidence and claims that came before them. Therefore they were usually local men, as these looked to be, dressed in their best doublets, gowns, and hats in a bright array of greens and blues and reds, trying to keep solemn demeanor but their heads bobbing toward each other in eager talk and turning over their shoulders to see who else was being let into the hall.

Lady Agnes, having nudged Nichola along the gallery railing toward Stephen and Master Haselden, put herself between her and Frevisse and set to cheerfully telling her who each of the jurors were and her opinion of them. Frevisse neither particularly cared nor particularly listened but gathered that, since there were no witnesses to the actual murder to serve as jurors, Master Christopher had given order for the eight male householders nearest to the nunnery to take the duty of viewing the body with him and coming to conclusions about the murder.

"Ah, but there's Master Gruesby," said Lady Agnes

with more interest, pointing. "Montfort's clerk. The little, uneasy man with the pair of spectacles there, being shown to the bench behind the jurors by one of the crowner's men. Remember I told you he found Montfort dead?"

He was, indeed, the man Frevisse had always seen as Montfort's clerk and now she had his name. As the finder of Montfort's body, his testimony would be maybe the most awaited, something some men would have enjoyed, but he gave no sign of being comfortable to be there, sitting on the very edge of the outer end of the benches where he had been put as if he expected it to burn him, adjusting with both hands his wooden-rimmed spectacles, held on by loops of ribbon around his ears and then adjusting them again and altogether seeming to wish he were somewhere else.

But, "Ah!" Lady Agnes said with great satisfaction. "Here comes the widow, and better yet, Domina Elisabeth is with her. That's good. She'll be a comfort to her, poor lady."

And be able to tell Lady Agnes everything about her afterward, Frevisse thought wryly. Accompanied by Domina Elisabeth and a maidservant, Mistress Montfort was escorted by one of the men now done with the jurors to a cushioned place on a bench well to one side, where her son would not readily see her whenever he looked up. Certainly now, as she shifted the cushion a little further along the bench and sat down, the maidservant on one side of her, Domina Elisabeth on the other, mother and son traded no look, her head still bowed too low for Frevisse to see her face, Master Christopher busy in talk with his clerk at the table end.

"Letice," Lady Agnes asked impatiently, "where are her children? Didn't I hear some of her children had come with her?"

From where she stood a proper few paces behind her lady but still able to see nearly everything and hear all,

Letice said, "Two daughters and two other sons came with her is what I heard, but she didn't want them here for this, it's said. They're at the nunnery."

"They'll hear all about it anyway. Servants talk, even if no one else does," Lady Agnes said. Then she stiffened, with a hissed intake of breath through her teeth, fierce with an anger that both startled Frevisse and turned her gaze with Lady Agnes's to the man and woman just being let into the hall. There was nothing particular about them, a middle-aged couple, soberly dressed, with a certain stiffness to them perhaps, the woman's hand resting on the man's raised one more as if they were making formal entrance to the royal court at Westminster than to a crowner's inquest in a country town, and with maybe an excess of cloth in the woman's skirts and a little too much length in the liripipe swung down from the man's broad hat and around his shoulders, but surely nothing worth Lady Agnes's open ire at seeing them.

It was Stephen who said over his wife's head, laughter behind the words, "Steady on, Grandmadam. You knew they'd be here."

"That doesn't make seeing them any the easier, the slinking weasels."

"If you frown like that, you'll give yourself wrinkles," Stephen suggested, "besides letting them see how much they irk you."

Lady Agnes flashed him a look of dislike to match what she had given the man and woman but he went on cheerfully, "Besides, you don't want to waste all your fury on them. Rowland and Juliana are here, too."

With another furious intake of breath that left Stephen laughing, Lady Agnes whipped her look from him back to the hall where a younger man and woman were entering in the first couple's wake, following them up the hall to the bench in front of Mistress Montfort.

"Oh, yes, putting themselves to the fore," Lady Agnes

said with rich dislike. "That's just their way."

"You'd like them none the better for sitting in the back," Stephen pointed out.

"What I'd like is them standing outside in the cold until they're needed," his grandmother returned sharply.

"What you'd like is them in the Thames up to their necks, with hopes there'd be a flood," Stephen answered, then laid his hand over Nichola's resting on the railing and said, because she was looking worriedly from him to Lady Agnes and back again, openly uncertain whether anger or laughter had the upper hand between them, "It's all right."

"Not while they're breathing it isn't," Lady Agnes snapped.

Frevisse held back from asking who they were for fear of rousing Lady Agnes more but watched with interest as the older of the two women paused to say something to Mistress Montfort who briefly raised her head to answer and then looked down again, leaving the two couples to sit ahead of her, the two women in the middle, the men at either end.

A few others had been let in behind them, to take places on the rear benches, but apparently they were the last who were meant to be there by right or necessity because way was now being given to whoever else would come in and the hall's orderly quiet broke under the hurry and talk of men and women crowding in, trying for a better place than someone else at the hall's far end and along the sides; but before it came to elbow-pressing, the guards at the door lowered their halberds to bar the way and exchanged a few short, sharp words with the foremost of those they had cut off before Master Christopher rapped once on the bare wood of the tabletop, bringing sudden silence to the hall except for the scuffle and shift of people still settling themselves.

Ignoring them, Master Christopher in a voice pitched

to be heard without being raised, said, firm with authority, "The inquest into the matter of the death of Master Morys Montfort, esquire and of this shire, is now begun."

With most sudden deaths there was little question of how they had come about, whether by accident or open murder, but in any where there had been real question, his father's preferred method of inquiry had been to gather as quickly as possible enough facts or seeming-facts to allow him to come to a conclusion that suited him and thereafter overbear the jury into agreeing with him. That Master Christopher's way differed from his father's was immediately clear. In a level, easily carrying voice he said to the jurors, "You have all viewed the body and the site of the murder in company with me?"

They agreed with scattered "Ayes" and head-nodding that they had.

"Would one of you be pleased, then, to describe what was seen and concluded by you all? Master Wilton."

Master Wilton had been agreed on beforehand, to judge by how readily he stood up, an underbuilt man with a reedy voice and the forward manner of someone always overready to put himself forward before others could. Eager with his brief authority, he told in careful detail that they had all seen where the deceased's body had been found, in the small garden of St. Mary's priory, and looked at the said body where it presently lay in St. Mary's priory.

"What did you conclude?" Master Christopher asked.

"That the deceased had been stabbed once with a long-bladed weapon too narrow to have been a sword and therefore likely to have been a dagger or knife." Master Wilton was firm and clear about it and equally firm as he went on, "Nor did the body seem to have been moved from where it fell. We therefore judge from that that the deceased was probably killed there."

Frevisse bit down on the urge to say, if only to Lady

Agnes, that if the deceased was indeed dead and his body not been moved, then yes, "probably" that's where he had been killed.

Either unnoticing or undisturbed, Master Christopher asked, "When would you judge that this murder took place?" And added a shade more quickly than Master Wilton could open his mouth, "We know it was the twenty-first of January this year of God's grace. The time of day is what we need."

Master Wilton caught back what he had all too clearly been going to say, swallowed with a large bobbing of his Adam's apple, and said instead, "We judge he was killed in the afternoon of the said day, shortly before the body was found."

Rather than after it was found, Frevisse thought, curt with impatience.

Master Christopher thanked Master Wilton and bade him sit, then spoke to his clerk, who left off his busy scratching of pen on paper to call on Master John Gruesby, finder of the body.

Slowly, maybe hoping the whole business would go away if only he took long enough, Master Gruesby rose to his feet, looking nowhere but at some papers clutched with both hands. But his hands did not tremble, Frevisse noticed, and though his voice did not rise much above a whisper, it held steady as he confirmed he was John Gruesby, late clerk to Master Morys Montfort, subeschea-tor of Oxfordshire, and that he had found Master Montfort's body the afternoon of the twenty-first of January just past as had just been said.

"How did you come to happen on the body?" Master Christopher asked.

"I was in search of Master Montfort."

"Did you know he would be in the said garden?"

"I did not know for certain he would be. I was told he had gone that way and followed him."

"Why were you looking for him?"

"A message had come for him. When he could not be found in the priory's guesthouse, where I expected him to be because that was where we were staying while here, I began asking after him. Someone had seen him go out of the guesthouse. Another had seen him going toward the nunnery's stableyard. A man there told me he thought he'd seen him going toward the way to the infirmary garden. I went that way and found him dead there."

"Isn't the infirmary garden part of the cloister?"

"Yes. I believe so."

"But it's open for anyone to come or go as they choose?"

"I believe not. There is a door to it inside the cloister and another, the way by which I entered, from the stableyard through a door said to be kept always locked."

"Did you find this door locked?"

"No."

"How did it come to be unlocked?"

"I don't know."

"You and the priory's infirmarian dealt with the body before anyone else. You found no key on him?"

"No."

"Did you look for one?"

"Yes. I also looked in the garden. There was none there, either."

Frevisse wanted to hear more about the unlocked door but Master Christopher turned his questions to where and how the body had been lying. Nothing that Master Gruesby said varied from what Frevisse had already heard from Lady Agnes, except that Master Christopher asked if he had seen any weapon there that might have been used for the murder, either when he first found the body or when he had searched the garden for a key. To that Master Gruesby answered he had not. He had yet to look up.

There were other things Frevisse would have asked but Master Christopher moved on to, "Why was Master Montfort here in Goring?"

"He was come in his office of escheator."

"In what matter?"

"The inheritance of Henry Lengley, esquire of this shire, lately deceased."

"Was there dispute in the matter?"

"There has been disagreement," Master Gruesby murmured.

"Between whom?"

"Between the said Henry Lengley's younger brother Stephen Lengley . . ."

Frevisse had readily understood that nothing he was being asked was any surprise to Master Gruesby nor were his answers any surprise to Master Christopher but now she looked sharply aside, past Lady Agnes and over Nichola's head to Stephen standing with all his attention on what was passing below but faintly smiling, as if it was a show put on particularly to entertain him.

". . . and his late mother's sister Cecily Bower, presently wife to James Champyon, esquire of Henley."

The couple who had stirred Lady Agnes's ire sat a little straighter, conscious of heads and murmurs turned their way. But Frevisse noted that the only surprise seemed to be her own. The matter was generally known, then. Except to her and perhaps Domina Elisabeth.

But Master Christopher was now asking, "Do you know of anyone who might have been interested enough in Master Montfort's death to murder him?"

Master Gruesby ruffled through his papers uneasily and must have whispered something that reached not even to the table because Master Christopher asked, "What?"

A little louder, enough to be heard, Master Gruesby said, "There have been people angry at him over the years."

That was gravely mis-saying it but all Master Christopher asked was, "Was there anyone angry at him now? Here?"

Master Gruesby shook his head, then probably remembered from his own clerking that the clerk writing away at the table would not see that and said, barely to be heard, "No one. No, there wasn't anyone. He'd only just begun here."

Goaded by his uncertainty, Frevisse would have prodded him for more. Master Christopher only said, "Thank you. You are welcome to sit down," and Master Gruesby did, with the heavy suddenness of legs giving way.

The priory's gardener, Master Garner, was called next, an elderly man who rose stiffly from his place on a rear bench and came forward to stand before the jurors and answered Master Christopher's question as to his name and all with a briskness that suggested he more probably demanded his plants to grow rather than simply encouraged them. When asked, he swore to deal in no lies and when questioned agreed that, yes, there was a lock to the side door to the infirmary garden and, yes, it was kept locked and there were but two keys to it, that he knew of.

"Who has those keys?"

"The infirmarian be one who does, I understand. The other be my lady prioress. It's my lady gives it to me when there's work needed in that garden there. Turning garden beds, carrying out refuse, things like that. Only she didn't have the key that day, I know."

That made an interested stir among most of the onlookers but Master Christopher merely asked, "Do you know who did?"

"She did." Master Garner pointed up at Lady Agnes. "Still does, for all I know."

All heads turned and lifted to look at her. Undiscomfited, Lady Agnes slightly bowed her head to Master

Christopher who slightly bent his in return but turned back
to ask Master Garner, "So you were never at the door that
day and so far as you know, it was locked or should have
been?"

"Aye, sir, it should have been."

Master Christopher thanked and dismissed him and
held out a hand toward his clerk, who handed him a paper
from which he read a sworn statement from Sister Joan,
presently infirmarian at St. Mary's priory, that the key to
the infirmary garden's door had not been out of her pos-
session that day nor any other and to the best of her knowing the door had been locked as it should have been. That
done, he handed the paper back to his clerk and turned
again to look up at Lady Agnes.

"My lady, rather than ask you to come down, may we
give you oath and have your answers from up there?"

"With thanks for your kindness, sir, yes," Lady Agnes
granted.

When she was sworn, Master Christopher asked, " "Is
this true you presently hold the prioress's key to the door
in question, my lady?"

In a carrying voice, easily heard throughout the hall,
she answered, "It is."

"Why?"

She explained with admirable briefness about her visits
of kindness to Sister Ysobel.

"Has the key ever been out of your keeping?"

"Not since Domina Matilda trusted it to me. I keep it
with my own household keys and they are always with
me."

"Did you use the key the day that Master Montfort was
killed?"

"Did I go to the infirmary garden, you mean. No, I did
not."

Master Christopher thanked her, she welcomed him, and
the stableman was called who had seen Montfort cross the

stableyard; but, no, he swore it was only Montfort he'd seen go that way until Master Gruesby came and, yes, he'd been there in the stableyard, at one task and another, a good half of an hour and more and would have noticed anyone else going that way, he was certain, sir, and was certain, too, that no one had come out from there either, not until Master Gruesby did, calling for help, almost as soon as he'd gone in.

He was thanked and dismissed in his turn and Master Christopher looked at a paper in front of him, then looked to Master Wilton as master juryman and asked, "Have you made inquiry if anyone was seen entering the garden from the outside of the nunnery?"

The man stood up again. "No one says they saw anyone anywhere near there through the midpart of that day."

He sat down again without being bidden. Master Christopher nodded thanks to him, then nodded to his clerk, who had been waiting and now straightened in his place to declare to the hall, "Master James Champyon is called before the court."

The man on the forward bench rose from beside his wife, took a pace forward, ignoring the rustle of people shifting and craning to have better view of him, and announced firmly, "Here, sir."

"And be damned to you," Lady Agnes said under her breath. Nichola twitched with a suppressed laugh.

Master Christopher's questioning of him was brief and to the point, neither man seeming to expect much of it. He affirmed that he was indeed Master James Champyon, esquire of Henley-on-Thames, and that he was presently husband of Cecily Bower, widow of Rowland Englefield and sister of the late Rose, who had been wife of the late Sir Henry Lengley, knight. No, he and his wife did not live in Goring but were come, with her grown children by her first husband—here he somewhat turned and made a small nod at the younger man and woman beside his wife—in the matter of his wife's manor of Reckling . . .

"His wife's manor?" Lady Agnes hissed under her breath. "I think *not*."

". . . presently in dispute," Master Champyon rolled on, "after the death of my wife's sister's son, Sir Henry Lengley's heir, Henry Lengley the younger."

"Tedious bastard," Lady Agnes muttered.

Stephen leaned behind Nichola to whisper with smothered laughter, "Grandmother, no. It's me, not him, who's supposed to be the bastard."

Lady Agnes made an angry noise at him, while below them Master Christopher asked, "This is the matter that the escheator Master Montfort was here to deal with?"

"It is," Master Champyon agreed.

"But no decision had yet been reached?"

"No. He had only come to town the day before his death."

"Did you see him the day of his death?"

"I saw him in the morning, at the inn where my wife and I are presently staying. The Swan in High Street."

"Did you see him in the afternoon of that day?"

"No, sir. I spent the day at the inn with my wife and never went out."

"And were seen there by various servants and other folk, I suppose?"

"Yes."

"Thank you. Pray, be seated. Clerk."

Frevisse saw Master Gruesby's head twitch to attention before he must have realized he was not being summoned. It was Master Christopher's clerk, as Master Champyon took his seat again, who declared, "Master Stephen Lengley is called before the court," and looked around and up.

So did everyone else in the hall, and Stephen calmly moved to the head of the stairs, made a slight bow toward the clerk or maybe the onlookers in general, then leaned

forward, grasped the rope railings on either side of the
steps, and in a single, long movement, swung himself out
and down, to land gracefully and a small flourish at the
stairfoot. A ripple just short of open clapping ran through
the onlookers while Stephen, seeming to notice nothing,
strolled around to the front of the table, bowed deeply to
Master Christopher, and said, "Here, sir."

"Yes," Master Christopher observed flatly. "Thank
you," and set to questioning him much as he had done
Master Champyon, with Stephen's answers coming as
readily as Master Champyon's had. He affirmed he was
indeed Stephen Lengley, younger son of Sir Henry Lengley, knight, resident here in Goring, and, yes, he was on
the opposite side from Master Champyon in the dispute
over this manor of Reckling but, no, he had not seen Master Montfort the day of his death. "He questioned both
Master Champyon and me the day before and told us he
would summon us again when he'd found out more. That
was the last I saw or knew of him until after he was dead."

"Where were you the afternoon that he was killed?"

"Here, visiting my grandmother, from dinnertime until
the servants came exclaiming there was a man killed at
the nunnery."

"And you were seen here during that time?"

"Neither my grandmother nor her servants being blind,
I was certainly seen here, yes."

There was laughter at that. Ignoring it, Master Christopher said, "Thank you," and dismissed him.

The questioning of both Master Champyon and Stephen
had been a makeweight, Frevisse decided, watching Stephen bow and return up the stairs two at a time. She could
see the outward purpose of it—they were the foremost
concerned in the matter that had brought Montfort to Goring—but their testimony had done little more than add
bulk to the inquest. Why? she wondered. Unless Master
Christopher wanted, for some reason, to have on record

where they claimed to have been when Montfort was killed.

With a wink for Nichola and a grin at his grandmother, Stephen took his place again, Master Haselden whispering something from his other side that made Stephen force down a smile and Nichola giggle, while below them Master Christopher was asking the jury if they could come to a conclusion based on what they knew by their own seeing and what they had heard here. Obediently, the men twisted around and toward each other on their benches, bringing their heads together. Around the hall a buzz of talk started up, only to fall away a few moments later when the jurors straightened themselves around into their places again and Master Wilton rose from among them to say into the waiting hush, "My lord crowner, from what we know and have here heard, we conclude that Master Morys Montfort, esquire and of this shire, was murdered by someone unknown and at present unknowable."

It was as safe and unfortunately as fair a conclusion as could be made from what had been presented to them here, unless they wanted to bring accusation against Master Gruesby, the only person known to have been in the garden with Montfort that afternoon and apparently they did not. Master Christopher accepted their conclusion as if he had expected nothing else, thanked the jurors for their service, and formally closed the inquest.

What Frevisse expected then was a great deal of standing about and talking, but several of the crowner's men moved from their places near the door, one of them going to open it wide, the others beginning to shift the onlookers toward it, skillful as sheepdogs working a herd of sheep. Even Master Champyon and his wife had just time to speak briefly to Mistress Montfort before one of them was beside them, courteously urging them away and Mistress Champyon's son and daughter with them. They went, Master Champyon and his stepson in immediate talk together and no backward look from either of them or the daughter. Only Mistress Champyon paused to cast a long glare upward to the gallery, at Lady Agnes and Stephen, Frevisse thought, returned in kind by Lady Agnes though Stephen met it with a slight bow from the waist that probably accounted for the increased anger with which Mistress Champyon turned and swept after her family.

"Ill-bred b—" Lady Agnes began but broke off with a glance at Frevisse and said instead at Stephen, "Help me down the stairs, boy. I want to have a word with Mistress Montfort if I may."

"My lady," Letice put in. "You've been on your feet a long while. Should you maybe lie down before dinner?"

"I've never needed to rest before I ate in my whole life and I'm not starting now," Lady Agnes snapped. "Stephen."

Her tone left the choice between quarreling or agreeing. Frevisse saw Stephen exchange a look with Master Haselden, who shrugged, holding in a smile, and Stephen said cheerfully, "As you wish, dear Grandmadam."

He went down the stairs as he had before and turned around to wait while Lady Agnes turned around, too, to make her way down backward, saying aside to Frevisse as she went, "Slow but certain. That's how I am these days."

Beyond them the hall was almost emptied and Master Christopher had given over being crowner and gone to his mother, had taken her by the hands and was speaking to her as he led her toward the door, Domina Elisabeth left behind. Over Lady Agnes's slowly descending head, Master Haselden said, "I'm afraid her son is seeing Mistress Montfort out. The nun is coming this way, though, if that helps."

"Fie." Lady Agnes looked over her shoulder "She won't have visitors and she won't stay to talk. What ails the fool woman?"

"She's in mourning?" Nichola ventured.

"For the likes of Montfort? Then she's a fool indeed," Lady Agnes said. "No, Letice," she added to something her woman hadn't said yet. "I'm not coming back up. They'll be setting tables for dinner soon. I might as well be down and be done with it. Stephen."

Obediently, now that she was in his reach, Stephen held her by the waist, steadying her down the last few steps to the floor, where she turned and batted his hands away, saying, "Leave off, youngling. I'm not a two-year-old," and demanded up at Master Haselden, "Hand me my staff, Philip, and get out of Dame Frevisse's way, you silly man."

"My lady," Master Haselden said, obeying with a deep bow and a smile.

They were all enjoying themselves, Frevisse realized as she made her own careful way down. That the inquest had dealt with a man's death seemed of no matter to anyone; it might have been no more than a show put on as a pastime for them. Of course, that Montfort was the dead man probably had much to do with that. Was anyone at all sorry for his death? Even his widow? Or his son?

Master Christopher and his mother were both gone now, last from the hall except for his young, sandy-haired and freckled clerk still at the table gathering up papers, pens, and ink bottle, unheeded by Lady Agnes's servants come to ready the hall for her dinner. Lady Agnes was gone aside to question Domina Elisabeth, and Nichola was paused at the head of the stairs to gather her skirts with one hand before starting down, gripping the rope railing tightly with the other while Stephen urged her, "Just jump. I'll catch you." And added when she started carefully down anyway, "I've never dropped Grandma-dam and you weigh far less than she does."

"I heard that, boy," Lady Agnes called, "and when

you're in reach I'm going to give you a good thump to show you I did."

Laughing, Stephen caught Nichola by the waist, swept her off the stairs, her squeal of surprise changing to laughter, too, as he swung her around in a swirl of skirts, gave her a swift kiss on the cheek, and set her down. In return and as swiftly, she caught his face between her hands and rose on tiptoe to kiss him firmly on the mouth.

"Here, here, here!" Lady Agnes declared in feigned indignation, rapping her staff on the floor. "What kind of wanton carrying-on is that for servants and nuns to see? Enough!"

Frevisse, drawn well aside from all of them but watching with pleasure, found suddenly the sandy-haired young clerk at her side, carrying papers, pens, and inkpot and saying in a low, hurried voice as he passed by her, for no one but her to hear, "Master Montfort hopes you'll meet him in the church after Nones, please you, my lady," and before she could answer had moved on to Lady Agnes, to give her the crowner's thanks for the use of her hall this while.

Chapter 5

Even in the startled moment before she realized that the Master Montfort the man meant was Christopher, not his dead father, Frevisse noted that no one seemed to have seen his brief word to her. Stephen was saying something to Master Haselden intent on coming down the stairs and Nichola had moved away to join Lady Agnes and Domina Elisabeth, neither of them looking Frevisse's way as Christopher's clerk finished with his thanks to Lady Agnes, bowed, and withdrew. Only Nichola looked around at her and shyly smiled while Domina Elisabeth said, seemingly continuing from something said before, "She'd surely be pleased for the courtesy of your asking her but I doubt she'll come, things being as they are."

Lady Agnes tapped her staff on the floor. "She can't really be cast down by being rid of him, can she? Is she that great an idiot?"

"I've only talked with her hardly enough to know what she feels or how she is, only that she's behaving seemly," Domina Elisabeth answered moderately. "Was he truly as ill-mannered as everyone says he was?"

"That and more," Lady Agnes said without hesitation.

Domina Elisabeth had never had the mischance to encounter Montfort, probably did not even remember he was the crowner who had dealt with a death near the nunnery a few years ago, nor did Frevisse intend to be drawn into talk about him. Instead, she merely stood, head a little down, listening with Nichola while Lady Agnes detailed a few of Montfort's rudenesses and, a few paces away, Master Haselden and Stephen discussed the likelihood that last year's increase in wool sold abroad was going to hold for this year, too. The servants had quickly finished setting the trestle and tabletop in the hall's center and a maidservant was going along it laying out bread trenchers, the man Lucas following after her with a pitcher in one hand and a stack of wooden cups in the other to set a cup and fill it between every two trenchers. Emme was smoothing a white linen cloth over the high table, finishing as the maid who had laid the bread trenchers brought pewter plates from the sideboard set along one wall of the hall and laid six places along the upper side of the high table, followed again by Lucas bringing three pewter cups, one to set between each two places, with Emme in her turn coming back from the sideboard with white linen napkins and pewter spoons to set beside each plate. That done, Letice, who had been overseeing it all, came to tell Lady Agnes, "All's ready, my lady."

"Then shall we sit?" Lady Agnes said graciously to her guests, took her own place at the center of the long, high-backed bench that was the high table's seat, and pointed everyone to their places, Domina Elisabeth and then Stephen on her right, Master Haselden on her left, and Frevisse and Nichola beyond him.

"And no throwing of bread pellets at one another," Lady Agnes added with a warning look first at Stephen, then at Nichola, who smothered laughter while Stephen said, all injury, "It's hardly kind to mention our youngling indiscretions in front of guests, Grandmadam."

"Nor would I if I thought you'd outgrown them," Lady Agnes returned. "Pray, be seated, all of you."

That was sign for Letice to sit at the near end of the lower table and beckon a rough-dressed man who probably saw to whatever outside work there was to come forward to a place at the lower table's end and the first remove to be brought to the high table by Lucas, Emme, and the other woman servant—roasted quails, onions fried in egg and butter and seasonings, custard tarts with raisins, and bread still warm from the oven—while for the lower table there was a thick pottage and more bread. That much of their duty done, the three of them sat with Letice and the other man and fell to their meal along with them.

Since supper had been a private thing in Lady Agnes's solar and breakfast the same, this was Frevisse's first chance to see Lady Agnes's household at the full, though there was surely a cook in the kitchen. A very good cook, Frevisse amended as she tasted the quail set before her. Because conversation was expected, Master Haselden and she agreed between them that the weather was mild for this time of year and were moving on to discussing the condition of the road between Wallingford and Goring before Lady Agnes claimed his attention with a question about whether it was wool sales abroad or to clothmakers hereabout they should be looking to sell to this year, but that merely meant, equally for politeness' sake, that Frevisse should take up talk with Nichola on her other side, and forgoing the overtried weather, she asked the only other bland thing that came readily to mind, "Have you been married long?"

With a shy smile and happy eyes, Nichola said, "Six months the morrow of Epiphany just past." And blushed a little and added, "I'm older than I look, truly. I'll be sixteen come St. Mark's."

Frevisse agreed graciously that she did look younger than that but kept to herself the thought that even so she was young to be a wife and, if things went as usual, probably soon a mother. It also meant she had almost certainly been married to Stephen by others' decision rather than her own.

Nichola, concentrating on neatly removing bones from her quail, said lightly, as if in answer to Frevisse's unspoken thought, "It was because of the inheritance, you see. Lady Agnes held Stephen's wardship but Father had his marriage." And therefore the right to choose whom Stephen married and to make what profit he could from it. "With Stephen coming of age, we had to be married lest the chance be lost for it." The chance that Stephen, left to his own choice, might have chosen to marry elsewhere when he was of age and his marriage out of Master Haselden's keeping. It was common enough for orphans not yet come of age to be given in wardship to a kinsman by whoever was immediate overlord of whatever lands were their inheritance, as Stephen had been given to his grandmother; and it was at least as common for their marriage right to be sold or given to someone else for separate profit; nor was it any surprise that Master Haselden had chosen to marry Stephen and his inheritance to his daughter, seemingly with Lady Agnes's good will, to judge by the friendship between them.

"How long has Stephen's brother been dead?"

"Harry? A little over a year."

"Was he of age or did his grandmother have his wardship, too?"

"She had both boys' wardships, and Harry's marriage, too. She had him betrothed and he would have been married just before he came of age but he died. Everybody was terribly unhappy about it. Especially Anne, the girl he was going to marry. Everyone liked her. But she's married to an esquire over Reading way now, so that's all right."

"But Lady Agnes didn't have keeping of Stephen's marriage," Frevisse said, almost too lightly for it to be a question, as if she were not much interested.

"Oh, no. She meant to, along with his wardship, after Sir Henry her son died," Nichola chatted on happily, picking raisins from one of the tarts to eat one by one, "but Lord Lovell saw to Father having it instead. But I think Lady Agnes would have agreed to our marrying anyway. There was halfway thought of Harry and I being married but then she had a chance for Anne."

Following after the one part of that that interested her, Frevisse asked, "Lord Lovell is overlord of the Lengley lands then?"

Nichola paused with a morsel of quail on the tip of her sharp knife halfway to her mouth, thinking about it, frowning more uncertainly. "No. The Lengleys hold from the king. But Sir Henry and young Harry after him, they were feoffed to Lord Lovell." Meaning they had been pledged his followers and he pledged to help them if there was need. "Sir Henry was in his retinue in France, in the war with him. So was Father. He and Sir Henry were friends."

Emme and Lucas had left the lower table a few moments ago. Now they returned with the second remove— dishes of ground pork mixed with bread crumbs, spices, and cheese and cooked to firmness in a light golden crust that were set between each two of them along the high table; and parsnips thinly sliced and fried in oil; and a thickened mix of figs and raisins cooked in spiced red wine to go with a red gingerbread.

In the way of good manners it was the gentleman's duty to serve the lady beside him. Dame Frevisse and Nichola, paired with each other, had served themselves, while Stephen had seen to Domina Elisabeth and Master Haselden to Lady Agnes who now slapped him on the back of the hand as he made to put a portion of the pork on her plate, telling him, "I taught you better than that. You move the goblet well aside first, that you can make the serving gracefully. Not all cramped in like you're doing."

"Yes, my lady," Master Haselden said, like a chided schoolboy but smiling as he returned the pork to its dish, set down his knife, moved the goblet aside, then set to serving her again.

Frevisse, dividing the parsnips with Nichola, looked around the edge of her veil at Master Haselden, wondering if he was as unangry as he sounded. Nichola, catching her look, said with a soft laugh, "Lady Agnes had the raising of my father for a few years in her husband's household when he was a boy. That's why she treats him that way and he let's her. Nobody else would dare."

But he must have a deep affection for Lady Agnes, too, Frevisse thought. Little else was likely to make a man as well possessed as Master Haselden have such tolerance of Lady Agnes's ways. And to keep up her side of the talk she asked, "Were you in Lady Agnes's household like your father, Mistress Lengley?"

"It still doesn't sound right to be called that," Nichola complained, smiling. "It makes me sound like I'm Stephen's mother. No, I was with Lady Agnes but only for a while. Mostly I was with the nuns." Nichola brightened past courtesy into open pleasure. "They taught me my reading and numbers and needlework and I liked it there. Then I was with Lady Agnes and then Stephen and I were married and now Mother is teaching me all the other things I need to know."

"You and Stephen live with your parents?"

"Oh, yes." Nichola was blithe about it. "I'm almost ready to have my own household, Mother says, but not yet. Besides, it makes better sense we don't start to live as if Stephen has his own until he does. Have his own, I mean." Nichola had kept steadily at her food, neatly tucking words between bites with the hearty appetite of the young but the good manners of the well-raised, but now she stopped, looked at Frevisse, and asked, "Do you know about those people trying to steal his inheritance?"

Used to eating far less at a meal than had been offered to her in even the first remove, Frevisse had mostly been only picking at her food, trying to give the seeming of eating without doing much. Now, to hide her interest— quickened despite herself—she spooned more of the figs and raisins onto the last of her gingerbread while answering, "Only what I heard here today at the inquest. That someone disputes his right to inherit."

"The Champyons." The name was not an easy one to spit but Nichola managed it, sounding something like a kitten being fierce. With a glance past Frevisse to be sure no one was heeding them, she leaned nearer, saying very low but still fiercely, "They're such liars. They want to take his mother's land away from him. Only, to do it, they have to say he's a bastard. But if he was, then he couldn't inherit his father's lands either. He wouldn't have anything at all. They're so nasty."

Nasty was probably a milder word than Lady Agnes used on them, let alone Stephen's feelings in the matter, and it was just as well that curiosity was not a sin because Frevisse was about to give way to hers by asking more when a shifting along the table said the meal was done. Emme and Letice brought basins of warmed water and towels for everyone at the high table to turn in their place and wash their hands, then at Lady Agnes's asking, Domina Elisabeth gave thanks and they all rose, Lady Agnes saying she was minded to lie down for a time, adding to Master Haselden, "Give your wife my greetings, please," and to Stephen, "Come, kiss your old grandmother."

"My grandmother, yes," Stephen agreed, taking her by the hands and kissing her cheek. "But old? Never."

Lady Agnes patted his cheek, smiling. "There's a good, flattering boy." She turned and held out her arms to Nichola. "You next, my dear."

Nichola went readily to her embrace, Stephen saying past them, "No need to glower, Letice. We're going."

"And none too soon," the woman grumbled, come to stand behind her lady with muted impatience to have her away.

"Hush," Lady Agnes said, drawing back from Nichola with a gentle touch to her cheek. "I've reached such an age that my every lying down may be my last, so don't rush me to it."

"Oh, Grandmother, no," Nichola protested.

"Oh, Nichola, yes. I only pray you may live so long," Lady Agnes said cheerfully.

Frevisse had noticed often enough ere this that while people knew of their own mortality, there were very few who truly believed in it. Frevisse suspected Lady Agnes did not. She might say what was proper to say at her age but her own dying was no more real to her than theirs were to Stephen or Nichola, bright with young years and love. And still cheerful, Lady Agnes added at her grandson, "And long years to you, too, Stephen, rascal though you are."

"You're a one to talk about rascals," Stephen returned, his arm lightly around Nichola's shoulders. "It's being a rascal that's kept you alive so long and don't deny it."

"I admit and deny nothing," Lady Agnes said, "except

you've never learned to keep a civil tongue in your head to me. Now away with you."

Emme had brought their cloaks by then and, with Stephen's promise to visit her tomorrow, they left, and Lady Agnes turned to Domina Elisabeth to ask, "How do you purpose to spend your afternoon, my lady?"

"I thought to see how my cousin does."

"And give her all the news of this morning," Lady Agnes said. "Very right. That will cheer her some. And Dame Frevisse?"

"With Domina Elisabeth's leave, I mean to pray awhile in the church."

Domina Elisabeth readily gave that leave, and while Lady Agnes labored her way up the stairs with Letice, Emme was sent to fetch their cloaks from their room. Then, at blessed last, Frevisse followed Domina Elisabeth out the hall door into the houseyard's shadows, the afternoon sun already slipping away behind rooftops. The day was noticeably colder than yesterday had been, and Domina Elisabeth said with an upward glance, "There's a change coming. We may have snow yet before we're done."

Frevisse made a murmur of agreement but no comment to keep a conversation going. She had not known how deeply tired of talk she was until now when she was so near to being free of it. For most of her years in St. Frideswide's the rule of silence had held, no talk allowed the nuns except during the hour of recreation at day's end or when there was absolute need. That discipline had slacked of late, even more under Domina Elisabeth than the prioress before her, and Frevisse direly missed the freedom there had been in that silence, a freedom from need to deal with others' thoughts and chance to go deeper into her own, searching out new places in her thoughts and moving into wider reaches of prayer.

So she made no effort of talk now and the cut of the

air did not encourage lingering, despite their cloaks and their fur-lined gowns they had both put on this morning. Together, they briskly crossed and went along the street and through the priory's gateway and to the cloister door where Domina Elisabeth's knock brought a servant who, after a quick look through the grill set high in the door, promptly let them in, curtsying as Domina Elisabeth swept by. Frevisse followed in her wake into the cloister, where Domina Elisabeth paused to say, "I'll join you at Nones," and went on her way, leaving Frevisse to go her own toward the door, deep-set in the stone wall's thickness, that opened from the cloister walk into the church.

Letting herself in with a turn of the heavy, round, iron handle, she entered the choir with its nuns' stalls where they prayed the Offices ranked in double rows facing each other and, beyond them, the altar, with the lamp always burning above it the only light in the church besides what fell through high, small windows, many-colored from the painted glass but dim with the afternoon's overcast sky, leaving both choir and nave more in shadows than not. Not that it mattered. It was to the altar she gratefully went, bunching her skirts and cloak to make a little padding under her knees which did not take to floors so easily as they used to do, before she sank down, clasped her hands, bowed her head over them, and drew a deep breath, not praying yet but letting quiet flow into her and her thoughts flow out, clearing her mind for prayer, the better to reach past the passing troubles of the world and body toward the bright, eternal freedom of God's love.

This quieting of her mind rarely came on the instant. Instead her thoughts usually strayed and wandered, hithered and thithered, unable to settle. In her early years in St. Frideswide's she had fought it, trying to hold her mind to where she wanted it to be, and her failure at it had been her constant trial and torment until she was finally forced, humiliated, to confess it to her then-prioress Domina

Edith. A nun for longer than Frevisse had been alive, her body frail with age even then but never her mind, she had said, "Oh, that. It's not something you need worry on."

Frevisse had opened her mouth to protest, then closed it as Domina Edith went mildly on, "My prioress called it butterfly-mind. She said just to let it go its way and not worry on it, it's no great matter, and so I've always done. Because one should obey one's prioress, yes?" she had added with a sharp, unsolemn look at Frevisse, who could not help a smile because both of them knew that obedience was not the easiest-come of her virtues. "Not that I always succeed, even now," Domina Edith had sighed. "Nor will you. But it's not something you need struggle with. Simply let it happen and go on your way. That's all you need do with it."

And surprisingly enough it was as almost exactly that simple, Frevisse had found over the years since then. When she set to praying and her butterfly-mind began its fluttering, she did not follow it among her own scattered thoughts, trying to curb it, but let it go its way and went her own, into a farther part of her mind where prayer came almost as easily as breathing, lightening her soul of the worldly dross that mere daily living gathered to her day in and out.

But today proved to be one of the days she did not go so readily into prayer as she wished, distracted for a while by the lately learned tangle of other people's lives. Montfort's murder was only part of it. Wherever the truth lay concerning the Lengley inheritance, someone was lost in greed-driven lying, but who? Montfort had been here because of it and someone had killed him. Was his death because of it? Master Christopher's questioning of Master Champyon and Stephen showed he had considered that possibility. But it could be because of something else altogether. Was . . .

Like taking a willful child by the hand, she inwardly

drew herself aside from that, said low but aloud, *"Dominus me adest"*—Lord be with me—and left her other thoughts to go their way while she set to wending herself into the shining paths of prayer.

Gone far along them, she could not have said how much time passed before the bell began to call the priory to Nones. Unlike St. Frideswide's, St. Mary's church had a true-toned bell. Its notes fell strong-edged and clear through the far reaches of Frevisse's praying, drawing her back until, with a deep-breathed sigh and regretting her knees, she rose and moved away from the altar, going to stand aside from the cloister door in wait for Domina Elisabeth as St. Mary's nuns came singly or severally from whatever they had been doing to take their places in the choir stalls, each in her familiar own. Then Domina Elisabeth swept through the door in company with Domina Matilda, the two prioresses parting with cordial nods, Domina Matilda to go to her more finely wrought choir stall set at one end of the facing rows of her nuns, Domina Elisabeth to go to the far end, Frevissse following her, to the two stalls given over to them this morning.

Like St. Frideswide's, St. Mary's choir stalls outnumbered the nuns there were to sit in them, but while at St. Frideswide's that was because there were insufficient lands and properties to support many more than the ten nuns there presently were—the widow who had founded it dying before she had endowed it as fully as she had meant to—Frevisse understood from Lady Agnes's talk that St. Mary's had been founded by a lord some few centuries past and upon a time there had been as many as forty nuns. Now, however, there were but eight, leaving empty choir stalls in plenty, and Frevisse was grateful both for her place there and to go gladly into Nones' prayers and psalms.

For courtesy's sake, neither she nor Domina Elisabeth tried to join their voices with those of St. Mary's nuns who through months into years of praying together blended smoothly into a whole with hardly need for thought about it. It was the same in every nunnery, making each nunnery's Offices a thing particular to itself despite the words remained much the same all over Christendom, and therefore Frevisse was content to pray only on the edge of her own hearing, with Domina Elisabeth's murmur beside her, under the rise and fall of the other nuns' voices rising and falling around them, and was nonetheless caught as easily as usual into the pleasure of Nones' particular psalm today—*Sed tu salvasti nos ab adversariis nostris, et eos, qui oderunt nos, confudisti. In Deo gloriabamur omni tempore . . .* But you saved us from our enemies, and those who hated us you silenced. In God we gloried for all the time . . .

Only regretfully, as the Office came to its end, did Frevisse surface back to the chill church but signed herself with the cross, head to heart and side to side, along with everyone else and quietly joined Domina Elisabeth in going last out of the choir and out into the cloister walk where Domina Matilda had seen her nuns on their way and was waiting for Domina Elisabeth again. But Frevisse stopped before they reached her and said, "My lady, I'd stay in the church awhile, if you please."

"Of course," Domina Elisabeth granted without question. "And go back to Lady Agnes's afterward?"

"If it please you, my lady. Or else simply walk in the cloister here."

"Either would do. Though take care or with all this praying you'll be as holy as Sister Thomasine," Domina Elisabeth jested, meaning the one nun at St. Frideswide's whose devotions were so intense that there was wary speculation she might be bound for sainthood.

Frevisse obligingly managed a smile and lowered her eyes in what might have been seemly humility but also served to hide her discomfort, because prayer was not her intent nor had she said it was. Instead, returned into the church, she went along the tall rood screen that divided the church, one end from the other, separating the choir that was the nuns' part from the nave that belonged to the town. The rood screen's finely carved fretwork allowed little to be seen of one side from the other; only the open doorway in its middle allowed clear sight of the altar from one end of the church to the other and a way to come and go between nave and choir, a wooden-grilled gate as the boundary between cloister and outside world but only hooked closed now, not locked during the day, to make easier the priest's coming and going, and Frevisse passed through without pause into the nave.

However many people might have been there to hear Nones, there were only three now, Master Christopher and—less expected—Master Gruesby and—even less expected—young Dickon from St. Frideswide's, standing together beside one of the thick stone pillars near the door into the outer yard, the townsfolk's way into the church. But only Master Christopher came forward to greet her as she went toward them, bowing to her as they met, saying, "Thank you for coming. I wasn't sure you could. Or would."

Frevisse bent her head to him in return courtesy. "It's good to see you again, Master—" she hesitated—"Montfort."

"Christopher, please," he said quickly. "I'm very weary of being 'Master Montfort.'"

"Christopher, then," she agreed, and indeed it did come far easier and they both smiled to it, with Christopher's smile ridding him of all resemblance to his father save for his reddish hair. There had been no occasion for smiles the other time they had dealt together, Frevisse recalled, and thought that despite his smile he looked older than his years. With good reason, she also thought, so many things weighing on him just now—his duties as crowner, his mother's widowhood, his own grief. At least she supposed he grieved to some degree; whatever Montfort had been, Christopher had been his son, and she said, "My regrets for your father's death."

Christopher's smile faded. "Thank you. Though I'm afraid it's because of his death I asked to see you."

She had been afraid of that, too, but hoping she hid her wariness, she said, "Your father has my prayers." Difficult though they were to make and the effort probably of more benefit to her soul than to Montfort's.

"My thanks for that," Christopher said. His voice dropped, too low for Dickon, standing a little behind and to one side of him, to hear, "But I needed to see you about more than prayers."

Firmly avoiding what she feared was coming, Frevisse said moderately, "Judging by what I saw at the inquest, you have the matter as well in hand as could be hoped for."

"I have," Christopher agreed. "But it was a false inquest."

Chapter 6

Frevisse held silent, too taken by surprise that he'd admitted to what she had already thought to answer him, and defending nothing, only explaining, Christopher said, "So far as the jurors know, it was fair. But they didn't ask all the questions that could have been asked. Nor did they look at the body so closely as they might have. And I didn't tell them differently."

"Necessary," Master Gruesby said, come forward to just behind Christopher's right elbow, the word hardly above a whisper and his eyes toward the floor.

"It was necessary," Christopher agreed. "And they made it the easier by being more impressed with themselves for being jurors than with what questions they might be asking. But it was my duty to tell them. I didn't."

Frevisse looked past both of them to Dickon. Left to himself, he was edging forward, interested. Christopher looked around at him, too, and said, "I asked him to come with us. One of your own people. To make it proper you were here."

Frevisse doubted being alone in the church with three men—and Dickon could count as such at his age—was more proper than being alone with two but it was not beyond bounds, being a public enough place, she hoped, and said with a nod of her head toward the bench along the opposite wall for the sitting of those too old or ill to stand through Mass or Offices, "Dickon, go sit there and don't try to hear us."

Even from three yards away she saw his chest heave with a disappointed sigh before he turned away, obeying. She looked back to Christopher and asked, suspecting she should bite her tongue instead, "Why didn't you tell the jurors differently?"

"Because it wouldn't have given us any better answer and would have told someone we knew more than he now thinks we do. If he's still here."

"The murderer, you mean."

"We don't have enough to know who he is. So we've kept some things to ourselves. Master Gruesby and I."

"That was why there were questions missing from the inquest that I would have asked," Frevisse said. "Such as where Champyon's stepson, I forget his name, was that afternoon."

"Rowland Englefield."

"He has as direct an interest as James Champyon and Stephen Lengley in this inheritance. It's considerable, I gather?"

"A fair-sized manor. Near Abingdon. It's where it is that counts as much as it's worth," Christopher said.

"Why didn't you question him?"

"We know where he was. He . . ." Christopher hesitated

and looked around at Master Gruesby who looked up at him, his eyes owlishly large and worried behind his thick, wooden-rimmed spectacles. To whatever Christopher silently asked him, he lifted his shoulders slightly, let them drop, and went back to staring at his shoes. Left to make his own choice, Christopher said, "Master Rowland was somewhere his mother would not approve of. A house here in Goring."

Either bawdy or for gambling or both, Frevisse supposed while being briefly diverted, as usual, by what was thought nuns wouldn't know or shouldn't hear about, as if because they chose to live aside from the world's general ways they were therefore ignorant of them, even by someone like Christopher who had had occasion to know better about her. But all she asked aloud was, "How do you know?"

"He told me," Christopher said. Frevisse raised her brows to him and he agreed, "No, not the best wellspring for truth if he's the murderer. Nor does it help that the . . . woman . . . of the house swears he was there. He could have bribed her to it. But he said he'd lie if we asked him openly at the inquest. Therefore we didn't."

Fair enough, Frevisse supposed, especially since the jury had not thought to ask about him either, though it seemed to her that Rowland Englefield was a grown enough man not to be all that worried over what his mother would approve or not, but she let him go, asking, "And Philip Haselden. You overpassed him, too."

Christopher smiled somewhat ruefully and said aside to Master Gruesby, "You were right. She didn't fail to note that."

Master Gruesby made a small, twitching nod of agreement without raising his head.

"Master Haselden," Frevisse said, "has an interest in the Lengley inheritance almost as strong as the Champyons, doesn't he? Because of his daughter?"

"If Stephen Lengley's claim is good, then Haselden has made a very good bargain in marrying her to him. Otherwise, he hasn't. How much have you heard about it?"

"Only that the Champyons claim Stephen Lengley is a bastard, with no right to the manor."

"That's all? You're staying with Lady Agnes, aren't you?"

"Since yesterday, yes. But she hasn't talked of it. No one has. I had this much and no more from Stephen's wife at dinner today."

Christopher looked aside to the bench along the wall on their own side of the church and asked, "Shall we sit?"

Frevisse agreed with a nod and they went and did, though Master Gruesby would have gone on standing to Christopher's far side if Christopher had not pointed firmly at the bench while going on to Frevisse, "It goes this way. Sir Henry Lengley was a well-propertied knight. He had lands both here and in Berkshire and near Minster Lovell. He married once. To Rose Bower."

Frevisse inwardly winced at the name though Christopher seemed not to have heard what he had said but went on, "She and her sister were the heirs of another knight. There were no sons and his lands at his death were split between the sisters."

"The entail," whispered Master Gruesby. Meaning the restrictions put by law on how land could be inherited, and though there were diverse of ways land could be entailed, once a particular way was fixed to a particular property, that way was supposed to be inviolate for all time to come. It might not be but it took considerable influence and costly legal work to change it.

"Yes," Christopher agreed. "The entail. That's where the trouble lies. By it, the two sisters each received half their father's properties. But if either sister's line fails— if the time comes that there are no more of the blood of one or the other of the sisters—then the share of the property that went to her must needs revert to the other sister or to those of her lineage who then live. You see?"

Frevisse saw. There were entails that allowed property to pass only along the male line, never along the female, come what might, even shifting everything to remote male cousins if there were no directly descended sons. Other entails, such as this one, allowed property to be divided among daughters if sons were lacking, with provision that the divided lands be reunited should either line die out.

"Rose is dead, I take it," said Frevisse.

"Over twenty years ago."

"But she left two sons."

"According to Lady Agnes, she left two sons," Christopher agreed. "Henry, who died last year . . ."

"Naturally?"

"You mean, is there suspicion he was helped to his death? No. He'd been in ill health since very young, it's said."

Beyond Christopher, Master Gruesby nodded agreement to that. His hands, laid unquietly one on either knee, looked to be longing for pen and paper, and Frevisse had the passing thought that today was the first time she had ever seen him without them, even as she went on, "Which left Rose's younger son, Stephen, to inherit."

"So Lady Agnes and Master Stephen claim. But Rose's sister, now Mistress Champyon, claims Rose had but the one son. Young Henry. She says Stephen is not her nephew but Sir Henry's son by one of his mistresses."

"*One* of his mistresses?"

Momentarily discomfited, Christopher said toward somewhere beyond her left shoulder, "He seems to have been noted for them."

"But there have to be records and witnesses as to whether this Rose had one son or two. There had to have been people at his birth—servants, midwife, friends, a priest—that can say who his mother was. There has to be someone."

"You'd think so," Christopher agreed with no joy. "But it's been more than twenty years. It seems Stephen was born at one of Sir Henry's manors away in Berkshire. No one here and now outside the family knows anything. And Lady Agnes says he's her grandson by Sir Henry and his wife. Mistress Champyon says that her sister never had a second child. But they've neither been able to give any proof, thus far. One way or the other."

"Why did she wait so long to challenge his legitimacy? If she'd done it from the first, there would have been witnesses easily come by, one way or the other."

"She claims she didn't know he existed until now. Until after her admitted nephew, young Henry, was dead and she made to recover the manor. Then she was told her sister had had a second son."

"Where had he been all this while? Or where had she been, not to know of him?"

"She says she never liked Sir Henry or Lady Agnes. She made no effort to know anything about them after Rose died."

"Or her nephew? The one she knew she had? She didn't want to know about him, either?"

"No. Her sister was dead and he was Sir Henry's son and no concern of hers, she says. Nor, after her sister was dead, were there any family links to here. For her to hear more."

"Bedfordshire," Master Gruesby murmured.

"That's the rest of it," Christopher agreed. "Her first marriage took her into Bedfordshire."

Where she was not likely to hear anything by chance about the Lengleys and she must have left no friends behind to tell her anything, Frevisse supposed. She assuredly didn't sound like the sort of woman who had long-lasting friends. "Then it was only after young Henry, the nephew she says she knew she had, was dead ... How did she come to hear about that?" Because somehow Frevisse did not see Lady Agnes bothering to send her word.

"Her second marriage lately brought her to Henley. Not so far off. She heard talk. Or someone wanted to make trouble. I don't know."

"It might be worth finding out who saw to her knowing," Frevisse suggested, and Christopher turned his head and made a single nod to Master Gruesby, who gave a small nod in return, note dutifully taken despite lack of pen and paper, Frevisse gathered while she went on, back to where she'd been, "So where was Stephen all this while, after his mother's death? If she was his mother."

"With Lady Agnes. His father gave him over to her as almost a newborn baby and she raised him. That's sure. It also seems that, whoever was or wasn't his mother, Rose Bower did die about the time he was born. Lady Agnes says it was at his birth and that's how he came to be given over to her. She says that Mistress Champyon ..."

"Englefield," Master Gruesby said at the floor.

"She was Mistress Englefield then, by her first husband, yes," Christopher said. "Lady Agnes says word was sent to her both of the birth and her sister's death. Mistress Champyon admits she was told of Rose's death but denies ever hearing of a second son."

"Still, whether she was told or not, there has to be someone who was at Stephen's birth or knows certainly about it," Frevisse insisted. "If nothing else, he was surely baptised."

"The priest is dead. So is the midwife."

Frevisse paused, a side consideration thrusting in. "Christopher, how do you come to know so much of all this? You only came here yesterday, didn't you?"

"With my mother, yes. All this is mostly from the proofs readied by both sides for the escheat inquest. Master Gruesby sent word of it all to me while I was readying to come here. It's everything my father knew before he was killed."

"Stephen's godparents. They'd know as well as anyone who his mother was. Please don't tell me they're dead."

"No, they're alive," Christopher said, not looking happy about it. "They're Lady Agnes and Master Philip Haselden."

Startled, Frevisse protested, "Then how could his daughter marry Stephen?" Because the bond of a god-parent to godchild was considered so close that any such marriage was incest and against church law.

But as she could have foretold with an instant's thought, Christopher answered, "By dispensation." Whereby the Church declared a thing acceptable to God that otherwise was not. But dispensations were not had cheaply or easily. That he had gone to the trouble and expense of one meant Master Haselden's stake in Ste-phen's legitimacy was even higher than it had seemed.

None of this was her problem or business, Frevisse pointed out to herself. It was all no concern of hers except out of curiosity, and while curiosity did not figure on the list of deadly sins, neither was it among the sovereign virtues. This matter of who inherited a disputed manor was not something with which she need deal, was some-thing she would leave behind her as soon as Mistress Montfort and her people took Montfort's body away home for burial and she and Domina Elisabeth were able to stay properly in the nunnery. But nonetheless she heard herself saying, "Then as it stands now, there's no proof on either side? Only Lady Agnes's word against Mistress Cham-pyon's?"

On Christopher's other side Master Gruesby hunched a little deeper into his shoulders as if it were some way his fault and glumly Christopher said, "Even so. And one of them has to be lying."

Or both of them, Frevisse thought but did not say. In truth, there could well be a mix of lies and truth from both of them, and all of it made worse because the man who had come to find out one from the other was murdered.

Of course, given the kind of man Montfort had been, he might well be dead for some other reason than the matter of Stephen Lengley's inheritance, but . . .

"What questions should the jurors have asked that they didn't?"

It took Christopher a moment to shift backward in their talk to where they had been, but Master Gruesby said toward the floor, "The way in."

"The way into the garden you mean?" Frevisse said.

Christopher caught up. "How the murderer came into the garden. And how he left without being seen. Yes."

"Through the infirmary," Frevisse offered. "The key hangs beside the door inside. But . . ." She immediately saw objection to that. "That would mean the murderer was likely a woman because no man could have passed through the cloister unnoticed. Do you think a woman could have killed your father?"

"I think I don't know. Not who killed him or why. And until I know more, I'm trying to suppose nothing."

A far different way than his father had taken. Montfort as crowner had always preferred to grab hold of the obvious choice—or the profitable one—and not let go unless forced to it.

But Christopher was going on, "The thing is that Sister Ysobel says no one went into the garden that way."

"Would she have heard if they did?"

"What she said when I asked her was that it's her lungs that are rotting, not her ears."

"She might have slept and not known it."

"Coughing," said Master Gruesby to the floor.

Christopher agreed. "She said her coughing kept her

from rest all that day. It probably did. She wasn't resting well when I talked with her either. Talking came hard and I didn't press her."

"Did she hear anyone, anything from the garden?"

"She says she heard two men, speaking too low for her to know what they said or who they were. It seems they did not raise their voices, nor was there any outcry. They talked and then were quiet and the next thing she heard was Master Gruesby shouting."

Frevisse looked at Master Gruesby who raised his head for a quick, startled look back at her as if the thought he had ever shouted was as impossible to him as it was to her. Then his gaze went down again and she asked of Christopher, "How long afterwards was that?"

"She was saying a rosary slowly. When she heard Master Gruesby, she was half the way through the second time since hearing the men in talk."

"How long a rosary?" Because a rosary could be either a loop of beads or a straight string of them and either one could be of any size. "Did she show it to you?"

"It was six decades." Six sets of ten beads each for Ave Maries, with a single bead for Paternosters between each ten, and said slowly, that could be time enough for whoever had done the killing to be well enough away that anyone hearing the outcry might fail to link the outcry with having seen him.

"Did the jurors think to ask Sister Ysobel about what she might have heard?"

"They did," Christopher admitted. "I said I'd asked her and she'd heard nothing."

"Safer," Master Gruesby said. "For her."

Frevisse silently granted that was true enough. The murderer had come and gone unnoticed from the infirmary garden once. If he thought there was need to be rid of Sister Ysobel, why wouldn't he try again? "But if not through the infirmary, then how?" she asked. "Not through the stableyard and other door, it seems. Nor over the fence." Which she remembered was of wicker, not able to hold much weight beyond a squirrel's.

"Through it," Christopher said.

"Through the fence? Leaving a great hole no one has bothered to mention?"

"It's of hurdles." Large but light-weighted pieces of withy-woven fencing easily handled by a man, meant to be moved around for making sheep pens and such-like things, kept up by being tied end to end with each other to make a pen, or else, as in the nunnery's garden, made into an uncostly but sufficient wall by fastening to firm-set uprights. "The twine holding a fencing to its post along the back side was cut," Christopher said.

And with that done, the murderer needed do no more than simply push or pull the hurdle enough open to let himself in and out.

"What lies beyond the fence there?" Frevisse asked.

"The mill ditch runs just outside the wall, fed from the Thames, with an open meadow beyond it all the way to the river."

"Nothing overlooks the ditch, the meadow?"

"Some nunnery windows and the mill. But no one says they saw anyone along there that day. Not at the needful time or anywhere near to it. Our best hope was some workmen at the mill that day but they were at their hot dinner in a tavern up the street all the time we need someone to have seen something."

"Footprints?" Frevisse asked without much hope. Even in raw mud, shoes and boots, soft-soled as they mostly were, would hardly leave prints that mattered.

"The bank is well grassed. All Master Gruesby found was somewhere on the far side where a foot might have slipped and torn the grass a little. Otherwise nothing."

Nothing seemed to be almost all there was so far

but . . . "What else did the jurors not ask that they should have? Or not notice?"

"The dagger wound was not the only hurt to the body."

"Christopher!" she protested. "How could they not notice that? Or you not point it out?"

Her protest did not unsettle him. After years of his father, it would probably take more than someone's mere protest to unsettle him, and steadily he said, "I doubt any of them had seen a man violently dead before this. They weren't minded to look closer than they had to this morning. They could see the dagger wound had surely killed him and that was enough."

"But you should have pointed out . . ." She stopped, regarding him, his level look meeting her own. More quietly, she said, understanding, "So as it stands now, the murderer doesn't know what you know and thinks everything is over and he's safe. Giving us"—she noticed the "us" too late to change it—"a small advantage."

"A very small advantage. Maybe none at all. But yes, that's what I hope."

"What are the other wounds?"

"A small cut in the right corner of the mouth. A scrape on the back of the head. Bruises on either side of the death wound."

"The tree," Master Gruesby murmured from behind Christopher.

"The tree where the body was found," Christopher said. "It's . . ." He made a ring with his hands maybe four inches wide.

"I've seen it," Frevisse said. The young, slender-trunked ash tree in the grassy midst of the garden.

"There was a narrow cut to the bark on one side. Where the edge of a dagger might have sliced along it. At about heart height for my father."

He said it coolly, keeping distant from it, probably the only safe way he could say it, and Frevisse matched him, keeping thought away from actual torn flesh to mere considering of the cut tree, saying after a silent moment of thinking, "It could be guessed, from that, that the murderer forced Master Montfort back against the tree with a hand put over his mouth hard enough to cut it with probably a ring, keeping him silent while he was stabbed." It was a narrow tree; with Montfort's body centered on it, a dagger thrust through his heart and on through him would very likely have sliced the bark the way Christopher said. She could see the rest of it, too. How the murderer had probably gone on holding Montfort there, weight leaned onto the dagger still through Montfort's body, Montfort's head still shoved back against the tree, hand still over Montfort's mouth until Montfort was fully dead. Then his murderer would have stepped back, jerked out the dagger, and let the body slump aside and fall.

But all that ugliness she left unsaid. By the look on Christopher's face he could see it clearly enough for himself, though he said steadily enough, "That's how we guessed it, too. Master Gruesby and I. It had to be someone strong."

"Someone strong or else very angry," Frevisse said. Anger's strength was never a thing to be discounted.

"Or very angry," Christopher granted. Angry enough to drive a dagger through a man to the hilt.

"The bruises," Frevisse said. "You said there were bruises to either side of the wound. Did you mean to the sides or at the ends?"

Christopher paused as if sorting out what she meant. Behind him Master Gruesby said to the floor, "At the ends."

"I see." Christopher drew an imaginary slit in the air. "At the ends, yes." And then added, "Round bruises."

Now it was Frevisse's turn to pause. "Round bruises?"

"Like two knobs had been driven against him."

Frevisse drew a sharp breath. "A ballock dagger."

Christopher nodded agreement. "Neither Master Gruesby nor I can think of anything else that would do it. And they're not common."

No, they were not. Usually heavy-bladed and often unusually long for a dagger, their handguard was shaped not in the usual outstretched quillons but, most often, into two rounded lobes. Sometimes there was only one lobe, sometimes there were three, with no reason Frevisse had ever heard as to why the shape was particularly desirable at all except for the sake of being different. Or lewd. She only knew they were indeed not common, and carefully putting aside thought of how much anger—or hatred—there had to be behind a thrust hard enough to leave those bruises with it, she said, "You said nothing about it at the inquest so that whoever it was will go on wearing it. Your men"—and you, she did not say aloud—"were watching for it today, in hopes the murderer would be here."

"Yes."

But they'd seen no one, or she and Christopher would not be having this talk; and because it was probably better that they be done and part company before someone saw her in talk with the crowner and wonder why, she asked, "What do you want of me?"

Christopher did not hesitate over his answer. "To listen and to watch. You're likely to hear talk of things no one would say to me. You're likely to find questions to ask that I wouldn't."

She did not argue that. She knew herself well enough to know that with all that Christopher had told her, she would be listening and seeing differently, both at Lady Agnes's and here in the nunnery, and she would be asking questions, if only of herself, so that all in all there seemed no point to refusing Christopher her help and she bent her head to him with, "As you wish."

Christopher smiled with a relief that briefly made him look as young as he probably was. "Thank you."

But she already had a question she wanted to ask and said past him, "Master Gruesby, the letter you were taking to Master Montfort that afternoon, what was it about?"

At his name Master Gruesby jerked up his head and now stared at her over Christopher's shoulder with much the look he might have had if sentence of death had just been pronounced upon him. "The letter?" he whispered.

"The letter."

He fumbled open his wide leather belt pouch with one hand and rummaged in it while still staring at her, rustling paper and parchment as if in search of a writing he could consult before he managed to say without help, "It was from Lord Lovell."

Frevisse waited until she realized that was all he meant to say, then insisted, "What was it about?"

Master Gruesby's eyes widened. "I didn't open it."

"Where is it?"

"With the other papers, waiting for whoever comes to finish the Lengley escheat."

"It had to do with that?"

"I don't know. I didn't open it."

"But it was addressed to Master Montfort?"

"To Master Montfort as escheator, yes."

And might very well have nothing to do with his murder but she said anyway to Christopher, "You should maybe read it."

His look asked her why, to which she could only answer, "Just to see if Lord Lovell needs answer to something, I suppose," and rose to her feet to show she was ready to leave.

Christopher and Master Gruesby rose with her and across the nave Dickon leaped to his feet, plainly willing to do something besides sit. Frevisse beckoned to him while adding to Christopher, "How will I get word to you of anything useful I might hear?"

"I'll send Master Gruesby to you sometime. Or make occasion to talk with you myself."

"What excuse will you make for staying here longer, now the inquest is done?"

"There's still my father's funeral. The in-gathering of folk to it and the funeral itself will keep me here at least four days more, I think."

"Here?" Frevisse barely covered her alarm. "He's to be buried here?" Rather than in his own parish church, the more common way.

Christopher made a small shrug and said, giving away neither one thing nor another, "Mother thought here would serve as well as anywhere."

Because it did not matter to her where her husband was buried so long as she was rid of him? Frevisse lowered her head in hope of hiding both that unkind thought and her dismay at after all not being soon done with Lady Agnes.

Chapter 7

ith bows, Christopher and Master Gruesby left her and Dickon came forward, curiosity writ large on his young face. The weak, long-slanted light through the nave's south windows patchily brightened the nave's gray shadows but told Frevisse that if she were at St. Frideswide's she would about now have been finishing her day's tasks before Vespers. Here there was only blank time to be filled, and tucking her hands more deeply into her opposite sleeves for warmth against the church's cold creeping into her, she said, "Thank you for waiting this while, Dickon."

He had grown suddenly this past year, was all long bones and boyish angles and could have been awkward with it but was not. Instead, he reminded her of his father, contained and certain in both manners and movement. He was more given to smiling than Frevisse had ever seen from his father, though, and he was smiling now, a boyish grin as he made a bow to her and answered, "You're welcome, my lady," with a glance at the door closing behind Christopher and Master Gruesby, inviting her to tell him what it had been about.

With the thought that it was better he knew something than be left to his own devisings, she said, "We were discussing his father's death. If anyone asks, you're welcome to tell them that."

Dickon brightened. "You're going to find out who did it, aren't you?"

"*That* is something you're *not* welcome to say."

"But you're going to."

"As God wills."

"The way you did when—"

"I think it would be better if that's not talked about," she said quellingly.

Dickon sobered with quick understanding. "Better if they don't know to watch out for you. Yes."

That was not the way she would have said it but she let it go, saying instead, "You can go now."

"You're staying here?"

Frevisse suppressed a smile of her own at that. Dickon, like his father, wanted to understand what he was being told to do, rather than simply obeying. It made his father a difficult man with whom to deal but a good steward to the nunnery and she said, "I mean to pray here until Vespers. After that, I'll be with Domina Elisabeth. You can be about your own business."

Dickon accepted that with a grin and a bow but hesitated before he turned to go and asked, "Shall I listen for . . . things?"

In her turn Frevisse hesitated, then said, "Listen, but

don't ask anything. Or be caught at listening."

Dickon nodded with quick understanding, bowed again, and headed cheerily out.

Frevisse closed her eyes, drew a deep, relieved breath at being alone again, slipped one hand from her sleeve to cross herself, then tucked the hand away and went hurriedly up the nave into the blessed quiet of the choir, into the choir stall presently hers, to kneel on the cushion there. The sacrist would come probably soon, to be sure all was in readiness for Vespers, and the bell would begin its steady calling, the nuns would come, there would be the rustle of pages turning, a pause full of waiting and then the Office, with voices raised to evening prayers and psalms; but for now there was only uncomplicated silence and softly deepening shadows, and Frevisse, resting her elbows on the book ledge in front of her, bowed her head onto her clasped hands, shut her eyes, and sank into the shelter and delight of prayer.

Or meant to. From years of daily saying of the psalms woven into each day's Offices, the cycle of them completed every week only to be done again the next week, they were become as familiar to her as the Paternoster, their passions both guide and shelter in her own reaching toward God, that endless questing of the soul that was the only thing she had ever found worth her whole heart's longing. Now she slipped softly into, *"De caelis respicit Dominus: videt omnes filios hominum ... Qui omnium eorum corda finxit, qui attendit ad omnia opera eorum ..."* From heaven the Lord beholds: he sees all the sons of men ... He who shaped the souls of them all, who knows all their works ...

What she intended was to wind herself further and further from the world into the deeper places of heart and mind. What she found in a while was that somehow she had slid away, back to a psalm from Nones, and was whispering, *"Per te adversarios nostros reppulimus, et in nomine tuo calcavimus insurgentes in nos . . . Eos, qui od-erunt nos, confudisti."* Through you we drove back our enemies, and in your name we trampled on the rebels against us . . . Those who hated us you silenced.

Worse, she was thinking of Montfort while she did and, startled and discomfited, she opened her eyes to stare down at her clasped hands without seeing anything but the dark way her thoughts had gone when she was not attending to them. At different times and places before now she had dealt with deaths of one kind and another. With ordinary deaths, come simply at the end of living, when the body was done and the soul had to move on in the natural way of things, there was sorrow to one degree or another, depending on what affection there had been for the dead. In her own life she had had some sorrows that had soon dimmed while others were with her yet and would be, even to her own death. Those were reasonable sorrows for reasonable deaths. The sorrow that came for deaths brought on violently was a different kind, because such deaths came out of the right way of things, before their time and never for sufficient reason but because of greed or lust or simply cruelty's sake. For those there was anger as well as sorrow, that such wrong could be done by someone to anyone else.

There should be at least that much sorrow and some-thing of anger in her for Montfort's death, and in a way there was—sorrow at least for a soul gone unprepared and violently to judgment. But that Montfort was gone from the world . . . no. For that she felt no sorrow at all. His never-swerving greed, his ever-unmindful cruelty made the loss of him more benefit than pain.

Eos, qui oderunt nos, confudisti. Those who hated us you silenced.

And yet . . .

. . . it had been wrong. However good it was to have Montfort gone, it was not by God's will he had died. It was by murder, and Christopher had asked her help in finding out the murderer and she had committed herself to it because, by God's grace, the finding out of things was a skill she had. Somewhere, probably near, there was a murderer freely moving among men, his corruption a taint to those around him, and with the deep sigh of taking up a burden she knew would be both heavy and unwieldy, Frevisse closed her eyes and set to praying again—*Dirigatur, Domine, oratio mea. Exaudi nos in die qua invocaverimus te.* Guide, Lord, my prayer. Hear us in the day that we call to you—and this time held her mind to it better, only breaking off when she heard the sacrist moving among the choir stalls. She was late to her task, it seemed, because overhead the bell began to call to Vespers and with relief Frevisse settled back into her seat and bowed her head, to wait silent-minded for the in-gathering of nuns.

The Office's prayers for peace of soul and mind through yet another night gave to her the comfort and quieting they always did but at their end she and Domina Elisabeth were, as it were, cast out from the nunnery's quiet and peace to return through the gathering gray darkness of the overcast sunset to Lady Agnes's, hurried on with more haste than grace by a nipping wind into Lady Agnes's candle-lighted hall, where the maidservant said Lady Agnes would dine in her solar tonight, would they be pleased to join her or be served in their own chamber or the hall?

"With Lady Agnes, surely," Domina Elisabeth said for both of them, which was well enough with Frevisse. For the sake of somewhere to start, she was going to suppose that Montfort's death had to do with Stephen's inheritance and surely Lady Agnes could be supposed someone from whom things might best be learned.

What was talked of first, though, over spiced pork cooked with apples in a thick crust, was the matter of

Montfort's widow staying longer than expected. Domina Elisabeth had heard of it from her cousin and so had Lady Agnes by way of servants' talk brought to her by Letice. "So you're welcome here," she said, "for however long until she goes and longer if you like. You make a change for me. Now, tell me how Sister Ysobel does."

From there the talk went to whether both nuns were recovered from their journey and how well Lady Agnes had rested that afternoon, with Frevisse finding no way to lead away to where she wanted to go until, as they finished the baked apples stuffed with raisins and walnuts, Domina Elisabeth asked lightly, "But what was that at the inquest this morning about trouble over your grandson's inheritance?"

"Peascods and sour grapes," Lady Agnes said with a dismissing wave of one hand. "Stephen's greedy aunt on his mother's side is claiming Stephen isn't her sister's son. It's all so she can lay hold of what isn't hers." One of the windows rattled heavily in its frame, shaken by a wind gust, and Lady Agnes looked away to it, clucking her tongue. "The weather is changing and not for the better, I fear. Will it be rain or snow tomorrow, do you think?"

Domina Elisabeth thought icy rain was likely but snow if it turned any colder, and Lady Agnes began to tell how difficult the ferry crossing was when the Thames ran high and how she preferred to cross by the bridge at Wallingford whenever she had had to visit the more northward Lengley manors.

"Not that I've had to trouble with those or any other for a while now. We traveled something much, my husband and I, seeing to them while he lived, and I did the like again after my son died, God keep his soul, until his young Henry came of age. Thank St. Paul they're all Stephen's to see to now and I needn't anymore."

Frevisse swept quickly through ways to turn that toward a question about Stephen but Lady Agnes was gone on to, "Let's go sit by the fire, shall we, and Letice will bring us warmed clary. Will you read to us over it, Dame Frevisse? You have such a soothing voice."

Frevisse was surprised to hear that, not remembering any other time she had ever been called "soothing" by anyone, but leaving the two chairs to Dame Agnes and Domina Elisabeth, she settled on a floor cushion rather than a stool, took the book Letice brought from a chest at the bedfoot, and found herself with a large, leather-bound *Canterbury Tales* and a slight sinking of her heart. But her uncle, from whom she had learned the pleasure there could be in the sound of words themselves as well as in their meanings when they were well set together, had also taught her, "Read true to the words, and let the rest fall as it may," and if she followed that, she could not do badly by Geoffrey Chaucer's work and very mildly she asked, "Where would you have me begin, my lady?"

"Choose as you wish," Lady Agnes granted graciously.

Frevisse began uncertainly to turn pages but then with her regrettable (she had been sometimes told) tendency toward the perverse turned deliberately to the "Tale of Sir Thopas" and launched forth with solemn vigor into its deliberately thumping verse and equally thumping action. Her uncle Thomas had used to say, about his father who had written it, "He found it quite down-heartening the number of people who did not see the jest. But then they're likely the same who do not see the jest in his retraction at the *Tales'* end, so what can one do?"

At least this time the jest went over, with laughter from Lady Agnes and Domina Elisabeth and even from Letice across the chamber, and when Frevisse had ended the tale with The Host's irked interruption—

> *"Mine ears ache . . .*
> *Now such a rhyme to the devil I give!*
> *This is rhyme doggerel . . ."*

—Lady Agnes clapped, saying, "That was most—I don't think 'beautifully' is a word to be used here—most happily done. Thank you, my dear."

Frevisse closed the book and handed it to Letice, taking a chased silver goblet of warm, spiced clary in return as Domina Elisabeth said, "She's distant kin to this Chaucer, you know."

"Is she?" Lady Agnes's interest was mild.

Preferring it stay mild, Frevisse said, "By marriage. An aunt of mine married his son."

"Chaucer," Lady Agnes repeated, her interest sharpening. "Alice Chaucer. The earl of Suffolk's lady. Is she your cousin?"

Frevisse took a long, deliberately slow, sip of the wine, trying not to have ill thoughts at her prioress for bringing up what need never have been mentioned, before saying as if it were a little matter, "Yes."

"Are you close?"

"Dame Frevisse's gown was a gift from her," Domina Elisabeth offered, proud of it as always.

"Ah!" Lady Agnes eyed Frevisse's habit, her interest fully caught now.

Frevisse, sharply conscious of the wealth she wore in fine wool lined with fur, refuged in taking another long sip.

"When Dame Frevisse visited her in London," Domina Elisabeth went on.

"Several years ago," Frevisse said.

"Ah." Lady Agnes's tone was considering. "Will you be visiting her again, while you're so near? Is she at Ewelme, do you know?"

"I don't know," Frevisse said. "I doubt it." And added, to put more distance between herself and Alice than there truly was, "I've not seen her since then nor do we much write."

They did not much write, not for lack of affection but

because their lives lay so far apart that there was usually little to be said between them.

"A pity," said Lady Agnes, sounding not so much disappointed for her as eased. "You've heard nothing from her lately?"

"No."

Frevisse was braced for more but Domina Elisabeth, overtaken by a yawn, covered it with her hand and said when it was done, "I think we've overstayed our bedtime hour, Lady Agnes. By your leave, we'd best to bed."

Lady Agnes said she had better do the same, it had been a long day, and Letice led them with a candle across the dark gallery to their own room on its other side. There she lighted a candle waiting on the flat top of a locked chest against one wall, bade them good night, and left them.

It was a plainly furnished room, with a single, shuttered window and besides the chest a curtained bed, a joint stool, and a wooden wallpole for the hanging of clothing, with presently their cloaks hanging from either end. A thickly braided rush mat made the floor a little warmer but everything was half-lost in the shadows beyond the candle's small reach of draught-wavering light. Not that any of that much mattered to Frevisse, since all she wanted was to say evening prayers and after that to be asleep as soon as might be. The nunnery's hour for Compline had rung while they were still at supper and they were now well past the hour when they would have been abed in St. Frideswide's. It was reasonable to suppose they would say the Office and then in silence ready for sleep but Domina Elisabeth, beginning to unpin her veil, said, "I think we can forgo prayers tonight. God surely understands our weariness. I should maybe ask your pardon for mentioning you were related to the Chaucers. I didn't think until too late that Lady Agnes might take offense."

With the thought that Lady Agnes had seemed more wary than offended and already offended herself at having Compline so lightly dismissed, Frevisse asked more sharply than she meant to, "Offended? Why should she be offended?"

Folding her black veil with great care, not seeming to hear or else not heeding the sharpness, Domina Elisabeth said, "Ysobel has been telling me about this quarrel over the grandson's inheritance. Remember there was something about it at the inquest this morning?"

Frevisse, unpinning her own veil now, managed to answer evenly, "Oh. Yes."

"It isn't just about the land, it seems. There's some rivalry for power between my lord of Suffolk and Lord Lovell."

Frevisse's hands went momentarily still before she said again, "Oh?"

Domina Elisabeth turned away to lay her folded veil on the chest well away from the candle's dripping. "Something about who will hold the most influence in this part of Oxfordshire. It's presently Lord Lovell, I take it, but Suffolk is powerful with the king now and is using his power to make himself more powerful elsewhere."

"And Lord Lovell is trying to hold on to his own here," Frevisse ventured, pretending more interest in laying her own folded veil on the joint stool than in what she was saying but silently weighing up the possibilities inherent in a conflict between two powerful lords.

"I gather so, and not just here in Oxfordshire," Domina Elisabeth agreed, unbelting her habit.

Frevisse, her wimple now off, shivered as an ice-touched draught fingered along the bare back of her neck. "But this Lengley inheritance is the present great trouble between them?"

"From what Ysobel says. Oh mercy, I don't want to

take this gown off. It's going to freeze tonight for certain. Has the bed been warmed at all?"

Frevisse lifted a bedcurtain aside and ran a hand under the turned-down coverlet and sheet to find there were indeed two smooth, large, warm-to-the-touch stones there, one on each side of the bed, taking something of the damp chill from the sheets, and she said, "Yes. All we need do is be fast in getting in."

Talk stopped as they made haste then to strip off their outer and inner gowns, carefully but quickly hanging them over the wallpole, Frevisse waiting then for Domina Elisabeth to slip, chemise-clad, under the covers on the far side of the bed before blowing out the candle and going swiftly to crawl in on her own side, to reach the hot stone's warmth before the room's chill could reach her bones. Only then, well under the covers, did she ask, stiff with trying not to shiver but unwilling to leave off learning what she could, "How does Stephen Lengley's inheritance come into their contention?"

"It's somewhere near here," Domina Elisabeth said through cold-clenched teeth, "where Suffolk is looking to make one of his centers of power because he holds Wallingford for the king and his manor of Ewelme nearby is one of his great holdings. As you know."

And as Domina Elisabeth was unlikely to forget, Frevisse thought but could not altogether blame her. A gift of money or land from Alice, Countess of Suffolk, would be very much to St. Frideswide's good, both for the nunnery's finances and for its fame, and Frevisse was the priory's surest way to come by such a gift; but she held to the present point with, "So the trouble with the inheritance must be that Stephen is Lord Lovell's man."

"Even so. The Lengleys have been enfeoffed to one Lord Lovell after another for generations and one reason Stephen's father married the Bower heiress, Ysobel says, was to have this manor brought into Lord Lovell's interests." Domina Elisabeth rolled onto her side away from Frevisse and curled up into a ball, much as Frevisse was on her own side. "Oh, I do miss my own bed!"

Which would have been thoroughly warmed all over by a maidservant with coals in a covered pan just before she slipped into it. Frevisse's bed in her cell in the dortor would not have been, would in fact have been far more chill than this one was, but she missed it anyway and the dortor's quiet and the deep sleep she would have probably been in by now if she were there, but she turned her thoughts away from that to say, "Then Suffolk has probably put this James Champyon to claiming the manor in his wife's right as a way to have it away from Lord Lovell's interests into his own."

"Ysobel says it's less that Master Champyon is one of Suffolk's men than that he wants to be. Having the manor is the way he hopes to make Suffolk interested in him."

A lesser man playing his ambitions toward a greater man's, Frevisse thought, and all the more dangerous for that, because what might be a small gain for someone like the marquis of Suffolk would be a great gain for someone like Master James Champyon and therefore worth a greater price. Maybe even a man's life.

Beside her, Domina Elisabeth settled deeper into her pillow with a deep, sleep-ready sigh, murmuring, "Ysobel says it's wonderful how, now that she can go nowhere and do nothing, she hears more than she ever did when she was up and about, from all the people who come to talk to her."

Wondering who besides Lady Agnes came, Frevisse asked before Domina Elisabeth was lost to sleep, "What does she say about the Champyons' claim that Stephen is a bastard?"

Probably too far gone toward sleep to wonder where Frevisse had heard that, Domina Elisabeth murmured, "She says he's been known as Sir Henry's son and young

Henry's full brother all his life and nobody has ever questioned it before now. What can be said beyond that?"

Nothing that Frevisse could think of but she went on staring at the featureless darkness of the bedcurtain while Domina Elisabeth's breathing evened into sleep, then set herself, alone and silently, to Compline's prayers, asking for a safe and peaceful night and God's blessing on all.

Chapter 8

The trouble, Frevisse realized upon awakening near dawn, roused by sounds of the household starting to stir, was that asking questions of Lady Agnes about the Lengley inheritance and other things would be awkward now that she knew Frevisse was, however distantly, kin to my lord of Suffolk. At this time yesterday it had seemed the stay with her would be simple and brief. Now it was become a tangle of lordly ambitions and questions that were not going to be easy to ask.

Someone rattled the latch, then came in, light from a carried candle showing through the drawn bed curtains before the maidservant said, "Good morning, my ladies. There's snow come at last," as she crossed the room to light their candle on the chest. Briefly Frevisse gave way to hope that it was maybe early enough there was chance of being dressed and across to the priory for Prime, but even as she thought it, the priory bell began to call to the Office and Domina Elisabeth stirred toward awake with a slow unwillingness that told there would be no hurrying to prayers this morning.

In truth, the only hurrying was into their cold clothing and down to the hall where a fire was built up and burning high on the hearth. Bread and ale and some of last night's meat pie were brought to them there and a bench pulled close for them to sit with their feet toward the fire. With its welcome heat on their faces and gradually warming through their gowns, they said something of Prime's prayers and psalms, but for Frevisse it was heavy going, the day all out of order with breaking their fast before they prayed and no Mass afterward and servants coming and going behind them . . .

She brought her thoughts up short, took firm hold on them, and set them to where they should be—*Scrutare me, Domine, et proba me; explora renes meos et cor meum.* Search me, Lord, and try me; test my soul and my heart—deliberately unknotting her thoughts and weaving them into prayer.

When they had finished, she judged it likely near the time Lady Agnes, up by now and dressed and breakfasted, would ask for their company and they would not escape her until they went to Tierce. Then Domina Elisabeth would go to her cousin and Frevisse would . . . what?

Before she had found answer to that there came a rapping at the hall's outer door. Lady Agnes's manservant, just come from kitchenward with an armload of logs for the fire, dumped them on the hearth and went to find out who was there, shutting the inner door behind him to close off the draught when he opened the outer so that it was a few moments more before Domina Elisabeth and Frevisse saw who was come, as he hurried in ahead of the servant following him with equal hurry away from the cold.

"Master Gruesby?" said Frevisse in surprise and stood up as the clerk, bundled deep into a cloak, his hands buried in its folds and snow dusted over his dark hat and shoulders, went hesitant between one step and the next, slowed, but managed to come the rest of the way and bow to them both while the manservant went to his task of adding logs to the fire.

"My . . . my ladies," Master Gruesby said unevenly, whether from chattering cold or uneasiness. He made another bow to Domina Elisabeth. "By . . . by your leave, please, may I speak with Dame Frevisse?"

"Of course." Domina Elisabeth gestured him closer to the fire. "Here, move nearer the warmth, pray."

That seemed to unsettle him worse but he obeyed, pulling off his gloves and putting his hands out toward the flames while saying at Frevisse, with little, uneasy looks at Domina Elisabeth, "My lady asks pardon for asking anyone out into the cold but since you'd be coming to church anyway, she supposed, she was wondering, if you would come to see her this morning. If it please you. If you would do her the courtesy."

"Your lady?" Frevisse was momentarily puzzled, then understood. "Mistress Montfort?"

"Mistress Montfort, yes." Master Gruesby rushed at his words, as if to have them done as soon as might be. "It was Master Christopher's thought. He's been called away to another death. At Moulsford. Word came late yesterday. He rode out at first light."

"What happened?" Domina Elisabeth asked.

Looking anywhere but at either of the women, Master Gruesby managed, "It seems someone dropped a tree on himself. Likely an accident but there was no one there to see it and Master Christopher must serve as crowner to say whether that's all it was or no."

"God have mercy on their soul," Domina Elisabeth said.

She crossed herself, and Frevisse, Master Gruesby, and the manservant just standing up from the fire did likewise before Master Gruesby went on, still at a rush, "Master Montfort's funeral won't be delayed because of it, he thinks. He'll be back tomorrow. But if you'd give a little time to his mother, Dame Frevisse, it would divert her, Master Christopher thought. He thought that with him gone, it would be well for her to be . . . diverted."

Frevisse looked to Domina Elisabeth. "Might I?"

If Domina Elisabeth was wondering why Frevisse instead of herself was asked, she hid it. "There's no reason why you shouldn't. If you wish, please do."

Frevisse quite wished, for several reasons, but all she said aloud to Master Gruesby was, "Pray, say I'll be pleased to come to her after Tierce."

Master Gruesby bobbed a low bow of thanks, drawing back a step even as he did and another step while he said, "Thank you, my lady. Please you, I'll await you at the cloister door after Tierce to see you to the guesthall."

Frevisse held back from saying she thought she could find her own way to the guesthall, merely said in answer to his courtesy, "Thank you."

With another bow, Master Gruesby made his escape and Frevisse turned to ask Domina Elisabeth, "How was Mistress Montfort yesterday while you were with her?" Because curious though she was about a woman unfortunate enough to be married to Montfort and bear him children—five, she thought Christopher had once said— time spent with someone in deep mourning for the man might be more than she could well face.

"Quiet," said Domina Elisabeth. "But we only met at

the priory gate as we were coming to the inquest, hardly a time for her to be much given to talk."

"You sat with her through it."

"She hardly stirred, barely raised her head, did not cry at all that I saw, but very possibly her grief was drained to the dregs for a while. At the end she bade me farewell and we parted. That was all, and if she's the same today, you'll have a dull time of it."

It sounded so but still it gave something to which she could look forward. Besides, in the brief time it would take Master Gruesby to see her to the guesthall, she might have time to question him a little or at least tell him what little she had so far learned, doubtful though she was that any of it was going to be new to him.

But Letice called to them from the gallery then, asking if they'd come up to Lady Agnes and they did, keeping her company until it was time to go to Tierce and Emme brought their cloaks. Outside, a harsh wind helped them across the street and through the priory gateway, a slight snow in large flakes flighting around them and blown into little drifts along the base of walls but the ground frozen; the two of them came dry-footed into the cloister, safe out of the wind if not the cold, in time to join the last of the nuns hastening into the church.

Tierce went its usual way, today's psalms and prayers strong with hope for God's help in time of peril—*Deus, audi orationem meam; auribus percipe verba oris mei . . . Deus adjuvat me; et Dominus susceptor est animae meae.* God, hear my prayer; with your ears hear the words of my mouth . . . God helps me; and the Lord protects my soul—giving both comfort and strength even in times unperilous. Afterward, in the cloister walk again, Domina Elisabeth turned toward the infirmary and Frevisse back toward the priory yard, letting herself out the cloister door in a flurry of wind-pushed cloak and skirts and veil and pulling the door hard shut, making sure it was tightly latched before she turned to find Master Gruesby huddled into his cloak and waiting for her as she had been sure he would be. He did not seem the sort of man who would ever be late to anything if he could help it.

"Master Gruesby," she said by way of greeting.

More toward the cobbles than her, he answered, "Dame Frevisse," and "This way, please," and would have hurried away except that, catching and holding close the flapping ends of her veil with one hand, she refused to fight her skirts to walk more quickly into the wind, forcing him to unhurry and then fall back to her side, giving her the chance to ask, "Yesterday Master Christopher said what matters most about this contested manor is where it is. He knows then about the part it has in the contention between Lovell and Suffolk?"

Master Gruesby was shorter than she was and kept his head so down, with the thick wooden rims of his spectacles to hide much of his face, that she bent a little over as she asked and so saw him blink and make two false starts before he forced out, "Yes. He knows."

"And Master Montfort knew?"

"He knew."

From cloister door to guesthall stairs was not that far. They were nearly there and she asked more quickly, "How much did he know?"

Master Gruesby scuttled a little faster, reaching the stairs ahead of her. Set side-on to the yard, they a little blocked the wind—very little, Frevisse amended as a gust made her cringe more deeply into her cloak but she stopped where she was, forcing Master Gruesby to turn back to her and answer in a reluctant rush, "He knew that my lord of Suffolk hopes Master Champyon will have the manor. But that Lord Lovell wants it for Master Lengley."

"How much pressure have Suffolk and Lovell put toward having their own way about it? On the escheator or anyone else."

Master Gruesby blinked rapidly. "I don't know."

Frevisse had a sudden wondering whether that was true or not but now Master Gruesby had a question of his own. "Have you found out anything?" Even looking at her as he asked it.

"Only about this, and that Lady Agnes doesn't mean to talk about any of it if she can help it. Nor will I be able to ask much while around her because she's knows I'm cousin to Suffolk's wife." To Master Gruesby's quick questioning look she added, "No, I didn't tell her. My prioress did."

Master Gruesby gave a slight shake of his head and what might have been a regretful sigh and would have started up the stairs again but Frevisse said before he could, "What was in Lord Lovell's letter?"

The question seemed to startle him though it could hardly be unexpected. "I don't know. I've not read it yet. Word came that Master Christopher was needed and after that . . ." He made a vague gesture. "There's hardly been time."

"You'll have time now," Frevisse said curtly and started up the stairs, impatient with him and deliberately making him have to hurry to reach the door and open it ahead of her. The hall into which he ushered her was large, meant for a gathering, eating, sleeping place for usual guests but far from crowded this morning, two plainly black-dressed women sitting with some embroidery beside a window and a black-doubleted youth leaning against the wall near them, balanced on one leg and kicking backward at the wainscotting, all of them probably in attendance on Mistress Montfort but with presently nothing to do but pass the time, it seemed.

"This way, please," Master Gruesby said and led Frevisse the room's length to a shut door at its far end. After a wary knock and someone's call from inside, he opened it and went in, Frevisse following him. Montfort's widow turned toward them from where she stood at the fireplace as Master Gruesby said, "Dame Frevisse is come, my lady," giving Frevisse her first near, clear sight of her, dressed as she had been yesterday in full mourning-black except for the white wimple tight around her face between the thick fall of layered black veils. Her close-fitted sleeves came down to her fingers, nearly covering her hands laid quietly, one over the other, in front of her, and the rich stuff of her gown, falling about her unwaisted in graceful folds to the floor and spreading outward around her feet, caught even the day's dull light with a sort of sheen. It was all meant to show that her late husband had been a wealthy man, well worth being mourned, but of Mistress Montfort herself only the pale oval of her face showed, showing nothing as she and Frevisse exchanged slight curtsies to each other while Master Gruesby drew back, closing the door as he left.

The chamber was small and nunnery-plain but with a tall bed and table, joint stools, a cushioned bench under the window, and set at the bedfoot, two chests of the sort used for travel and likely come with Mistress Montfort. In a corner across the room from the fireplace and its fire crackling among thick logs there was a brazier burning charcoal; between them, the chamber was actually warm rather than merely unchilled, to Frevisse's pleasure as she unclasped and took off her cloak.

"Just lay it there," Mistress Montfort said, pointing toward the bed, and added, catching Frevisse's look around the room in mute surprise to find they were alone, "I sent everyone out. I was tired of their talk that went the same ways all the time and never anywhere." Her voice was pale and even and her face matched it, with pale eyes and lashes and brows so fair she almost seemed to have no features at all. Besides that, she was slightly built, both in height and body, and would hardly have come to Montfort's shoulder, Frevisse judged, with the added, unkind thought that might have partly been why Montfort married her—she would have been most easy for him to overbear in any way he chose.

But Mistrell Montfort was gesturing toward the window bench with, "Pray, let's sit, if you will," and together they moved that way, Frevisse far more easily than Mistress Montfort, who had to deal with her gown trailing half a yard on the floor around her feet and needing to be gathered and lifted out of her way before she could move at all. At last seated on the window bench facing Frevisse, spreading and settling her skirts in graceful folds around her feet, she said with a shading of bitterness, "My husband's choice," and looked up in time to see Frevisse's uncertainty at that and added, slightly smiling, "He bought all this some few years ago. He said that if he died ere me, he wanted me mourning him in something worthy of him, not some poor excuse for widow's weeds." She smoothed a hand down the rich cloth. "Of course he also said that if I died ere him, he could sell it all for as much as it was worth, not having been used, and cut his losses."

With nothing to say to that but need to say something, Frevisse tried, coming as close as she could honestly come to offering regret for Montfort's death, "I'm sorry for your grief."

With a small shrug and no particular feeling, Mistress Montfort said, "It's little enough but thank you." And again must have seen Frevisse's momentary uncertainty at what to say to that because she added kindly, "My grief. It's very little, I'm afraid. I grieve he died the way he did, cut off without even chance to cry out for God's mercy, but I can't mourn that he's gone." She looked down again, still smoothing at her skirts, then raised her gaze to Frevisse and asked, "I pray you, can you tell me how to go about mourning a man like him? What do you do when you know there's a soul in desperate need of prayer but all you can manage are thanks to God that you're free?"

Frevisse, unready for their talk to go that way, momentarily had no answer, knowing that so far she had slacked prayers for him herself, but finally said the best she had to offer, "I'd pay a priest to say a great quantity of masses for him and, hoping for the best, go on with my life."

Mistress Montfort gazed full at her, eyes wide and considering, for the length of a long-drawn breath. Then all unexpectedly she began to smile. "Yes," she said. "Yes. That much I can do." And even more unexpectedly she laughed, soft but truly, as if some tightly wrought cord in her had eased. "I thought, from what I've heard of you from my son and Master Gruesby, you might be someone I could talk to. I never meant to be so open, though. Pardon me."

"You needed to say it all," Frevisse said, unhesitating, "and I am, after all, safe."

"From what Christopher and Master Gruesby have said about you, safe is hardly what you are. But someone who would understand, yes. Thank you."

Discomfited at thought of being talked of, Frevisse said, to go another way, "You have a fine son in Christopher."

"A very fine son, I think," Mistress Montfort smilingly agreed, before the smile faded as she added, "The others are more like to their father."

Not a happy thought, and all that Frevisse could find to say to it was, "They all came with you, didn't they?"

"They're all here but John." She didn't seem to take much comfort from it. "Just now Edward has gone with Christopher on this crowner business and one of the servants has taken Anne and Joan to see something of Goring. They've found little else besides their crying to do here and are finding it tedious." There was the faintest dry edge to her voice on that. "John will be here with his wife's family sometime tomorrow morning. In time for the funeral."

"And Christopher?" Frevisse asked, realizing how little she actually knew of him. "Is he married, too?"

Mistress Montfort's eyes suddenly shone. "No. He's not. I stopped it. Every time." She must have read a-right Frevisse's suddenly shuttered face because she went on, "Oh, no, not against Christopher's desire, ever. Against his father's. If Christopher had wanted anyone his father eyed for him, it would have been different. But all Montfort ever considered was what the marriage might do for *him*. Never what it might do to Christopher. His first choice, when Christopher was fourteen, was half Christopher's age and born half-witted but her father could have been useful. Then, a few years later, there was a senile widow thrice his age who had a brother Montfort was dealing with. And finally, three years ago, a woman known to take any man to bed who caught her eye, but she would have come with a fine stretch of lands, both by dower and of her own and was hungry for a young husband after her second elderly one was lately dead, so my husband saw no trouble."

Mistress Montfort's clasped hands still lay lightly in her lap and her voice was even, her eyes lowered. Someone careless—and Montfort had ever been careless of people over whom he had power—would not have noticed her seeming-quiet body was rigid with an anger that showed only when, now, she looked up with it burning in her eyes, though none of it showed in her voice as she said, "*That* is what my husband would have wished on Christopher."

Because this was not only what Mistress Montfort wanted to talk about but what she *needed* to say, Frevisse asked, "How did you stop the marriages?"

Again there was the faint curve of her mouth and warming in her eyes. "Easily, as it happened. All I did was talk on about how wonderful whichever marriage it was would be. How the half-wit would surely bear witted children.

That the talk I'd heard about the aged widow being secretly at odds with her brother was surely only talk. That undoubtedly the whore would take great care to get with child only by Christopher, not just any man. I approved so much that my husband had to start doubting, and when he came to doubt enough, then he found his own reasons for breaking off the match."

Where strength is lacking, wits will serve, as the old proverb went, Frevisse thought. Wives more than anyone probably proved it true. But aloud she only asked gently, "Did he know how much you hated him?"

"How much I still hate him." Mistress Montfort did not hesitate over that cold, soul-deep answer. "No. Nor would it have mattered to him if he had. What I felt never mattered, so long as I was serviceable. So long as I made his home comfortable. Provided him with sufficient children. Was there for his use. What I *felt* about it didn't matter."

Her hands were clenched into white-knuckled fists in her lap. "Oh, yes. I hated him. I was married to him when I was fourteen. Had his first child when I was fifteen and was already hating him by then. He was a mean-minded, small-hearted, pushing man, and I was someone he felt most free to push all that he wanted to."

Still gently, understanding more with every word that Mistress Montfort said, Frevisse offered, "And you're telling me these things because you've never said them aloud but need to and it's best if they're said to someone you can trust to hold silent and will likely never see again."

Mistress Montfort nodded, her hands still tightly clasped together in her lap. "From what both Christopher and Master Gruesby's said of you, I thought you would do."

Setting aside her unease at the thought of Master Gruesby saying anything at all about her, Frevisse said, "Your hatred at least has to be confessed to a priest."

Mistress Montfort bent her head slightly, agreeing. "It

does, and now that he's gone, I'll confess it, do penance for it, hope to purge my heart of it. I couldn't before because . . ."

She made a small, helpless gesture and Frevisse finished for her, "Because confession and penance are done with intent never to sin that way again, and you knew that so long as Montfort was in life, you'd go on hating him."

Mistress Montfort nodded, pleased to have it said for her. "Yes. I would have. But now he's dead and damned and I'm alive and able to purge my soul of hatred for him. Which is the worse, do you think? My sin in hating him or his sins that brought me to my hatred?"

Frevisse hesitated over an answer to that but thoughtfully, bitterly, Mistress Montfort answered it for herself with, "Not that it much matters toward his damnation, I suppose. He had sins enough of every kind that adding the weight of those more to his soul will hardly matter."

It was a cruel epitaph. But Montfort had worked long and hard to have it and Frevisse could find no urge in herself to refuse it to him.

Chapter 9

ith Dame Frevisse safely left with Mistress Montfort, Master Gruesby went out into the cold and along the yard again, back to the cloister door where his knock brought a servant. Like any nunnery too small to have a constant porteress at the door, whoever was nearest came to the task but the servantwoman who opened the door to him did not question his being there. He was known from other visits and she only said, "I'll see you there. Come on, then," and led the way to the small parlor off the cloister kept for the nuns to receive guests. With a small, bouncing curtsy and "I'll find someone to fetch your things," she left him at the door and went off, supposing he could see himself in.

He did. It was a bare place, furnished for purpose, not comfort, with a bench, two low-backed chairs, and a slight table but no fireplace or brazier, nothing to take the edge off the raw air nor any light except what might come through a high, small window and the door if they were left open. Today the window was shuttered but the woman had let the door stand open for the sake of what gray light the day offered, and Master Gruesby set to pacing the room across and back for what warmth there was in moving, his arms clamped to his sides and his hands tucked under them, until the woman's return with a three-wicked oil lamp that she set well toward one end of the table, then stepped aside, out of the way of the nun following after her with a small wooden chest.

On Master Montfort's arrival at St. Mary's, he had made prompt demand at the prioress that she give over to him all documents and deeds concerning Lengley-held lands that he knew she had in the nunnery's keeping, only to be told promptly back that they were not his to demand. Master Montfort had started to swell toward outburst but it seemed the prioress had taken his measure more quickly than he had taken hers and liked him none the better for it because she had added, curt as he was, that she was, of course, willing to send someone to ask if Lady Agnes would allow him to see them.

"Allow me, madam?" Master Montfort had bridled. "*Allow* me?"

"If Lady Agnes graciously allows you," she had answered, matching him snappish for snappish, "then, on my terms, you shall see them as often as you wish."

"Your terms, madam? Who are you to make terms to me?"

"The person who has what you wish to see under lock and key and chain," she had said back, and it had ended that while Master Montfort went off to other business, Master Gruesby had waited; and when Lady Agnes had sent back word, "Yes, let him look at whatever he wants and be damned to him. We've nothing to hide," the prioress had given leave for Master Gruesby not only to see them that day but at any reasonable time he needed, with Sister Maud the sacristan to bring them and watch over everything he did.

And accordingly here was Sister Maud, thumping the chest down on the table's other end from the lamp and bidding the servant leave with, "Pray, close the door as you go," adding to the priory's novice, come in behind her so she would not be left alone with a man, "Sit there," pointing to the bench beside the door.

This was as it had been the other times. The novice would sit where she was told and Sister Maud would stand across the table from him, able to watch everything he did—her suspicion seemed to be that he would stuff his sleeves full of scrolls and papers and carry them off secretly if he could—while he ignored them both, for once unbothered by being under someone's eyes because Sister Maud was not noticing him in particular, only what he did, and as soon as he was doing nothing with the chest and its documents, she would cease to notice him at all, he was certain.

That certainty made him very comfortable. He did not like being noticed. It was one of the reasons Dame Frevisse made him uncomfortable. She noticed him, and he knew full well that when she noticed things she thought about them, and he did not like being thought about. He preferred being un–thought about and it was for comfort against the unease Dame Frevisse made in him that he was come here, rather than for any work that needed doing. He had no delusion about that, no delusion that he was anything but hiding as he unhasped and set open the chest's lid.

But there was nothing wrong with hiding if it kept him safe from being thought about, and to keep Sister Maud from thinking about him he started to sort through the chest's scrolls and folded papers as if looking for something in particular. He was not. He knew well enough all there was there from the other times he had gone through the chest. Knew too well, but it was something familiar to do and he liked the familiar.

That was the worst of Master Montfort's death—that it had ended almost everything familiar about Master Gruesby's life. Nor did he have much hope it would better, because people tended to employ their own clerks and whoever took Master Montfort's place as subescheator would almost surely not want him for clerk and about how he was to go about finding a new master he did not want to think.

The only good thing was that whoever took Master Montfort's place, or else their clerk, would go through all these same documents and deeds, and that would end at least one of Master Gruesby's problems.

As for finding work again, well, there was always place to be had for a clerk with a good hand, and so long as he was allowed to work he'd be at least somewhat content. He liked his work, liked words and the writing of them— the clean flow of well-made ink, the skritch of pen point over parchment or paper, the clear black shaping of letters. He enjoyed the making of something where there had been nothing and the satisfaction of how words set rightly down made a thing firm and certain.

Or as certain as people let anything be, even words. Because it was never words by themselves that made trouble, Master Gruesby had found. It was people who made trouble and used words to do it. That was why he preferred words to people. Words stayed what they were. He liked things to stay what they were. That was why his secret hope was that Master Christopher would have place for him, so that he could stay with the familiar. That had been what made Master Montfort endurable. He had been the same, year in, year out, never giving anything Master Gruesby's way except orders, yes, but never wanting anything back, either, except Master Gruesby's work. He had wanted no talk, no thought, no trouble, just Master Gruesby to go on steadily writing. Being with him had been simple. There was never doubt about him.

Equally, that was what made being with Dame Frevisse so *un*simple a thing. She was hardly ever, with her thinking and what she did, where one thought she was or expected her to be. It was because she made him uneasy that he was here now, trying to calm himself by dealing with papers rather than people, but to keep up the seeming he had some other purpose, he took up and unrolled one of the scrolls. A brief look at it told him it was a perfectly correct lease of meadowlands from Lord Lovell, good for another eight years, no quarrel or question about it. In truth, from his other times of going through them, he knew there was no quarrel or question about any of these documents. They were, for the most part, simply deeds, leases, agreements having to do with the long-term holding and inheritance of all Lengley properties, and very probably—no, certainly—no one had bothered to have them out since Sir Henry's death nor possibly for some while before then. They said what they said and until now there had probably been no need for anyone to look closely through them. Land was the safest of all things to hold and most of those who held any at all knew well what they held and by what rights they held it, down to the last square foot of messuage for a peasant, the last acre of meadow, wood, or arable for a lord. Sensible men took expense and trouble when they acquired any property to be sure the legalities were completely and correctly met.

Even the agreement over the Bower manor on which the present argument hung was clear enough. It said exactly what Lady Agnes claimed and Mistress Cecily admitted it did. The trouble did not lie with the agreement. Its words were clear, its meaning certain. The trouble lay with people. With who was Stephen Lengley's mother and who was not. There was where the quarrel and question lay. With who was lying and who was not.

Putting the rolled documents to one side on the table, Master Gruesby shuffled through the folded papers in the bottom of the chest. Like the scrolls, they were of all ages, some going back the two hundred years and a little more to when the first Lengleys had risen to knighthood and began to hold property. Some even had seals still hanging from them, or parts of seals whose wax had gone brittle with age and broken. They were the seals of the men and women who had made or witnessed the agreements, men and women long dead and mostly forgotten except for their names here; and so were the clerks' hands also long gone that had written the words, and their names were gone with them unless, for some reason, they were here in a document they had written those years upon years ago. Master Gruesby fingered what he knew to be the newest seal among them, the seal of Goring Priory itself, showing the Virgin seated with the Child on her lap under a fretted canopy. It did not seal the paper closed but was fastened to the letter by a ribbon, not meant to keep secret what was written there but testifying that the prioress of Goring—Domina Nichola Inglefield then, it seemed—had witnessed what was written and swore to its truth.

He did not open it. He had read it when he had read all the others and knew what it said. He simply wanted to see it again, to be certain it was still there and satisfied of that, left it where it was and chose another to unfold and read, a list made over seventy years ago, for some reason long passed, of who held what manors in some corner of Berkshire. So Sister Maud would not think he was wasting time here, he seemed to read it with great care and at the end nodded to himself as if satisfied of something and carefully put it and all the rest back into the chest, closed and hasped it, and nodded that he was done to Sister Maud without looking directly at her.

"Good," she said and turned away to lead him out of the room and see him out of the cloister.

With still no decision made of what he ought to do, he followed her.

Chapter 10

istress Montfort settled to more usual talk after their strange beginning, as if an infected sore had been lanced and the poison in it drained. She asked how Frevisse's journey to Goring had been and talked a little of her own journey, far shorter. With a few mutual questions they determined they knew no one in common but Christopher, about whom Frevisse could say pleasant things and his mother be pleased, and Master Gruesby, about whom neither of them had much to say at all. Frevisse ventured that she had never known his name until now. Mistress Montfort returned, "He's hardly needed one, being my husband's shadow. I don't know what will happen to him unless

Christopher takes him on," and brought their talk back to Christopher.

Frevisse quickly found she need only listen and was willing to it, letting Mistress Montfort talk on about the one person she seemed to care for, until her daughters returned, two half-grown girls who looked far more like their father than they did their mother and had his manners, too, thrusting into the room complaining of the cold as if somehow their mother were at fault for it. Mistress Montfort tried to quell them, pointing out they had a guest, to which one of them said, "A nun. We've had enough of nuns for the while."

"You'll nonetheless make her a curtsy and say 'Good day, my lady,' " Mistress Montfort directed, stiff-voiced, and they obeyed, albeit with little grace, and Frevisse was glad both for her own sake and Mistress Montfort's when a little later the bell rang to Sext, freeing them from each other's company. If she had had chance, she would have told Mistress Montfort she did not see her daughters were her fault. Even if they had not so much resembled their father in face and manners, Frevisse had encountered their sort before now—children who seemed to have come fully molded with no impress to be made on them by either love or discipline. This was sometimes to the good, sometimes to the bad, but with these two Frevisse's thought was that the sooner Mistress Montfort married them off her hands, the better for her.

Unable to say that, the girls crowding close while she and Mistress Montfort made their farewells, ready to claim their mother for themselves, Frevisse merely thanked her for their talk and went gratefully to Sext. Domina Elisabeth did not come, presumably staying with her cousin, and with no one to suggest what else she might do, Frevisse remained awhile in prayer after the other nuns had gone, until even with her cloak and fur-lined gown the cold became too much and she had to move or freeze. Walking in the cloister had no appeal, for the same reason, and for lack of anywhere else to go, she returned to Lady Agnes's, finding as she came out into the foreyard that the snow and wind had stopped and the sun was trying for a feeble yellow glow through the thinning clouds.

Its effort made the day no warmer. At Lady Agnes's hall door she knocked sharply only for courtesy's sake and went in without pause, eager for the hall hearth's fire. That she had not waited was just as well; she was to the hearth, holding her hands out to the flames and beginning to unchill, before Emme came from kitchenward, curtsied to her, and said, "Please you, my lady, Lady Agnes said you and Domina Elisabeth were come to her directly you're here, if you would. She's in her chamber."

With her unwillingness to be in more talk balanced by the thought that except for the kitchen, Lady Agnes's chamber would be the warmest place in the house, Frevisse thanked her, went up the stairs, and left her cloak in her own room before crossing the gallery to rap lightly at the solar's door. At Lady Agnes's bidding, she went in and was surprised that Emme had not said there was another guest, not only Letice, seated at the far end of the window bench with embroidery in her hands and a sour look on her face, but another woman seated at the fireside with Lady Agnes. Making no haste, Frevisse crossed the room toward them, the other woman standing up to meet her as Lady Agnes said, "Dame Frevisse. Lady Juliana Haselden."

Lady Juliana was young but, unlike Nichola, well into her womanhood, Frevisse thought as they greeted one another. Her smooth face, as finely proportioned as a painter's madonna and lovely with a light flush from the fire's warmth, was the sort that kept its youth through more years than many women's did, but there was a confidence and grace in even the slight curtsy she exchanged with Frevisse that youth usually lacked.

There was also an awareness of that grace, Frevisse thought. Too much awareness. Just as there was awareness, probably, of the single curl of dark golden hair escaped from the side of Lady Juliana's wimple to curve against her cheek. But with courtesy as smooth as Lady Juliana's own and no sign of her thoughts, Frevisse accepted her offer of the chair, leaving her to take one of the stools instead, and asked as she sat, "You're kin to Master Philip Haselden?" for the sake of conversation.

"Only distantly. I was wed to an uncle of his."

Was wed, Frevisse noted, and therefore was now a widow but not lately because rather than black or even mourning gray, her gown was a deep-dyed wintergreen with a high-standing collar lined with a fine brown fur, a scarlet belt around its high waist.

"Her husband was Sir Laurence," Lady Agnes said. "A godchild of mine, though I saw little enough of him after he was grown."

"And little of me, either," Lady Juliana said, "for which I've come to make excuse and ask pardon."

"It's more than excuses you'll be making to your mother when she finds out you've been here," Lady Agnes said tartly.

Lady Juliana laughed. "That's one of the advantages of being once-wed and now widowed. I'm not my mother's to tell what and what not to do."

"Not that you'd likely listen to her anyway. Nor anyone else either," Lady Agnes answered.

"Very likely not," Lady Juliana granted, still smiling. "You don't, do you, once you're set on your own way?"

Lady Agnes acknowledged the truth of that with a small, smiling bow of her head. "Not of late," she agreed.

They may have rarely met but there seemed to be a kind of understanding between them—an accord of spirit if nothing else. But no ease, Frevisse sensed. No more than between two men sparring with daggers to try each other out but not in deadly earnest. Yet. And abruptly Frevisse realized she had seen Lady Juliana before this. At the inquest yesterday she had sat between Mistress Champyon and Rowland Englefield and, yes, as Lady Agnes had said, her mother would very likely object strongly to her being here.

Lady Agnes must have caught Frevisse's sudden widening of eyes because she said, tinged with somewhat bitter mirth, "Yes. Juliana Englefield she was and her mother is trying to declare my grandson a bastard but here she sits instead of being turned from the door with a rude word."

If being frank was to be the way of it, Frevisse saw no reason to hold back. "Why?" she asked.

"Because my idiot man let her in. She told him I was her god-aunt, of all improbable things, and that her name is Juliana Haselden."

"And so it is," Lady Juliana said. "Besides, why should he turn me away? You like me and I like you and always have."

"Things change," Lady Agnes said. "Don't go presuming I haven't."

"Besides," Lady Juliana said to Frevisse, "I don't back my mother's claim to this manor of Reckling, so why shouldn't I come here?"

"You don't?" Frevisse said, neither to one side or the other but interested to see Lady Agnes up against someone as openly strong-willed as she was.

"No." Lady Juliana smiled. "It's a foolish claim and a waste of money and time."

"Ah!" Lady Agnes said. "So you admit Stephen is her sister's son, just as he claims, and your mother is lying."

"What I admit is that you and Stephen are known and liked here and hereabout. My mother is hardly known at all and, courtesy of you, probably not liked. If it comes to people swearing to the escheator that Stephen has been known for years to be Sir Henry's son by my mother's sister, there'll be more than enough people around here who'll swear so and very likely none who'll swear otherwise."

A deep-set satisfaction on Lady Agnes's face agreed with her. They were both, it seemed, well-satisfied women—Lady Agnes with the truth of what Lady Juliana said, Lady Juliana with her own clear-thinking to have seen it, but not satisfied about a great many things and seeing no reason to waste this chance to learn something, Frevisse said, "I've gathered your mother and her sister weren't close."

Juliana laughed. "To say it gently, no, they weren't. In truth, according to Mother, they could never abide each other and gladly went their separate ways once they were married."

"To the point of your mother not knowing whether her sister had a second child?"

"Rose sent her word of young Henry's birth, for certainty, and was bitch-spirited enough, my mother says, that if she'd had a second son she'd have sent her word of that, too, just to let her know Rickling was that much farther out of her reach."

"Rose died at Stephen's birth," Lady Agnes said. "I sent her word of both."

"What Mother says," Lady Juliana answered, "is that she had word that Rose had died but no mention there was any birth, Stephen or otherwise."

"She'd be bound to say that, wouldn't she?" Lady Agnes returned.

"She would indeed," Lady Juliana agreed, her smile like warm honey.

Lady Agnes smiled back with verjuice and be damned to honey. "That still leaves us with the question of why

you aren't with her in this. After all, whatever the truth
may be, there is a whole manor at hazard. Not to mention
your stepfather's ambitions."

Lady Juliana lifted a shoulder in a graceful, disclaiming
shrug, rose to her feet, and crossed the room toward the
window, saying as she went, "For one thing, I think wanting to be one of my lord of Suffolk's dog pack is a mistake on my stepfather's part."

"Do you?" Lady Agnes asked with real interest.
"Why?"

"Because Suffolk doesn't have staying power. Lord
Lovell does." She turned to Frevisse. "My mother and
aunt were in ward to Lord Lovell when they were small.
He made the Lengley and Englefield marriages for them."

"And you were a lady-in-waiting to Lady Lovell for a
while after your marriage to Sir Laurence," Lady Agnes
put in. "Your loyalty to the Lovells is very pretty." And
much doubted, her voice if not her words said.

It was unclear whether Lady Juliana's slight bow of the
head acknowledged her loyalty or admitted to the doubt
as she answered, "Of course, it has to be considered that
Lord Lovell doesn't presently have Suffolk's power with
the king, but in the long run, to my mind, he's the better,
steadier man to follow, rather than haring off after johnny-
jump-up Suffolk. As for the manor, what am I to care
about it? I'm not the one who'll benefit from it, am I? If
Mother makes good her claim, it goes to my brother, not
me. It's all wasted effort and expense so far as I'm concerned."

"Ah." Lady Agnes leaned an elbow on her chair's arm
and shook a finger toward Lady Juliana. "The Bowers
have never been strong breeders. Your brother, now. He
looks to be more Bower than Englefield, if you ask me.
Five years come spring he's been married and that wife
of his isn't breeding yet, is she? And if he has no issue,
the manor comes to you, doesn't it?"

Lady Juliana laughed, turned back from looking out the window again. "You've been asking about us!"

"Small need to ask," Lady Agnes retorted. "Once your mother decided to make this hornets' nest, people have been only too glad to tell me things whether I ask or no."

The high curve of Lady Juliana's eyebrows arched higher. "Have they indeed? Well, fair's fair, I suppose. We've heard things about you and yours, too."

"I warrant you have," Lady Agnes agreed. She smiled and Lady Juliana smiled back at her and there was nothing friendly at all between them, smoothly laid words or no.

But it was Lady Juliana who looked away first, out the window, before turning back to the room and saying as if giving up the challenge laid down between them, "Time I went, I think. Before I outstay my welcome." She crossed to take up her richly blue cloak from the chest at the bedfoot. "Unless I have already?" she added with a smile.

"By no means," Lady Agnes said graciously, almost no razor edge behind the words. "You've made my morning delightful."

Cloak over her arm, Lady Juliana returned in kind, "Thank you," and added to Frevisse, as if it might actually have been, "A pleasure to have met you."

"And you," Frevisse answered, as blandly as if she had noted nothing beyond courtesies between them.

"See her out, please, Letice," Lady Agnes ordered, and Letice, already on her feet, obeyed, going to open the door ahead of Lady Juliana and following her out, leaving a silence where Frevisse had nothing she wanted to say and Lady Agnes seemed waiting to be certain they were well alone before finally she burst out in disgusted mockery, " 'God-aunt.' And 'I don't care about the manor.'" She looked to Frevisse. "Did you ever hear such foolery? And don't tell you have because I won't believe you. How was the widow? Grieving?"

"Only over having been married so long to Master Montfort."

Lady Agnes snorted. "At least she's neither fool nor hypocrite then. Have you been with her all this while?"

Frevisse began to tell in detail of her going to Tierce and later to Sext, in hope of being so tedious that Lady Agnes would dismiss her, but she had not succeeded before Letice returned and Lady Agnes interrupted to ask, "Is she gone?"

"Gone," Letice confirmed. "The back way, though. Through the garden."

"The garden? Why?"

"She said she'd come through the alleyway and meant to go back the same in hopes no one would notice her."

"The day that one wants to go unnoticed will be the day Hell's flames turn cold," Lady Agnes said.

"And Master Stephen has just ridden in."

Lady Agnes brightened. "Has he?" She looked past Letice as if she were somehow hiding him. "Where is he?"

"Not come in yet."

Lady Agnes's heed snapped back to her. "Why not?"

"I couldn't say." But said, as if to the side of Lady Agnes's question, "Lady Juliana was just going into the garden when he rode in."

Lady Agnes went narrow-eyed with thought but only for a moment before slapping both hands down on the arms of her chair and pushing herself up to her feet with a small grunt at the effort but saying briskly enough when she was up, "Dame Frevisse, would you care to walk with me in the garden awhile?" Adding before Frevisse could reply, "Letice, fetch my cloak. And yours, too."

With for once no protests of worry over her lady, Letice hastened to obey. Frevisse, at first minded to refuse, decided to be curious instead, fetched her own cloak, and waited at the stairhead while Lady Agnes made her way laboriously down, Letice waiting at the bottom in case of

need. That done, Lady Agnes set off briskly enough for
the outer door, thudding her staff against the floor with
the force of her going. As Letice was opening the hall's
inner door ahead of her, Frevisse overtook them and
moved past to open the outer, standing aside for Lady
Agnes, then falling into step beside her, asking no questions as they crossed the narrow yard to the penticed gateway into the garden, past a saddled chestnut palfrey
tethered by its bridle to a wall ring on the yard's far side
with no sign of its rider.

The morning's overcast was breaking away into high
white drifts of cloud across a scoured blue sky, and Letice,
sniffing the air, said, "Warmer again tomorrow."

"Or not," Lady Agnes rejoined at a harsh half-whisper.
"We could be to our elbows in snow by tomorrow for all
you know. Now hush, the both of you."

For Frevisse, with nothing to say, that was easy enough,
but Letice's mouth was shut into a tight line over obviously a great deal she wanted to say as she moved ahead
of them to open the gate and stood aside to let them go
into the garden ahead of her.

"And close that gate quietly," Lady Agnes ordered as
she went in.

There was no trouble over which way to go. On its left,
the path was bounded by a waist-high, wide-latticed fence
between it and what was surely the kitchen's garden, its
long beds waiting for spring's planting, with here and
there a snow-covered hump of something not cleared
away last autumn, while on the right was the high stone
wall between Lady Agnes's garden and her neighbor's.
Only further on, past where the kitchen garden ended, did
the garden open out into the common pattern of square
beds and paths, here bounded on both sides and at the far
end by tall walls hiding it from its neighbors. A turf bench
ran along the rightward wall where there would be shade
on summer afternoons; along the other, lean trees were

spread and tied where they would catch the sun most of a summer's day; and at the far end was a vine-covered arbor almost full across the garden's width, only stopping short of a low door at the corner of the wall that must lead into whatever back way ran behind the houses there. In summer, grown over and green with leaves, it would be a private place but like all the garden it was naked now, its barren, brown vines unable to hide anything and assuredly not the man and woman standing within it, close-entwined to one another.

Frevisse and Letice both stopped. Lady Juliana, though her back was to them, was easily known by her bright cloak but Frevisse did not know Stephen until he raised his head and, over Juliana's shoulder, saw Lady Agnes stalking down upon them. Briefly he was startled. Then his face lighted with laughter and he bent his head to say something into Juliana's ear that made her look around at them with laughter, too. She was flushed with a different warmth than the fire had given her indoors as she took a step backward out of Stephen's arms and turned to stand beside him, neither of them looking either abashed or contrite. Indeed, Stephen said, chiding, as Lady Agnes stopped in front of them, "There now, Grandmother. Since when have you been wont to go for walks in the snow?"

"Ever since I was hard put to believe Lady Juliana came to see me out of the mere goodness of her heart," Lady Agnes snapped. She was short of breath and leaning on her staff but none the less waspish with anger. "Especially when that was followed by a wondering why my grandson was seen to ride into the yard but didn't come into the house, he being no more given to cold strolls in the snow than I am that I've ever noticed."

"Grandmother, Grandmother," Stephen said with a regretful shake of his head. "Remember what's said about curiosity and the cat. If you catch your death of cold by coming out here about what's none of your business, don't blame me."

"I'll blame you for anything I choose to. If it's proverbs we're about, best you remember, 'It's ill to sin and worse to continue.' And I decide what's my business and what isn't. Don't meet your wantons in my garden if you don't want it to be my business."

Merry reproach lighted Juliana's face. "I'm not his wanton, my lady. I'm his paramour. His love."

"Like Lancelot and Guinevere," Stephen said, drawing her closer to him with an arm around her waist.

"Hah! You're not Lancelot, boy, and that"—Lady Agnes pointed her staff at Juliana—"is no Guinevere, make no mistake."

Frevisse was suddenly angry at them all, Lady Agnes as much as Stephen and Juliana, because while there was no shame on their part, neither was there real anger on Lady Agnes's. Despite all her outward wrath, she was enjoying the quarrel as much as they were, with a sharp pleasure in the heightened moment that made it worse, and Frevisse, with her feet growing colder and her anger hotter, was ready to turn around and walk away, back to the house and warmth, but Lady Agnes made abrupt end to it, probably feeling the cold herself, saying at Juliana, "If you want a man, best find you one you can marry for yourself, not sport with someone else's husband. Now off to your mother with you and stay out of my garden with your nonsense."

For answer, Juliana only laughed and reached out a hand to Stephen, who took it, raised it, kissed it, and stepped aside to open the door through the wall there, then saw her through with another kiss of her hand and a gallant bow to which she beautifully smiled into his eyes before she took her hand away from him and turned and left. Only as Stephen closed the gate behind her did Lady Agnes show her first deep displeasure, demanding, "How came my garden door to be unlocked, boy?"

Stephen was ready for that, already taking a heavy key from his belt pouch under his cloak, answering, "With this." Lady Agnes made an angry tching sound and held out her hand for it but Stephen, locking the door, laughed at her. "You still have yours, Grandmother. I had this one made years ago." He put it back into his pouch. "You'd never have known about key or door if I hadn't been late today and Juliana decided to make up her waiting time by visiting you."

"What I know now is that you've no scruples and no care, either, leaving my garden open for anyone to wander in that wants to."

Stephen came to her and with a hand under her elbow turned her back toward the house, saying kindly, "Don't you know, Grandmother, that it's peril gives sweetest love its sweetness?"

"It's supposed to be your peril, not mine, boy." But she let him lead her along the path, Frevisse and Letice standing aside to let them pass, then following while she went on at him, "Though you'll have peril enough if you're found out by someone besides me. What do you think Philip is going to think of your playing his daughter false?"

"Not much. He knows how these games go."

"You think that's going to make him more mellow at your betraying of his daughter? You're a fool, Stephen. How did you and this Juliana meet at all? In Lord Lovell's household, I suppose?"

"Of course. When I had my month-duty with him a year ago last summer. She was lately widowed and come to have Lord Lovell's assurance of her dower lands. We took each other's fancy, and here we are."

"You set to it with her a goodly while before you were married to Nichola then."

"Yes."

"Why not marry this Juliana instead, then, while you still had the choice?"

"Choice? You know the fine Philip would have had from me if I wanted to buy him out of choosing my marriage. Besides, Juliana is to be enjoyed, not married. And you, Grandmother, of all women, surely don't hold that a man can't love more than one woman well?"

"Don't tell me what I hold and don't hold, boy. What I'm telling you is that you're putting yourself into peril for no purpose. You're better off playing safe instead of foolish."

" 'Safe' becomes 'dull' after a time, I find. After all, even Adam had Lilith as well as Eve."

"Remember how that turned out?" Lady Agnes returned. They had reached the gate into the yard now and Stephen moved ahead to open the gate for her, but instead of going through, she stood still and asked at his back, "Does Nichola know?"

Stephen faced her as if startled by the question, pausing before he answered, "Of course she doesn't. I don't mean for her to."

"Hah." Lady Agnes went past him, rapping her staff against his ankle as she did. "What you mean is that you don't think she knows and that, let me tell you, boy, means nothing."

Chapter 11

hether because of his grandmother's chiding—though he seemed singularly unbothered by it—or because he had not meant to be here for long, Stephen made his farewell to Lady Agnes there in the yard, giving her a kiss on her cheek that she received peaceably enough before he bowed to Frevisse, grinned at Letice, untethered his horse, swung into the saddle, and with a cheerful wave, rode out of the yard and away.

While Lady Agnes watched the few moments until he was gone, Letice hasted toward the hall door, ready to open it when Lady Agnes at last moved to go in, Frevisse following her, all of them ready to be indoors again. But as Lady Agnes paused for Frevisse to open the inner one ahead of them, Letice took the chance to say from behind her, "What with him riding in and then riding out again so soon instead of staying to dinner, rumor will be all over town the two of you have quarreled. What then?"

"Everyone knows we always quarrel and that it means nothing. Thank you," she added to Frevisse, going into the hall ahead of her. "At most our friends will shake their heads and regret it. Everyone else will be glad of it. For what that's worth. What matters is what I say, and I say be damned to them all. Hurry up. You're letting the cold in."

Letice was already hurrying into the hall after Frevisse, shutting the inner door as she came, persisting, low-voiced now they might be overheard, "And Stephen and this Lady Juliana?"

"Be damned to them, too," Lady Agnes said, not low-voiced at all.

Caught between them, Frevisse considered her chances of escape. There was no bustle of tables being set up for dinner, only the man Lucas sweeping the floor around the hearth, though it was near to dinnertime. That meant Lady Agnes meant to dine in her chamber, Frevisse supposed, and that she'd be expected to dine with her and could find no sufficient excuse to avoid it as Letice hurried ahead to take Lady Agnes's cloak from her. To be useful rather than merely there, Frevisse offered to take both women's cloaks and Letice gratefully gave over Lady Agnes's with her own, freeing her to help her lady's labored climb up the stairs. The effort of that ceased all talk until, safe at the top, Lady Agnes said to Letice, "Tell them we're ready to eat," and asked past her to Frevisse, "I gathered this morning that Domina Elisabeth meant to stay all the day with her cousin?"

Climbing the stairs, awkward with her own cloak as well as the others to manage, Frevisse said, "She planned so, yes."

"Then there will be only the two of us and I'm hungry. Go tell them so, Letice."

"Yes, my lady," Letice said on a heavy sigh and took herself back down the stairs.

Lady Agnes, taking for granted that Frevisse would come with herself, headed for her chamber, leaving the door for Frevisse to close and saying, sharp with annoyance as she crossed the room toward the fire, "Young fools. What did they hope for, meeting like that at this time of year? Too much risk they'd be seen and no hope of satisfying each other. Young idiots."

Frevisse, going to lay the cloaks on the chest at the bedfoot, made no answer, nor did Lady Agnes seem to want one, going on as she poked a log further into the fire with her staff, "No sense at all. All they could hope to do, all they did, was inflame themselves to nothing but high discomfort. What were they thinking of?"

Frevisse, less and less pleased that all Lady Agnes's anger seemed for the foolishness of it, not the wrong, said curtly, "I doubt they were thinking at all. Haven't you found that when lust comes in, thinking goes out?"

Lady Agnes laughed. "True enough."

Joining her at the hearth, holding out chilled hands to the warmth, Frevisse suggested with forced mildness, "You could warn your grandson more strongly about what trouble he's heading into."

"Best save my breath to cool my soup." Lady Agnes prodded the log again. "It's in his blood. His father and grandfather, God keep their souls, were the same and likely his son will be and grandson after him."

"And Nichola?" Frevisse asked, keeping anger out of her voice with difficulty.

"She'll learn to live with it the way other wives have learned. At least she has the comfort that her husband loves her along with his leman."

Frevisse held back from saying that what Stephen felt

for Juliana was hardly love, led by the loins as it was, rather than by the heart. What she said instead was, "Then if you mean to do nothing to stop them, why did you go out purposefully to catch them at it?"

"Ah. You're the cunning one, aren't you?" Lady Agnes did not sound completely pleased to be called to account. "I went because they'd best learn they're not as clever as they think they are. And to let them know that I don't intend to lend myself to their dalliance."

Letice came in then with Emme, to set out the table with a clean white cloth embroidered in red and yellow spirals around the hem and well-polished pewter dishes and cups, and both Lady Agnes and Frevisse held silent while they did, finishing just as the other maid and Lucas brought in two cloth-covered trays and a pitcher of warm, spiced wine that Frevisse welcomed for its warmth's sake as much as she welcomed the food.

The meal was a pleasingly simple one of rabbit cooked in a sauce of spices and raisins, followed by risshewes of figs mixed with spices fried in a fine pastry crust; and Lady Agnes kept the talk pleasingly simple, too, first with a little mild speculation on who and how many might come to Montfort's funeral—"The curious and the required for the most part, I'd guess. Real mourners will likely be few," was her judgment—and, her good humour restored, went on from there to talk about St. Mary's.

"Though there's woefully little to say about it," Lady Agnes complained, only half in jest, Frevisse thought. "Last year Bishop Lumley made one of his visitations to learn of all the wrongs and whatever there might be. That's when scandals and complaints come out, everybody tattling on everybody else. But there was nothing. Not a thing. Not even one nun tattling on another. No backbiting, no scandals, no reports of any sinful doings or complaints of poor managing. Nothing."

"Whatever are they thinking of?" Frevisse said dryly.

"Their prayers, I suppose. More's the pity. How goes it in your nunnery? Is it is as dull as this one?"

Frevisse suspected that was the question Lady Agnes had been aiming at all along, undoubtedly with the hope that, with Domina Elisabeth not there, Frevisse would turn to tale-telling. But rather than giving any sign she had understood the chance she was being offered, she took her time over a last small bite of a risshewe before saying so mildly butter would have barely melted in her mouth, "Oh, it's much the same, I'd say."

Lady Agnes let her doubt of that show. "All honey and warmth, is it?"

"Well . . ." Frevisse paused as if for thought. "Dame Perpetua *was* upset lately over a batch of ink that didn't turn out well. And Dame Claire was maybe a little too persevering at Domina Elisabeth about something she wanted brought from Oxford when we returned. You know how infirmarians are."

Lady Agnes gave a sharp laugh. "I see how *you* are anyway, Dame. Have it your own way. Tell no tales and no tales will be told about you, you think? Well, will you read to me awhile, before Letice begins to remind me I should lie down for a time?"

Frevisse would have preferred to leave Lady Agnes to her rest but the warmth near the fire and lethargy after the meal kept her, as much as for courtesy's sake, brought her to say, "I'd be pleased to. What would you like?"

Lady Agnes waved a hand at Letice, waiting to clear their dishes now they were done with eating. "Bring the *Lais*. It's wherever you put it in the chest last time."

"I mind where it is," Letice answered, already moving to fetch it.

Clear in the cold air, the nunnery bell began to call to Nones. All three women crossed themselves but that was all the heed either Lady Agnes or Letice gave it and Frevisse took the book when Letice brought it to her without comment, merely asking, "Which would you like?"

"Where the marker is," Lady Agnes directed, settling herself against her cushions with eyes shut and hands folded over her stomach. She did not nap, though, but listened well, with occasionally a laugh and sometimes a soft snort at something more unlikely than the rest; and when there was a light scratching at the door she opened her eyes on the instant to demand at Letice, "Go and see who it is."

Unbothered at being ordered to do what she was already doing—but if she was going to be bothered by Lady Agnes's ways, she would have left her years ago, Frevisse supposed—Letice crossed the room and opened the door, said with pleasure, "Mistress Nichola," and stood aside to let the girl enter as Lady Agnes wiggled up straighter in her chair and called, "Ah! Good! Come here, sweetling."

Her cheeks prettily bright from the cold, Nichola obeyed, smiling, asking as she unfastened her dark green cloak and gave it to Letice, "Is it all right I'm here? You're done with dinner, aren't you?"

"Long since," Lady Agnes said. "Nor would it matter if we weren't. I'm always glad to have you here. You know that. Letice, has the wine kept warm? The child is chilled, surely. You didn't walk, did you?"

Shaking out the skirts of her simple, dark red gown before curtsying to Lady Agnes and Frevisse together, Nichola said with a small, breathless laugh, "No. I rode. See."

She had kept her gloves when she gave up her cloak and now held them out. Lady Agnes gave a sharp, approving nod. "Good. Show them to Dame Frevisse."

Nichola obediently did and Frevisse duly looked at them. They were lovely, made of pale, soft doeskin, with long cuffs meant to protect a rider's forearms, the back of each hand intricately patterned with embroidery and beads in greens and blues.

"Father said I wasn't to wear them except when I ride," Nichola offered shyly. "That's why he gave them to me. So I'd ride."

"Nichola is afraid of horses," Lady Agnes grumbled.

"I'm not," Nichola protested. "I like horses. I just don't like to *ride* them."

"You'll make no miles by looking at them," Lady Agnes pointed out crisply.

Apparently used to being scoffed at for it, Nichola said easily, "But I don't need to make miles to visit you," and added, smiling, to Frevisse, "We only live a little beyond the top of High Street. No long way to walk at all."

"Or to ride," Lady Agnes said. "You'll come to no harm over that short stretch of road. Letice . . ."

But Letice had already brought a stool, was setting it down behind Nichola and offering to take her gloves. Nichola gave them to her and sat, while Lady Agnes left off jibing at her and said, smiling, too, "Now, child, what brings you here besides simply the pleasure of my company? Our company," she amended with a slight bend of her head to Frevisse. "Are they fretting at home and you decided to escape for a time?"

"Oh, Godmother." An unwilling smile tugged at Nichola's mouth. "They're always fretting, you know that. Mother . . ."

She stopped, to take the cup of wine Letice had poured for her, and Lady Agnes asked, "How is your mother?"

"Fretting." But Nichola smiled as she said it. "You know how she is."

"Is she done with that rheum she had at Twelfth Night yet?"

"Nearly."

"You tell her from me to drink a strong brew of peppermint with honey thick in it. That will clear it." Lady Agnes turned to Frevisse. "She's a narrow-chested woman so these things always take her hard. The sweetest of women but not strong. Bearing four sons and two daughters was too much for her, I think. But they all lived and so did she and that's more blessing than God sometimes gives . . ."

She seemed likely to go on that way, but Nichola, having probably heard it too often to more than be half-listening now, asked, "Godmother, was Stephen here today?"

Without change of countenance or pace, Lady Agnes turned from procreation to husbands, answering easily, "He was indeed. For a pleasant while I had both him and Dame Frevisse for company."

Nichola glanced at Frevisse who, wary of where this might be going, nodded very slight agreement that she had been here. Looking back to Lady Agnes, Nichola said with obviously forced boldness, "It's being said you quarreled."

"Fools say a great many things. Whether you heed them or not is your choice." Lady Agnes dismissed them all with a wave of one hand, then leaned forward to tap Nichola firmly on the shoulder. "And on the whole you'll find that any word that runs as fast as that one did is usually false."

"You didn't quarrel, then?" Nichola persisted.

Lady Agnes sat back in her chair. "Of course we quarreled. We always quarrel. It's what we do for sport. You know that by now and that there's never harm in it."

Nichola smiled, again as if unwillingly. "That's what Stephen said, too."

"You asked Stephen?" Lady Agnes sounded both surprised and pleased.

"Just before I came. Mother said I shouldn't, but who else should I ask first if not him?"

"Quite right," Lady Agnes approved. "Sensible girl. Keep him that bit off balance."

"Oh, no . . ."

"Oh, yes, my child. If you let husbands keep their balance all the time, they become impossible to govern, and Stephen will be worse than most if you let him. What did he answer?"

"He said I shouldn't be a ninny."

"There then. You listen to him. He's your husband after all. Just don't always heed him, mind you. But do listen." Nichola laughed.

"Now drink your wine while it's still warm and will do you some good," Lady Agnes ordered.

Nichola obeyed, raising the cup with both hands like a child, but to Frevisse the look in her eyes looking at Lady Agnes over the cup's rim said she was not yet altogether reassured, and when she had lowered the cup to her lap and was gazing down at it, Nichola asked, "You had other company this morning, too." She hesitated. "Mistress Champyon's daughter?"

"Ah. Lady Juliana." Lady Agnes took a long sip of her own wine. "Yes. She came to pay her respect because I was her late husband's godmother. She said. What she really wanted was to see if I was as witless with age as her mother hopes I am and, if I was, to judge how much to her mother's advantage it would be."

"She didn't!" Nichola protested.

"She did indeed. I was a disappointment to her, I fear."

It was a neat bit of lying, Frevisse granted, and all the better for not being quite altogether a lie, but Nichola asked with a lightness not quite light enough, "Was she here when Stephen was?"

"She was going out as he was coming in, I think." Lady Agnes's lightness was much better done. "They probably passed each other in the yard. Letice." She held up her cup to be refilled and, while Letice fetched the pitcher, asked in her turn, "What do you hear about your brothers, Nichola?" as if moving on to something more interesting.

Left with the choice of answering or being rude, Nichola settled to telling they'd heard that both her two older brothers and their wives were well, that Robin at Westminster was complaining of his law studies being too long, and that Ned had written from Oxford just after Twelfth Night to say he was short of money.

"Young Ned would be short of money if he were the archbishop of Canterbury," Lady Agnes said. "He's no sense that way. Wherever he becomes priest, they'd best look to their altar plate, that's all I can say, or they'll find it pawned."

"Oh, Grandmother!" Nichola laughed. She had given over being the worried wife, was again simply the cheerful girl she had been at dinner yesterday.

"And your sister?" Lady Agnes asked.

"The baby is expected to come about Ladymass day. Mother and I mean to be there for it, if the weather holds good for riding."

Lady Agnes nodded approvingly. "Very good. And you?" She leaned to pat Nichola's stomach. "What about you?"

A duskier red than what the cold had brought to her cheeks flooded Nichola's face. She looked quickly down into her lap, her hands suddenly tight around her wine cup as she murmured, "Nothing yet. You know that."

"I just wanted to be certain Stephen is still behaving himself. Put your head up, child. You're not a servant."

Nichola raised her head, face still flamed. "If he . . . if I . . . he might not need then—"

Lady Agnes cut her off with another tap on her shoulder, saying firmly, "You put those thoughts right out of your head, child. Stephen loves you best of anyone and that's all you need to think on. Now, we've left Dame Frevisse out of our talk too long. Tell her about your plans for your manor when you and Stephen finally move there."

Obedient, Nichola swallowed down whatever she was

hurting to say but stood up and said instead of Lady Agnes's bidding, "Another time, please you. Mother will be wanting me and I'd best go."

"Off you go then. Give me a kiss."

Lady Agnes tilted her head and Nichola affectionately kissed her cheek, then turned to make curtsy to Frevisse with, like the well-bred child she was, "It was good to see you again, my lady."

"And you, Mistress Lengley," Frevisse answered with a bow of her head.

"Mind you come again to see me soon," Lady Agnes said. "Mind, too, that you ride the long way around to home. Up Mill Street, if nothing more. The more you ride, the easier you'll feel at it."

"Yes, Grandmother," Nichola agreed but whether to the longer ride or not wasn't clear.

"Letice," Lady Agnes said, and with Nichola's cloak over her arm and gloves in hand, Letice went to open the door, letting Nichola pass through ahead of her, then following after, shutting the door as she went, probably to see the girl all the way across the hall to the yard, and with them safely gone, Lady Agnes slumped back in her chair with a deep sigh of relief and, "There. That's trouble done."

Or at least fended aside for a while, Frevisse thought, because to her mind Nichola had been turned aside from worry rather than talked out of it; and despite she knew she should leave it lying, she said, "She knows about Juliana. Or suspects."

Lady Agnes straightened. "Very likely. People talk where they shouldn't, and wives hear what they wouldn't. But hopefully she has wit enough to realize how much better it is *not* to know. She's not too young to learn that not-knowing and not-seeing are two of life's most desirable skills."

"What the eye doesn't see, the heart doesn't grieve at?" Frevisse said dryly.

"Yes." Lady Agnes thrust her staff fiercely at the crumbling coals at the fire's edge. "Besides, whatever Stephen does, she's no call to complain of him. She's had her rights of him. Her father made certain of that. She's fully married, fully his wife. There's nothing can change that, even if he's taken care not to get her with child while she's still so young." She poked ferociously at the coals again. "That's kinder than most husbands would be."

And the more surprising, given the open affection Frevisse had seen between them yesterday. Stephen's forbearance spoke better of him than his lust for Juliana did, but Lady Agnes rubbed at her forehead as if there were an ache there and said, "Mind you, if Philip ever finds out, there'll be trouble. Until Nichola has a child, he can't be sure of the Lengley lands."

"Sure of them?" Frevisse asked. Whether Nichola had a child or not, Stephen's lands were Stephen's lands, not Philip Haselden's. Unless, Frevisse amended, Nichola had a child and then Stephen died. Then, very likely, her father would be given wardship of the child and its lands— and their profits—until the child came of age.

There, if for some reason Stephen did not fully trust his father-in-law, was another reason he might hold back from getting his wife with child.

And there, Frevisse thought uncomfortably, was one of the corruptions caused by murder: until the murderer was known, suspicion spread out poisonous roots into places where it would never have gone without being fed by the certainty that someone unknown had killed and could kill again.

But Lady Agnes was saying easily, with no trace of troubled thoughts, "What Philip wants is to be sure of them staying in Lengley hands. There's been alliance between the Lengleys and Haseldens for three generations

and more. My husband and Philip's father were like
brothers, and before Philip and my son went off to the
French war together, the young fools, they swore in St.
Thomas's church here that if either of them died, the other
would see to his family like his own. Philip feels still
bound by that oath, I think, just as my Henry would, did
he still live instead of Philip. Stephen is the last Lengley
heir, and until he has sons, Philip won't feel he's kept all
as safe as he would have had my son keep things for his
sons, if things were different."

"Was it for that Lord Lovell gave him Stephen's marriage?"

"Partly, but also because Philip has long been Lord
Lovell's man and had earned it."

With assurance, too, of his continued faithful service,
Frevisse guessed. That was the purpose of lordship and
service after all—to bind lord and man to each other to
their mutual benefit and the general good, because not
only could a lord well served by others better serve the
king, but a man in good service to a lord was less likely
to make troubles where he should not. It was a power that
could be likewise turned to ill-purpose in the hands of an
ill-skilled lord or ill-intentioned, but that she had never
heard ill of Lord Lovell meant he was likely a lord who
used and governed his power and his people well.

Unlike the earl—no, marquis, now—of Suffolk, who
seemed ever at the edge of ripples of rumor and trouble.

But Lady Agnes was still going her own way. "Not that
the right to the marriage didn't come to Philip in good
time. What with buying good marriages for two of his
sons and setting the other two up in the world and managing a sufficient dowry for his older girl, paying out for
another marriage would likely have been too much for
him. It would have to have been the nunnery for Nichola
for certain. Not that Stephen looked to be all that good a
take. Until his brother died, he only stood to inherit the

least of the Lengley manors. But when young Henry died, well, there, Philip couldn't have done better for the girl, and Stephen is no loser by it either."

His grandmother's casual mention of her grandson Henry's death made Frevisse wonder how much less loved than Stephen he had been. He had never been strong, she remembered someone saying, and Christopher had had no doubts about his death, but still . . .

But shame on her, sitting here as Lady Agnes's guest and thinking again of murder, especially when the likelihood was so little. Heirs often died and their deaths were usually convenient to someone without there being more to it than that mortality was the lot of every man.

But Montfort was dead. Was murdered. Very probably because of the Lengley inheritance. By someone familiar enough with Goring to make use of the infirmary garden. Someone . . .

Lady Agnes shifted, resettled herself discontentedly in her chair, and said, "I'd best tell Stephen to take better care in his dealings with this Juliana woman, I suppose. Being a man, he'll doubtless never suppose Nichola has guessed at it. Nor he won't have thought past a glimmer of how badly she may take it when she's certain. Her mother is a mouse, sweet but a mouse nonetheless, and I don't think Nichola will be the same, St. Waldetrudis be thanked. Stephen doesn't need a mouse. Though why she thought I'd tell her anything . . ." Lady Agnes broke off with an impatient shrug.

"Because she trusts you?" Frevisse asked, with a sharper edge to the words than she had meant to show.

Lady Agnes eyed her a moment before answering, "You've a shrewd edge to your tongue when you choose, don't you? Yes, she trusts me, and that's to the good because it makes her more likely to believe me when I lie to her."

"The question then is, Should you lie to her?"

"Most surely, yes. I know from all the lies there were between my husband and me that there's often far more comfort in them than in the truth."

"A false comfort."

"Better false comfort than none," Lady Agnes snapped. With her staff she broke the nearest burning log down to glowing bits in the fire's heart, scattering sparks. "Haven't you found that most things of the world are false and the best to be hoped for is to deceive yourself into thinking you're happy for as long as may be before having to face that you're not?"

Frevisse's first urge was to anger at such a cruel view of the world, but even as the anger rose in her, she saw the bleakness of Lady Agnes's stare into the fire and the strained, tired downturn of her mouth and her anger slipped sideways into pity, because whether Lady Agnes truly believed or not in what she said, it gave her a shield against a hurt so long a part of her she would probably, in life, never be rid of it.

But in the moment Frevisse thought that, Lady Agnes put her pain away, back to wherever she kept it, and said with a sudden, sharp look at her, "What I said about Stephen not meaning to get Nichola with child yet, that's not to be said outside this room to anyone. You understand? Philip would be furious at them both and they don't need that while living under his roof. There'll be children in good time, not before, Stephen says."

"What does Nichola say?"

Lady Agnes waved a dismissive hand at that. "It's not for her to say anything, any more than it's her business to say anything about any other women he may have. That's simply a man's way. Let her be satisfied with knowing he loves her and she loves him. That's more than many women have and St. Anne knows she won't be the first wife and she won't be the last who's loved her husband despite he's indiscreet." She pointed a finger at Frevisse. "Nor don't try to tell me where I'm wrong in this. I know things about men you'll never know because you've been Christ's bride all your life and he's a far easier husband to have than one of flesh and blood, let me tell you."

Frevisse was so taken by surprise at the thought that being wed to Christ was easy that for a moment she simply stared, then gave up and laughed aloud in open merriment. Christ was, beyond doubt, to be preferred to a spouse of flesh and blood, but as for it being easy to be wed to him . . . it was and it wasn't, and there were days when "wasn't" was very strong.

Except that, unlike with earthly husbands, she could be ever sure of his unfailing love and faithfulness.

But hopeless of making an answer Lady Agnes, probably already offended by her laughter, would believe, Frevisse stood up, saying, "I'm sorry, my lady. I didn't mean to be rude. I must be more tired than I knew. I pray you, pardon me. By your leave, I'll withdraw for a while."

Lady Agnes made a dismissing movement of one hand. "As you say, my lady. We're likely both tired or I'd not have been so free of speech."

"It's more than likely you're tired," Letice put in, come back into the chamber without their noticing her. "You're past time for your afternoon rest by more than a little."

"I am, I am," Lady Agnes agreed and was making to rise from her chair as Frevisse took her cloak from the chest and left with a nod and a smile to Letice.

The smile faded as she crossed the gallery. She doubted Lady Agnes was judging Nichola rightly and very possibly so were Stephen and even her father. They all of them apparently presumed she could be shaped as each of them chose, but it had taken daring all her own to come to Lady Agnes today, and she had tried with more a woman's need than child's to have answers from her. That made Lady Agnes's deceiving of her all the worse, because whatever amendment Stephen might make would have to come by his own choice and will, but if Lady Agnes were sensible—and although she was not wise, she was not a fool and could be sensible if so she chose—she would help Nichola toward becoming the woman Nichola needed to by giving her truths, not thwarting her with lies under the guise of calling them necessary.

Angry on Nichola's behalf and at the troubles people made for themselves, she shoved shut the bedchamber door somewhat more forcibly than need be and was finally fully alone for the first time all that day.

Chapter 12

he bed had been made since Frevisse and Domina Elisabeth had left it that morning but nothing had been done to warm the chamber. Frevisse eyed the open window, its shutter lowered to let in fresh air, but decided against bothering to shut it. Simply closing it would do nothing toward warming the room, nor was she minded to call for a warming pan or anything else that would, even briefly, bring her company.

Instead, she wrapped herself in her cloak, sat on the bed with her feet tucked up under her safe from the floor's draughts, and turned to thinking while she had the chance, beginning with what Christopher had told her of Montfort's death and then about what she had learned on her own. Set out and looked at, there was not much. Of what she had learned, most was on the Lengley side, with very little about the Champyons, and none of it bearing plainly on Montfort's murder.

But Montfort was dead. He had either angered someone sufficiently or been threat enough to someone that this person had killed him, and that anger or threat most probably had to do with this manor of Reckling.

It might not, of course. There was always the possibility he had been killed because of something else. But if he had been, the likelihood of discovering the murderer was even less than it already seemed to be. So, like Christopher, she would work at the problem from the only sure way they had, and that brought her to the question, What *was* the threat that had been worth Montfort's death? If it came from something he had found out, then likely the threat still existed, a danger to whoever else might find it out.

Unless it was some sort of written proof and Montfort had had it with him when he was killed and now his murderer had it. Or more likely, had by now destroyed it. In which case threat and proof and hope of learning anything about them were all gone together.

But proof of what? The most damning, to one side or the other, would be something that showed Stephen was— or else was not—Sir Henry's legitimate son.

So . . . who was most concerned with that?

Stephen, of course. To have the manor of Reckling, the Champyons had to prove he was illegitimate, and if that was proved against him, then he lost all claim to any inheritance at all from his father. All the Lengley lands would cease to be his.

That made it Lady Agnes's problem, too. Frevisse suspected she had the fierceness to want a man dead and she was openly bound, both by oath and love, to the claim that Stephen was the son of her son Sir Henry and his wife. That she had a key to the garden's gate was no use, because no one but Montfort and then Master Gruesby had been seen or heard to go in that way, and besides that, she was hardly strong enough to have driven a dagger through Montfort, let alone have managed to come into the garden by way of the fence.

Stephen could have done both those things, and Lady Agnes and her household were the only ones to say he had been with her that afternoon. But neither was there anyone who had yet said they had seen him elsewhere, and there was a large part of the problem, no matter whom she considered—no one had seen anyone along that side of the priory at the necessary time that day.

Where had Master Philip Haselden been then, she wondered. To him it mattered that Stephen be kept legitimate both for his daughter's sake and because of his service to Lord Lovell. If Stephen was proved illegitimate, Nichola's marriage to him would turn from being a profit to an utter loss, and if Lord Lovell were displeased enough over the loss of the manor, it might cost Master Haselden his favor with him, a favor that Frevisse gathered had been very profitable to him over the years.

And then there was Master Champyon's ambition. He was said to want the manor as a way into favor with Suffolk. How great was that ambition? Great enough for him to go to the trouble and expense of taking the matter to law, at least. Did he have any other way to come to Suffolk's notice or was the manor his only one and therefore his interest the more desperate? But then how did he come to have sufficient knowledge of Goring to know about the infirmary garden and where it was in the nunnery and how to reach it unseen? Did his wife know? And if she did, then how? She wasn't from here, it seemed. But Frevisse knew so little about her or her dead sister and had only other people's word that her ambition to power matched her husband's. Not that it needed to. Simple greed to have the manor could be as powerful a force as greed for influence with powerful men.

Come to that, why not suppose she could have gone to meet Montfort herself? Nothing had yet been said about where she was when he was killed. For all Frevisse knew, Mistress Champyon might well have the strength to kill a man and so might Juliana, come to that. But where would either of them have come by a ballock dagger? It could be carried concealed under a cloak, that was no problem, but it was hardly a woman's weapon, hardly something either of them would happen to have with them. So it would have to be someone else's—husband, son, brother, even a servant—who either did not know it had been borrowed or else knew it had but did not realize that it mattered. . . . or else *did* realize and was keeping silent anyway.

Christopher must ask more openly about that dagger. It might be in the Thames by now but it might not. It depended on whether the murderer thought he was better rid of it and maybe have someone wonder where it had gone than to keep it and deny having aught to do with Montfort's death if he were asked.

The cold had begun to slip through Frevisse's cloak and habit and undergown. She was not chilled yet but soon would be and rather than wait for it she uncurled her legs, slipped stiffly off the bed, and began to pace the chamber without letting loose of her thoughts. There was still Rowland Englefield to consider. He wasn't well accounted for the afternoon of Montfort's murder. Despite not questioning him at the inquest, Christopher had surely checked the brothel or wherever Rowland claimed to have been, to learn what was said there. That was something she would ask Master Gruesby when next she had chance. Or Christopher himself, though she doubted chance for that would come until after his father's funeral. In the meanwhile, how could she go about making acquaintance with both the Champyons and Rowland? More acquaintance with Juliana she did not want or even need because, despite she might have been able to kill Montfort, there was no open reason why Juliana would have bothered herself with having Montfort dead. She had pointed out herself that she did not stand to gain anything by her mother having the manor, and Juliana had not seemed to Frevisse someone who would trouble herself on anyone's behalf but her own.

Unless, of course, having disposed of Montfort, she planned next to dispose of her brother and thereby clear her own way to inheriting the manor and possibly other things, depending on how the Englefield lands from their late father were entailed.

Maybe she should consider Juliana a little further. The question of the dagger was the same for her as for her mother, and she knew Goring well enough to come and go the back way to Lady Agnes's garden. But Stephen had very likely told her that, and even supposing she somehow knew how to reach the infirmary garden, it was hardly likely she—or her mother, come to that—could have gone there and come back without being noticed and remembered by someone and more probably several someones. It was possible, Frevisse was willing to grant, but hardly a chance a murderer would care to depend on, surely?

The only thing made simpler by considering Juliana as the murderer was that she would have had no trouble coming near enough to Montfort to use the dagger if she had chosen to let him think she was attracted to him . . .

Frevisse pulled back from the pointless unkindness of that thought. Juliana was already too unkind to herself to need more unkindness from anyone else.

But had Christopher even asked about where she was that afternoon?

That was something else she would have to ask him or Master Gruesby when the chance came. She equally wanted to see the letter that had come to Montfort from Lord Lovell, though how a letter he had not yet read could have brought on his death she did not try to guess. And another thing she should have asked about before now was how Montfort had been lured to the garden at all. There had to have been a message. Why had nothing been said about it or about who had brought it?

Frevisse rubbed at her face with both hands, her mind beginning to congeal with too many questions still to be asked. She was warm again, though, and curled back onto the bed. To fill some of the time until she could ask the questions, she should spend at least a while in prayer for Montfort's soul after letting the uneven and disjointed past few days serve as excuse not to, needful though she knew it was. Given Montfort's greed and uncare for anyone but himself in life and the suddenness of his death, his soul was likely lost beyond hope in Hell, but there was always the chance there had been some small piece of virtue in Montfort, enough to have rescued him into Purgatory where at least there was hope of winning through the torments there to Heaven. And if there was the smallest chance of saving a man's soul, even Montfort's . . .

With more grimness than grace, Frevisse brought herself to, *"A porta inferi, Domine, erue animam eius. Domine, exaudi orationem meam. A porta inferi, Domine, erue animam eius . . ."* From the gate of Hell, Lord, rescue his soul. Lord, hear my prayer. From the gate of Hell, Lord, rescue his soul . . .

She had always believed that a prayer with her heart and mind behind it was worth more than one of merely words but though she tried now for better than only the sound of her own voice, she did not feel she had much succeeded by the time the nunnery bell freed her to go to Vespers.

Chapter 13

t Vespers' end, while St. Mary's nuns hurried off to their supper in the refectory, Frevisse went out with Domina Elisabeth into the last of the day, with swathes of creamy clouds across the pale sky and a faint-orange sunset fading down behind the westward hills as they made haste back to Lady Agnes's, into the warmth and ordered hurry of the tables being set up for supper in the hall there. Although there were no other guests and only a single remove of beef and mutton pie, a fish tart cooked with fruit and spices, garlic boiled to tenderness and savory with saffron, salt, and cinnamon, and yesterday's gingerbread with warmed honey and nutmeg poured over it, the meal went on longer than any nunnery meal might have done and by its end Frevisse was stifling yawns and grateful when, as they rose from their places, Domina Elisabeth asked Lady Agnes's pardon because she and Dame Frevisse wished to withdraw to their chamber to say Compline and go to bed nearer to their usual hour than they lately had.

"We've had days busier than is our wont and been keeping late hours into the bargain," she said, smiling. "By your leave, a night closer to our proper way of things will do us well."

"An early-to-bed will do me no harm either," Lady Agnes said, adding with a look at Letice, "So I'm told," and they parted with mutual wishes for a good night and sound sleep.

Frevisse, at least, after she and Domina Elisabeth had said Compline together and hastened into their warmed bed, had both the good night and sound sleep but found the morning none the easier to face. Hurriedly dressed and with Prime's prayers hurriedly said, they descended to the hall's fire-warmth and breakfast, to learn that Montfort's funeral would be that afternoon, for a certainty.

"His son's to be back this morning," Emme said, setting wedges of cheese next to the bread already on the table, "and what with the dozen people I've heard came in yesterday and some more expected this morning, there's enough to do it proper. There's been no stinting on the feast neither, from what I've heard. The inns and bakers are beside themselves with readying it all. But won't Domina Matilda be glad when it's all done with and things are quiet again?"

Domina Elisabeth agreed she would be indeed. Silently so did Frevisse because, when it was all over and done, Mistress Montfort and her people would leave and maybe by tomorrow night there would be place for Domina Elisabeth and her in St. Mary's.

"Even the weather is to the good," Emme went on,

taking up the pitcher to pour more ale for Domina Elisabeth. "Not nearly so cold today. There's some friends of Lady Agnes will be here to dinner and they'll be glad of the better riding. Oh, and Mistress Letice said to tell you Lady Agnes will be lying in this morning, to be rested for when they come and for this afternoon."

She left them then and while they ate and drank Frevisse wondered how it was at the nunnery, with the Office of the Dead to be said at the usual hours of prayer and the funeral to be readied for, but was turned from her thoughts by Domina Elisabeth asking if she would spend the morning with her and her cousin. "To give her different company the while, please you?"

"Of course," Frevisse said, as courtesy demanded, but found, once the words were out, that she did not mind doing it. There would be small chance she could ask questions of Master Gruesby today and no chance at all of talking with Christopher. Nor was she much minded to be caught in talk with Lady Agnes and her friends and there would be no sheltering in the church, busy with final readying of the grave and all. To be out of the way of everything for at least a few hours seemed the best chance the morning held.

It held other chance, too, beginning when they discovered as they came outside, cloak-wrapped and ready to hurry, that there was small need. Just as Emme had said, yesterday's freezing cold was gone, the air almost mild, with a soft dripping from eaves and the rising sun a red-orange ball through thin white clouds. Giving up hurry, they crossed the street into the nunnery foreyard and along it toward the cloister door through the early morning come-and-go of servants about their business, until Frevisse saw Dickon standing in the further gateway through into the stableyard, holding a pitchfork but only busy at watching people, not doing anything himself except, when he saw them, to raise a hand in greeting.

With a sudden thought Frevisse said, "My lady, there's Dickon. May I have a word with him? It's his first time so far away from home and I wonder how he's doing."

Domina Elisabeth glanced toward him. "Master Naylor's boy? Of course."

She could have beckoned him to come to them, but not wanting Domina Elisabeth to hear what else she wanted from Dickon, Frevisse went toward him, quickly enough that although he promptly set the pitchfork aside and came to meet her, they were well away from Domina Elisabeth and as by themselves as they were going to be in the busy yard when they met and she asked as he straightened from his bow to her, "How goes it with you and the others? Is everything well?"

"It's crowding up in the stable, there's so many folk come in now." He was cheerful about it. "Keeps it warmer at night. We're fed well, too."

"Straw," she said, pointing at bits of it caught in his hair.

He brushed it away and asked in his turn, "How goes it with you, my lady?"

"I'm beset with too much talking and not enough to do." Surprised at herself for saying that aloud and at Dickon's laugh, she went on quickly, "There's something I'd have you do for me."

Dickon brightened even more. "Surely, my lady."

"I'd know how easy or hard it is to go along the back wall of the nunnery from outside without being seen. There's a part of the wall along there that's only wicker hurdles. I'd like to know about that part especially. How easy it is to come to and anything else about it you can see. Without you being noticed at it. Without anyone else knowing what you're doing."

"Especially the murderer," Dickon said. "That's what it's for, isn't it? It's about Montfort's murder."

Dickon would have been small use to her if he weren't

sharp-witted but Frevisse said quellingly, "Yes. So be careful."

"Careful as a king in his counting house, my lady," he said, cheerful as if she'd given him a holiday. "I promise."

She left him with hope he'd keep his promise, rejoining Domina Elisabeth who asked, "All's well with him?"

"With him and with the other men, he says. They're keeping warm and are well fed."

Domina Elisabeth laughed. "Then all's well."

But not with Frevisse, busy with being displeased with herself for not having asked Dickon to do this two days ago, in the church when she'd had the chance and should have thought of it, rather than letting it go until now. What else wasn't she doing? Of what else hadn't she thought? And was she not thinking of them, not doing them, because she cared too little about finding out Montfort's murderer? With that thought troubling her, she followed Domina Elisabeth through the cloister, this morning almost as busy with servants as the yard had been, preparations for the funeral and afterwards leaving no peace even here until they reached the infirmary and its quiet, not even the infirmarian there.

"Ysobel may be sleeping," Domina Elisabeth said softly. "Wait here while I see."

Careful of the inner door, she let herself into the next room and Frevisse waited, content where she was beside the work-marred table among the mingled, familiar, pleasant odors of herbs and oils and other things, but the respite was brief before Domina Elisabeth returned to the door and nodded for her to come on.

There was need in all nunneries, since all sleeping and living spaces were shared, only the prioress having any privacy, for somewhere the ill could be kept apart, either to avoid contagion or simply to spare the nunnery the disturbance that inevitably came with caring for the ill. Like St. Frideswide's, St. Mary's room for this was plain, with white-plastered walls and a few beds—four of them here, with a small table between each pair of them—and a single, shuttered window.

That much Frevisse saw before Domina Elisabeth closed the door, returning the room to a gloom broken only by the fierce, low glow of burning coals in a brazier set near the first bed inside the door. By that little light Frevisse could see only a little of the woman slowly, possibly painfully, shifting herself higher on the pillows there, until Domina Elisabeth lighted a splinter at the brazier, and sheltering its burning tip with her hand, returned to the table to light the oil lamp waiting there. In the small yellow spread of light from the low lamp flame Frevisse saw Sister Ysobel more clearly, lying back against her pillows now with her eyes shut while she recovered from the effort of moving even that slightly. She wore a long-sleeved winter undergown, her head was wrapped in a white kerchief, and her age was difficult to judge, wasted with illness as she was, her face sunk into thin flesh stretched over blunt bones, her eyes into hollows under her dark brows. She might have been Frevisse's age or much older. Or possibly much younger. Not that age much mattered by now. What mattered more at this far end of living was how good or ill someone had lived the life they had had and how well they would see it out.

And how much more suffering the body would have to endure before the soul was able to go free.

Domina Elisabeth laid a hand on her cousin's lying on top of the blanket and asked gently, "Is there anything you'd like? Anything I can get for you?"

Sister Ysobel opened her eyes. There was far more life in them than in her wasted body and her whisper was strong as she answered, "What I'd like is the window opened."

Domina Elisabeth drew back from the bed, distressed. "Oh, Ysobel, you know that wouldn't be to the good."

Clear air in a sickroom was unhealthy, a danger to the ill, but, "What's it going to do?" Sister Ysobel asked, laughter tinging her voice. "Kill me? Dame Frevisse, if you would be so good."

Without comment, Frevisse went to the window, set high enough in the wall that she had to stretch to reach the shutter's catch, slipped it aside, and lowered the shutter, letting in the early morning's light and a draught of cold air. Behind her, Sister Ysobel began to cough and Frevisse turned around to see her with a handkerchief pressed over her mouth, struggling with the spasm while Domina Elisabeth hurriedly poured a cup of water from the pitcher on the table beside the lamp, turned away from her cousin so she did not see—perhaps purposefully did not see—when her cousin's coughing stopped and Sister Ysobel sank flat against her pillows again, her hand with the handkerchief dropping weakly to her side. But Frevisse saw and wondered into what terrors she would fall if ever there was that bright-red spotting of blood on a handkerchief of her own, before Sister Ysobel recovered strength enough to close her fingers around the handkerchief, hiding it.

Maybe she was past the terror of knowing she was going to die. She was calm, anyway, as she sipped from the cup Domina Elisabeth held to her lips and she smiled when she was done and said to them both, "Thank you." She moved a hand slightly toward the bed beside her own. "Sit, if it please you." And when they had settled side by each on the bed's edge, she asked, "What have you done since I saw you yesterday, cousin?"

"Nearly nothing," Domina Elisabeth answered. "Talked with your prioress. Had supper. Went early to bed and slept. And here I am again."

"What a dull world I'm leaving. Sister Joane told me when she brought my breakfast that the funeral will be this afternoon. You're going, the both of you?"

"It seems best we do, since we're here."

"Then you can tell me all about it afterwards." Spare of movement, either too weak or else saving what strength she had for when she had greater need of it, she smiled toward Frevisse without turning her head. "My cousin tells me you've had to do with murders before this one, yes?"

Silently accepting that Domina Elisabeth had had to find things to talk of through the hours she had spent with her cousin, Frevisse granted, "Sometimes, yes."

"She says you've skill at finding out murderers."

"By God's grace, yes," Frevisse admitted.

"Have you been doing aught to finding out our murderer here?"

There were times when lying would be comfort and convenient but even then a sin and Frevisse said, ignoring the interested turn of Domina Elisabeth's head toward her, "I've thought about the murder, yes."

"And you'd rather I didn't ask you about it," Sister Ysobel said, smiling more.

Frevisse smiled back. "Much rather."

"Then I won't." She paused for breath. "On the other hand, you're welcome to ask me whatever you like about it."

"Oh, Ysobel," Domina Elisabeth protested, "you don't want to think about such a thing now, do you?"

Sister Ysobel turned her smile toward her cousin. "Come now, Elisabeth. You have to know that presently I have a particular interest in death."

Frevisse had noted before now that the dying were often able to speak more lightly of their mortality than those around them could. Domina Elisabeth was silenced for the moment by Sister Ysobel's question as Sister Ysobel said to Frevisse, "Is there anything you want to ask me?"

If nothing else, it would pass the time, both for her and Sister Ysobel, and Frevisse said, "Your rosary. Could you show me how you were praying with it that day? How fast or slow you were telling the beads."

Sister Ysobel reached toward the table where a rosary of both dark and silver beads lay waiting. Domina Elisabeth hastily handed it to her and Sister Ysobel smiled her thanks, took it, closed her eyes, and began, *"Ave Maria, gratia plena..."* Hail Mary, full of grace... deliberate over the words as if each one were precious.

After four Aves, one to a bead, Frevisse stopped her. "That's the way you always say it?"

Sister Ysobel opened her eyes. "Always." She handed the rosary back to Domina Elisabeth but kept her gaze steady on Frevisse. "Always," she repeated.

Then there would have been more than time enough for the murderer to be well away before Master Gruesby raised an outcry.

For that matter, there would have been time and enough for Master Gruesby to have killed Montfort, left through the fence, and come around and through the stableyard to "find" the body.

Frevisse found she was not uncomfortable with that possibility, able to believe easily enough that Master Gruesby, after his years in Montfort's service, might have reached the point of hating him enough to kill him. He could have lied to Montfort to arrange the secret meeting, giving him the chance both to kill and to keep suspicion from himself. Where was he supposed to have been when Montfort was killed? Did Christopher know whether he had actually been where he said he was? Had Christopher even considered he might be lying?

Putting that thought aside for later, Frevisse said, "You told the crowner that no one entered the garden through the infirmary door. That you heard voices of, you thought, two men about the time Master Montfort was murdered. That you know how long it was until the outcry was raised because you were saying the rosary in that while. What else should I ask you about? Unless you've remembered something more."

"It's not that I've remembered more. It's that I never finished what I had to tell that young man."

"Didn't finish? Why?"

"Because I began to cough, and before I'd done, he thanked me and left." Sister Ysobel could put little force into the words but she bit them short with displeasure. Then she unwillingly smiled. "Sister Joane was glowering at him from the doorway. She frightened him off, I think. And I made no matter of it afterwards because what little else I had to say wasn't enough to change anything, I doubt."

But she wanted the chance to say it anyway and Frevisse obliged by asking, "What else was there?"

"The door from the passage into the garden. It creaks a little, hardly to be noticed unless one has nothing else to do but lie here and listen to whatever there is to hear. Before I heard the men talking together, it opened and shut only once. Nor was it open long. Only long enough for one person to pass through."

"A creak as it opened, a short pause, another creak as it closed," Frevisse said. "Like that? Not long enough for two people to have come through it?"

Sister Ysobel made a small, agreeing nod. "The next time I heard it was just before the dead man's clerk made his outcry."

There was nothing helpful in that. It was already certain, from the witnesses in the stableyard, that only Montfort and Master Gruesby had come that way, but before Frevisse had to say that to her, Sister Ysobel went on, "I suppose the murderer must have come through the fence. That's an easy guess, though no one's said so. It was the other thing I wanted to tell that young crowner. About hearing the murderer."

Frevisse's heed sharpened. "You heard him?"

"I heard him walking. Well, heard someone walking and afterwards knew it must have been him."

"You're certain it was a man?"

"The walk was too heavy and long-strided for it to have been a woman. Skirts, you know."

"You didn't wonder why there was a man in the garden?"

"I wondered but supposed we had a new gardener and no one had told me. There was no one else he was likely to be."

"But you're certain you didn't hear him come in?"

"I slightly thought he must have come in by the gate and that I somehow hadn't heard him. You know how one does, wanting an answer and taking one that's simple rather than right."

Frevisse knew. It was a common, sometimes perilous trick everyone sometimes played on themselves, herself included. "And you're sure he hadn't come through the infirmary?"

"I wasn't fevered or drowsing that afternoon. When I'm not . . ." She paused, maybe to catch her breath—her dying lungs made even so little as she was asking of them difficult—but also she sounded a little ashamed as she continued, "When I'm awake and unfevered, I'm always listening. In hopes someone is coming to see me."

Domina Elisabeth leaned forward to take her hand. Sister Ysobel returned her hold with a slight squeeze and went on, "I'm certain no one came that way. When the gate creaked with Montfort coming in, I thought it was the other man going out and wondered how I had missed hearing him when he came in."

"I'll speak to Sister Joane about having the gate hinges greased," Domina Elisabeth said.

"Oh. No, don't," Sister Ysobel protested. "It gives me something to hear. Until spring comes . . ." Her pause then, as if something in her had suddenly hurt, betrayed how surely she knew there was likely to be no spring for her this year or any other, before she went on, ". . . there'll be something more to hear in the garden than sparrows quarreling sometimes. But until then, with so little to hear, I'd rather the gate went on creaking."

"Of course," Domina Elisabeth murmured, meaning to be soothing, Frevisse supposed.

But she also supposed Sister Ysobel would prefer to be distracted rather than soothed and said, "So you heard the man who must have been the murderer walking. For how long, do you think, before Master Montfort came in?"

"I heard him walking not long after Nones started. I started the Office when the bell stopped. When everyone would have started it in the church. I'd reached *Olim locutus es in visione* by the time I heard Master Montfort come in."

About a quarter of an hour, Frevisse could guess. Unless Sister Ysobel had been praying at a running pace and it was doubtful that she had.

"I was maybe slower than usual," Sister Ysobel said, as if picking up her thought. "Prayers pass the time and I never make haste over them anymore."

Frevisse could not see yet that knowing how long the murderer had been there made any difference. But it might count for something later. There was the chance with every small piece that it might count later . . .

Sister Ysobel made a soft sound that was probably as near to laughter as she dared to come and, when Frevisse looked at her questioningly, said, "The way you were staring away to somewhere else, your mind gone far off and everything here forgotten. Did what I said help you any?"

"It might," Frevisse said, the only truthful answer she had, and was saved from saying more by a nun coming into the room, breviary in hand, and the bell to Tierce beginning to ring. Forestalled from speaking by the Rule that enjoined silence when the call to an Office came but understanding readily enough the other nun was come to say Tierce with her cousin, Domina Elisabeth gave Sister Ysobel the breviary from the table beside the bed and, with Frevisse, silently rose and left, to go to the church for their own prayers.

Frevisse found small satisfaction in the Office, try though she did to put Sister Ysobel and what she had said from her mind for the while, and at the Office's end she returned to the infirmary willingly enough with Domina Elisabeth, to find the other nun already gone, the breviary laid aside, and Sister Ysobel lying narrow under the blankets with flushed cheeks, her eyes fever-brightened, and her breathing more labored than it had been. But she said as soon as she saw them, "I've been thinking about what I heard," then had to pause, fighting to find enough breath to go on, restlessly turning her head away from the hand Domina Elisabeth laid on her forehead.

"You're hot," Domina Elisabeth said. "Sister Joane showed me where the borage mixture is kept. I'll ready some for you."

When she was gone out, Frevisse asked, to give Sister Ysobel something to think about besides her dying body, "What have you thought of?"

Unsteady with her ragged breathing, Sister Ysobel whispered, "The other thing . . . I didn't tell the . . . young crowner. That when Master Montfort came into the garden . . . he said something angrily. A word. No more. Then went to the waiting man. There were only his footsteps, going from the gate. The other man, wherever he was, didn't move. Then they talked."

"But you heard nothing they said," Frevisse said.

"There was hardly . . . anything to hear." Sister Ysobel closed her eyes, waited until her breath caught up to her words, and went on, "They hardly . . . spoke at all."

Domina Elisabeth returned with a small basin of water, saying as she set it on the table, "The borage is brewing.

A few more minutes," before she went out again, leaving
Frevisse to take and wring out a cloth from the cool water
and wipe Sister Ysobel's hot face.

Sister Ysobel, used to having that done, kept on from
where she had been. "One of them said something. The
other one asked what sounded like a question. An angry
question. That was the longest thing either of them said.
The other man answered him back, angrily, too, and only
a few words, and that was all."

"That was all? They didn't quarrel? A greeting, a question, an answer, and nothing else?"

"Nothing else."

Frevisse considered that before finally saying, slowly,
"The other man was there to kill Montfort. From what
you say, there was no quarrel. One of them asked a question, the other answered and then, whoever the other man
was, he simply stabbed Montfort. We don't know why
Montfort was there, but the other man came for no other
reason than to kill him."

Sister Ysobel made a small, agreeing movement of her
head. "Yes," she breathed. "Yes."

"But I doubt it would have helped the crowner any,
even had you been able to say it to him."

Worry clearing from her brow, Sister Ysobel said on a
sigh, "No. I don't suppose it would."

It did not even make clear that Montfort had come to
the garden to meet someone he knew, although he'd be
unlikely to agree to a secret meeting with a stranger.

Unless the stranger was a messenger from someone he
did know, someone whose asking or order for such a secret meeting he would accept.

Who had asked the question Sister Ysobel thought she
had heard? Had Montfort asked something and the murderer answered him, then stabbed him? Or had the murderer asked and killed Montfort when his answer had been
wrong? Her guess would be the murderer had asked it

and, when Montfort's answer had not been what he wanted, had killed him. But either way was possible. And did it matter?

Trying to find something to ask that might lead some-where useful, she asked, "Did you hear the murderer leave?"

"I heard footfalls on the gravel again. Briefly." She paused to work at breathing before going on, "Then there was only silence until the gate creaked again. I thought they had moved further away . . . and were speaking too low for me to hear anything."

"But you didn't go on with the Office?"

Sister Ysobel's smile was small and bitter and tired all at once. "I'd lost my place and couldn't . . . bring my mind back to it. It's hard to think sometimes. I took up the rosary instead."

Domina Elisabeth returned with the borage mixture in a shallow cup. Sister Ysobel tried to sit up and Frevisse helped her with an arm behind her back and a careful pushing of the pillows, then moved aside for Domina Elisabeth to hold the cup to Sister Ysobel's lips, patient while she drank in small sips between long pauses, until the cup was empty. Worn out with the effort, eyes closed, Sister Ysobel whispered her thanks to Domina Elisabeth, who asked as she set the cup down, "Would you like us to leave you to sleep now?"

Sister Ysobel moved her head slightly side to side on the pillow. "Stay," she whispered. "Talk and let me lis-ten."

Domina Elisabeth and Frevisse traded looks, and as they sat down side by side on the next bed, where they had sat before, Domina Elisabeth said, "You've heard me more than enough these past few days. Dame Frevisse, do you talk for a while."

That was fair and Frevisse cast quickly through her mind for something to say. There had been enough said about the murder for now and other people surely brought talk about nunnery matters. Better to find something far different, and on that thought's heels Frevisse asked, "Have you ever been to Spain? On the pilgrimage to St. James at Compestela?"

Sister Ysobel's lips made the word "No," and Frevisse let the story take itself, building partly from her own very small-child memories of riding in a woven pannier on the side of a quiet ass led by her father along pale, dusty Spanish roads, the smell of orange blossoms in the air, but mixing it with other people's haps and hazards heard over the years—including the pack-ladden mule who fell while crossing a flooded stream and, even though it was rescued from drowning, refused ever to cross running water again and had to be sold to the nearest farmer who would take it.

Sister Ysobel's laughter over that brought on a brief heave of coughing that jerked her forward, drove her back into the pillow, and left her struggling with quickened, shallow breathing and blood flecked at one corner of her mouth. Wordless, Domina Elisabeth squeezed out the cloth in the basin and wiped away the blood, and Sister Ysobel after faintly smiling thanks whispered, "Go on, please."

Frevisse did, more carefully this time, telling how in Compestela's streets and market a pilgrim could buy St. James's badge of a scallop shell made of everything from gold to pewter to poorly glazed plaster. "The only kind of scallop shell you can't buy there is a real one, I think," she said, though she did not remember for herself, had only heard her father laughing about it sometimes over the years afterwards.

Lying white and still against the pillow but smiling, Sister Ysobel whispered, "Isn't that always the way?" And then, "I think I'll sleep awhile now."

"Of course, my dear." Domina Elisabeth rose and

leaned over to kiss her forehead and Frevisse could see the family resemblence there must once have been—a shape of nose and cheek—before disease had brought Sister Ysobel down to dying flesh sunk slack over bones.

"I just wish"—Sister Ysobel whispered—"that I could stand one more time . . . on a high hill . . . in sunlight and the wind."

For a moment Frevisse thought what a strange longing that was for someone who had chosen to live out her years cloistered inside nunnery walls. And then thought that after all it was not so strange. Life's end was the time when longings were most likely to rise up for things left behind or undone. Even if they had been left behind in favor of a greater longing, left undone because of a greater need, now was when they came, the ghosts of a life unlived. But useful ghosts, because how was anyone to know the true value of a thing except by knowing what it had cost them? How could anyone make final peace with all they were leaving unless they looked at it, judged it, valued it?

For herself, Frevisse could only hope that when her dying time came, her own last longing and regret would be as simple as a wish to stand one last time on a high hill in sunlight and the wind.

Quietly, careful of their footfalls and the door, they left Sister Ysobel to her sleep.

Chapter 14

By midday the world was soaking, with mud underfoot and every eave steadily dripping when Frevisse and Domina Elisabeth picked their way across the street to Lady Agnes's to find four more guests had come, three men and a woman, friends of Lady Agnes ridden in for the funeral, though Frevisse gathered from their cheerful talk as they stood together in the hall waiting for the tables to be laid for dinner that they were here more for curiosity's sake than out of mourning for Montfort. When all was ready and they moved to be seated at the high table, Lady Agnes bade the men—Frevisse had not tried to keep their names in mind—to sit all together on her right because, she said, they would talk of things the women would not want to and therefore she would have the women on her left, the better to talk without the men.

For herself, Frevisse was pleased to be put to the table's far end with Domina Elisabeth between her and the other woman and Lady Agnes. From there she would hardly be part of any talk and able to listen or not, as she chose. Mostly she chose not. The nearest talk, between Lady Agnes and the woman and sometimes Domina Elisabeth, was as easy to foretell as Lady Agnes had said the men's would be—of the weather and neighbors and children. Frevisse, sitting with eyes lowered and all her heed seemingly on the well-spiced, roasted meatballs and creamed parsnip soup, found herself listening past Domina Elisabeth's agreement that indeed the snow was melting fast today, who would have thought it after yesterday's cold, to the men's talk at the table's other end. If the meal had been a full feast, the hall full of people, there would have been no hearing them, but there were only household folk at the lower table today, speaking quietly in the presence of their betters, while the men were trading comments on Montfort, boisterous with each other's company and most of what they said coming clearly over the women's talk. The surprise for Frevisse lay in how little ill of Montfort they had to say. The times she had encountered him, his stupidity had seemed exceeded only by his rudeness, but among the three men here there was a kind of grudging respect for the way he had been rising in the world.

"He was sharp enough," the farthest man granted to something one of the others had said. "Look where he started from and where he ended."

"He ended dead," the man beside him said.

They all laughed but the first man went on, insisting, "So will we all, but in the meanwhile Montfort did well enough. Look at him buying that manor two years back."

"And this year he bought his way into the escheatorship," the third man said. "Word is that he was looking to be sheriff one of these years soon."

God forbid, Frevisse thought, while the second man said, "He'd been making warm with Suffolk, the word is."

"Oh, aye. Suffolk." The first man's tone carried a burden of unsaid things and a moment's silence among the men agreed with him before the third one said, "Have you heard he's been given keeping of the Norwich bishopric until a new bishop is made?"

"He'll make a pretty penny off of it, that's sure."

"He does off of everything else."

Frevisse was grateful that if Domina Elisabeth or Lady Agnes heard any of that, neither of them saw fit to offer comment on her own tenuous link to Suffolk. For her own part, she would as soon forget it but it was unsurprised that Montfort had been trying to attach there.

Just as James Champyon was.

His purpose and Montfort's had been running the same way, it seemed. Had they run together? Because if they did, then neither Master nor Mistress Champyon had had anything to fear from Montfort, no reason to want him dead. Never a man to be put off from his own ends unless forced to it, Montfort would have found in their favor over the contested manner, whatever the truth might be.

But what if Master Champyon had been Montfort's rival for Suffolk's interest? Or Montfort been playing to some other end than the plain one and somehow against Master Champyon's interests? Then Master Champyon or even his stepson Rowland might have had reason to want him dead rather than treacherously alive.

But to what other end than Suffolk's favor could Montfort have been playing?

And how would Master Champyon or anyone else have known of it, been certain enough of it to go to the length and danger of murdering Montfort?

She knew too little and had to depend too much on

things overheard or happened on by chance, as with these men now—and following her own thoughts, she had lost what they were saying—or with Sister Ysobel this morning.

Losing hold a little on her patience, she scooped her spoon forcefully into a browned-almond-topped white rice pudding, tired of time spent eating and thankful that since there would be food after the funeral and therefore no point to feeding full now, the meal was shorter than it might have been. Once done and making ready to go out, Lady Agnes and her woman guest held brief debate on whether they should wear the thick wooden patterns that would put them dry-footed above the snowmelt and mud, but mindful of the clatter they would make on the church's stone floor or the bother of dealing with them if taken off and carried, they decided against, despite Letice's frown at Lady Agnes. Instead, with Frevisse slightly trailing behind everyone else and their busy talk, they all made their way into the street and along it with much swerving from puddles, the women with lifted skirts.

There was drier going across the priory's cobbled yard and into the churchyard with its wide, graveled path between the graves, leading from its penticed gateway to the wide gathering place outside the church's north door. With the door still closed, no one was going in yet, the perhaps two score other folk standing around in clusters, most of them knowing each other, to judge by the steady on-go of subdued talk among them and how widely welcomed Lady Agnes and the men and woman with her were welcomed. But Domina Elisabeth had fallen back from among them to Frevisse's side when they came into the churchyard and now she drew Frevisse aside with her, saying low-voiced, "I think it best that we're seen to be here on our own, rather than with Lady Agnes. Because of this inheritance matter. It wouldn't be seemly to give appearance of being somehow entangled with it."

Frevisse slightly bowed her head, willingly agreeing
with that and, more than willingly, followed Domina Elisabeth's quiet sideways drift to a lee behind one of the
larger clusters of people, not far from the church door but
out of the way and people's notice, in their black cloaks
and veils unremarkable among the rest of the dark-clad
mourners.

Outside the cloister and among so many strangers,
Frevisse should have had her head deeply bowed and her
eyes lowered. Instead, she bowed her head only enough
to seem looking downward while able to cast quick looks
around the yard, finding she knew few among the people
gathered there. Besides Lady Agnes and her friends now
in talk with several men Frevisse thought had been jurors,
paired with women probably their wives, the only others
familiar to her were Master and Mistress Champyon
standing well away across the yard, with Juliana and her
brother Rowland beside their mother, the four of them
noticeably by themselves. Others there would be mostly
relatives of Montfort or his wife, Frevisse guessed, or else
unrelatives of sufficient acquaintance—she never seemed
to think of friendship as part of Montfort's life—to feel
they should be here. Others, like Lady Agnes and her
friends, were there for no more than curiosity or because
they felt their importance required their presence. Some
of that latter sort were easily picked out from among the
others, standing with a puffed awareness of themselves,
their voices a little too loud, their gestures a little too bold,
to make certain they did not go unnoticed.

Master Champyon was of their kind, Frevisse judged,
though presently restrained because no one was giving
him any notice save his wife and stepchildren. Nonetheless he stood with his feet set firmly apart, as if claiming
that space of yard for his own, with his thumbs hooked
into his belt and his elbows cocked wide to spread his
cloak open, showing his fine, dark-blue houppelande

trimmed in black fur and the ornate, gold-shining—but brass, Frevisse guessed—buckle of his wide, black-dyed leather belt.

His wife well-matched him. Her fashionable padded headroll, set over cauls rather than a wimple, was that little too wide, the layers of veil draped over it that little too full, and she stood with the same over-boldness as her husband, a lift to her head as she looked around the yard with sharp, determined eyes that suggested she was going to be offended soon at being so completely ignored.

Her son, standing on her other side from Master Champyon, had neither his stepfather's arrogance nor his mother's sharp eyes, only the set face of someone who wished he were somewhere else. Broad-boned and of good height, he was somewhat wide-girthed for so young a man and likely heading toward what would be fat in a very few years. If he had been named after Rowland, Charlemagne's great hero of legend, his mother must be displeased with how he was going, but more likely his namesake and probably godfather had been a wealthy uncle, or neighbor who might be hoped to remember his godchild generously in a will.

Frevisse chided herself for judging Mistress Champyon without knowing her except by guesses grown from other people's words. As for Rowland himself, she had even less by which to guess anything about him. All she could really say with any certainty was that he was of a size to have been able to drive a dagger into Montfort.

And then there was Juliana.

Frevisse took some comfort that, by openly acknowledging her dislike of her, she could at least try to work against it toward being fair. But her good intent was not helped by Juliana being the only one of her family who looked at ease with being here, as if wherever she was should be pleased that she was there. Slender and bright in her blue cloak, she had an assured grace in even the slight turning of her head as she looked around the yard. Like her mother, she wore cauls and padded headroll rather than merely wimple and veil but the cauls were neatly proportioned to frame the delicacy of her face, the headroll only wide enough to spread the short veil draped over it into soft wings that drifted gracefully on either side as she turned her head back to say something to her brother.

Rowland bent his head toward her, said something in return that Juliana seemingly answered with something else because he broke toward laughter that changed his glooming face to that of a younger, brighter man before he stifled it with a hand over his mouth and their mother said something at him that brought his gloom back. Juliana turned her head away, removing herself again from their company. A moment later her look sharpened and Frevisse turned her own head to see Master Haselden entering, trim in black doublet and hose, one side of his cloak thrown back over his shoulder to leave his left hand free, held at waist-height for the woman beside him— surely his wife—to cling to with one hand while holding her skirts clear of the ground with the other. Only when she was safely through the gateway, but still clinging to her husband and her skirts, did Mistress Haselden look up and around with a rapid little glance that made Frevisse think of a mouse caught out of its hole, too frighted to know which way to run. Nichola and Stephen were just behind them and the likeness between mother and daughter was easy to see, though Nichola was pretty with a youth her mother had long since left behind, nor did she have any of her mother's shyness. Very likely she had never met Montfort; his death could hardly mean anything to her; she was maybe too young to believe much in anyone's dying, let alone a stranger's, and though she was trying to keep a mourner's face, she was looking about her with hardly inheld eagerness as Stephen led her in her parents' wake toward Lady Agnes.

It was slow going, with constant pausing for greetings and brief talk with various people. Their way took them nowhere near the Champyons, Rowland, and Juliana, which was just as well. Likewise to the good, they made not even a look toward Master and Mistress Champyon's proud and bitter glares.

Rowland, on the other hand, was studying either his toes or the ground in front of them and Juliana . . .

Her look was both aching and angry as her eyes followed Stephen across the yard, but all Frevisse curtly thought was that if it hurt that much to see him, then she should not look—unless seeing him with his wife would serve to remind her that neither should she touch.

"We're going in," Domina Elisabeth said.

Frevisse gladly turned both herself and her thoughts away from living troubles to the needs of the dead, with hope that Montfort's funeral would help her find way to pray more whole-mindedly for him than she yet had. She and Domina Elisabeth were among the last to go in, passing from the day's thin sunlight into the church's twilight and column-shadows, stopping not far inside the door with no pretense of right to any forward place, here by chance and only because it was more seemly that they be than not. Through the shift and settle of people ahead of her, Frevisse briefly saw Mistress Montfort standing, veil-draped, in a cleared place in front of the rood screen, her two daughters on her left, Christopher and another man and a half-grown boy on her right. They made a black-clad cluster of mourning with their equally black-clad household folk gathered behind them, Master Gruesby probably among them.

Somewhere beyond the rood screen, near the altar, was Montfort's body and, beyond the altar, the place readied for its burial beneath the chancel floor. From where she

stood behind so many people Frevisse could see only the
altar itself, shining in a halo of candlelight, with a glimpse
of St. Mary's nuns in their choir stalls, before the priest
in gold-embroidered black vestments moved into his place
at the altar. The Mass for the dead went its slow, mourning way, carried on the priest's strong voice and the nuns'
singing, with incense from the swung censors making a
golden nimbus in the many candles' light around the altar,
drifted among the rafters and down among the crowd.
Carried on the wonder of the prayers wound through with
the dark mystery of death and the golden hope of life
eternal, Frevisse found that at last she had slipped past
any troubled effort to pray for Montfort into the glory of
praying a soul toward God. Death was the journey beyond
journeys, and whatever Montfort had been in life, his soul
was on it now, gone into eternity, and she could only wish
him mercy, as she hoped for mercy in her turn when her
own journey came.

At the end, when all was finished, she stood with bowed
head, returning only slowly into the day, into ordinary time
and where she was, grateful that Domina Elisabeth stood
unmoving beside her until they were crowded back by others crowding out of the way of Mistress Montfort being escorted out by her household, Christopher beside her, the
other children behind them, the two girls weeping as if they
owed it to themselves to be as openly grieved as possible,
the youngest boy stiff-faced with knowing he was being
looked at by a great many people whom he did not wish to
see him crying. When they were out of the church, people
began to mill and talk, voices rising and interest turning,
somewhat too openly among some of them, to what there
would be in the way of food and drink in the guesthall now
but no one making haste out the door, giving Mistress
Montfort and her people time to be there ahead of them. For
herself, Frevisse wanted to go the other way, following the
nuns filing out through their own door into the cloister's

quiet, and nearly said yes when Domina Elisabeth, a little loudly against the mounting voices around them, said, "I promised Ysobel I'd tell her how the funeral went. Will you come with me?"

But this might well be her only chance to find a way to speak with Master or Mistress Champyon without being too noticeable about it. She might well have chance to talk to Master Gruesby, too, and regretfully she said, "By your leave, my lady, I think I'll go to the guesthall with the others." And added, not untruthfully, merely inadequately, in answer to Domina Elisabeth's faint surprise, "I'll be able to bring all the talk I hear there to Ysobel tomorrow."

Domina Elisabeth smiled and nodded, satisfied by that, and turned cloisterward, leaving Frevisse to join the drift of folk now leaving the church, although once outside she made no haste across the churchyard back toward the nunnery's foreyard and the guesthall but took time to gather herself, breathing deeply the sharp-edged air so welcome after the incense-laden church.

That excess of incense and candles had surely been Montfort's doing rather than anyone else's. As with his wife's mourning clothing, he had probably provided for them beforehand by orders and money to their purchase, to be sure his funeral would suit him, and just as well he had because no one else was likely to care as much as he had about it, Frevisse thought.

And so much for where she had gone in prayer during the Mass, she added wryly. Already and easily she was, alas, as uncharitable as ever toward Montfort.

Nor was she much further—if any further—toward learning who had killed him, and the uncomfortable thought rose into her mind that maybe it was not lack of chance holding her back from knowing more about his death but lack of care. Maybe she cared so little that he was dead that it hardly mattered to her who had killed him.

As she passed through the penticed gateway from the churchyard, someone said, "Dame Frevisse?" and she turned to find Dickon standing a little aside from it, plainly waiting for her but looking unsure he should be there until she said, letting him know she was pleased to see him, "Dickon. How goes it with you?"

His unsurety vanished with a grin and he jerked his head toward the guesthall, saying, "That depends on how much they leave for the rest of us."

He and the other St. Frideswide men, like most of the guests' servants, had not been in the church for the funeral but neither would they have any part in the feast except for whatever leavings might come their way afterward.

"I'll eat as little as may be," Frevisse promised, walking on that way.

Falling into step beside her, Dickon laughed and said, still grinning, "I've done what you asked."

"Good! What did you find?"

"That bank that closes in the garden on that side, it's for the millstream."

"The millstream?"

"The mill is there." Dickon pointed toward a building's thatched roof showing over the high wall at the other side of the churchyard, not far off from where they stood. "There's been a deep ditch cut to bring water from the Thames past the mill and then the nunnery," Dickon explained. "The ditch and the piled-up bank run all along that side of the nunnery before curving back to the Thames near the ferry crossing."

That was something toward which she might have at least made guess if she'd thought about it, Frevisse realized. To run water through or beside a place was a common way of dealing with a common problem. At St. Frideswide's the water to carry off kitchen and privy wastes came from a nearby stream by way of a wide, shallow ditch dug past the nunnery and back to the stream.

Here the water came from the Thames and served first to turn a mill's waterwheel as well.

"Is there a path along it?" she asked.

"Not on this side. On the other side there is, beyond the up-banked earth but no way from one side to the other and on their in-sides both banks go down steep, into the water. And the water's deep. It took a stick almost as tall as me to reach the bottom. And flowing fast, too."

Frevisse could well believe that, what with the mill to drive and all the force of the Thames behind it. "But someone could make their way along the top of the bank on the nunnery side if they wanted to?"

Dickon shook his head. "There's barely toes-room at its top. The buildings crowd right up to it and the bank is all grassy anyway. I wouldn't even try it, for thinking I'd not go far without I'd slip off of it."

"That's sensible, then," said Frevisse. And if a boy could not do it, neither could a man.

"But . . ." Dickon paused, trying to hold down the smile that wanted to be broad across his face.

"But?" Frevisse asked.

"From the other side of the ditch, looking across, I could see something."

He was drawing it out, pleased with himself, and patiently Frevisse asked, "What could you see?"

"Below that withy fence, in the grass on the bank where it goes down into the water, there's stones sticking out."

"Stones," Frevisse repeated, failing to see how that mattered.

"Worked stones. Big ones. Like from a wall that had fallen." He was open about his excitement now. "Not a lot of them. At least not a lot that show. The ones I could see look to be mostly buried in the bank, with the grass grown up and nearly hiding them."

Frevisse caught up to what he was saying. "You mean someone could have used them to climb up the bank that's otherwise too steep to climb. They would have been hand and foot holds."

"Yes!"

Her own rising excitement faded. "There's still the matter of how he reached them across the ditch."

"A rope," Dickon said promptly. "If he had a rope, he could have stood on the meadow side of the ditch, tossed a loop of it over the top of one of the posts the fence is tied to, they're heavy things, by the look of them, and held on to it to keep from being swept away while he crossed over. He could have gone back the same way and pulled the rope free, and just walked off."

"It's possible," Frevisse granted, slowly. "How well can that part of the bank along the ditch be seen from anywhere? Did you think to notice?"

"Of course I thought to notice." He sounded a little offended and somewhat scornful that she thought he might not. "Upstream, there's an upstairs window in the mill looks that way and another one in the gable end of whatever cloister building it is that overlooks the garden and two more in the same building where it runs along the bank. Downstream towards the ferry there's the only blank back of barns. You'd have to be on their roof to see anything. Then the ditch curves back to the river, keeping this side of Ferry Road, and you'd think you could see from there but you can't because everything is all grown with willows that way. To hold the banks there," he added kindly, as if she could not be expected to know something like that. "They're pollarded and so thick that even with the leaves off you can't see beyond them very well. You'd have to be standing right in among them to tell much about what's on the other side."

"And toward the river?"

"There's a wide meadow that doesn't look to even be grazed lately. Probably resting for the winter, to be used for milch cows come the spring." There spoke the well-taught son of a steward. Frevisse could almost hear Master Naylor's voice, but it was with a boy's eagerness that Dickon went on, "There's alders and more willows and such like all along the river's bank, of course, and there's a bank diked up against flooding, that anybody on the path there is along the river would have to climb to see the nunnery."

Frevisse saw fairly clearly what he was describing. If everything was as Dickon said, the murderer had run some risk of being seen coming and going from the garden but a limited one and apparently worth it to him.

"The thing is," Dickon said, having thought along the same way she was going, "with the steep banks of the ditch nobody would be seen, unless from the mill maybe and those nunnery windows, except when he was right at the fence and he wouldn't have had to be there long, cutting his way in or coming out. And coming out, anyway, he could have taken time to be certain no one was in sight in the open at least."

And that lessened his risk by a great deal. But there was still the going to where he crossed the ditch, when he would have been in the open for a long way, and although anyone seeing him there might not have thought about it at the time, once word of the murder had spread, they would have said something about it to someone, wouldn't they? Frevisse was not easy yet, either, with how he had crossed the ditch—a rope was a bulky thing to carry—and thinking aloud, she said, "It seems he could have done it with no one seeing him. But would anyone, when he was doing murder, be willing to trust so much to chance?"

Dickon scrunched his forehead into a frown before reluctantly admitting, "If it was me, I wouldn't."

"Nor I. But we're not murderers."

Dickon laughed at that, as she meant him to. They were nearly to the guesthall steps; she thanked him and they parted, he to wait for whatever would be left of the funeral feast, she going up the stairs behind two men in warm talk about the embassy come last month from France— "So do we call the Dauphin king of France now or don't we? That's what I don't see yet"—and ahead of three women intently sharing their ways of dealing with winter rheums—"If it's an old cough, I favor hazel milk in honeyed water, with a good dose of pepper to clear the head. That's what I've found best."

Once through the door, she slipped aside, out of the flow of people to stand for a moment and look about her. Mistress Montfort was still on display, seated at the near end of the hall in a high-backed chair probably brought from the prioress's parlor for her, to judge by its size and carving, keeping widow's court with her children ranged on either side of her, her daughters less tearful now, only sometime having recourse to their handkerchiefs, her younger son rather openly copying his two older brothers in solemn dignity to the people doing their duty to the widow, giving her and her children consolations on their loss before moving on to the food and drink laid out in generous array along several trestle tables down the middle of the hall.

No attempt was being made at seating anyone. People helped themselves and, except for those who had found a place on the benches rowed against the walls and looked unlikely to shift anytime soon, stood around in talk with food and drink in hand, voices beginning to rise and laughter breaking out here and there now that duty to both the dead and the living was done and the shift started away from death's ceremonies to everyday life again. Except for the saints and greatest mystics, turned as they already were in life to the wonders and joys that could come when they were done with the flesh, awareness of the body's mortality did not linger long in the forefront of men's thoughts. It might be better for them if it did, but it was maybe more merciful it did not. Surely here it seemed that Montfort buried was Montfort forgotten.

Coming behindhand as she was, almost last of those to reach Mistress Montfort after a few pointless words to her daughters, Frevisse expected to find her worn down by the difficult day, but she was sitting straightly upright, dealing with people's murmured consolations with quiet assurance and no particular care to look the downcast widow, only a deep-willed intent to see it through and have it done. And when they were face to face, Frevisse instead of false words about the sorrow of her loss said, "Only a little longer and then you're free."

In the same level, low voice with which she must have been answering one comment and another all through this, Mistress Montfort said, "Yes. Thank you." But into her eyes, meeting Frevisse's just for a moment, a gleam of delight danced.

Frevisse, reassured that all was as well with her as it might be, moved on to her sons, leaving her to a swag-bellied man who, to guess by the crumbs on two of his chins, had been to the tables before bringing his consolations to the family.

This was neither time nor place to talk to Christopher, but although he was shadowed under his eyes with weariness, he gave her somewhat better greeting than either of his brothers did, not knowing her at all, and she said the only thing she could truthfully as well as courteously offer, "It was a very seemly funeral."

He bent his head to her in acknowledgment and said, "Thank you," but as he raised his head, he met her gaze and then very deliberately shifted his eyes to the side, drawing hers away to Master Gruesby hovering uneasily on the edge of a cluster of other Montfort household folk further down the hall, aside from the shifting crowd around the tables. Frevisse, with another slight bow of her head, moved away.

Chapter 15

either hungry nor feeling like hiding behind food or drink, Frevisse circled somewhat wide from the tables and through the crowd toward Master Gruesby, masking her purpose, she hoped, by going slowly, taking time to look about her and pleased to find Master and Mistress Champyon not far off from her, without Rowland or Juliana near them this time but again standing apart and ignored, each with something to eat in one hand, a cup in the other, and sour looks on their faces, no longer waiting to be noticed, it seemed, only waiting to be out of here. A small shift in her way through the crowd brought Frevisse to them. There was unlikely to be better chance than this to meet them but, unable to think of any clever reason whatsoever she could give for pausing to talk, she simply stopped in front of them and said with the bright voice useful for such moments, "You're as much out-comers here as I am, aren't you? First that inquest and now this. With all of it and everything, how has your stay in Goring been?"

"Too long." Master Champyon's answer was terse with displeasure, at life in general rather than at her, Frevisse judged; and when his wife twitched an elbow sideways against his arm, he managed to add with somewhat better grace, "At least the weather hasn't been too bad. Mostly."

Frevisse agreed, aware that Mistress Champyon was studying her, sharp-eyed, and therefore not surprised when the woman said, "You're a friend of the Lengleys, aren't you?"

Without hesitation Frevisse said, "Praying your pardon, no. My prioress and I met Lady Agnes when we first came to Goring and had just found there was no place for us at the nunnery. When she offered to take us in, my prioress accepted, thinking an honorable widow's house better than an inn for us."

" 'Honorable,' " Master Champyon scoffed.

Mistress Champyon's elbow pushed against him again while she said at Frevisse, "But you've heard since then what's going on between us?"

Glad to be saved the trouble of bringing the talk around to that, Frevisse said mildly, "Between you and her grandson, you mean?"

"Between us and the old malkin herself, more like," growled Master Champyon. "Her and that lying bastard Haselden are the ones . . ."

"We think," Mistress Champyon put in moderately, "that young Stephen is maybe unknowing of what wrongs they've done."

"In a pig's ear," Master Champyon grunted.

Like his wife, Frevisse ignored him, merely granting to Mistress Champyon, "I've heard a little about it all."

"A little?" Master Champyon seemed to take that as some sort of offense, too. "Only a little?"

Mistress Champyon balanced her nibbled piece of cake on top of her cup, freeing a hand to lay on her husband's arm. "It's hardly something to be talked of much in front of guests, my dear. Is it?" she added to Frevisse with what she probably meant to be subtle prompting toward telling more.

Choosing not to be prompted, Frevisse said with a smile as false as Mistress Champyon's own, "No." Added, "By your leave," and moved away, having judged Mistress Champyon was too intent on learning what she could for there to be much chance of learning anything from her in return.

But if the woman had gained nothing by their talk, Frevisse took away an increased dislike of both her and her husband that now she would have to work against in judging anything she learned, either to their favor or not. And worse, at the moment, was that her way to Master Gruesby was going to take her past Juliana and her brother standing in talk with another woman farther along the hall. A careful steering among other people would keep her well clear of them but the woman with them had been among the Goring couples in talk with Lady Agnes and the others outside the church before the funeral, and curiosity made Frevisse curve her way to pass behind them.

She did not slow her going, for fear of being noticed, but as she eased around a broad woman complaining to a narrow one that whoever had made these honey cakes had stinted on the honey, she was near enough to hear Rowland say, "Let it go, Juliana," as if he had said it before.

"You let it go, Rowland," Juliana mocked back at him impatiently.

Frevisse was able to see between them now to where they were looking across the hall and table to Stephen and

Nichola standing with another girl and young man, food and drink in their hands and laughter a-light in all their faces.

"You have to grant, they're very sweet together," the Goring woman offered, nothing sweet in how she said it.

She was much about Juliana's age, a well-gowned, amply-wimpled wife of a prospering townsman by the look of her, with no plain reason for her voice's venom edge. A venom Juliana matched in, "That much sweetness makes my teeth ache."

"Juliana," Rowland said wearily. "He's not yours."

Past them, Frevisse looked again toward Stephen, so guilty in this, and Nichola who at that moment turned her head to look, as if she had felt the burn of eyes on her, directly back at Juliana with a stare that betrayed, to Frevisse if no one else, that the girl knew far more than Stephen or Lady Agnes thought she did. Then Stephen said something that brought laughter from the others and Nichola turned back to them, laughing, too.

Juliana must have said something because Rowland said again, "Let it go, Juliana," not as if he thought it would do any good this time either.

Then Frevisse was beyond hearing anything else said among them, but not beyond wondering how much how many other people knew of what was between Juliana and Stephen. And how long it would be before Nichola was certain of it, if she was not already.

Unhappy with that thought, she threaded the few yards and half-dozen more people to Master Gruesby, who had not moved from where she had first seen him, a mostly undrunk cup of wine in one hand, a barely nibbled, crust-wrapped piece of meat in the other and his usual huddle-shouldered seeming of trying not to be where he was.

"Master Gruesby," she said as she reached him.

"Dame Frevisse," he offered in return, mostly toward

his feet but with a sideways, upward glance at her through his spectacles' thick lenses.

Bypassing any attempt at pointlessly light talk with him, she asked, "When will I likely be able to talk with Master Christopher?"

Master Gruesby cast a hunted look from one side to the other, as if answer to that might be lying about, waiting to be found, before he finally said as if it were a desperate secret drawn from him by force, "Tomorrow. His mother means to stay one more day before he sees her home. He'll have chance tomorrow to see you."

"She's staying over another day?" Frevisse said before she could stop herself. Another day and night she and Domina Elisabeth would have to spend with Lady Agnes and out of the nunnery?

Master Gruesby huddled his shoulders a little higher, into a small shrug. "To let everyone else leave ahead of her. So she won't have to ride with anyone but her own people. She says she's tired of people."

Sharing that feeling all too readily, Frevisse pried loose from her own disappointment to ask, "Have you read the letter from Lord Lovell yet?"

Master Gruesby gathered himself, not happily, and managed to answer, "It was only an asking that Master Montfort let my lord know quickly, once the Lengley decision was made, how he'd decided."

"Did it say which way Lord Lovell wanted him to decide?"

Master Gruesby lifted his head enough to look at her reproachfully. "That would hardly be seemly. Or"—his gaze dropped again and his voice fell to a whisper—"necessary."

That told her what she had only supposed so far—that Lord Lovell was taking an interest in what shifts in power there might be here. From that she could guess that surely so was Suffolk.

Which meant Montfort had been caught between them. There was a certain black-livered humour to that, she supposed. Ever more devoted to his ambitions than to truth, Montfort had finally worked his way up from crowner toward being escheator only to be immediately caught between the ambitions of two far more powerful men.

Men powerful enough to bring on a man's death?

But almost any man had that much power. If not to kill by his own hand, then to hire another man to do it. In which case it was only a matter of the cost. And some men came cheaply.

Not that cheap or dear would matter that much to either Suffolk or Lord Lovell. They could both afford to pay well for a task well done. The trouble was that she did not know—had no way of knowing—whether either of them was so base as to buy a man's death, had no way to know whether this manor of Rickling was worth that much to one or the other of them. Had Montfort already decided which way he meant to go and the losing lord somehow learned of it—or knew Montfort well enough to suspect it—and decided to be rid of him in hopes that the next escheater might be more inclined his way?

That was possible. But how probable? And somewhat sharply she asked, "Had Master Montfort made up his mind on the Lengley matter?"

"He'd not have told me." Master Gruesby was reproachful again, then unexpectedly had a question of his own. "Have you learned anything of yet?"

What she had mostly gained thus far were questions but she gave him what she could. "I've talked with Sister Ysobel, the nun in the infirmary."

"Master Christopher had already done that," Master Gruesby said with a firmness that surprised Frevisse and she returned, a little shortly, "There was more to be had from her than Master Christopher waited to hear. She says very few words passed between Master Montfort and whoever else was there, nor did it sound like there was a quarrel between them. That means that almost certainly the murderer came ready to kill him. Came meaning to kill him."

For once Master Gruesby's eyes were fixed on her face. He even seemed, from what she could see of his brow above his spectacles' thick rim, to be frowning slightly, as if listening very hard as she went on, "Also, the murderer has to know Goring and the nunnery well. That he knew of the garden and how to reach it unseen and was certain he could safely kill Master Montfort there all argues that. Or else there's someone else, who told him what he needed to know."

Master Gruesby blinked at her from behind his thick lenses. "Someone else," he said, seeming to like that thought no better than she did. His gaze slipped away from her face and past her shoulder, to hang for another moment before he brought himself to look at her again and say, "A woman. It would more likely be a woman than a man who knew so much about the garden. And all. It being a nunnery."

Frevisse had thought of that, too. Nor would the woman have to be a nun. Besides Lady Agnes there would be any number of other women over the years who might, like Domina Elisabeth, have been there while visiting an ill friend or kin. Or girls now grown to women who might have been at school in the nunnery. Like Nichola. Like the woman with Juliana just now.

"But then," Frevisse went on, "it surely had to have been someone Master Montfort knew or had been given reason to trust or he'd not have met with him secretly?"

She made it a question, to see how Master Gruesby would answer, and after a moment's hesitation he granted, "Yes." He hesitated again, then offered, "Or else he thought he knew who he was meeting. But someone else came."

A well-taken point which brought up another and she asked, "Have you learned yet who brought him the message, written or otherwise, that sent him to the garden?

Master Gruesby blinked. "No."

"But you or someone else has tried to find out."

"Yes. Of course. Yes. It's one of the things . . . one of the things Master Christopher tried to learn right away."

"What did he find out?"

"No one says they know anything of any message brought to him here. Master Christopher thinks it must have been given to him during the morning, while he was out."

"He was out during the morning? Where?"

"Here in Goring. To talk with various people. About the Lengley matter. With Lady Agnes and Master Lengley and Master Haselden. And with the Champyons."

"He went to them instead of having them come to him?"

Master Gruesby bobbed his head up and down.

"Did you go with him?"

"One of the yeomen did. I didn't."

"The man's been questioned?"

"Of course. Master Christopher asked him about everything. But he was left outside every time and knew nothing."

"Every time?"

"Every time."

"He never heard anything that was said?"

"Never. He only knows that Master Montfort came away cheerful at the end of it all. I saw that, too, when he came back to the guesthall. That he was cheerful. It was . . ." Master Gruesby gave a small, vague flutter of his hands.

"Unusual," Frevisse finished for him. Unusual and worrisome, because the only times she had seen Montfort anything like cheerful were when he had thought he was going to have his own way about something. What had he succeeded at this time? "When Master Christopher talked to Stephen, Master Haselden, and the Champyons, did he ask about this?"

Master Gruesby bobbed his head again. "But all they said, all of them, was that he'd asked things about the inheritance and the Champyons' challenge, and nothing was said that wasn't already known, by him and everyone."

So Montfort had somehow had a message of which there was no trace, from someone he might or might not have known, whom nobody else had seen.

Frevisse's jaw was beginning to hurt with holding her voice so forceably level as she said, "Then there's also the question of how the murderer came to the garden wall at all. There's still no word that anyone was seen along there about the time Master Montfort was killed?"

"Questions have been asked." Master Gruesby sounded almost reproachful that she would doubt it. "Nobody saw anyone. It was a cold day. With a wind. I remember. People weren't out."

"So whoever it was wasn't seen." Frevisse supposed she must resign herself to that. "But at some point he had to cross the ditch that's there and the water would have been cold and it flows strongly, I'm told. However he got across it, he would have been cold and soaking wet afterwards and had to have gone somewhere. Why wasn't he noticed then?"

"Oh." Master Gruesby's gaze veered away from her and back again. "He wouldn't have been. There wasn't any water in the ditch that day. Or very little. At most he would have wet his feet. Would have muddied them. Probably nothing more."

Only desire not to be overheard kept Frevisse's

"*What?*" between her teeth in a harsh but hushed demand.

"The mill," Master Gruesby said. "The wheel needed repair. It was being done that day. The sluice was closed. The ditch was drained from early morning until late afternoon. All there would have been was some water standing in the bottom of it. And mud."

She had been troubled over a problem that was no problem, Frevisse thought. Worse, another problem took its place, because it would hardly have been a secret in Goring that the mill was shut down for the day, the ditch emptied. It was the sort of thing everyone in Goring was likely to have known. But, "How far ahead were the repairs decided on?"

"How far ahead?"

"That day? The day before? Longer? Was it because of a sudden-come problem with the wheel or something foreseen and planned?"

Master Gruesby's eyes widened as he understood. "You mean, did the murderer have a long time or a little to plan the murder. I . . . we don't know. I don't think Master Christopher has considered that."

"Then you'll find out."

"Yes."

Something else came sharply to her. "Wait. If the mill was being repaired, where were the workmen? Didn't they see anyone along the ditch?"

"The workmen." Master Gruesby shrugged unhappily. "They were at dinner. They'd been given a hot meal as part of their day's wages. In a tavern up the street from the mill."

Another question returned to her. "Has Rowland Englefield's story of where he was that afternoon ever been better looked at?"

Master Gruesby made a small sound that might have been a fretful sigh before he said, "Master Christopher sent a man there. Into that place. He didn't say he was there for that. He just . . . made talk. And listened. From what he heard, Master Englefield was there. Just as he said."

"At the time Master Montfort was killed?"

Toward his toes Master Gruesby whispered, "I don't think anyone keeps close time there."

No, they probably did not, Frevisse thought and held back from saying tartly they probably wouldn't notice, either, if Rowland had come in muddy-booted and dripping as if just back from a stroll in the mill-ditch, would they? Instead she went another way, asking, "The lands that were divided between the two Bower sisters, Rose and Cecily, how are they entailed? What ways can and can't they be inherited?"

Master Gruesby brightened. Happy to be on sure ground, he said confidently, "The lands are entailed to descend in the right blood, entire by the male line or, if the male line should fail, to be divided equally among such female heirs as there may be."

Frevisse sorted that out. "That means if Rowland Englefield has no children, at his death his properties will go to his sister."

"Yes. Except for such as are dowered to his widow for her lifetime. And if there are no males by a collateral line."

"Which there are not or there would have been no division between Cecily and Rose at their father's death."

Master Gruesby bobbed his head in agreement to that.

She had gathered most of that already from other people's talk but it helped to have it plainly laid out and she asked, "If it's proven that no heir to Rose is yet living, then her share—this manor of Rickling—reverts to her nephew Rowland or else to his heirs, yes? Meaning his sister Juliana if he sires no legitimate children."

Master Gruesby bobbed his head in further agreement.

Which meant that for Rowland the straightest way to

have this manor of Rickling would be not by way of Montfort's death but by Stephen's.

And for Juliana the straightest way to it would be over both her brother's and Stephen's dead bodies.

Not that it was Stephen's *dead* body she wanted.

Frevisse removed her mind firmly from that uncharitable thought, to turn the problem another way. Since it seemed that Montfort's death did not directly serve the Englefelds, did it serve Stephen? Or Master Haselden, for that matter, because his stake in Stephen's legitimacy was high. And the answer to that was that if Montfort had determined to decide against Stephen, then, yes, his death might be useful, in the hope his successor would decide otherwise. But how would either Stephen or Master Haselden—or anyone, come to that—have known what Montfort was going to decide?

Unless his business with them all that morning had been to tell them so. Or to ask for reasons—meaning bribes—why he should favor one side over the other. If that had been what he was at, then someone might very well have decided his death was a simpler way to go than bribery.

With nothing else she thought she could learn of Master Gruesby, she said, "I'd best go. Please, I pray you, tell Master Christopher I want to talk with him." Master Gruesby bowed and she added to the top of his head, "Tell him, too, that he had better ask more strongly after that dagger."

Chapter 16

 he had learned what she could for now, Frevisse
thought, but escape was most of the hall's
length away through the crowding of people. By
weaving her course carefully, she kept well clear of where
Lady Agnes was in heads-together talk with several other
women but instead came face to face with Nichola just
turning away from two other young women now drifting
away toward the tables for more food or drink. As momentarily without anything to say as Frevisse was, Nichola paused, before good manners caught up to her and
she said, "My lady, you haven't even anything to drink?
Would you like me to bring you something?"

"No. Thank you, but no," Frevisse said, returning the
courtesy, only just stopping herself from speaking as if to

a child. Nichola was very young but not a child, was a wife and well along toward being a woman, and of everyone Frevisse had yet met here, she and Sister Ysobel seemed to be the best-hearted and least given to doing harm. "In truth, having done my duty here, I'm trying to escape."

Nichola smiled with delight. "I'd go with you if I could. Isn't it dull? I thought there'd be someone different to see. The sheriff maybe or even Lord Lovell or that maybe he'd send his son. That would have been reasonable, I think. Master Montfort was escheator, after all. But it's all just people I've seen before."

"There's Master Montfort's family," Frevisse pointed out.

"They're all dismal and weeping. And what can you talk to them about except Master Montfort being dead? And that's no good. I didn't even like him."

"You met him?" Frevisse asked, carefully not showing great curiosity.

"Oh, yes. The times he came to visit Father. They knew each other from Lord Lovell's and when he was hereabouts he'd stop in to talk and be fed. Mother always hated it when he came. I don't think even Father liked him but Master Montfort was someone you didn't want to not like you, if you see what I mean."

Frevisse saw. Montfort had had power to make other people's lives difficult and had never paused, that she had ever seen, over using his power to do exactly that if he had the chance. It had indeed been better to keep on his good side. Even if she had never managed to do it.

"Stephen says we'll maybe go to Lord Lovell's for Christmas next," Nichola chatted on. "Just he and I. He says that I should be one of Lady Lovell's ladies for a while sometime and that would be lovely, I think. He says we'll go to London sometime, too. I wish I could have been there for the queen's coming." When there had been processions in the streets and ceremonies everywhere to welcome Margaret of Anjou, a girl hardly older than Nichola but brought from France to be young King Henry's wife. Nichola sighed. "Though even going to Oxford would be a change. I've never been further than Wallingford and that was just for one day and a night, and then straight back here we came and it was all some business of Father's anyway."

Frevisse almost said something tedious about the time would come for Nichola to go places and see things but remembered how much she had disliked having things like that said to her when she was young, and before she found something else to say, Nichola looked past her and stiffened into sudden silence. Frevisse turned her head to look, too, and saw Stephen and Juliana standing together in talk together farther along this side of the tables. Or not so much in talk together, Frevisse amended, as Juliana talking at him, her hand on his arm to keep him there while Stephen, with a small, round cake in one hand and a goblet in the other, looked more as if he wanted to be somewhere else.

"I don't like her," said Nichola stiffly. "She won't leave him alone."

Frevisse held back from asking, "Does he want her to?" and managed to say instead, "They've met before this?"

"Oh yes." Nichola's voice was cold with scorn. "She came up to him before the inquest, when we were on our way to Lady Agnes's, and spoke to him. There in the street, in front of everyone. Before that, she even came to see him at home but he wasn't there and Father wouldn't have her in. He just kept her in talk in the hall awhile and saw her out again. Mother says that to do those sort of things she must have no manners."

"What does Stephen say?" Frevisse asked, knowing she should not.

"Oh, he says it's because he knew her husband in Lord

Lovell's household that she likes to talk with him, but I think it's because she wants him and Mother says that, being a man, he's probably fool enough to be flattered that she does."

So much for keeping thoughts out of Nichola's head, Frevisse thought wryly but aloud said only and mildly, "Just now he looks as if he might want rescuing."

Nichola brightened. "He does, doesn't he? Should I, do you think?"

"Most assuredly." And again knowing she should not, added, "It will annoy Lady Juliana."

Nichola smiled with mischief. "I'd like that. She annoys *me*. If you'll pardon me, my lady?"

Smiling, too, Frevisse nodded her pardon and Nichola went, making her way among people toward her husband and Juliana. Frevisse, for her own part, went on toward the door again, reaching it but lingering before going out, long enough to see Stephen, as Nichola came up to them, move to meet her, smiling and holding out the cake and goblet to her. Nichola, sensible girl, smiled up at him as she took them and was still smiling as she turned to speak to Juliana, who was no longer smiling at all.

Frevisse's last sight of them was of Nichola standing very close beside Stephen, her claim to him clear, and Frevisse took out-of-doors with her the thought that the girl seemed likely to hold her own far better than Lady Agnes thought she could. From what Frevisse had seen of her, she was not weak, merely young, still learning life, but had already discovered she need not obey everything she was told to do and shown she could think for herself. At a guess, there was more of her father than her mousey mother in her, and very possibly the time would come when she would surprise them all. And maybe Stephen more than anyone.

Frevisse meant to return to the church, to try to pray for Montfort's soul better than she had so far. Thinking about Nichola, she even made it to the nave door and a few steps in before she stopped. The smell of incense still hung in the air and the pale, thinning cloud of it among the rafters, but from where she stood there was no other sign there had been a funeral here. A man's passing from earthly life had been noted and dealt with and those who had been there were moved on, were even now eating, drinking, and making merry in the guesthall, in the full knowledge—willfully though they might ignore it in the forefront of their minds—that tomorrow might come their turn.

At the thought Frevisse made an impatient sound at herself. There were few things so true as old proverbs, but come what may—including tomorrow—she did not feel like praying for Montfort just now. Let him fend for himself, she thought, knowing she was in the wrong even as she thought it but nonetheless turned away, left the church, and crossed the nunnery yard to the gateway. A few poor folk were clustered there, waiting for whatever alms of food or money might be given out as was usual at rich funerals. Doubtless they did not wait in vain. Just as there would be enough and more left from the funeral feast for Dickon and any other servants in the nunnery, Montfort would have seen alms to the poor as necessary to his after-death glory as masses, candles, incense, and his wife's mourning clothes.

Guilty that even now she could not think charitably toward him, Frevisse passed among them and into the street and turned not toward Lady Agnes's but away. By right and Rule she should be out nowhere alone unless merely to Lady Agnes's house, but she had suddenly had enough of this going back and forth from Lady Agnes's to the nunnery to Lady Agnes's like a feathered cork in a badly played game of shuttlecock. When she had chosen to become a nun, she had made willing trade between the freedom she would gain for her soul against the freedom

she would lose for her body, but here in Goring that bind-
ing to other people's will was coming between her and
being able to do much at all toward finding out Montfort's
murderer. If she was slack at that task because she did
not greatly care that he was dead, then she was grievously
in the wrong and to put herself in a different kind of
wrong by going to the mill alone was nothing compared
to the wrong of being so uncaring over a man's death.

Even Montfort's.

So, at a firm walk, meaning not to tarry over the business, head bowed and hands tucked into her sleeves to
maintain something of propriety, she went along the street
and turned at its corner into the street leading down to the
timber and white-plastered mill. That street ended at the
mill ditch and the high-railed wooden bridge across it into
the millyard, and because her curiosity had more to do
with the ditch than the mill, Frevisse stopped on the
bridge to see what could be seen from there. From at the
upstream railing, with the rush of white-foamed water
loud below her, she could see at least one island in the
river there and that the mill ditch had been dug off the
river's narrow curve around it, with still force enough
from the Thames's strong flow to drive the millwheel but
probably the sluice gate that controlled the flow into the
ditch easier to maintain without the full force of the river
against it.

She crossed to the bridge's other side, into the shadow
of the mill and its tall, undershot millwheel, driven by the
force of the water flowing against its blades down in the
ditch, turning it steadily, steadily, the dark wood rising
wet and glistening out of the deep ditch's shadows into
the daylight and around and down again with the familiar
groan of wood and gears that went with all millwheels.

Looking first down into the ditch with its dark swiftness
of water and then along it toward the nunnery, Frevisse
knew she had been right to think no one would easily or

readily have crossed it; but according to Master Gruesby, the ditch had been drained the day Montfort was murdered. That would have left it vilely muddy and undoubtedly with some water still in the bottom but not the obstacle it would be today. That day there would have been only the steep ditch sides to be overcome, and sliding down into it would be easy, while the stones that Dickon said were half-buried in the bank would maybe have been enough to make climbing up to the garden fence and down again possible without too hard a scramble at it. And afterward? For leaving the ditch? A scramble then would serve, she supposed, with a toehold here and there and a dagger thrust into the bank for a handhold, with a moment lying flat just below the crest of the bank, clinging to the grass while looking over the top to see if it was safe to go the rest of the way.

Once out of the ditch and on the path along it, there would only be overly muddied boots or shoes and maybe clothing to explain but with soft weather there would have been mud enough in more places than the mill ditch for a man to be muddied honestly.

Satisfied of all that, she crossed the bridge and the mill-yard to the mill's door and pulled the rope on the bell— meant to be heard over the grinding stones—hanging there. The miller opened to her almost immediately, and while he was still staring with surprise to find a nun on his doorstep—and not even a Goring nun, as he could easily tell by her habit—she said, "I want to look out your upstairs window," and started forward, supposing he would get out of her way.

She supposed rightly. He moved aside, saying, "Aye, my lady. If you like, aye," as she passed him. Open-backed, thick plank steps went steeply up the near wall to the hole in the mill's loft floor. The miller was still bemusedly saying, "Aye," as she climbed them, to find that the loft was where the miller lived, a single, sparsely furnished room to which she gave no heed as she crossed to the window in the south-facing wall. The shutter was down, letting in what there was of the day's thin sunlight and giving her a clear view of the nunnery's whole west side and the length of the ditch, too, as well as the wide meadow that lay between it and the Thames and, at the meadow's far end, the willows that blocked sight of Ferry Road, all as Dickon had said, and look as hard as she might, it told her no more than she knew already. There was everything she had expected to see and no more. Just that and no answers.

Nor were any answers to be had for certain about the nunnery windows she could see from here. Except for one, they all looked to her to be set too high for anyone to have sight of anything from inside them except sky. But the one nearest this end of the nunnery, looking out from the second storey of a steep-roofed building set against the church tower. . . . She studied it and judged that from it there would be view of the ditch and meadow and she wondered how to find out to what room it belonged.

With seemingly nothing else to be gained from here, she returned down the stairs to the miller still standing beside his open door and asked him, "The day the man was killed in the nunnery, did you ever happen to look out your window up there? At any time?"

She could see him wondering why she was asking as he answered, "Nay, my lady. I didn't. I wasn't here. There was no point, the mill not running. I'd went to visit my daughter over in Streatley. She's married to the miller there."

"You were gone all day?"

"I made sure of the sluice gate at dawn, that it was tight shut, and was away on the first ferry of the day and didn't come home until just at sundown."

"The mill hadn't broken down unexpectedly then? You'd planned to shut it down?"

"Oh, aye, my lady. Order'd been given for the workmen a good week ahead. It was just some cracked blades of the wheel that needed seeing to and better it be done before they were worse than later, that was all."

She thanked him and left, with him looking no clearer than when she had come as to why she had been there at all. Since that could not be helped, she forgot about him before she was across the bridge, was only wondering as she went back up the street what she had gained and decided it was very little. Nothing she had seen had changed anything Dickon had told her, and if it helped to know the miller had not been there that day, she did not yet see how. That he would be gone to his daughter's was something that could have been as easily known through Goring as that the mill would be shut down for the day, not limiting at all who could be suspected.

What she wanted now, she realized as she turned the corner into the street between the nunnery and Lady Agnes's, was to be alone for a while without need to think about anything, most especially Montfort. She was worn down by the day, tired and not particularly happy, and if she had thought she could reach her room at Lady Agnes's without having to talk with anyone, she would have gone there. The church would have been her next choice if she could have sat there quietly without feeling dutybound to try yet again to pray for Montfort's soul but what she wanted just now was to be without need to think about anything for a while, most especially him.

But since she had small hope of rest at either Lady Agnes's or the church, she would settle for a chance to have more answers to questions and took her way back through the priory gateway and past the guesthall toward the cloister door. People who must have ridden in today for the funeral and hoped to be home before dark drew in were scattered about the yard in their various groups, their horses being brought for them, and she passed among them with her eyes down, to avoid being seen. That was an illogical thing but she had found over the years that it worked well and certainly no one spoke to her here before she reached the cloister door.

Her light pull on the bell rope was answered almost before she let go of it by a servant who stared a moment and then stepped quickly aside with a bobbing curtsy, saying half-laughing, "Pardon, my lady. I thought it would be someone's kin again. They've been so coming in and out all the day to see one or another of the nuns that I've been set as doorkeeper, you see."

"A busy day all around," Frevisse said politely. "Might I go to see Sister Ysobel, do you think?"

"Surely. You know the way, yes?"

"Yes. Thank you," Frevisse said over her shoulder, already on her way.

Today, after so much coming and going as the servant woman said there had been, the cloister felt fraught with it, even though there were only a pair of nuns in low-voiced talk on the other side of the cloister walk. Frevisse went the other way around from them, quickly and with her eyes down, just as she had crossed the nunnery yard, into the side passage and to the infirmary, entering without even a knock to find it blessedly empty of anyone else. The murmur of someone reading aloud beyond the shut door to the bedsroom told her Sister Ysobel was not alone but here there was only herself and she leaned with both hands on the battered worktable and closed her eyes, drawing a slow, deep breath, taking the chance to quiet herself, if only for the moment.

Steadied after a few moments, she straightened and went on and at her slight scratch at the door the reading broke off and Domina Elisabeth bade her come in. She did, to find not only Domina Elisabeth there but Lady

Agnes, the both of them seated on the bed beside Sister
Ysobel's, with Sister Ysobel lying higher on her pillows
than yesterday, her face bright with interest rather than
fever as she greeted Frevisse before anyone else could,
saying with a gesture to the foot of her own bed, "Pray,
sit, my lady. How good of you to come! Have you
brought me more talk of what's gone on today?"

Frevisse sat, careful not to jar her, but admitting, "I
doubt I can add much. You've surely heard of the funeral
from Domina Elisabeth, and Lady Agnes probably saw
and heard more in the guesthall afterwards. I talked
mostly with Master Montfort's clerk, Master Gruesby."
She tried to think of something she could say about him
but a man with less to be said about him than Master
Gruesby she had never met.

"You were talking with the Champyons," Lady Agnes
said and was a little unfriendly in the saying.

"I was." Frevisse had not thought those few moments
would go unnoted, if not by Lady Agnes herself, then by
someone who would tell her of it.

"What about?" Lady Agnes asked, almost demanded.

"The only thing they're presently interested in. That
manor of Rickling."

Indirectly that was the truth. If truth could be indirect.
She would have to give thought to that later but the an-
swer satisfied Lady Agnes. More friendly, she said,
"Humph." And then, "What did you think of them?"

To that Frevisse could straight enough answer. "I found
them unpleasant."

"They're that, right enough," Lady Agnes agreed
curtly.

With a smiling, sideways look toward Domina Elisabeth, Sister Ysobel asked, "How is the widow doing?
Lady Agnes says grief hasn't bowed her down."

"She'd be a fool if it did," Lady Agnes muttered.

More judiciously, Frevisse said, "So it seems for now. How she'll be later . . ."

"When she won't have to keep in her glee anymore," said Lady Agnes.

"Lady Agnes, that's hardly charitable," Sister Ysobel remonstrated with a flicker of laughter.

"I wasn't trying to be charitable. Unless she's a fool, she can't be grieving over being quit of Montfort. He was a petty man, come to a petty end."

"He was murdered, Lady Agnes," Domina Elisabeth murmured, "and needs our prayers."

"He does indeed, after earning so many curses in his life. The wonder will be if he gets any. Prayers, I mean. The curses are assured."

As much to go away from that as toward her own ends, Frevisse said, "Sister Ysobel, a question. There's a window overlooks the garden here from its north side. Where does it look out from?"

"The nuns' dorter," Sister Ysobel said. She smiled. "So it therefore doesn't truly overlook the garden or anything else." Because windows in a nunnery's dorter were usually set too high for looking out of.

And besides that, no nun was supposed to be in the dorter during the day. At the hour when Montfort was murdered, whoever had killed him would have been doubly safe from being seen from there, not only in the garden but as he came and went along the ditch because the dorter's other windows were those small, high ones Frevisse had seen from the mill.

That left only the one, large window to wonder about but she held back from a question about it with Lady Agnes there to hear her, lest questions be asked back at her about why she was interested—and how she came to know about it at all.

But now she had to wonder who, among those most possibly Montfort's murderer, would have likewise known it was the dorter overlooked both the garden and the way the murderer had to come to it.

"As for curses," Lady Agnes went on, back to where she had been, "the Champyons have their share of them, too, right along of Montfort. If ever there was a pair worth the cursing, they're it. And that son and daughter of hers, too. Strutting at the funeral was as if they belonged there."

"Cecely may feel she does have some claim to belong here," Sister Ysobel ventured.

"It's been—what—thirty years since she was at school here," Lady Agnes scoffed.

"Surely not that long, has it been?" Sister Ysobel demurred.

Lady Agnes shrugged. "Near enough. The point is that she and Rose were both at school here when they were girls, and Cecely hasn't been seen or heard from by any of the nuns since she left."

"You mean Mistress Champyon was here in the priory as a girl?" Frevisse asked, careful to sound barely interested, a little discomposed to be given information that she wanted but for which she had not asked yet.

"Yes," Lady Agnes said. "Just as I was. Years before her, of course, but I made friends then, both among the nuns and the other girls, that I've kept to this day." She paused on a thought. "Well, not to *this* day. All the nuns I knew then are dead, God keep their blessed souls, save for Sister Margaret. She yet lives but we never agreed together. Nun or no, she's a pushing woman and always has been. But I've other friends I've kept since then, women I've known all our lives. And now their daughters and grandchildren, too." Lady Agnes paused, momentarily turned inward, before adding, "That shows how old I've grown, doesn't it? But the point is that Cecely was here at school and has the priory or anyone in Goring heard aught from her since she left? Does she have any friends from when she was here? Has she been to see anyone

since she has come back? No and no and no again. All
she's come for is to make trouble and what does that say
about her?"

"It's maybe her husband who wants her to have naught
to do with anyone here," Domina Elisabeth suggested.

"It would have to have been her first husband as well
as this second one who wanted it," Lady Agnes pointed
out sharply. "I'd like to think a husband has ever had the
upper hand with her, but I'll lay no money to it. No matter
how much this one looks like he's at the forefront of this
business, never think for a moment that she's not the one
pushing to make it happen. All for that lump of a son of
hers and never doubt it."

"What about her daughter?" Frevisse did not resist asking.

Lady Agnes opened her mouth to snap some answer
back but stopped, with a sharp look at Frevisse, before
saying tartly, "She's a whole other set of problems and
not mine, thank God." She rose stiffly to her feet. "Well.
I think we'd best be going, my ladies."

As she said it, the bell for Vespers began and Domina
Elisabeth said, reaching out to lay a hand over her
cousin's, "I've said I'd stay to pray here."

"Ah." That was hardly something with which Lady Agnes could quarrel but she asked at Frevisse, "You, too?"

"If I may," Frevisse said toward Domina Elisabeth, who
answered, "Most welcomely."

"I'll see you at supper, then, will I?" Lady Agnes asked,
wrapping her cloak around her.

They agreed she would and she left as Domina Elisabeth took up the breviary from the table and Frevisse
moved to sit beside her, that they might share it. There
was enough westering sunlight slanted through the high
window for them to make out the familiar words—*Deus,
in adjutorium.* God, be my help—but the very familiarity
of the prayers worked against Frevisse this time, her

thoughts sliding away toward what she had learned from Lady Agnes just now.

That Mistress Champyon had been at school here in her girlhood meant she knew the nunnery well enough to have told either her husband or her son whatever he would have needed to know about the garden and the dorter. Or told both of them. That the murderer might not have worked alone was something she must needs consider, too, she supposed.

But if those stone blocks that Dickon said were half buried in the earth bank did indeed mean there had been a garden wall that had fallen, when had it fallen? If after Mistress Champyon's time in St. Mary's, she would not know about it. But the stones were well buried, Dickon had said, so the wall might have gone down that long ago, or longer. No one was in any haste to repair it, that was sure. Who could she ask about it? Not Lady Agnes. Almost the last thing Frevisse wanted was to awaken her curiosity by asking too many questions of her or around her . . .

"Domine, miserere mei," Domina Elisabeth said. Lord, have mercy on me.

"Sana animam meam, quia peccavi tibi," Frevisse heard herself answering—Heal my soul, for I have sinned against you—and realized how little heed she was paying. With an effort, she let go the tangle of questions and set her mind to Vespers' prayers and psalms with their reaching toward God that was the mind and soul's eternal quest, until by Vespers' end—*Fidelium animae per misericordiam Dei requiescant in pace.* May the souls of the faithful rest in peace—she was quieted she would have been content to sit awhile with bowed head and in silence.

But Domina Elisabeth closed the breviary and set it aside with a brisk, "There. We'll be going now, I think, Ysobel. Your supper will be coming soon and Lady Agnes will be waiting ours."

Looking sunken and tired again but with a smile, Sister Ysobel held out a hand for Domina Elisabeth to take. "Tomorrow?" she whispered.

"Tomorrow," Domina Elisabeth assured her.

She stood up and Frevisse rose with her, going to wait beside the door while Domina Elisabeth kissed her cousin on the forehead and whispered probably a blessing over her. Then in silence, leaving Sister Ysobel to the shadows until someone would bring an evening light and her supper, they went away, out of the infirmary and into the darkening cloister where there was candlelight through the choir windows of the church and, distant beyond the stones, the rise and fall of the nuns chanting toward their own end to Vespers.

There was no one at the door into the yard but it was not locked yet, only left on the latch, and they let themselves out, Domina Elisabeth waiting while Frevisse took the time to close the door silently and be sure the latch fell into place so that there would be no going in that way tonight by anyone unless someone opened the door from inside. Then, making haste because of both the dark and the cold now swiftly drawing in, they started toward Lady Agnes's, Frevisse finding the comfort of Vespers was quite gone from her. Instead, she was realizing that if Lady Agnes had not told her about Mistress Champyon, she would have been left with only Stephen and Master Haselden to suspect—and that she would have been very uncomfortable with that, because if she chose whom she liked and whom she disliked in the matter, the Champyons lost out even against Stephen.

That thought made her take hard, half-angry hold on herself. She had no business taking sides in this, especially for no better reason than her dislike of what little she had seen of the Champyons.

She was still confronting that thought as she and Domina Elisabeth passed through the nunnery gateway into the street, with no one among the few people still out and about near enough to hear Domina Elisabeth say suddenly, "You give very little of yourself away, do you, Dame?"

Frevisse came to a startled stop, looked at her, then quickly looked away toward the houses across the street as if intently interested in the thin lines of light around their shut shutters as she answered, "There's very little of me to be given."

"Sister Thomasine is someone with little of herself to give away," Domina Elisabeth returned. "She's given so much of herself to God there's little of her left here in the world. You, on the other hand, have a great deal of yourself still here. But you keep it to yourself."

Still toward the windows, Frevisse said, "It's never seemed my place . . ."

"You wouldn't know 'your place' if it bit you on the ankle, Dame," Domina Elisabeth said; then said with quick contrition, "That isn't fair. Or true. It's not that you don't give. It's that you don't take, the way most people do. Whatever it is you're at now, with your odd questions and long looks at people, I shouldn't ask about it, should I?"

More startled, unaware until then that she had been so noticed, Frevisse looked back at her before saying softly, "If it please you, my lady."

"I think it had better," Domina Elisabeth said as quietly. "Please me, I mean." She started forward again. "Though you understand that I'll probably have to ask you about it later."

Humbly following her, Frevisse said, "Yes, my lady."

Chapter 17

he dawn next morning was a narrow bar of rose behind the black shapes of Goring's eastern rooftops when Master Gruesby crossed from the guesthall into the churchyard and toward the church, hurrying behind a few late-coming townsfolk through the stone-fretted patterns of candlelight thrown to the path through the high choir windows. Behind him in the hall and beyond it in the stables there was yellow lamplight and busyness and beside the church door a single lantern was hung to show feet the way over the threshold, but once inside the nave everything was shadows, the goodly number of people gathered to hear Mass only dark shapes, shuffle-footed in the cold and crowded in small groups for better warmth.

He was in quest of Dame Frevisse, certain she would be at Mass and therefore here in the nave rather than the choir because one of the guesthall servants had told him that the cloister door would not be unlocked until full light. He thought he saw her but there were too many cloaks and veils and women among the shadows for him to be certain, and since there was anyhow no way to have her out of here before the Mass was done, he patiently sidled into the lee of the pillar nearest the door. Wary as always of what the world and the day might have in store for him, he tried to take his usual comfort in the Mass, in its reminder that just as the candlelight around the altar, distant beyond the rood screen, was promise that all of life was not darkness and cold and uneasy shadows, so the Mass was promise that however far life might seem from holiness, God was as near as the bread and wine that could become His body. But today the comfort did not come. Master Gruesby was too aware of Master Mont-fort's body laid to its corruption there beyond the altar, his soul gone to a judgment for which Master Gruesby had no doubt it had been unready. Alive, Master Montfort had been a trouble. Dead, he still was, and Master Gruesby was only glad when the Mass was done and he could set to what he had been sent to do.

By the gray light growing through the nave's windows now he could be certain of Dame Frevisse, tall for a woman, as she moved with her prioress not toward him and the door into the yard but toward the door through the rood screen. He saw they meant to go into the cloister and hastened forward along the wall, skirting everyone going the other way, and along the rood screen, over-taking them just before they were beyond his reach.

"Dame Frevisse." he said low-voiced and made them a low, hurried bow as both women turned around. "Please you, my lady, Mistress Montfort wonders if you could come to her presently." He ducked another bow, this time directly to her prioress. "By your leave, of course, my lady."

Surprised but not apparently put out, her prioress asked, "Do you want to, Dame Frevisse?"

"If you please, my lady," she said quietly. "I can join you with Sister Ysobel later, if that would be all right."

"And maybe be a comfort to Mistress Montfort in the meanwhile. Yes, go on." Her prioress dismissed her with a brisk nod. "Come and join us when you can."

As she turned away, Master Gruesby made her another quick bow to her back, then yet another to Dame Frevisse, who said in answer, "Lead on, then."

She was not, he thought, in the least deceived that it was Mistress Montfort who had asked to see her, and with no wish to answer any questions she might have of him, he hurried away, his head bowed in the hope that he looked merely respectful, his hands tucked deep into the folds of his heavy overgown as if he could tuck away the unease she always made in him. He succeeded at least in not being spoken to while they left the church and church-yard, back into the nunnery yard now busy with horses, servants, and guests preparing to leave. At the guesthall stairs he had to thread his way upward against the outward flow of baggage and people but Dame Frevisse kept close behind him there and through the hall—loud with bustle and talk—to the door to Mistress Montfort's chamber. There, he knocked in a way Master Christopher would recognize, opened the door, and stood aside, bowing to her to go in ahead of him. She did, and relieved to be quit of her, he followed, nothing more he need do but close the door and take a place beside it while she crossed to Mistress Montfort and Master Christopher waiting for her beside the fire.

The three of them made a dark gathering, Master Gruesby thought—Dame Frevisse in her Benedictine black, Master Christopher and Mistress Montfort in their mourning—and of the three of them, only Mistress Mont-fort's face was at variance with it. These past days of dealing with Master Montfort's death and funeral she had held herself in well, nor did Master Gruesby doubt that if she was to go out into the hall or someone else came in here, she would take on her expected widow-look readily enough; but without that need to satisfy others, she was a-glow with gladness, free of any pretense of grief.

It was otherwise with Master Christopher. All that he had had to do and feel these past days was weighing on him, and even though that other inquest had meant he had not been here to keep the vigil beside his father's body the night before the funeral, young Denys said he had instead kept it in the church where he had been. That had meant little rest that night, and if he had slept well last night the gray shadows under his eyes this morning belied it. Besides that, Master Gruesby was worried for him on account of what more trouble might come of his having asked Dame Frevisse's help. He doubted Master Christopher understood that she was not a woman easily put aside once she had turned her mind to a thing. She might well have kept aside from dealing in the matter of Master Montfort's murder, given her dislike of him—and of that dislike Master Gruesby had never had doubt, try though she did to hide it behind seeming respect and woman-hood—but now that she had been started on it, she would not let go and what trouble that might draw down on Master Christopher was a worry.

Master Christopher was pouring wine from the silver pitcher into the goblets waiting on the small table close to hand while Mistress Montfort said, "You'll have some warmed, spiced wine with us, Dame? To take off the morning's chill?"

"Yes, thank you," Dame Frevisse answered and added in the dry voice that always made Master Gruesby more wary of her than ever, "I'm pleased to see you're still doing so well against your grief."

With a deepened smile, Mistress Montfort acknowledged, "I do what I can." Master Christopher offered her the first goblet but she nodded it away to Dame Frevisse, going on, "I've sent John and Edward and the girls to bid folk farewell and good journey on my behalf and Christopher's. It's understood I'm too stricken down to show myself and Christopher is comforting me. I suppose that's why you're here, too, if anyone should ask. But in truth it's Christopher who must needs talk with you. I"—she swept her skirts around to one side and sat down in the chair beside the hearth—"am merely here."

She took the goblet Master Christopher now offered her, smiled on him and on Dame Frevisse, and turned her head away toward the fire, showing she was leaving them to whatever business there would be between them.

Master Christopher took up the third goblet of wine and brought it to Master Gruesby. Discomfited, Master Gruesby fumbled toward thanking him but Master Christopher said with a smile, "You're in this with us, sir," and returned to the table, leaving Master Gruesby in confusion because that was altogether more courtesy and kindness than he could remember ever having from Master Montfort even once in all the years he had served him.

Fortunate for what quiet he had left, no one was heeding him. Instead Master Christopher was pouring wine for himself and saying to Dame Frevisse, "Master Gruesby said you wanted to talk to me."

"And you to me, I trust," she returned. "Master Gruesby told you what I gathered from talking with Sister Ysobel?"

"That whoever was there in the garden, they came purposing to kill my father?" Christopher turned from the table to face her, wine in hand. "Yes."

"We agreed, too, that someone had to know the nunnery well to have chosen the garden as the place to kill him. That made both Master Haselden and Stephen Langley more likely than Master Champyon or Rowland Englefield."

"That was also in my mind."

"I've since learned that Mistress Champyon was at school here in her girlhood. She'd know the nunnery enough to tell her son or her husband about the garden."

Christopher's face darkened. "Damn."

"There's the matter of the fence, though. I had Dickon—he's one of my . . ."

"I remember Dickon."

"I had him go to look at the nunnery from outside. He says there seem to be stones half buried in the bank below the garden, almost hidden in the grass. Worked stones, he said."

"I saw them, too. They would have served the murderer in climbing the bank, I thought."

"Yes. But they're worked, as from a fallen wall. When did it fall?"

Master Christopher cocked his head, silently asking why that mattered, then straightened with a jerk, understanding, and said, "If it fell after Mistress Champyon was familiar with the garden, then she wouldn't think of that as a place to lure my father because she wouldn't think there was an easy way into it."

"Even so. So we need to know when the wall, if there was indeed one, fell. I'll ask about it today. I couldn't yesterday, there being only so many questions I can ask at a time." Without giving away to anyone what she was doing, she meant.

It made Master Gruesby ill at ease how often he understood what she meant even when she did not say it. As always when he was uneasy, he wanted to busy himself with pen and paper but lacking that refuge, he took an incautiously deep drink of wine. There proved to be too much nutmeg among the spices and the effort not to choke on it noticeably occupied him while Dame Frevisse went on to Master Christopher, "Could you find out if Mistress Champyon has gone out walking while here in Goring, that she might have seen the change in the wall? It's hardly been walking weather nor does she seem to me someone given to pointless wandering along the back ways of places. If she's gone out, the inn servants will likely remember it."

"I'll have questions asked," Master Christopher said.

"The trouble is that all we know so far are odds and ends and apparent nothings. We lack what would fit them all together into sense. Would you have questions asked, too, about where everyone most concerned in the Lengley inheritance was that day? All that day but most especially at the hour Master Montfort was killed. Women as well as men."

Master Christopher nodded in agreement to that.

"Everyone with a near concern in the Lengley inheritance," Dame Frevisse repeated. "Including Master Gruesby."

She looked across the room to him as she said it and he froze, the goblet raised for another drink, staring back at her over the rim of it before he hastily lowered it and said, shaken, "I've nothing to do with the Lengley inheritance!"

"Master Montfort was dealing with it, and you as his clerk were therefore dealing with it, too," she said back at him. "Just as any of the Lengleys' or Champyons' lawyers and their clerks are."

"Following that way of seeing it," Master Christopher protested, "we must needs ask where all their servants and wives and children and maybe distant in-laws were that day."

"If they were anywhere near Goring, yes." Dame Frevisse's gaze was still fixed on Master Gruesby. "For a beginning, where were you when Master Montfort was killed?"

She was not using him merely for example, Master Gruesby realized. She wanted to know because she was truly willing to suspect him. But why shouldn't she? They had no certainty yet as to why Master Montfort had been killed. She could well suppose he himself had as good a reason as the next man, and steadied by how reasonable it was for her to ask, he answered with hardly a shiver, "I was here in the guesthall all the morning and through dinner. Until I began to search for him to give him Lord Lovell's letter. There are servants who'll say so, surely."

Dame Frevisse turned back to Master Christopher. "You'll ask?"

"I'll ask," Master Christopher said with a glance at Master Gruesby that asked pardon.

"And about the women. Mistress Champyon. Juliana." Dame Frevisse paused a moment, then added, "Lady Agnes, too. Not simply where they were but if they sent a message to anyone. Though a sent message is unlikely. Master Montfort saw all of them that morning. Whatever took him to the garden that afternoon could have been set then, with no need to pass word by way of anyone else." She looked at Master Gruesby. "You still say no message came to him that day except the one from Lord Lovell?"

He blinked rapidly but managed to nod.

"Nor the day before," Master Christopher said. "We've asked."

"And you've read that letter from Lord Lovell and there's nothing in it that helps?"

Master Christopher paused. Master Gruesby guessed he was considering how much to say, but when he answered he held back nothing. "Without saying it in so many words, it makes plain that Lord Lovell supposed my father knew which way his decision over the manor should go. If he were to please my lord Lovell."

Mistress Montfort had seemed at ease this while, leaned back in her chair and sipping occasionally at her wine, removed from all of them in her thoughts if nothing else, but now of a sudden she asked, "What if the killing was for something other than this inheritance?"

Master Christopher looked at her bleakly. "Then our chances of finding the murderer out are even less than they already seem to be."

"Oh," Mistress Montfort said as if a little surprised but not much concerned.

Dame Frevisse turned her head to stare into the flames and after a short silence said, slow with thought, "Since it seems he had no messages and talked to no one that day but those concerned with the Lengley inheritance, we're in safe bounds to think his death has to do with that. Given that, the questions about who was where and when can be centered on those most concerned with it." She moved away from the fire, toward the table, and set her goblet with its untouched wine beside the pitcher and turned back to Master Christopher. "What have you done toward finding out about the dagger?"

"I've had men asking about it through the town and looking for it. But only quietly and by the way. No one knows anything, it seems."

"You may have to ask less quietly. There might be use, too, in knowing how much beforehand people generally knew the mill would be closed that day, the ditch drained."

"You want to know how long ahead the murderer had to plan."

"Yes."

"Master Gruesby," Master Christopher said. "Find out, please."

Master Gruesby gave a small bow, not letting show how pleased he was to be treated as if he were still crowner's clerk instead of not. There was still young

Denys to consider, but as often as not these past few days, it had been himself and not young Denys to whom Master Christopher had turned. He had not enjoyed being an escheat clerk, because dealings over property too often led to arguments and angers. Crowner's work was usually with people either grieving or wary or both but on the whole far less troublesome than those involved in escheats. He did not like trouble.

The thought of trouble made him think of Dame Frevisse, and with his head bent as if he were staring into his wine cup, knowing his spectacles' thick rims hid his eyes, he watched her where she stood beside the table, silent again, her hands folded out of sight up her opposite sleeves. He had sometimes wondered if she so often hid her hands because they gave away what her carefully still face did not; even now, here with Master Christopher, whom she seemed to trust, both her face and voice were mostly bare of anything except quietness as she raised her head and said, "I can't see what else we should do for now."

"Nor do I," Master Christopher said. "But thank you for all you've managed so far."

"Little though it's been." Briefly her voice gave away how much that annoyed her.

"It's the little pieces brought together will tell us finally what we want to know."

"True," she said and smiled at him, to Master Gruesby's startlement. Had he ever seen her smile before this? She never had in Master Montfort's presence, that was certain.

There came a knock at the door and Master Christopher sighed, raised his voice to say, "I'll be there," then said more quietly, "I must needs go and make farewells to people too important to be neglected. If you'll stay awhile longer with my mother, it will give color to why you're supposedly here. If you will."

"Of course."

He set down his goblet, slightly bowed to her, and went to kiss his mother on the cheek. With no wish to be left here to Dame Frevisse, Master Gruesby quickly set aside his own drink, and with his eyes carefully down, followed Master Christopher out of the room.

Chapter 18

eft behind, Frevisse sat and made talk with Mistress Montfort over how long a ride she would have to home tomorrow—it would take more of a day than not, Mistress Montfort said—and about how long Frevisse thought she and Domina Elisabeth would stay here in St. Mary's—Frevisse was unsure—before a small silence fell between them, until Mistress Montfort said, "I think we've served to cover my son's purpose well enough, if you want to go."

Frevisse did, only paused when they had both risen to their feet, to ask, "What's Master Gruesby's place now? Is he become your son's clerk or is he working for him only this while?"

"I don't know if they've made decision or if what's

happening is simply happening. My hope is that Christopher will take him on as a crowner clerk again. Because if he doesn't, I'll have to think of giving him place in my household."

"And you'd rather not."

"I'd rather not," Mistress Montfort agreed.

Because he made her as uncomfortable with his silences and watching as he made Frevisse? Or for some other reason? Or reasons?

Abruptly impatient with herself for conjuring up yet more questions she could not answer, Frevisse moved toward the door. Mistress Montfort moved with her, following thoughts of her own but in the same direction because she said, "I think he makes me uncomfortable because he never seems happy nor unhappy. He never seems much of anything. He's always just simply there."

For something to say rather than because she had considered it, Frevisse offered, "Mayhap it's because he's happier than any of us. It may be he's so settled into it he's past need to show it." Once said, though, there was a kind of sense in it—that there might be small outward sign of someone's happiness if they were so deeply happy as to be past the need for seeking out of pleasures and bursts of merriment.

"Much like you, I might guess," Mistress Montfort said musingly.

Because they were at the door, Frevisse was spared trying to find some answer to that. Instead, hand on the handle, she asked, "Should I send someone in to you?"

"No." Mistress Montfort was both quick and sure of that. "They'll come soon enough, thinking I shouldn't be left to myself. Until then a few moments of peace . . ." She smiled and made a small gesture meant to show Frevisse had not troubled her peace. Frevisse smiled to show she understood, slipped out the door, closed it and turned all in one quick movement, and was still barely in time to hold back the two Montfort daughters and the woman ready outside to knock and enter as soon as she was out of the way, saying to them in a hushed voice, "Best let her be for a time, I think. She's in prayer." Which was close enough to truth; she was probably praying to be left alone a little longer.

Outside, full day was come, with the thickness of clouds that had darkened the dawn broken into drifting fluff high overhead and clear morning sunlight slanting long across the yard. Not far from the guesthall stairs Christopher was in talk with several men and women, their servants standing nearby with their horses, ready to leave. Master Gruesby seemed to be nowhere in sight but neither did Frevisse much look for him as she passed along to the cloister door. Her knock brought the same servant as yesterday, who said as soon as she saw her, "Oh, good. Your prioress is with Domina Matilda in her parlor. I was to bid you join them, if you would."

Frevisse felt she would rather not, but good manners did not permit that choice and she said only, "Of course," and followed as the women led her into the cloister walk and around it, past the church to stairs up to a door where the woman scratched lightly and, at someone's bidding to come in, opened it and stood aside to let Frevisse go into the room beyond it, a large, comfortably furnished chamber. Because among a prioress's duties was the receiving of particular visitors, often for the sake of dealing with matters beyond what could be dealt with in the daily chapter meetings, her parlor presented the best a nunnery could offer and St. Mary's could offer much, it seemed. Besides beautifully braided reed matting for the floor and glass in the upper quarter of the two windows that let light in even though the shutters were closed, there was a bright, fringed cloth over the broad table in the middle of the chamber, beautifully embroidered cushions on the window seats, a woven tapestry covering one long wall show-

ing the Three Christian Worthies with their banners
unfurled above them, and a wide fireplace where the two
prioresses were seated in high-backed chairs, a small,
silky-haired spaniel curled against Domina Matilda's
skirts.

They looked to have been in comfortable talk, each
holding a mazer bowl of what Frevisse feared was more
spiced wine, and indeed it was, she found, after Domina
Matilda had welcomed her, gestured to a third chair beside
Domina Elisabeth, and bade her help herself to the wine
and cakes from a nearby table. Frevisse hardly wanted
more wine or any food but took both for courtesy's sake
and to occupy herself, pouring only a little of the wine
while answering Domina Elisabeth's asking how Mistress
Montfort did, and taking the smallest cake before she
joined Domina Elisabeth and Domina Matilda, talking together of the troubles that went with being prioress.

Frevisse had long since seen enough of the duties and
worries that came with being a prioress to be purged of
any desire she might have had, when she was young and
foolish, ever to be one herself. Worse, as if the usual
burden of seeing to the spiritual and bodily well-being of
her nuns at St. Frideswide's was not enough, Domina
Elisabeth also had the repairing of all the damage left by
her predecessor, both to the nunnery's worldly well-being
and its spiritual health. St. Mary's looked to be in altogether better circumstances although presently Domina
Matilda had the pressing problem of yet another day of
feeding guests. "Though, thank St. Anne, there'll be almost only Mistress Montfort's household folk and the escheator's men before the day is out. A few more days of
so many as there were and I'd be going door to door
asking for alms instead of giving them out. Happily, Master Haselden has promised us a roedeer. Or maybe two,
if the hunt goes well today."

"Venison," Domina Elisabeth said on a sigh. "How lovely."

Domina Matilda's sigh matched hers. "Especially since we'll soon be having naught but salt fish." Because Lent would soon be on them. "How many barrels of stockfish do you find sufficient for a year?"

They were away on practical matters then, leaving Frevisse with chance to think about what had passed between her and Christopher this morning. Faced squarely on, it seemed to her they were trotting in circles, on the move but going nowhere, unable yet to close on one person more than another for the murderer. Somehow, some way, Montfort had been threat enough to someone for that someone to want him dead. And the threat had most likely to do with the Lengley inheritance. But what was the threat? Who had been threatened? How had they lured him to the garden and come and gone from there themselves unseen?

The same few certainties. The same returning questions. Around and around.

She finished both the wine and the cake, set the bowl aside, and folded her hands into her lap, to sit with downcast eyes and not much listening to Domina Matilda and Domina Elisabeth, who were comparing the prices of London spice merchants and whether the added cost of carriage from London made it more reasonable or less to buy from a merchant nearer to home. Uninterested, Frevisse drew her mind back to Montfort. If the supposed threat had to do with the Lengley inheritance, then it was almost surely some sort of proof—something firmer than one person's word against another's—of whether Stephen was legitimate or not, because that was the one thing on which everything else hung. If Montfort had found certain proof that Stephen was—or was not—legitimate and then had, for whatever reason, told the wrong person of it, yes, his murder could have come easily from that.

But what proof? From where and in what form?

Her own guess would be it was something written.

And that brought Master Gruesby and his perpetually ink-stained fingers immediately to mind.

But if he had known of anything to do with the Lengley matter, he would surely have told Christopher about it long before this.

"Are you well, Dame Frevisse?"

Frevisse raised her head to find both prioresses looking at her and said hurriedly, "Yes, my lady. Only tired." Which was maybe not a strict untruth. She was tired of too much thinking up questions to which she could find no answers, was tired of other people's troubles . . . She brought herself up short and made a small beckon toward the room's windows. "May I look out?"

"Of course," Domina Matilda said graciously. "If you see the hunt coming home, tell me, please." And added to Domina Elisabeth, "Everywhere near here was fairly well hunted out at Christmastide. Master Haselden thought that rather than spending the day riding far enough afield for good hunting and then having the long ride home afterwards, the hunt could ferry over the Thames to hunt closer to hand. You can see the ferry from my window there." She nodded toward the room's far end.

"But given the cost of ferrying hunters and hounds and horses . . . ?" Domina Elisabeth questioned.

Domina Matilda laughed. "St. Mary's owns the ferry. I gave them all free passage both going and coming back, since they're hunting to our good."

While Domina Elisabeth asked how well the profits from the ferry balanced against its costs, Frevisse rose and went to the nearer of the room's two windows, finding when she had set back one of the shutters, that it overlooked a little of the churchyard but not much because the parlor was built out from the church's west end and the church's tower and the townfolk's porch and door into the nave blocked sight of most of the yard, leaving only a narrow slice of it to be seen along the millstream bank, with the mill's roof and millwheel showing above the wall not far off.

She closed the shutter and went to the other window, opening its shutter with better hope and was not disappointed. This was the window she had seen from the mill. From it she could see across the water meadow to the Thames and the Berkshire hills that in the pale, winter-misted morning air seemed distant and unlikely, as if they might dissolve away with the mists. The loveliness held her a moment. Then she leaned forward onto the wide stone sill and looked down into the dark-flowing ditch, deep within its banks below her, and then leftward along the priory's buildings, able by leaning a little further out to see the garden's withy fence.

Behind her, Domina Matilda was saying, "One of the useful things about owning the ferry is that at least we don't have to pay to have our grain hauled over to our mill and brought back as flour. Isn't it foolishness we don't own the mill right outside our walls but the one over the river at Streatley? You can see it from there, Dame Frevisse."

Frevisse could, high enough here to see over the pollarded trees along the river to Streatley and its mill and the ferry landing not far from it. Behind her, both prioresses rose and came to join her at the window, the spaniel padding beside his mistress, Domina Elisabeth asking as they came who owned the mill in Goring if not the nuns.

"Oh, the earl—only I must say marquis now; such a foreign word—of Suffolk. He's lord of the town, you know."

Domina Elisabeth said no, she had not known that, and Frevisse braced for her to say more, but they had reached the window, Frevisse moving aside to make room for them, and Domina Matilda said, pointing toward the path along the millstream's other side, "Isn't it strange to think that Master Montfort's murderer very possibly walked right past here? I might even have seen him if I'd been here and happened to look out."

"You weren't here?" Domina Elisabeth asked.

"We were all at Nones, I gather, when it happened. Look." She leaned a little out, as Frevisse had done, and pointed, leftward this time. "You can even see the garden fence from here."

Domina Elisabeth leaned out to look and Frevisse took the chance to ask, "How long ago did the wall along the garden there fall down?"

"Oh, goodness, let me think," Domina Matilda said. "How ever did you know of that?"

"Someone mentioned it," Frevisse vaguely answered.

Domina Matilda, busy reckoning, was not curious enough to ask who, and said, "Twenty and some years ago, it must be. No, longer than that. Oh, my. The bank gave way and the wall collapsed the year before Agincourt. I was just out of my noviate and remember we were gathering money to rebuild it and instead had to pay it all into our tithe toward our late King Henry, God keep his soul, going into France. Afterwards, we just never bothered with it. It's been one withy fence after another. I suppose it's something I should take in hand, shouldn't I? But if there's ever money to spare, it's always needed somewhere else more."

"Isn't that always the way of it?" Domina Elisabeth said. "More things to do than money to do them with."

Before they could go off on that, Frevisse asked, "Wasn't Mistress Champyon at school here then?"

"After that, by a little, I think." Domina Matilda made a face. "Cecely Bower and her sister Rose. We none of us much liked them." Then she thought better of being uncharitable and asked more moderately, "Do you know her?"

"No. It's only that she's being talked about so much."

"She's doing her share of talking, too, if she's anything like she was."

However long since Cecely had been there, it seemed Domina Matilda's feelings toward her had not warmed. "Not even her sister liked her much."

"Nobody seems to now, either," said Domina Elisabeth, moving away from the window, back toward the comfort of the fire.

Domina Matilda followed her, saying with a laugh, "Well, her present husband and her children must—or maybe—do. But that makes one wonder about them, doesn't it?"

Left to herself, Frevisse leaned out the window and looked down again, thinking that the drop from there to the top of the bank would not be too long for a man if he slid down and hung by his hands from the window's sill before dropping. Before he did, he would have been able to see if anyone was in sight, too, and judge whether or not he could go unseen for the brief moment it would have taken him to be out the window and drop to the bank and slide into the ditch. To a desperate man, the chance of being seen would have been little enough, and he must have been desperate to take the chances he had taken.

But the problem with having him drop from the window was that he would have had to be in the prioress's parlor and how he would have come there Frevisse did not yet see. Even given all else he had dared to have Montfort dead, even depending on all the nuns to be at Nones, still the hope he could pass through the nunnery to reach the parlor unnoticed by any servant seemed one chance too many.

Unless Domina Matilda was with him in planning Montfort's death.

Frevisse eased back from the window and turned to look at Domina Matilda, seated again by the fire, stroking her spaniel's ears and sharing with Domina Elisabeth the constant costs of keeping up a nunnery's buildings. What interest could she possibly have had in wanting Montfort dead? Nothing Frevisse had heard so far linked her in any way with the Lengley inheritance. Unless her friendship with Lady Agnes ran so deeply she was willing to help toward murder . . .

It made better sense to think she might not have known it was going to be murder and was holding quiet now out of fear.

But also holding quiet at peril of her soul, and what would be worth that?

A promise of lands or goods or money to the priory in payment for her silence?

That was possible, Frevisse supposed. She had known a prioress who had imperiled her self and soul for worldly gains. But Domina Matilda did not seem that kind. She seemed more like Domina Elisabeth, firm and able in her duties, now asking Domina Elisabeth, "Do you think Mistress Montfort might want to aid the rebuilding of the garden's wall as a sort of memorial to her husband?"

Frevisse looked away, out the window again. Then turned to face it fully, leaning forward as if that would be enough to help her see more clearly what was happening at the ferry landing across the river.

Something in her suddenness must have drawn Domina Elisabeth's notice because from across the room she asked, "Dame Frevisse? What is it?"

"I don't know. Would the hunters be coming home this soon?" That seemed the most likely reason for the milling of horses, riders, and—small with distance but no mistaking the surge and shift of them—a pack of hunting hounds in the wide space left among Streatley's low buildings for travelers to gather to the ferry.

"No," Domina Matilda said, rising and coming back to the window. "It's too soon, surely. They . . ." Her voice faltered as she reached Frevisse's side and saw what Frevisse was now seeing—a long shape wrapped in a dark cloak being carried toward the ferry by three men, and softly she said, "God have mercy. Someone's dead." She swung away from the window. "Or hurt. Please God, only hurt. I'll send someone to find out."

Chapter 19

t was Nichola Lengley. And she was dead.

Master Gruesby, standing behind and aside from Master Christopher and young Denys in the hall of the Haseldens' manor house, was doing what he could not to see her cloak-wrapped body laid on the trestle table set up for it hurriedly and crooked in the middle of the hall. Word of the death had spread through Goring in the time it had taken for her to be carried from the ferry to her home and Master Christopher had followed almost as soon as he heard and Master Gruesby had gone with young Denys after him. That Master Christopher had not turned him back was to the good but that did not mean Master Gruesby was pleased to be here nor did he want to think about the dead girl. Instead he had noted as they rode into the manor's yard how the Haseldens' house, proudly fronting its own lane off the Reading road, was all new-built, with pargetted plasterwork and thick-laid thatch. Now, here in the hall, he was purposely noting that all its furnishings were likewise mostly new, the painted tapestry on the wall at the far end of the best quality—French, he thought, and Master Haselden had been in the French war, so it was maybe booty rather than bought . . .

But none of all his noticing other things kept him from being all too aware of the body lying there. He did not like bodies. People alive made him uneasy, it was true, but he had perfected being forgotten, could be in a room and go unnoticed by everyone and was happy at it. What he was not happy about and had never been able to hide from was his pity for the dead. Even those he had never known when they were alive. What made this worse was that he remembered this girl alive all too well, both at the inquest and after Master Montfort's funeral. She had been pretty, he remembered, in the way young things often were, simply because they were young. Now she was not. Either young or pretty.

Not that her face was much marred. It was dirtied, yes, and with dried and darkened blood flowed out from both the corners of her mouth that her softly sobbing mother was even now carefully, carefully washing away with a cloth and warm water from the basin held by a loudly sobbing maidservant standing beside her. But the dirt and blood had not taken the prettiness out of her face. It was the emptiness did that. The emptiness where there had been someone alive and now there was nothing, only empty flesh already graying toward its decay. The brightness of her fair hair spread behind her head and falling over the table's edge now that her mother had eased off her veil and wimple and dropped them to the floor was almost an offense, looking so much more alive than she did.

And besides death, Master Gruesby did not like grief as raw and new as it was here. He didn't like grief at all, come to that, but as crowner's clerk he had mostly come to deaths after there had been time for the grief around them to be worn out a little. Here death and grief were both too raw, too hurtful—the mother crying as if something deep inside her had broken and she would never be able to stop; the father standing beside Master Christopher across the table from his wife, never quite looking at either her or his dead daughter but talking, talking, the words coming as if he couldn't stop them, saying again for Master Gruesby no longer knew how many times, "The stream bank was steep, it was muddy, yes, but everyone else made it, safe as anything. Nobody else fell. Nobody else."

And worst, the dead girl's husband simply standing at the foot of the table looking at her and nothing else. Not moving. Not speaking, only standing there. As if bereft of movement as his dead wife.

But guessing by his clothing, he had done something more than that sometime. Besides the expected spatter of mud over him from hard, muddy riding, he was mired with mud to his knees and the front and one shoulder of his thick, winter-padded doublet was smeared with not only mud but blood where, down on both knees, he must have gathered his wife's broken body against him.

"It was Stephen. He looked around and didn't see her," Master Haselden said, yet again telling how the hunt had been at full gallop away from the stream, crossing a pasture with the hounds in cry after a stag, when Stephen had missed Nichola. "He yelled at me and turned back and so did I and so did . . ." He named off two others, the men who had been standing muddy and white-faced in the yard with their horses when Master Christopher, Master Gruesby, and young Denys had ridden in. The rest of the hunt, it seemed, had made the kill before they realized they were short some of their riders and gone back to find them, not knowing until then that theirs had not been the day's only kill.

"It wasn't that bad where she fell," Master Haselden was saying again. "There was thicket all along the other side of the stream where we'd come down, yes, but where she fell on the other side was open. It was steep and muddy but open. And she was right at the top when she fell, when her horse went over. Everyone else made it, nobody else fell . . ."

He kept circling back to that. That nobody else had fallen. Nobody else. Only Nichola. But that was how it was with accidents, Master Gruesby had noticed over the years. They happened to one person when they could just as easily have happened to another. Or to nobody. They were the will of God. Or of the Devil. He had heard them called both but made no choice himself. For some reason—some fault by her or her horse or in the mud under its hoofs—she and her horse had slipped on a muddy slope and fallen and she'd been thrown and her horse while struggling to rise had fallen again and rolled on her, with probably never a chance for her, tangled in skirts and cloak, to scramble clear.

"She hated riding," Mistress Haselden whispered. Her husband flinched a look at her and away again. She had finished with the blood, was wringing the cloth out in the dirtied water. "Hated it. He'd have her go. He wouldn't take her no for an answer. But she hated it. The way I've always hated it."

Master Haselden began shaking his head, refusing that, insisting as he had insisted before, "She rode careful. She always rode careful . . ."

"Hated it," Mistress Haselden whispered again, beginning to clean the mud from her daughter's forehead now.

"... always kept behind everyone else," Master Haselden said. "That's why we didn't know she was down. We none of us saw . . ."

From what he had said and said again, the four men had come back and found her dead. The horse had been still alive but lying half in the stream and half out with a broken hind leg and someone had cut its throat to end its misery. Nichola had been more than broken, she had been crushed from her chest downward and Master Gruesby was glad it would not be his duty to pay heed when time came for Master Christopher to view the body. It was a crowner's duty to view a body before bringing the matter of the death before an inquest and it was his clerk's duty to write down what the crowner saw. Master Gruesby had always been careful to sit well apart from Master Montfort's viewing and kept his gaze to his pen and paper as much as might be, satisfied to write, not see. He wondered if Denys, trying just now to handle his writing box and its small inkpot and pens and paper suitable for carrying from place to place to use at awkward times like now, had learned the value of writing without seeing.

If he hadn't, he had better because there were so many ugly ways to die and, after seeing them, so many nights of nightmares about them.

Though for Stephen Lengley, by the look of him, the nightmare was here, no need to wait for night. What lay in front of him was mercifully mostly hidden in the folds of cloak wrapped and doubled around it but he had seen her freshly dead, had held the ruin of her in his arms, and by the look of him he was remembering that. Or what might be worse in this moment, how she had been and never would be again.

Master Gruesby had lived too far from closeness to anyone to understand fully what grief there could be in that much loss but knew he did not understand, knew he did not want to understand, and slid his gaze away from everyone, down to a pair of riding gloves lying beside the table on the floor that was, he determinedly noted, of good stone flagging under its clean scatter of rushes . . .

Far kinder at it than his father would have been, Master Christopher was disentangling himself from Master Haselden's half-unwitted, grieving circling of words by laying a hand on the man's shoulder to silence him long enough to say himself, "I understand. I'm sorry beyond words for your loss." And then, more to Mistress Haselden than her husband, "I'm sorry, too, but I have to view her body. Once I've done that, I'll go away."

He—and Master Gruesby with him—clearly expected she would give trouble over that but she only went on washing her daughter's face while she answered, her voice dead behind her soft sobbing, "I won't unclothe her here for everyone to see. We'll take her into my chamber. I'll ready her there and then you can see her."

"Thank you." Master Christopher matched her quietness and added to Master Haselden, "I'll speak to the other men while we wait."

"Yes," Master Haselden said vaguely, as if he had not been listening, did not know to what he was answering. "I'll . . ." He lost whatever he had been going to say and stopped, baffled by his grief.

It was his wife who said in her dead voice to the maid beside her, "I'll need hot water. A great deal of it. And the best kitchen knife. To cut her clothing off her. And some of the men to bring her to the room."

"I'll . . ." Master Haselden started again.

"Not you," his wife said. "Nor Stephen." To the sobbing maidservant she added, "See that someone gives Stephen something strong to drink. And that he sits down. I'll . . ." Her voice finally faltered, but as Master Gruesby looked up from the floor to her, she recovered it and said steadily on, turning away from the table, "I'll find clean sheets to lay her on."

Master Christopher turned his own uneasy look from her to Stephen back to Master Haselden and said, to no one in particular this time, "I'll question the other men now," and started to withdraw, with a gesture at Denys and a look at Master Gruesby telling them to follow him. But Master Gruesby met his look with a stare so strong that Master Christopher paused, surprised, and deliberately Master Gruesby lowered his gaze towards the gloves lying on the floor, then raised his eyes to Master Christopher. Just raising his own gaze from them, Master Christopher met his silent asking and after only the barest pause answered him with a quick, agreeing jerk of his head.

No one else saw it. Mistress Haselden and the maid were already gone. Master Haselden had turned away. A manservant was persuading Stephen aside. Young Denys was closing his scribe's box.

Nor did any of them seem to notice Master Gruesby bend and take up the gloves and tuck them, carefully folded together, away from sight in the folds of his gown as he followed Master Christopher out of the hall.

Chapter 20

ady Agnes's grief was fierce nor could the people best able to comfort her come to her need. Domina Matilda was dealing with her nuns' distress and prayers for Nichola's soul, Goring's priest was gone to the Haseldens, and Lady Agnes flailed out against anyone seeing her broken down and weeping— "I won't give them the pleasure!"—so that friends were turned back at the door and it was left to Letice and Domina Elisabeth to do what they could with her while Frevisse helped them as best she might, keeping her own grieving to herself. Not until late morning did Lady Agnes, with tears running down her cheeks along wrinkles that seemed to have sunken deeper since the ill word came, say suddenly, "There'll be some sort of inquest. I want it here. Send word."

"My lady," Letice started, "the crowner may have already chosen—"

"Then he can choose again. He knows the place. There's no reason Mistress Haselden should have the burden now and the nunnery's put up with enough these past few days. Here is where it should be. Send that louter Lucas to tell him so." Lady Agnes's fierceness broke, too much of her strength worn out of her with grief. Pitifully, a hand over her eyes, she said, "If it's not here, I won't be able to go. I can't. . . . I can't. . . ." She broke off, tears flooding again, and Letice fled, crying, too, to do her bidding while Domina Elisabeth set, again, to persuading Lady Agnes to drink more of the latest soothing drink Emme, weeping, had brought for her.

Whether for Lady Agnes's need or because it made best sense, Christopher sent word back, with thanks, that he would hold the inquest there, and that since there was no need for delay and something of a mercy in haste, it would be next morning.

"Good. Good. God be thanked," Lady Agnes said. She was by then enough tired out that Emme's drinks had begun to take hold. Domina Elisabeth was able to persuade her to lie down awhile, and once down, she slept a merciful part of the day away, to awaken in late afternoon too tired for more weeping until in the evening Stephen came to her, gray-faced and weary with his own grief but wanting her to hear from him what had happened. Domina Elisabeth made to leave the room when he came in, taking Frevisse with her, but Lady Agnes bade them stay as well as Letice. "This is something you'll know sooner or later and it might as well be sooner."

Frevisse trusted neither Lady Agnes's calm nor Stephen's but he pulled a chair close to his grandmother, took hold of her hands, and began steadily to tell her about the hunt and finding Nichola. There his tears began to come again but he struggled a few words more before he broke, let go Lady Agnes's hands, and slid from his chair to his knees, his arms around her waist, his face in her lap. Her own tears streaming, Lady Agnes bent over him, trying to give comfort where there was no comfort to be had until, probably more worn out than anything like comforted, Stephen ceased to cry and, sitting on the floor, leaning against his grandmother's knees, finished the dark telling while she stroked his hair.

Lady Agnes wanted him to stay the night but, looking worse than when he had come, he said, "Nichola is there. I have to be, too," and left.

It was a long while before Lady Agnes finally slept but in the morning she seemed done with crying for a while, calm outwardly at least, giving firm orders for what needed to be done before the inquest, including having her chair carried out to the gallery, admitting she would not have the strength to stand as she had through Montfort's inquest. But after sight of herself in her mirror as Letice readied her, she had the chair moved well back into the shadows where she would be able to see much without being easily seen herself. "Not looking like this," she said.

Whatever else might die, it seemed vanity did not.

But even vanity was no armor against grief. When time came to take her place in the gallery, Lady Agnes was grim-faced and unaccustomedly silent, maybe thinking, just as Frevisse was, of what sorry contrast there was between Montfort's inquest and today, with only Domina Elisabeth and Frevisse there to keep her company and Letice hovering behind, waiting to be needed. Given her own choice, Frevisse would have preferred to be somewhere else. She had heard enough from Stephen's telling last night, wanted to hear no more, and most certainly did not want to hear the kind of details that would come out at an inquest; but the choice was Domina Elisabeth's, not hers, and Domina Elisabeth would not leave Lady Agnes, to Letice's great relief. It was the necessary choice and the better one, Frevisse knew, and she made the best of it by watching the people in-gathering below her. Many of them were the same who had come to Montfort's inquest, but they were far more subdued for this one. Nichola must have been known to most of them all of her life and there were red-rimmed eyes and muffled sobbing among the women, no loud talk or jostling among the men.

Stephen and Master Haselden came in together, to be escorted by one of Christopher's men to a forward bench where two other men were already seated. If Stephen had slept at all, it had done him little good. He looked hardly better than his grandmother, and Master Haselden matched him, both of them dry-eyed at present but stiff with strain and looking to have been shaved and combed and dressed by force of someone else's will rather than their own. But while Master Haselden made effort to answer the men and few women who came forward to speak to him and Stephen before taking their places elsewhere in the hall, Stephen said almost nothing, looked at no one, sitting with his hands clutched to each other in his lap as if only by holding tightly to them could he hold together at all.

Of Nichola's mother there was no sign, but that was reasonable. Why would she want to be here to hear over what she already terribly knew?

The hall was nearly full when Juliana entered, followed by her brother, and Frevisse's displeasure was nothing to Lady Agnes's, who leaned forward with an inward hiss of breath and a movement toward rising to her feet but Letice stepped hurriedly to her side and said, low-voiced, "They're here as witnesses. They were on the hunt."

"What were they doing on the hunt?" Lady Agnes demanded, hardly less displeased. "It was no matter of theirs."

"Master Haselden gave out word it was open to everyone. He supposed some of Mistress Montfort's people might want a change and come along. He never thought *those* would dare. It's said he wasn't happy when they did."

"He should have turned them back at the start!"

But at that moment Christopher entered. What little talk there had been in the hall dropped away and perforce Lady Agnes sat back in her chair, everyone watching while he took his place behind the table and nodded to his clerk, who stood up from his place at the table's end, cleared his throat, and said, "All those present who were on the hunt with Nichola Lengley yesterday, please stand."

Besides Master Haselden and Stephen and the two men sharing their bench, three other men, a woman Frevisse did not know, Juliana, and her brother all stood up from the two benches behind them. The young clerk looked to Christopher who, very much Master Montfort the Crowner at that moment, said at them, "Those of you who were at the finding of the body will be sworn as jurors. The rest of you, who were on the hunt but not at the finding of the body, know you are charged to speak out if you hear aught testified here that is not truth as you think it to be. So swear."

With some glances among themselves, the men behind Master Haselden and Stephen and the woman and Juliana and Rowland gave their oaths. Christopher nodded for them to sit, his clerk gave the jurors' oath to Stephen, Master Haselden, and the two men with them, said, "Be seated," and set them example by sitting down himself.

After that Christopher made mercifully short business of the inquest, there being small question about what had happened. Step by official step, he took the juror-witnesses through their finding of Nichola's body and the viewing of it with him afterwards. They were more knowledgeable than their fellows had been for Montfort's inquest but nothing any of them had to say was new from what Stephen had told Lady Agnes last night, nor was what Christopher's young clerk read about the body un-expected—that it was neither marked nor marred beyond what would be likely from having fallen from a steep bank and been rolled on by a horse, save for a narrow cut across her face where probably a branch had caught her in riding down through the thicket on the stream's other side.

When all that had been testified to, Christopher asked, "Are you willing, the four of you, to rule that Nichola Lengley died of being crushed under her horse, fallen during the hunt yesterday?"

The juror-sworn men nodded, Master Haselden with his head bowed too low for his face to be seen, Stephen sitting so tautly upright he seemed barely able to move his head.

"Then you are thanked for your service and dismissed," Christopher said.

And there was an end to it. Nichola could now be buried and the bereaved left to somehow pick up their lives and go on.

Lady Agnes made to rise then and did not object when Domina Elisabeth on one side and Letice on her other helped her. Once on her feet, she ordered Letice, "Tell anyone who wants to come up that I'm seeing no one today. Only Stephen. And Philip if he's minded to come. None else. You mind that. None else."

She leaned all her weight to Domina Elisabeth's arm, gestured Letice away toward the stairs, and turned toward her solar. Frevisse went to open the solar's door ahead of them, then stood aside, letting them enter first.

Emme was waiting, with the fire built high and the bed turned down, and she hurried to take Lady Agnes's other arm, but Lady Agnes balked at sight of the bed.

"I'm not sick," she snapped. "When I'm dead or dying, you'll find me in bed in daytime and not before. When I'm dead . . ." She started to cry again and Emme with her.

Leaving them to it, Frevisse silently shut the door and returned along the gallery to the head of the stairs. Letice was on guard below, deep in talk and unhappy exclaims with three townswomen. Around the hall other low-voiced people were likewise still in talk, Master Haselden among them, bracketed in talk with four men; while others were drifting toward the outer door, including Juliana and Rowland, heads-together with the other woman from the hunt. Frevisse's swift look did not find Stephen anywhere but, more to her present purpose, she saw Christopher just leaving, followed by his young clerk and Master Gruesby, and she gathered her skirts aside from her feet and went down the stairs far more quickly than was safe, passed Letice and the women with her with lowered eyes to avoid being caught into talk with them, and keeping wide of Juliana, made her way the hall's length as swiftly as she could without openly running. If she had to follow Christopher back to the nunnery, she would but would rather overtake him here.

Her haste served her well. She came out of the hall and into the yard in time to see him going not toward the street but through the gateway into Lady Agnes's garden, Master Gruesby and Stephen with him. The young clerk was left behind at the gate and he stepped into her way as she approached, to stop her going in, but she called past him to Christopher, "Master . . . Montfort," sticking only a little over the name.

Already well away along the path, Christopher turned and, seeing her, raised a hand to tell his clerk to let her pass and she joined the three of them as Christopher was saying to Stephen in apparent answer to a question or protest, "Anything you would say to me you can say with her here to hear it."

Stephen cast her a look, openly uncertain what to make of that, but driven by something else too twisted tight inside him to be held back, he let it go and demanded at Christopher, "At the inquest, you ruled on how Nichola died but didn't rule her death was accidental. Why not?"

That was the question that had brought Frevisse after Christopher and she nodded agreement with it. Christopher gave a slight sideways look toward her but asked at Stephen, sharp with demand of his own, "How did your wife's gloves come to be on the floor of her father's hall?"

"Her gloves?" Stephen asked back, blankly.

"Your wife's riding gloves. When her body was lying in her father's great hall, the gloves were on the floor beside her. At least they were a woman's riding gloves. Of fine doeskin. Patterned blue and green. But your wife was still wrapped in her cloak. How did her gloves come to be on the floor?"

"Her gloves," Stephen repeated, groping backward in his memory. "Her gloves." He struggled and finally said, "Yes. Her father took them off her when we first found her. I was . . . I was holding her and he was calling to her and pulled her gloves off to rub her hands. He was trying . . ." Stephen stopped, his head twisted aside and eyes tightly shut, struggling again before he was able to say with strangled control, "He was trying to wake her. When finally the others . . . took her away from us, while they were wrapping her in her cloak, the gloves were lying there and I picked them up and tucked them through my belt. They'd been her New Year's present. She . . . took great care of them. I couldn't leave them. But when we were home again, there in the hall, it suddenly was stupid to have them when she was . . ." He shook his head, as if to escape the tears rising in his eyes. "I pulled them out of my belt and threw them down and kicked them aside."

He went abruptly angry. "She shouldn't have been on the hunt at all! She only went because we didn't want to anger her father. I should have . . . angered him and be damned. But I didn't. I didn't. I didn't."

That was something with which both Master Haselden and Stephen were going to have to live ever after. Just as Nichola was going to be ever after dead because of it.

But Christopher said, "Everyone says she hated riding. That she was afraid of it. What does that mean?"

"Mean?"

"Was she a poor rider?"

"No. No, she rode well enough. She just didn't . . . didn't like it. She was always afraid . . . something would happen."

"She kept well behind the other riders the whole hunt. That's what everyone is agreed on. Was that always her way?"

"Always. Sometimes I tried to stay back with her but in a hunt you don't . . . you don't hang back. You ride as hell after the hounds as you can."

"But Nichola didn't. She always kept well away from other riders."

"Yes," Stephen answered, his gaze fixed on Christopher's face as he tried to follow where the other man was going.

"Always?" Christopher insisted.

"Always."

"And carefully? Never 'hell after the hounds'?"

"Never." Even the thought of it made bitter laughter rise in Stephen.

"Then how did she come by that cut across her face?"

The laughter died out of Stephen, leaving only a bitterness that was mostly pain. "A branch," he said flatly. "A branch caught her across the face."

Master Gruesby cleared his throat, startling at least Frevisse, who had yet again forgotten him standing aside and silent, until he said now toward his feet, "It was a very precise branch. If branch it was."

"What?" Stephen said at him.

Master Gruesby huddled his shoulders a little higher as if asking pardon for having spoken, leaving it to Christopher to answer, "It was something Master Gruesby pointed out. The cut was laid straight across her brow. Straight and even. A branch might have done it. Equally, a branch might well have not. If, as you and everyone says, she didn't ride fast or ever close to other riders, how did it happen a branch came whipping back into her face that sharply? It didn't happen in her fall."

"No," Stephen agreed. "No. Where she fell it was open. There was nothing there that could have done it."

But something had.

Very quietly Frevisse asked Christopher, "Why did you want to know about her gloves?"

Christopher turned to Master Gruesby, "You saw it. You showed it to me. Tell them."

Frevisse thought Master Gruesby would rather have walked on hot coals—if he could have done it unnoticed—than obey that. As it was, he answered without raising his head, firmly toward the ground, "There were the long hairs of a horse's mane or tail caught in the beadwork of her left glove. Her horse was a bay. With a black mane and tail. The hairs caught on her glove were chestnut. A bright chestnut."

Stephen was no fool. He saw as quickly as Frevisse what that could mean and color rose in his face as he said at Christopher, "You mean you think her fall wasn't an accident."

"I have to have a doubt."

"You think someone crowded her there on the stream bank and she went over the edge because of it," Stephen pressed.

"There's nothing to say she couldn't have brushed

against someone else's horse at any time during the hunt," Christopher answered.

"Except she wouldn't have. She *always* kept clear of other riders. Even me."

"This time she might not have."

"She would have. It's someone else who didn't keep clear. That's what you're thinking, isn't it? That maybe it was because of someone else her horse went down that bank and they're keeping quiet about it."

"That's more than can be safely said." Christopher refused to shift from caution. "It's something that has to be thought on, but it's nothing more than that. As yet."

Stephen began to be angry. "Why didn't you say anything about it at the inquest?"

Without anger Christopher said back at him, "Because there's nothing can be proved from those horsehairs. There are only four of them. How many chestnut horses were on the hunt?"

"I don't know. Four. Maybe five." Stephen abruptly stopped, as if he saw the difficulty.

"With not much difference between one chestnut and another," Frevisse said. "Unless you're looking for a difference. You *are* looking for that difference, aren't you, Master Montfort?"

"Master Gruesby has been, yes," Christopher said. "That's one reason I held the inquest so quickly. To keep everyone's horses here and give him chance to see them all on the quiet. Since some of the people on the hunt are not of Goring and could leave."

"Why bother looking if nothing can be proved from what you have?" Stephen demanded, vehement with frustration and anger together.

Both Christopher's voice and look at Stephen were level. "Because I want to know."

"Why tell me about it if nothing can be done!"

"Because you asked."

Stephen stared at him, tried to say something and failed, then made a sudden flinging movement of his hands and spun around and walked away.

Frevisse, Christopher, and Master Gruesby watched him go in silence, back toward the house, letting him leave the garden before Christopher said, "Master Gruesby."

Without needing more, Master Gruesby gave a quick bob of his head and left them, too.

"To do what?" Frevisse asked of Christopher.

"To see where Master Lengley goes."

Trying to keep buried the sick feeling that went with the thought that Stephen could have had part in Nichola's death, she asked, "Does he have a chestnut horse?"

"No. His father-in-law does but it wasn't ridden yesterday."

"You really think Nichola didn't die by accident?"

"I think I'd like to know more certainly than I do that she did die by accident."

"Someone could have crowded her accidentally and not want to admit it."

But Christopher answered that with the objection already in her own mind. "How could someone accidentally crowd a rider who always rode behind the hunt?"

"And by having Stephen followed?" she asked.

"He has to know better than I do who might want his wife dead," Christopher said grimly. "If he had no part in it, I hope at least to find out whom he might suspect."

"Who on the hunt had chestnut horses?"

Christopher named three men whose names meant nothing to her, then, "Rowland Englefield and his sister."

Cold down her spine, Frevisse said, "Both of them?"

"An almost matched pair, I understand."

"And Master Gruesby has seen them?"

"Today, he intends."

"You know there's more than friendship between Stephen and Lady Juliana?"

Christopher's eyes narrowed. "No. I don't know that."

Keeping her own feelings to herself as much as might be, Frevisse told him what she had seen and heard said, both between them and about them. Christopher listened without comment and when she had finished said, "I'll make sure Master Gruesby looks especially close at her horse. And her brother's. For all the good it will do. Four horsehairs aren't enough to prove anything."

"If naught else, at least the suspicion will go with Juliana hereafter."

"You think she's more likely than her brother to have done it?"

"Would you kill a girl to help your sister more easily satisfy her lust?" But there could be more than lust to it now, she realized.

With Nichola dead, Stephen was free to marry again.

But if Juliana married him, her interests would then be completely opposite to her mother's hopes of proving him baseborn.

The tangle was worsening, and without need to hear Christopher's answer, she asked the next thing on her mind. "With all this, have you been able to go any farther about your father's murder?"

"Do you know, almost everyone else says 'your father's death.' You're almost the only one who says 'murder.' "

"Almost everyone?"

"Master Gruesby, like you, says 'murder.' "

"We share a certain scholarly desire to be precise, I suppose," Frevisse said dryly. "Have you been able to find out where people were that day?"

"Yes. Stephen Lengley was at home through the morning. Until after my father had spoken with him and Master Haselden. Then he went to dine at his grandmother's and was there until the alarm was raised after Master Gruesby found the body. Servants at both places all say the same thing. No one has been caught in contradiction to what anyone else says nor is there any sign of lying."

Frevisse nodded that she was satisfied with that. As satisfied as could be, because servants could be loyal and there was no reason they could not lie well, especially to strangers. But for now she would accept what Christopher said as he went on, "Lady Agnes did not leave her chamber that day. She saw my father there in the morning. She was the first of them all he visited. After he was gone, she stayed alone except for her woman until her grandson came. They dined together there in her room. Master Haselden went out from home not long after Stephen did. He was then out and about on various business into the afternoon."

"What business?"

"First, at the priory. He spent some time with Domina Matilda over priory matters."

"Why?"

"He's bailiff of Goring."

"How can he be? Suffolk is lord of Goring and Master Haselden is Lord Lovell's man," Frevisse protested.

Christopher raised his shoulders slightly. "Master Haselden is head of the gentry around here. Since Lady Agnes's son died a dozen years ago. He's prosperous in his own right and has local authority. Until this matter of the manor arose, there was probably no conflict in his interests that weighed against everything in his favor. So he's Suffolk's bailiff here and sometimes there are things to be decided between him on the lord's behalf and Domina Matilda on the priory's."

"So he was at the priory when your father was murdered. No." She corrected herself. "Domina Matilda was at Nones then."

"He left when Domina Matilda went to Nones. He spent most of the day afterwards upriver, riding the fields to see how much danger of flooding there was like to be."

"Who saw him go?"

"Who saw him go?"

"Out of the priory. Who saw him leave?"

Christopher held back before admitting, "I don't know."

"Someone rode with him around the fields?"

"One of his men. They were both seen by people we've questioned."

"Could anyone say exactly when they were seen?"

"Afternoon. That's all. It was an overcast day, no close telling of time by the sun."

"Ask who saw him leave the cloister. Find someone who certainly saw him walk out the cloister door into the yard." She forestalled the question she saw coming to that by asking, "What about Master Champyon?"

Almost, Christopher refused to be turned aside from Master Haselden; he hesitated but finally said, "My father talked with Champyon at his inn that morning. He won't say what was said between them. He claims it's for the next escheator to know, no one else. He says he left not long thereafter to ride to Reading on business. He and the servant who went with him claim that's all he did. That he rode out of Goring on the Reading road, nowhere near the nunnery and long before the time of the murder. They came back late the next day. I haven't learned yet when he reached Reading. I've sent someone to ask."

"Who heard what passed between him and your father?"

"Mistress Champyon and her son and daughter were there."

Which was almost the same as saying "No one" because they would long since be all agreed on their story. Unless, for Stephen's sake, Juliana deserted her mother. "Did your father have someone with him? Master Gruesby?"

"No. That morning he went alone to everyone."

"Why?"

"I don't know. Even Master Gruesby can't say."

"We know where Rowland Englefield was later, almost to a certainty. Where were Mistress Champyon and Lady Juliana after Master Montfort and then Master Champyon left them?"

"It seems they kept to their room at the inn."

"Seems?"

"Their servants say so. Inn servants were in and out, bringing their dinner and clearing away afterwards. No one saw them go anywhere, anyway."

"And Nichola?"

"Nichola?" The question stopped Christopher short. "Why her?"

"She had as much to lose as Stephen if he was found to have no claim to that manor. More to lose than her father does." Though Frevisse had not seen it that way until now.

Nor had Christopher. Slowly, considering, he said, "I'll find out."

Another new thought made Frevisse exclaim, "Lady Agnes!"

"I already said—"

"Not where she was. About the dagger. She's not always been an old woman who goes few places, and even now she has friends she talks with and is always hearing things from her servants. She very possibly knows as much as anyone about everyone and everything in Goring. She may well know who has something as unusual as a ballock dagger."

"To protect someone she might lie," Christopher said doubtfully.

"She probably would, if it were Stephen. Otherwise, she might not. We lose nothing by asking her, and best we ask her now, while she's still unsettled by Nichola's death."

Chapter 21

ady Agnes was seated at her window, a cloak wrapped well around her against draughts, the thin winter sunlight making paler her already pallid face, and when she turned her head from watching the street and whoever was presently leaving her house to regard Christopher and his question with a long level stare, her years were sitting more heavily on her than they had been two days ago. She had allowed him to come in because Frevisse had asked it but not given him so much as a look until now and looked more ready to bid him go away than answer it.

But after a pause, her stare still fixed on him, she said, "Ballock daggers are common enough. Why are you asking?"

"They're not that common, my lady," Christopher said.

She looked away out the window, determined not to be interested. "What does it matter?"

Evenly but with the weight of his authority as crowner quietly behind it, Christopher said, "There's been murder, Lady Agnes. A death where there need not have been. In the king's name, tell me what you know about any such dagger."

She turned her head to look at him again as if staring him down might end the matter before, abruptly, she faced forward and said at the wall in a low, half-angry voice, "Philip has one. Master Haselden. Or had one. After he came back from the French war with Lord Lovell, he used to always wear it until I told him it was coarse." She returned her look, sharp now, to Christopher. "That was years ago. It's been years since I've seen it. Anyone could have it by now. It could be anywhere."

"Thank you." Christopher took a step back from her, ready to leave.

"You're not particularly welcome." Distracted from her grief, Lady Agnes was becoming crisp, and more crisply her look going past him, she asked, "When did my solar become everyone's thoroughfare? Who are you?"

Frevisse turned with Christopher, Domina Elisabeth, and Letice to find Master Gruesby hovering with his usual unease in the doorway, as if uncertain whether he had come in too far or else not far enough or, when Lady Agnes snapped at him, should not have come at all.

"He's my clerk," Christopher said, going toward him, asking, "You heard?"

"Master Haselden," Master Gruesby murmured.

"He's likely returned home by now. Go and make inquiry after the dagger. Take someone with you. Where's Denys?"

"Gone back to the nunnery with everything."

"Is Jankyn still below? Take him with you. He'll be better anyway. Master Lengley?"

They were both too intent on what they were doing to think about where they were or Christopher would not have asked that, Frevisse thought. But he did, and Master Gruesby answered, low as always but not too low to be heard across the room, "He went to the inn where the Champyons are staying. He said something to a servant and waited while the servant went inside and came out again. I presume he sent in word to someone there and waited for the answer."

Christopher nodded agreement with that. "And then?"

"He returned here. He's in the garden again."

Lady Agnes snatched her staff from where it was leaned against the window seat and thudded it on the floor, flinching everyone around to face her as she demanded, "What do mean, having your man follow my grandson?"

Christopher gestured Master Gruesby to leave while saying, "Lady Agnes—"

"Don't 'Lady Agnes' me." She struck the floor again. "What are you at? And where's he going?" She pointed her staff at Master Gruesby's back as he scuttled out of sight. "I want him back here!"

"Lady Agnes . . ." Christopher tried again.

"Philip's dagger. My grandson. This is all about Montfort's murder, isn't it?" She threw the folds of her cloak aside from her legs and made to rise. "You young fool, let it lie. I don't care if he was your father. He was never, and isn't now, worth making trouble over." She tried to push herself to her feet but failed, too weak or else too shaken by her rage, but striking peevishly at Letice who had rushed to help her, saying still fiercely at Christopher, "Let it lie, I tell you!"

"You'll make yourself ill, my lady!" Letice protested.

Domina Elisabeth was gone to her, too, taking her a

goblet of something to urge on her while frowning at
Christopher who, unsettled by so much disapproval turned
on him, tried, "Lady Agnes, none of this may go anywhere—"

"Good," she snapped, shoving away Letice's attempt to
cover her legs again and refusing the offered drink. "Nobody cares who killed him, least of all me, just so long
as he's dead."

"Lady Agnes, *no*," Domina Elisabeth said.

Lady Agnes rounded on her but stopped, bit back whatever she had been going to say, and after a hard-fought
moment said bitterly instead, "You're in the right and I'm
not. Whatever kind of man Montfort was, murder can't
be let go." And at Christopher, more grudging than gra-
cious, "Follow my grandson if you think it will do you
any good. It won't. He was with me when Montfort was
killed and that's flat."

With barely a knock at the door, Emme entered, head-
kerchief awry, and with hurried curtsy tumbled out, "Master Stephen is quarreling in the garden with that woman
that was here the other day. I heard them when I went
out . . ."

"Damn her!" With the help of her staff and her anger,
Lady Agnes surged to her feet. "I'll have her head on the
garden path this time . . ." She swayed, sat heavily down,
and made to rise again despite it but Letice and Domina
Elisabeth closed on her, exclaiming that she must not, and
Frevisse, already moving toward the door, said, "Shall I
bring them here? Both of them?"

"Yes!" Lady Agnes cried. "The both of them. That
bitch in heat can at least let him be until Nichola's in her
grave!"

Frevisse escaped out the door, Christopher with her, but
in the gallery with no one to hear them she said, "It's
maybe best you stay here. Whatever Lady Agnes knows,

she's more likely to say it while she's angry. I'll bring Stephen and Juliana for you."

"Here? With Lady Agnes to hear everything?"

"Here and now, while they're all angry," she said over her shoulder, leaving. "They'll maybe drive each other on to betray more than otherwise they would."

Above her head as she went down the stairs, Christopher called to a man in his livery waiting beside the hall's hearth, the hall finally empty of everyone else, "Go with Dame Frevisse. She has my authority. Back her on whatever she does."

Frevisse let the man follow her without wasting explanation on him, thinking pointlessly as she left the hall and crossed the yard that it was as well she was wearing that unloved fur-lined habit today, given how often she was going outside without a cloak. Stephen's angry voice reached her as she went through the garden gateway. He and Juliana were not in the winter-barren arbor this time but on the path halfway down the garden and no sign of lust between them, Juliana clinging to Stephen's arm to keep him near her as he pulled away, saying at her, "Leave go. Just leave go. I don't want you."

"Then soon. There's no reason not to . . ." Juliana broke off, seeing Frevisse and the crowner's man and letting Stephen go as he turned and saw them, too.

Frevisse, not bothering with courtesy, said at Stephen, "Your grandmother wants to see you," and at Juliana, "You, also. Now."

Juliana drew back, gathering her cloak around her. "A pity, then, that I don't want to see her." She gave Stephen an unfriendly sideways look. "I'm not welcome here and I'm going."

"The crowner is with her and wants to see you, too. He's sent his man to be sure of it," Frevisse said, and when Juliana looked about to refuse again, Christopher's man took a purposeful step forward. She paused at that then shrugged with disgust and started toward the house. Stephen opened his mouth to ask something of Frevisse but she curtly shook her head at him and stepped aside to let him and Juliana and Christopher's man go ahead of her.

They returned to the hall in silence, with Christopher's man going aside to the fire again once they were inside and Stephen waiting at the stairs for Frevisse and Juliana to go up ahead of him. Frevisse, going first, heard Juliana behind her say something quickly and low to Stephen, who only answered, "No," and Juliana's face was sullen and unbecoming when she joined Frevisse in the gallery. Stephen's was no better and in continued silence Frevisse led them into Lady Agnes's chamber and then stepped aside, staying beside the door as they crossed together toward Lady Agnes still seated at the window, Christopher standing beside her and Domina Elisabeth and Letice drawn away to the fireside.

Watching them come toward her, Lady Agnes gave a short, barking laugh. "Is it a falling out of lovers makes you both so grim? Or just fury at me for interrupting a dog and his bitch at play?"

"No play, Grandmother," Stephen said back at her. "Not anymore."

"Finding lust an insufficient bond, are you?"

"Just because you're past it, you old bitch—" Juliana started.

But Stephen cut her off, saying at Christopher, "I've asked her about how the horsehairs might have come on Nichola's glove and she won't say. I haven't told her what else you know."

That was a neatly placed bluff but Juliana gave Christopher no time to play it, saying at Stephen scornfully, "Whatever he knows, he doesn't know enough or he'd be arresting someone."

"You're right. As always," Stephen snapped back. "But

I know enough. You made Nichola fall. You killed her."

"You *fool*." Juliana's anger was as vicious as his own. "She fell. There was nothing more to it than that!"

"You made her fall, Juliana."

"It was her own stupid clumsiness made her fall. Or her horse's. It doesn't matter!"

"Or a riding whip across her face! You tried that on me one time, remember? I said something you didn't like and I barely got my hand up in time to keep from a cut across the eyes. Nichola wasn't so quick."

Juliana took a step to bring her close to him, said up at him, furious and unfearing, "Don't be such a dolt. The little fool was hit by a branch."

"How?" Stephen demanded, his fists clenched at his sides. "She'd have to be riding close behind someone for a branch to hit back that hard into her face and she never rode that close, especially in rough riding like there was along that stream. What did you do, Juliana? When all the rest of us went charging up the far bank of the stream, you pulled back, knowing Nichola would be well behind us all? Did you try to shove her off her horse and she flung out her hand to save herself, grabbed at your horse's mane, and that's how its hairs were tangled in her glove? Was that the way of it?"

"You idiot, Stephen!" Juliana's fury was now matching his, made harsher with scorn and disgust. "Suppose I did take the chance there at the stream to say something to her. Suppose she laughed at me for it and said that whatever I did, whatever happened, you were hers and going to stay that way. Suppose she made me angry enough I didn't care what I did? You're guessing all of it!"

"She made you so angry that you hit her across the face, didn't you? And then what? While she was blind with pain, you swung your horse against hers and sent it over the bank? Was that the way of it?"

Juliana took a step back from him, suddenly cold in her rage. "You're such a fool, Stephen!"

"Why do it, Juliana?" Stephen asked, the words raw with pain. "She never did you any harm."

"She laughed at me. And she married you when you ought to be mine!"

"Our marriage was her father's doing and mine, not hers! It's me you should have killed. Or him. Not her!"

With fury uppermost in him, Stephen grabbed Juliana by the arms. Nothing of the lover was left in either one of them, only the desire to hurt, and Christopher started forward to stop him but Juliana twisted loose and out of Stephen's reach saying with a fury to match his, "You bastard!" She stopped and sudden, ugly delight sprang into her face and then her voice. "Yes! Bastard! You're as much a bastard as your grandmother is a lying bitch, and I'll tell the next escheator everything about it when he comes!"

Carried on her anger, she turned away in a swirl of cloak, past Frevisse and out the door before anyone could stop her. Frevisse, nearest, followed her, to call down to Christopher's man to block her leaving if need be, but Juliana was brought short at the stairhead by Master Gruesby who was just handing Mistress Haselden up the last step onto the gallery, with no way past them and no chance for them to be out of Juliana's way before Christopher had overtaken her with, "Wait on, my lady. There's more to say," and added to Stephen come close behind him, still angry and wanting his hands on Juliana, "Enough. The rest is mine to do," stopping him a few yards away.

For one long moment they all stood staring one at another. Juliana, Stephen, Christopher. Master Gruesby still holding Mistress Haselden's arm. Mistress Haselden still poised on the last step. Frevisse. Then Master Gruesby let go of Mistress Haselden and Christopher pointed first at

Juliana and then aside, saying, "Step away, my lady," and
gave a look at Stephen and for good measure at Lady
Agnes, Domina Elisabeth, and Letice just come out into
the gallery from the solar, warning them all to stay where
they were, while Frevisse quietly eased sidewards and
back, putting herself in the way of the other door from
the gallery to leave Juliana not even that retreat as, obeying Christopher sullenly, she moved away from the stairs.

Mistress Haselden, not understanding any of it, stared
at them all with tear-reddened eyes, seeming even slighter
a person than Frevisse remembered her from the day of
Montfort's funeral when at least there had been her husband to steady her. Here she was simply a worn wisp of
a woman in a plain black mourning gown and veil who,
openly desperate to be reassured, asked toward Lady Agnes, "What—?"

But Christopher stepped in front of her, interrupting
her, albeit courteously, not to fright her more, "My lady,
thank you for coming. Master Gruesby?"

That was an asking as to why she was here and Master
Gruesby hastily but to Christopher rather than at the floor
said, "Master Haselden was not at home. I asked Mistress
Haselden about the dagger and then thought that you
should hear her."

"Mistress Haselden," Christopher said, still carefully
courteous, "my clerk asked you about a certain kind of
dagger?"

Another woman might have questioned why but Mistress Haselden looked to be too dulled with grief to care.
"My husband had one, I know. I tried to find it just now,
when your clerk asked about it, but I couldn't. Then your
clerk said I should talk to you."

"Your husband wears this dagger?"

"Not for a long while. He said it was overlarge and
awkward for everyday wearing. He put it away in his
clothes chest a long time ago."

"He might have sold it since then and not told you. Or given it to one of your sons," Christopher suggested.

Mistress Haselden refused that with a small shaking of her head. "I see it every time I turn out that chest for the spring and autumn cleaning. It's always—"

"Allison."

She stopped short and turned her head along with everyone else toward Master Haselden at the foot of the stairs. Then she moved aside as he came up them, two at a time, to pause at their top to take in everyone with a quick look and a slight, puzzled frown before laying a hand on his wife's shoulder and saying, pleasantly enough though a little short-winded, "There now. I came home just after you'd gone. They said you were away with the crowner's clerk to see Lady Agnes. What's toward?"

"She was just telling us," Christopher said, "that a dagger of yours has gone missing."

"A dagger of mine?" Master Haselden laid his free hand to the pommel of the dagger at his belt. "I don't think so."

"Your ballock dagger," Mistress Haselden said. "It's gone from the chest."

"If it is, I don't know about it," Master Haselden said, still caught too off guard for even indignation yet.

"I had the thought," said Christopher, "that you might have put it elsewhere and not told her."

Sure of her housekeeping if nothing else, Mistress Haselden answered before her husband could, "He hasn't. He'd have said. It was there when I put his best doublet away after Christmas but when I looked just now, it's not."

"Then someone has taken it," Juliana cut in suddenly. "And who more likely than Stephen?" She pointed an accusing finger at him. "He killed Montfort. He probably killed Nichola, too. He was always saying to me how much he hated her."

"You lying bitch!" Stephen cried out. "I never did!"

He started for her but Juliana moved quickly behind Christopher who put a hand out in warning to Stephen, stopping him as Juliana went on, vicious with triumph, "He hated her! He even deliberately kept her barren all the time they were married so he could be rid of her someday. He never meant to get her with child, no matter what you wanted, Philip!"

Master Haselden swung angrily around on Stephen. "What? You kept her from breeding on purpose?"

Angry past caring and attacked too many ways at once, Stephen threw back, "For her sake, yes. She was too young—"

"Like hell she was!" Master Haselden boiled into higher anger. "She could have had one baby by now and another on the way if you'd done what you were supposed to!"

"Please, Philip," Mistress Haselden protested. "She *was* too young. Don't—"

"You knew," Master Haselden exclaimed, disbelieving and angry together. "You knew!" And slapped her across the face with full-armed strength, spinning her sideways against the gallery's rail.

"She didn't know!" Stephen made to go for Master Hasel-den but Christopher grabbed hold of his arm and held him where he was, shouting at both of them, "Stop it!"

They both did, probably because Christopher's man was coming at a run for the stairs, evening the odds, Stephen pulling back from Christopher, Master Haselden holding where he was, choleric and breathing heavily.

„4"Further off," Christopher said, pointing for Stephen to draw back a few more steps and gesturing for his man to come up and keep watch on Master Haselden. Mistress Haselden, crying almost soundlessly, was still clinging to the railing, leaning over it, sobbing. Only when Lady Agnes came to her, laid a hand on her back, did she straighten and turn, burying her sobs against Lady Agnes's shoulder as Lady Agnes put her arms around her.

Juliana, still venomous and not interested in any of that, said, "It was Stephen killed Master Montfort. It had to be."

"Give it over, Juliana," Stephen said, bitter and sounding suddenly weary. "I was here when it was done."

"Your grandmother is a liar and so are all her servants," Juliana snapped.

"Juliana," Frevisse said quietly.

As if startled to remember she was there, Juliana spun around to face her, demanding harshly, "What?"

Still quietly but the words weighted, Frevisse asked, "Why did you call Master Haselden 'Philip'?"

The question caught Juliana unready. "What? It's . . ."

She groped for an answer but Master Haselden, not so quick to see the trap, said impatiently, "It's my name."

"I know it's your name," Frevisse said. "But I'd never presume to call you by it, and I've met you rather more times than I thought she's ever done. Why did you call him Philip, Juliana?"

"For shit's sake, Juliana, it doesn't matter," Master Haselden said, more impatiently. "They know you're a whore. What does it matter if you were mine for a while? It was five years back."

Now it was on him Juliana turned, eyes slitted with fury. "I wasn't 'yours,' you weak-loined nothing. I made use of you for a while and that was all. Don't ever go saying I was 'yours.'"

"But it was Master Haselden killed Montfort, not Stephen, wasn't it?" Frevisse asked, still quietly.

The quietness seemed to grate worse on Juliana than Master Haselden did. "What? Yes, of course it was him, not Stephen," she snapped.

"Damn you, that's a lie!" Master Haselden swore. "I

wasn't anywhere near Montfort that day once he'd done yapping at me at my place."

"You were at the priory," Frevisse reminded.

"Yes, I was at the priory. I was with Domina Matilda in her parlor and there was some old nun muttering her prayers in the corner who'll say so along with Domina Matilda. I was nowhere near the garden."

"You know where the garden is, though? Where Montfort was killed?" Frevisse asked.

"Of course I know where the garden is. I had an aunt was a nun in St. Mary's. I went more than once to see her while she was dying, carried her out into the garden twice at least. But I was nowhere near it the day Montfort was killed." He rounded on Christopher. "What's she playing at? This is your business, not hers. Shut her up."

"She has my leave to make it her business," Christopher said evenly. "Tell her what she asks."

That was trust out of the ordinary since he did not know what she was doing, did not yet know he had told her something today that had finally brought things together in her mind, and she said at Master Haselden, "You're the bailiff for Goring. It would have been you who gave the order for the mill to be repaired the day Master Montfort was murdered, yes?"

Now finally wary, Master Haselden granted, "Yes."

"So you knew better than anyone that the ditch would be drained that day, giving a way to come at the garden there otherwise wouldn't be."

"Half Goring, if not more, knew the ditch would be drained that day."

"How many also knew the miller would be gone to visit his daughter?"

"More than enough. I doubt he kept it a secret."

"And that the workers would be out of the way, having a midday meal you paid for them at a tavern?"

"There's nothing in all that," Master Haselden said strongly.

"There's not much but there's something," Frevisse said back. "It's that you were in the prioress's parlor brings it all together. It's no great drop from the window there to the ditch bank."

"What?" Master Haselden's scorn almost rang true. "What do you think I did? Said 'Pardon me, my lady' and dropped out of her window and she never thought on it again?"

"I'm saying you set your visit to her just before Nones, knowing she'd go off to the Office and think nothing of letting you leave the cloister on your own, used as you both were to you being there as Suffolk's bailiff. All you needed do was go down the stairs with her and when she hasted off to the church along with the other nuns you turned around and went back to the parlor. If you met a servant, you said you'd forgotten something. Once out the window and into the ditch, you were safe from being seen from anywhere but the mill, where no one was likely to be."

"And after I'd done for Montfort, I somehow crawled back through her window, dirty with mud and dripping, and strolled out of the cloister, leaving no trace? Are you really supposing that's what I did?"

"No," Frevisse said coldly. "I think you went back along the ditch and came out at the mill where you knew nobody would be. If anyone saw you after that, going around to the gate back into the yard, you could say you'd been at the mill seeing how the work was coming on and had slipped into the mud. Not that anyone was likely to think much of muddy boots with all the mud there is around these days. Whether you did meet anyone who will remember when we ask doesn't matter. We only have to ask your servant left waiting with the horses which way you came back into the yard. From the cloister and through the gateway."

"He won't know," Master Haselden said. "He's doing good the days he can keep track of where his feet are."

Mistress Haselden had turned around a while before, keeping close to Lady Agnes but watching, listening, to everything, and now, faint-voiced and staring wide-eyed at her husband, she said, "That's why you took Walt with you that day, isn't it? Because he won't remember anything."

"Close your mouth and keep it closed!" Master Haselden took a step toward her, and despite Christopher's man moved into his way, stopping him, Mistress Haselden shrank back against Lady Agnes, a hand pressed over her mouth to hush herself.

It was Lady Agnes who said to Christopher angrily, "She means Walt is simple. He's serviceable for plain things, but if Philip had come bloody to the thighs and elbows, Walt would not have wondered about it or remembered long enough afterwards to say anything to anybody."

"Damn you!" Master Haselden said.

"How you got Montfort to the garden is plain enough," Frevisse said. "When he saw you that morning, you set up the meeting in the garden, for whatever reason you found to give him. The only great question left is why you killed him."

"The great question is why no one's killed you, with that mouth you have!" Master Haselden returned angrily. He faced Christopher. "There's no proof of anything in what she says, just guesses."

Scornful and disgusted, Juliana said, "There's proof enough. You never could see more than what you wanted to." She turned to Christopher and said impatiently, "Of course he killed Montfort. He told me so."

Master Haselden choked on his fury. "You set me on to do it, you bitch!"

"All I did was tell you that he said he was going to decide against Stephen. After that you couldn't wait to have him dead."

"You set me on to do it and, by God, I'll make that plain to any jury."

"You won't. What jury isn't going to believe me in my distress"—Juliana's voice took on a pleading innocence—"at the thought that anything I might have said could have set you on to do such a terrible thing?"

Chapter 22

That Juliana could succeed at persuading a jury exactly as she said was too real a likelihood. And possibly she was telling the truth, had done nothing more than tell. Haselden what Montfort purposed. But Frevisse doubted it. But where was there proof to the contrary? All the frustration of that was in the look she shared with Christopher before he asked at Juliana, "How did Master Montfort come to tell you so much of his business that Master Haselden would want him dead?"

"Oh, that." If Juliana remembered at all that Christopher was Montfort's son, it did not matter to her. "I came here with Mother and Champyon not because I care a snapped twig about that manor but in hope of chances to be with Stephen. The more fool me." She cast Stephen a look as baleful as his fixed on her. "Montfort came to see Champyon within an hour of his arriving in Goring. I stayed and listened. No one minded if I was there. I'm my mother's dear daughter, after all. She doesn't know about Stephen. Or about much of anything else, come to that. Montfort made it plain in just about so many words that he was already set to decide against Stephen as a way toward currying favor with my lord of Suffolk. He merely wanted Champyon and my mother to understand how grateful they were going to be to him. I should have left him to it."

"But you sent word to Master Haselden instead," said Christopher.

"A sealed message taken by an inn servant paid not to talk about it," Juliana agreed.

Christopher looked to Haselden. "Her message was enough to decide you to kill Master Montfort?"

Haselden, something of his balance recovered, answered tersely, "Of course not. What the note said was only that there was trouble and I should meet her in the church just ere dark. I did, damn me." He glared at Juliana, who smiled at him with a pleasure just short of open laughter, and he jerked his gaze back to Christopher. "That's when she told me what Montfort said he was going to do. I knew the man well enough to believe her and to know there was no way to stop him short of killing him. But she's lying if she says she didn't know that's what I meant to do. I worked it out while we were talking. The garden and how I could reach it and leave it with good chance of going unseen. Her share in it was to tell him the side way into the garden and get him there."

"It will be my word against yours on that," Juliana said, unbothered. "I think you said none of that to me. I'm very sure it never crossed my mind you meant to kill him."

"Didn't cross your mind? We talked it through. All of it!"

Juliana turned her smile to Christopher. "He talked about

needing to talk alone with Montfort, with no one to know they'd met. All I did was say I'd help and the next day told Montfort I'd meet him in the garden. He'd said the day before that he meant to go around to my mother and all the others in the morning, so I knew I had the chance. Covering the ground before the ploughing started, he called it. I listened while he talked with Mother and Champyon but went out of the room a little before he'd finished and waited on the stairs for him. After that, it was all easy." Unexpectedly, she laughed aloud and her voice took on the same silken undertone of lust she must have used to Montfort. "When he would have passed me, I laid a hand on his arm, looked at him from under my lashes, said I'd be in the nunnery's infirmary garden about the hour of Nones and wouldn't mind if he met me there. He promised me he would." She changed abruptly to disgust. "I've never met a man I couldn't lead by his privy parts like a horse by its halter. Montfort probably spent the rest of the morning holding his crotch." She swept a look around at Frevisse and all the other women there, showing she thought it was something none of them could have managed even in their best days, then fixed her smile toward Lady Agnes while still saying to Christopher, "The interesting thing is that he was all pleased that morning when he was talking to my mother and Champyon over something that he said made the matter of the manor all simple. He said"—she cast a sideways look at Stephen—"that he had proof after all that Stephen was a bastard beyond doubt."

Tight-faced with instant fury, Lady Agnes moved forward, leaving Mistress Haselden. "He couldn't have. There's nothing of the kind!"

"He seemed very sure about it," Juliana said happily. "He patted his belt pouch and said that what he had there was worth money and he wanted to think awhile on how best to use it."

To Frevisse that sounded a fool thing to have told anyone, but Montfort had never given sign of having much sense, only of greed. What he had probably wanted to think on was how best to extort the most money from both sides before doing what he meant to do all along.

"He didn't happen to say what this 'proof' was?" Lady Agnes asked scornfully. "Because he said nothing of anything like that to me."

"As if you'd admit it if he had," Juliana said back at her, equally scornful. "He only said that there was going to be less trouble than he'd thought about ousting the Lengley claim because he had the proof now that Stephen was a bastard."

"He was playing false," Haselden growled. "Or she was lying, to make certain I was angry enough to kill him when the time came. What she did was send me a message that morning, saying he'd said that. But he hadn't anything like it on him. I looked after I'd done for him and it wasn't there."

"That doesn't mean he didn't have it with him that morning," Juliana snapped.

"It means you're a liar, is what it means," Haselden returned harshly. "You wanted to make sure I'd kill him, that's all."

More interested just then in practicalities than angrily flung accusations without proof, Frevisse asked, "Where's the dagger you killed him with?"

More interested in his hatred of Juliana, Haselden tossed back, "In the ditch, of course. It takes good cleaning to rid a dagger of all blood and I wasn't going to have the time to do it with my usual one. So I took that one with me and dropped it into the mud afterward and treaded it down. A waste of a good dagger because of a shit of a man."

"How did you carry it unseen?" Christopher asked.

"Sheathed down my back so no one knew I had it." He might have been explaining something no more important than how he'd dealt with a broken bootlace. But that seemed to be about how much Montfort's life had been worth to him—far less than his lost dagger.

Sadly, softly, Lady Agnes said, "Oh, Philip."

What control Haselden had recovered broke. He turned on her savagely and said with all the sick rage and despair there was in him, "You think you're free and clear? You and your bastard grandson? When all I did has gone for nothing anyway?" He turned back to Christopher, with a vicious gesture toward Stephen, and said, "Proof or not, Montfort had it right. There's no more Bower blood in him than in a joint stool."

"Philip, don't be a fool!" Lady Agnes cried.

"I've already been a fool!" Haselden raged. He turned on Stephen. "You played me for a fool with my daughter, you treacherous bastard. I'll put you down so far you'll never crawl up again for that!"

Stephen tried for words that did not come, managed only to shake his head in refusal or denial. It was Christopher who said, "Proof, Master Haselden. Do you have proof?"

"My sworn oath on it. He was got on his father's whore. His father and I and Lady Agnes conspired to pass him off as legitimately born because Sir Henry's wife looked likely to die and all she'd had was one sickly brat to stand between Sir Henry keeping that manor and losing it. I'll swear it on the Bible seven times over."

Lady Agnes, ice now and settling to the fight, said, "I'll swear to the contrary as many more times as need be, and who'll be the more believed? Me, the boy's own grandmother, or you, a proven murderer out for revenge?"

"Or let's look at it," Haselden returned, "as you with everything to keep if you're believed, against me with nothing to lose."

"I've sworn on oath before that he's legitimate and I'll swear it again and go on swearing it until I die."

"Then you'll burn in hell!"

"I'll run the risk!"

Whatever Master Haselden might have said back to that was forestalled by a small cough from Master Gruesby, whom Frevisse had vaguely noticed ease away along the gallery behind her a while ago. Now he sidled forward to Christopher, holding a ragged-ended piece of paper in one hand and in the other a short quill pen and an inkhorn small enough to have fit in his belt pouch. Barely above a whisper and more to Christopher's shoes than Christopher he murmured, "Lady Juliana's statement against Master Haselden."

Christopher took the paper, swept it with his eyes, and said, "Good. Thank you." He handed the paper back to him and nodded toward Juliana. "Let her sign it."

Juliana looked half ready to refuse, then shrugged and held her hand out for the paper, read it quickly, and went to where Master Gruesby was now waiting at the railing, the only flat place to be had in the gallery besides the floor. With a careless flourish she took the readied pen from him and signed below his words and gave the paper and pen back to him with, "There. That's done. Now I'm going."

She started for the stairs but turned again to Stephen and said, low-voiced and gently, "All I wanted was for you to love me."

Hoarsely, strangled on too many feelings, Stephen said, "No. You wanted me to lust for you. But my love . . . you never wanted my love. It was Nichola wanted that. And it was Nichola I gave it to."

Juliana's look at him went cold, but before she could make to leave again, Christopher said, "There's still that for you to answer. Nichola Lengley's death."

Juliana raised her eyebrows in mocking surprise. "Her death? That's nothing to do with me."

"There's evidence says otherwise," Christopher said grimly.

Juliana hesitated. Then she smiled, bitter and brittle and mocking all at once, and answered, "Evidence? That as we crossed that stream I dropped back from the other riders to ride beside her despite she tried to keep away from me, even shoved at my horse? That I said something to her about her husband and she made answer back at me that he was hers and she would keep him no matter what I did? That she made me so angry I hit her across her pretty little face with my riding whip and she cried out and I knew she'd tell Stephen so I swung my horse against hers, forcing it sideways over the edge of that steep stream bank? Is that what you mean?"

"Exactly that," said Christopher.

Juliana's smile was now small and bright and hard with scorn. "For all of which I doubt you have evidence enough to hang a flea, let alone convince a jury against me. Therefore, I think there's nothing else about Nichola Lengley's death to be said between us." And she turned away again, arrogant in her triumph and with nothing to be done to stop her because what she had said about the evidence was all too true, and no matter how much truth there was in what she had said, she had not made confession of it.

But Mistress Haselden beside the stairs said as Juliana reached the top of them, "Lady Juliana."

And Juliana turned toward her. And Mistress Haselden put both hands against her and shoved. And Juliana with no chance to save herself, maybe not even time to feel afraid, fell outward and backward and the snap of her spine as it hit the edge of a thick oak step near the bottom came almost as one with the crunch of her skull into the hall's stone paving.

And into the frozen, horrible quiet of the moment afterwards Mistress Haselden said with terrible calm to no one at all, "She tripped."

Chapter 23

fterward, Master Gruesby never cared to think much about the rest of that day. There were outcries that brought servants running, with more outcries and confusion, but by then Lady Agnes had seized hold of Mistress Haselden and taken her into her chamber, out of the way, along with her woman and Dame Frevisse's prioress. It was Dame Frevisse who stayed to order the servants, quieting them and seeing to it that Lady Juliana's body was moved to lie flat on the hall floor and that a blanket was brought to cover it while Master Christopher sent his own man at a run to bring the rest of his men from the nunnery while holding Master Haselden under guard himself.

Master Gruesby hovered aside from all of that, making

sure he had Lady Juliana's statement safe in his belt pouch and keeping an eye to Stephen, who had drawn back until flat against the rear wall of the gallery, out of the way and out of sight of Lady Juliana's body, unheeded by anyone until Dame Frevisse went to speak low-voiced to him. He answered with first a sideways shake of his head and then a nod, and she turned from him to give order to one of the servant women, "Take him to the kitchen, Emme. Give him something strong to drink, keep him warm by the fire, don't let anyone make him talk about anything."

"Lady Agnes . . ." Emme started.

"Has enough on her hands just now. Nor does Stephen need to deal with women for the while. He needs quiet and something strong to drink. Go with her, Stephen."

Stephen went, not saying anything and his head turned aside from Lady Juliana's blanket-covered body when he had to pass it at the stairfoot. Master Christopher's men came then and Master Christopher sent one of them promptly out again to keep guard in the yard against anyone coming in, because if the screams and cries had not been heard, then the running to and from the nunnery had surely been seen and the curious would be gathering.

To Master Gruesby's relief, young Denys was given the task of going to tell Lady Juliana's family that she had fallen and was dead and to promise that Master Christopher would see them himself as soon as might be and tell them more. In the meanwhile he would keep with Master Haselden until somewhere was found to lock him up and keep him under guard until he was given over to the sheriff. It therefore fell to Master Gruesby to go with the men who carried Lady Juliana's body to the nunnery, where the nuns and nunnery servants would be better able to help her family with all that would need doing than anyone at the inn. But when he had told the nun at the cloister door what was the matter, she took him to explain again, to Domina Matilda, who granted the nunnery's help—"Of course"—and went to see what she could do.

He made his escape only barely in time. As he crossed back to Lady Agnes's, Denys was coming down the street toward the nunnery in company with Mistress Champyon, her son, and husband. For Master Gruesby that made it easier to go forward into the gathering of people already outside Lady Agnes's, their questions flurrying around him—What had happened? Whose body had been carried out? Who was dead? Had someone died?—his head bowed and shoulders hunched, thankful when Master Christopher's man let him into the safety of the yard.

But to be thankful was not the same as to be happy and he was not happy as he went into Lady Agnes's hall. Was even farther from happy seeing a maidservant on her knees at the foot of the stairs scrubbing Lady Juliana's blood from the stone floor, and he shied aside to the fire-place, to stand with his back to her and his hands out to the fading coals and gray ashes of the neglected fire. Not that he would have been any better warmed by flames. He was cold right through with a cold against which no fire had chance.

He had seen someone die before now. In the ordinary way of things it was natural for people to die. He had even taken comfort once in being beside someone he cared about until her end and thought she had taken comfort in his being there. But he had never seen someone killed before now. He had seen the aftermath of violent deaths often enough, of course. As crowner's clerk he had seen a great many bodies dead in any number of unpleasant ways. But by the time he had seen a body it had been . . . a body. Not a person anymore. Even little Mistress Lengley yesterday. He had seen her alive one day and then, when next he'd seen her, she had been dead and he had been able, as always, to keep the two things—the being alive and the being dead—apart in his mind.

With Lady Juliana it had been . . . was different.

Not that he had liked her. He had not. But he had watched her this morning laughing, being scornful, angry, proud . . . and then between one instant and the next, in the time it had taken her to strike the stair and floor, she was no longer there. Instead of Lady Juliana there had been only a sprawled body with blood spreading from under its head. No longer anyone at all.

And that was how it had been with all those other bodies he had seen. Upon a time each of them had been someone who had laughed and been angry, hurt, and happy. Had been someone as alive as Lady Juliana had been. And then they were not. No more than Lady Juliana was or ever would be anymore.

It was as if he had come around a corner in his mind where he had never gone before and instead of only knowing something he was *feeling* it.

Feeling anything much at all unsettled him. He did not like it and he was grateful to Master Christopher for coming at that moment through a nearby doorway into the hall, letting him leave the fire and his thoughts to go to him, a little guilty at being found idle, saying, "All's seen to at the nunnery, sir."

"My thanks. With Lady Agnes's leave, we've tied Master Haselden for now in a storeroom with a small window and heavy door."

"Mistress Haselden?" Master Gruesby ventured to ask.

"Lady Agnes has given bond to answer for her. Now I'd have you write me word to the sheriff that he's needed here. Tom will take it . . ."

Master Gruesby slid, pleased, into familiar duties. There was comfort to be had from duties. If one only held to them hard enough, they kept a great many thoughts at bay, and today they served to see him well into the afternoon, until Master Christopher could no longer put off going to see Lady Juliana's family. Mistress Champyon had been sending demands to him, that he tell her himself what had happened, and finally, with everything done that could be done for the day, he faced the task but took young Denys with him. "Because if you're there, Master Gruesby, she'll want to question you about it, too, and that would mean more talking," Master Christopher said, to Master Gruesby's great relief.

But it left him with no excuse against doing the thing he had to do and, unhappy at it, he returned to the nunnery and displeased the sacristan by asking to have the Lengley strong chest brought to him. At least he did not keep her long. There was only the one thing he needed from it and when he had it he stood for a moment over the open chest, holding it, then seemed to put it back among the other papers but in the doing somehow set the scrolled documents he had set aside on the table rolling over the edge to bounce and scatter on the floor toward the sacristan and servant, who moved to stoop and gather them and did not see Master Gruesby slip the folded paper up his sleeve before he came around the table to help them, begging pardon for his unhandiness. The sacristan was not much disposed to pardon him, instead snapped, "You're always doing this," as she snatched and dumped documents back into the chest, then asked if he were done, and at him humbly admitting that he was, slammed shut and locked the chest and went away with it, leaving the servant to see him out.

Clear away, he went back yet again to Lady Agnes's, half expecting to be told Stephen had returned to the Haseldens' manor but found that he had not, was still with his grandmother. Master Gruesby would have asked if he might speak with Master Stephen alone but the tiredly impatient servingwoman gave him no chance, showed him up to Lady Agnes's solar without question, announced, "It's the crowner's man," and withdrew, all in a bustle that frighted him off saying anything.

He immediately regretted his weakness. Not only was Lady Agnes there, sitting straight-backed in a cushioned chair close to the fire, looking weary and grim, with one age-thinned hand held out toward the flames and the other holding tightly to Master Stephen seated beside her, but so were Dame Frevisse and her prioress, seated across the hearth with hands folded in their laps, the both of them with the look of someone praying inwardly and hard. He had heard, during the day, that they had put off their remove to the nunnery, asked by Lady Agnes to be with her a little longer, but he had also forgotten he had heard it and the knot already in his belly knotted a little tighter. He would rather not have had Dame Frevisse anywhere near what he was going to do.

But there was no going back from his purpose now, and as the four beside the fire looked toward him, he bowed and said, close to a whisper but unable to help it, "By your leave, Master Stephen. I'd talk with you apart, please."

He had hoped Master Stephen would leave the room with him but he only rose, looking puzzled, and crossed to the window, where the late-afternoon sunlight was slanting in, long and golden. Perforce, Master Gruesby followed him but, once there, sidled a little sideways to put his back toward the women by the fire.

"Is something wrong?" Master Stephen asked. Too little time had passed yet for all of yesterday and today's happenings to be lined deeply into his face but the pain that would make those lines was there, along with a weariness that wanted only to be done with hurts both given and received as he amended his question to, "Is something else wrong?"

For answer to that, Master Gruesby drew the folded paper from his sleeve and held it out, more wishing he was elsewhere than at almost any time in his life before. Master Stephen took the paper from him, turned it over in search of a superscription that was not there, and asked, "What is this?"

Master Gruesby drew breath to answer that but could not, let out his breath, drew it again, and succeeded in saying toward Master Stephen's belt buckle, "It was with the Lengley deeds and documents. I found it. It's yours."

"Mine?"

Unnerved so badly he could hardly stand, Master Gruesby repeated, somewhat desperately, "Yours."

He had carefully refolded the paper with its attached wax seal safe inside it. There was no doubt that Master Stephen could feel the weight of it and indeed he unfolded the paper carefully, caught the seal as it slid out, and as he began to read, kept it in his hand rather than letting its heavy wax hang loose on the green ribbon that had been threaded through a pair of slits near the bottom edge of the paper and doubled over, both ends of the ribbon fixed firmly in the wax so that the seal could not be removed from the paper without destruction of the seal or tearing of the paper or cutting of the ribbon.

It was a short letter, considering what it had to say. In the days it had been his and no one else's, Master Gruesby had wondered how many times Stephen's mother had written it over, and with what effort and agony, to bring everything she had wanted to say down to those few sentences before she had left it to God's will whether it would someday come to her son or not. Now it had and the son she had hardly known was reading it more than once, guessing from the time that passed until he looked up from it to Master Gruesby and asked with a quietness worse than shouting, "How long have you had this?"

Master Gruesby cleared his throat. "It came from the strong chest in the nunnery within the hour."

With that same quietness, Master Stephen said, "I mean, how long have you known about it?"

With desperate effort Master Gruesby met his gaze and

answered steadily, "Since the day we first came to Goring. Master Montfort and I. Since then."

Master Stephen opened his mouth, shut it over whatever he had been first minded to say, paused, and finally asked, "Who else knows about it?"

"Master Montfort did. No one else. He set me to look through the Lengley documents as soon as we arrived. While he went to see the Champyons. I gave it to him when he came back." Master Gruesby's throat was so tight the words would barely come but there was relief in saying them, in not being the only one to know. "He took it with him the next morning. I th-think he liked the power he felt, having it. Over everyone he was talking to. You see. He gave it back to me when he returned. He said to leave it where it had been. Until he asked for it again."

Stephen's gaze had returned to the letter. "My God and Judas' blood," he breathed. "Juliana wasn't lying." And then, accusingly, "Why give me this? Why not to the crowner or escheater?"

"Because . . ." Master Gruesby stopped and gathered himself, and went on, "Because you should know. Because it should be your choice. Instead of someone else's." And also because Master Gruesby knew something of what it was to lose out on one's life for no other reason than one's birth. But that was aside from Master Stephen's trouble and he did not say it, and if the shadow of it was in his voice, Master Stephen did not hear it, eyes on the letter again. That morning, before Master Christopher's men had taken Master Haselden away, Stephen had asked of him, "If my mother wasn't my father's wife, what happened to her?" And Master Haselden had said back with angry pleasure, "Dead a long time ago. Your grandmother can tell you all about it. Make her."

Now there was far less Lady Agnes would have to tell him.

But from across the room she was become aware that

something more than a mere message was happening. Sharply she called, "Stephen. What is it?" And when he did not answer, she pushed herself to her feet by an arm of her chair and her staff, saying more sharply, "What is it? What have you there?"

Master Stephen looked over Master Gruesby's shoulder at her, a long-drawn moment passing before he said, level-voiced, "A letter from my mother."

Lady Agnes straightened, her mouth thinning to a harsh, determined line before she said, "Nonsense. There's no such thing." She held out a demanding hand. "Give it here."

Master Stephen made no move toward her. "It was with the documents you gave Master Montfort leave to look at."

"It wasn't. It couldn't have been."

Master Stephen stepped aside from Master Gruesby, as if clearing a tourney field between him and his grand-mother, and read, " 'I, dying with nothing of the world to leave to you, leave only this, a gift of truth, and knowing that neither your father nor your grandmother can be trusted to give it to you, nor feeling I should burden any living soul with it, I have persuaded Domina Aylenor to let me put it in the Lengley strong chest, that if it be God's will that it come someday and somehow into your hands, it will.' "

Lady Agnes struck her staff against the floor. "The treacherous whore!" She thrust her hand out angrily. "Give that thing to me. It's lies and nothing but lies. Give it here."

"No."

"It's lies! All of it!"

Master Stephen took his look from her and from near the bottom of the page, close to where the seal was attached, read, " 'I, Domina Aleynor Thedmarch, prioress of the nunnery of St. Mary the Virgin in Goring, do attest and swear that I have not read what is herein written but have taken oath from Mariota Coleshill that it is true . . .' "

" '*Stephen,*" Lady Agnes said in a voice that utterly forbade him to read more.

" '. . . and because she is near to death and has repented of her sins and made confession, I do believe her.' " Stephen raised his eyes to his grandmother. "It's sealed with the nunnery's seal."

"Mariota as always a liar. She was lying to Domina Aylenor. She's lying to you through that letter. Let me burn it."

"It isn't her lies I've been living by," Stephen said, coldly calm. "It's been your lies. And my father's and Master Haselden's. Her only lie was in letting you have your own way against her and she did that for my sake."

"Everything was done for your sake," Lady Agnes said back at him, angry but also, Master Gruesby thought, afraid.

"But for your sake and my father's and Master Haselden's first," Stephen answered. "I was simply the means to your ends."

For the first time Lady Agnes showed desperation. "Your father loved you, Stephen. *I* love you . . ."

And gently Stephen answered her, "I know you do, and I love you and ever will. But the lying has to stop. I want to take my own course instead of one set for me by others."

"Not this course. This is the wrong course." Lady Agnes turned to Domina Elisabeth. "She was an apostate nun. Utterly damned. She fled out of St. Mary's with a man. Not my son. Someone else. It was only after the first man deserted her that my son took her and then at the last she deserted him, went crawling back to the nuns begging forgiveness. How can anyone believe anything she ever wrote or said?"

"Grandmother," Stephen said, dangerous in his quietness. "Listen. She confesses she fled her vows and was later taken up by my father. Then she writes, 'We loved each other carnally but more than carnally. We loved with our hearts as well as our bodies and when the time came that I bore you, his second son, and knew even while my happiness was at the height, holding you in my arms, that I was dying without hope, I gave your father and grandmother their wish and let them have you in return for being allowed, weary of the world as I was become, to return to St. Mary's, to pray for the nuns' forgiveness and God's in my last days.' "

He stopped and, grim with remembrance, Lady Agnes said, "Your father was so bitter over that. His little bitchwife had been sickly for years but wouldn't die, while his paramour who had been so full of life died in a bare few months of lung rot. Only then and at almost the same time did his wife finally die, the useless woman." Lady Agnes jerked her staff toward the letter. "But that doesn't mean that has to be the truth there!"

" 'Dying,' " Stephen remorselessly read, " 'I leave you what I can of my love and the truth, and hope it comes to you. They say God's will is over all. That being so, I wonder why he willed this life, this death on me, but that is not the manner of question we are taught to ask. May God be with you, as I know he is now with me. Written by my own hand this seventh day of . . .' "

Now, finally, Stephen's voice twisted toward the tears he had been holding in and he stopped until he had them at bay, not shamed by them but in need of dealing with other things first, lowering the letter and saying to his grandmother when he had steadied his voice again, "There's been enough of lying. I'd rather live by the truth from here on."

"The 'truth' will cost you your legitimacy and your lands," Lady Agnes said back at him.

"Your lies cost Nichola her life! And have helped to

ruin Master Haselden and Mistress Haselden. And Juliana come to that. And even Montfort. I think that's enough. Don't you?"

Tears filled Lady Agnes's eyes. "We didn't think your brother would live, and to lose all because there was no other heir . . ." Her tears flowed over, down the long lines of her face. "It isn't only the Bower manor that you'll lose by this. It's everything. You'll be left with nothing, Stephen. Don't you see? You'll have nothing."

Stephen went to her, three long strides, and put his arms around her, taller than she was though she was tall, and held her to him, her face against his shoulder, and said to the top of her head, "Grandmother, Grandmother. I'm not a fool and I'm not a weakling. I'd rather make a life for myself that wasn't come from lies and people dying for it. Besides . . ." He set Lady Agnes back at arm's length from him and said with a smile for her sake and something like laughter, broken though it was on his own tears, "Besides, don't I remember that you have a manor in your own name, to will to whom you wish, and who better than your well-loved grandson?"

"A small manor," she protested. "Not worth a quarter of all you're giving up!"

Smile and laughter gone, Stephen looked into her eyes. "But without Nichola's death because of it," he said.

Chapter 24

he next morning, to Frevisse's relief, she and Domina Elisabeth parted early from Lady Agnes, moving with their few things into the nunnery's guesthall at last, with thanks and reasonable farewells and no protest from Lady Agnes at their leaving. With all else she had in hand at present, they were probably forgotten by now, Frevisse thought as she stood in front of the church's rood screen not much afterward, waiting for Christopher and a last chance to talk with him before he left Goring, to ask the things there had been no chance for yesterday. This early in the day, with the nuns at Chapter meeting and most other people about their day's business, she and Christopher would likely have the church to themselves except for the nunnery servant she had brought with her for seemliness' sake because this time she was here with Domina Elisabeth's knowledge and leave; but the woman was sitting on a bench along the wall near the rood screen, hands wrapped in her apron for warmth and her head bowed in what her heavy, even-rhythmed breathing told was sleep, not watchfulness.

That suited Frevisse well enough. To have the church's quiet and beauty to herself this while, with the long slant of the lately risen sun through the windows streaming colors down into the nave—ruby, azure, saffron gold. They were warmer to see than to feel, though, and shivering slightly in her furred gown, she thought wryly that she must be growing old, the cold came nearer her bones than it had used to. Or maybe it was the coldheartedness of these past few days that had chilled her so deeply she was not sure when she'd be warm again. Montfort's death and all the rest had come not of any hot passion of love but out of the cold passion of greed. Greed for power, greed for land, greed for flesh. Montfort's greed, Philip Haselden's greed, Juliana's greed. Greeds that had left Montfort and Juliana and Nichola dead and the Haseldens ruined and Stephen . . .

For Stephen at least she had hope. There were people who despite anything that happened to them, stayed small and shut without thought into the same endlessly repeating pattern of their feelings all of their lives. Come what might to them, they never grew. But there were also those who, besides feeling what happened to them, thought about it and thereby had chance to change, to grow. Stephen looked to be one of those. Whoever he had been a few days ago, he was someone else now, someone more than he had been before, and she would be ever thankful she had been there to see him make his choice to live by truths instead of lies.

It had been a costly choice in more ways than one and the price paid to bring him to it was a price no one would have chosen to pay; but having been paid, at least it was not gone to waste. As his mother's life had not, after all, gone to waste. There was no way to know whether trusting her letter to such chance as might come to it had been a foolish thing to do or an act of deepest faith but Frevisse preferred to believe that the woman had given the letter over to God's will in recompense for having so badly failed to give her life to him, and if it had been done out of faith, then her faith had been fulfilled. If anyone had bothered with those papers over the years—and very possibly no one had, there being no need until there was quarrel over the inheritance—that one paper had gone unnoticed, shuffled past because it was not what anyone was looking for, until Master Gruesby, of all unlikely people, had read it.

Or maybe, rather than unlikely, he was the likeliest of all, preferring words to people as she thought he did and probably reading everything that ever came his way.

The heavy iron latch on the nave door rattled as it was raised and she turned from the rood screen, expecting it would be Christopher coming in and not surprised to see Master Gruesby silent-footed behind him, head down as usual, turning back to pull the heavy door shut with a soft thud before he followed Christopher up the nave toward her. As they approached, she saw that Christopher's weariness looked to be as heavy on him as his dark mourning clothes and said to him, "May we sit?" as if she were in need of it instead of him.

"Of course," he granted and they went to the bench where they had sat together before, Master Gruesby following, and again Christopher had to tell him to sit.

As Master Gruesby did, Frevisse asked, not to waste what probably small time they had, "The question of Stephen's inheritance goes to whoever is now escheator, I know, but besides that, what's toward?"

Christopher leaned tiredly back against the wall and

sighed. "I've sent a messenger to the sheriff. To tell him he's needed here. When he comes, everything goes into his hands."

"And Mistress Haselden?" Out of all of it, it seemed to Frevisse she was the one who would suffer beyond her deserving, even allowing for Juliana's death. "Must she be put in goal?"

"Since there's no likelihood she's going to run, I've placed her under bond. To keep to her own house and do no violence from now until she's brought to trial. She'll have her own people to see to her. And Lady Agnes and Master Stephen. He's to stay with her still. To see her through."

"And when she comes to trial?"

"I'm crowner," Christopher said simply. "I witnessed her murder of Lady Juliana. I'll testify she was not in her right wits at the time. That she was driven out of them by her grief and the taunting of the woman who had killed her daughter."

"Which she was," Frevisse said.

"Beyond doubting. And because she was, she'll be found innocent of murder. Then it will be for her lawyer to prove she's recovered from her madness. Once that's done, she'll be allowed her dower lands. She'll have at least that much to live on. Even if all else the Haseldens hold is forfeited because of her husband's guilt."

Leaving Mistress Haselden with a life patched together out of the ruin other people had made around her. It was better than no life at all—but nothing could give her back her daughter.

"And Master Haselden?"

Christopher's voice hardened. "I'll do all I can to see that he hangs."

There was dark determination in that but a deeper darkness lay behind it, shadow of a thought Frevisse had already had, and she asked, "You think there's chance Lord Lovell will plead a pardon for him?"

Christopher nodded. "In Haselden's mind my father's death was as much for Lord Lovell's good as for his own. Lord Lovell, however much he'll decry the murder, will likely see it the same way. He's almost sure to see Haselden is pardoned."

"Even for outright murder?"

"Even for anything, the way things are now. Ten years ago, five years ago, he wouldn't have. Not for Haselden or anyone else except his own blood. But with the way things are shaping around the king, no lord is going to lose that loyal a follower. For any reason. Not if he can help it." Christopher straightened from the wall and leaned forward, elbows on knees, hands clasped tightly together. "Not that anyone will greatly care if . . . *when* Haselden is pardoned. Considering who he killed."

Frevisse could only, silently, admit that that was all too likely true. Master Montfort had worked too long and hard at caring about nothing except himself for anyone to care that he was gone. So she was taken by surprise to hear herself say, very quietly, "I'll care."

Both Christopher and Master Gruesby straightened to stare at her and, disbelieving, Christopher asked what was on both their faces. "Why?"

Frevisse paused, searching out her answer, before saying, "Because it was an unjust death. If it isn't answered with justice, then the unjustness grows. Once that begins— the bypassing of justice for whatever reasons we may find good in the moment—the law fails, and where will any of us be then except in chaos and danger?" She paused again, then added, "And you'll care."

"Will I?" Christopher said bitterly. "I neither liked nor trusted my father. I don't want him back, any more than anyone else does. I'm willing for Mistress Haselden to go free. Why should I care if my father's murderer does, too?"

"Because Mistress Haselden truly was wrought out of her right mind by grief and pain when she killed Juliana. When Master Haselden killed your father, he did it coldly, willingly, with thought beforehand. You'll care if he goes free because . . ." Frevisse stopped, her eyes on Christopher's face, leaving it for him to finish his answer.

And after a moment he did, simply and unbitterly. "Because, as you say, where will we be if law fails us? Truth and law. What else can we build our lives on?"

"On love," Frevisse said as simply. "Without it, what use is there in truth and law?"

"But there's Love and then there's love, isn't there?" Christopher said back. "That woman. Stephen's mother. She probably said that everything she did was from love."

She probably had, petty and ill-founded though her loves had been. Frevisse had thought of her now and again since yesterday—a nun who had broken her vows for the sake of satisfying her body's lusts—and prayed for her, too, the more so because Frevisse doubted that even at the last the woman's love had been unselfish. She might well have written that letter to Stephen out of either desire to leave him the truth or for love of him but equally likely she had written it because she had been dying and frightened and had not wanted to go unknown and unremembered into the dark. But despite of that and despite all the petty loves to which women and men both could sink, twisting lives out of their right shape the way Juliana had twisted her own and those around her, the Love that was more than all that, the Love that was more than the flesh, was still there.

And Christopher with an impatient, wordless, aching sound rubbed at his forehead with both hands, and said, "I'm muddled and tired. And wrong. It isn't love that's at fault. It's us and all the ill uses we put love to." And in the way of someone too tired to hold his mind to its course, he turned suddenly to Master Gruesby and demanded, "Come to that, speaking of truth, why did you hold back that letter all these days?"

Large-eyed behind his spectacles, Master Gruesby stared at him, then dropped his gaze, fumbled at and slipped loose their ribbons from around his ears, took the spectacles off, looked surprised to find he was holding them, put them back on, and said toward his knees, "Master Montfort ordered me to leave it where it had been until he asked for it again."

"But when he was dead," Christopher said, "why didn't you give it over? To me or to anyone?"

Master Gruesby looked from one side to the other as if the answer might be lying on the floor there, huddled his shoulders in a shrug, and said nothing. It was Frevisse who answered for him, impatient at Christopher for not seeing it and at Master Gruesby for not saying it. "Because Master Montfort had told him to keep it until he asked for it again, and he's been so used to obeying what Master Montfort ordered at him for years that even with Montfort dead, he went on obeying him. What Montfort had told him to do, he did."

Christopher turned to Master Gruesby. "Was that it?"

"I was his clerk," Master Gruesby said softly, as if that were answer enough; and for him it probably was.

"Then why give the letter to Master Stephen after all?"

Master Gruesby looked past him to Frevisse, maybe hoping she would save him again from having to answer it himself, but she could not. She had guessed at this unreasoning obedience to Montfort from what little she had ever noticed about Master Gruesby over the years and seen of him lately, but as to why he had given the letter to Stephen . . .

And then, suddenly, briefly but for long enough, she saw not the differences there were between herself and

Master Gruesby but where they were near to alike—two people who lived more inside themselves than out and had found their ways to the place they needed to be and held to it as strongly as they could. And although it was Christopher she answered, it was at Master Gruesby she said, "I think the answer to that is Master Gruesby's matter and none of ours. But partly it was because he's done being your father's clerk and is ready to be yours."

"Mine?" Christopher looked sharply around at Master Gruesby, who looked back at him, steady for once, and after a moment Christopher said again, "Mine," but without question now.

And something lighted in Master Gruesby's eyes that was as near to a smile as Frevisse ever expected to see from him, before he bent his head and said toward the floor. "Yes, sir."

Frevisse stood up and, perforce, so did both men, as she said, "By your leave, I have a promise to keep elsewhere."

They bowed to her, Christopher saying, "Of course, my lady," Master Gruesby saying nothing, his eyes down as she turned away from them toward the door through the rood screen, into the choir. Domina Elisabeth was with Sister Ysobel and both of them were waiting for her to tell them what she could of these past few days and soon she would go to them, but first there were prayers she must say. At Montfort's grave.

Author's Note

Some degree of circumlocution in describing Master Gruesby's behavior has been necessary because in medieval English "nerves" referred to ligaments and sinews and to say someone was "nervous" meant they were strong-bodied. Therefore, Master Gruesby is never "nervous," except on one occasion when, in the medieval sense, he is actually unnerved.

Although the fine grinding of lenses had not been perfected by the 1400s, spectacles—"eyeglasses" and "glasses" are later terms—can be seen in paintings of the time and at least one will of the 1400s refers to silver-rimmed spectacles.

As for using a plea of insanity to clear someone of

murder, such a plea was indeed recognized in medieval English law, though in the thirteenth century's *On the Laws and Customs of England*, Bracton warns that careful ward should be made against people claiming madness in order to take advantage of the law. Ah, yes, some things do stay the same.

The type of dagger used to kill Master Montfort tends to appear in modern reference books as a "kidney dagger." It seems that Victorian scholars were uncomfortable with the actual medieval name and changed it.

Concerning Lady Agnes's obvious independence and control of her household and business interests, something should be said about the myth of medieval women as helpless pawns in a male-dominated society structure. By the 1400s, before the Renaissance came to England, women had more legal and economic rights than at any time afterward until the late twentieth century. What uses were made of their possibilities varied according to the individual, just as now, but a competent, well-off widow was expected to run her own life and properties and she expected to have no more interference at it than a man would have. For pleasure as well as information there is *Medieval Gentlewoman: Life in a Widow's Household in the Later Middle Ages* by ffiona Swaby.

For an actual medieval legal case concerning bastard (or not) heirs there is *The Armburgh Papers*, ed. by Christine Carpenter.

That there are differences between this story and modern Goring in regard to street names and some river topography is accounted for by the passage of over five hundred years and the recent replacing of the medieval ferry by a bridge.

*   *   *

My particular thanks go to Eleanor Simpson of the Goring and Streatley Local History Society and Mary Carr of Goring (website: www.goring@lineone.net), who provided me information about medieval Goring and its nunnery that I would not have come by otherwise.